话语语言学与语言教学
Text Linguistics and Language Teaching

主　编：阳志清　曹志希

上海交通大学出版社

图书在版编目（ＣＩＰ）数据

话语语言学与语言教学／阳志清，曹志希主编. 一上海：
上海交通大学出版社，2008
ISBN 978-7-313-05254-4

Ⅰ.话… Ⅱ.①阳…②曹… Ⅲ.话语语言学 – 应用 – 外
语教学 – 研究 Ⅳ.H09

中国版本图书馆CIP数据核字（2008）第085251号

话语语言学与语言教学

阳志清 曹志希 主编

上海交通大学出版社出版发行
（上海市番禺路 951 号 邮政编码 200030）
电话:64071208 出版人:韩建民
常熟市文化印刷有限公司印刷 全国新华书店经销
开本:787mm×960mm 1/16 印张:16.75 字数:312 千字
2008 年 11 月第 1 版 2008 年 11 月第 1 次印刷
印数:1～2 050
ISBN 978-7-313-05254-4/H·738 定价:32.00元

目　录

FOREWORD

Language policy can be seen as part of educational linguistics. ① But I wish here to present the opposite argument, namely that educational linguistics provides the tools and techniques for language policy and more specifically for language education management. First let me outline the model of language policy that I have been developing (Spolsky 1996; 2004; 2005b; 2006a; 2006b; in press; Spolsky & Shohamy 1998). It does not offer ready-made solutions or advice so much as it tries to make clear the complexity of the factors that need to be taken into account in language management.

First a word of history. The earliest language management activities were particularly concerned with the preservation of sacred texts—witness Panini and the mediaeval Arabic and Hebrew scholars. An even earlier tradition of language management started in China, with two major trends: the development of a single writing system to serve the range of varieties that make up Chinese, and the parallel process of persuading speakers of the different varieties of the unity of Chinese. While the effort to establish a single approved variety, now known as *putonghua*, is much more recent, the 2000 years of persuasion has encouraged the belief that such a national variety is achievable and worth achievement. Language management in Europe, in practice the cultivation and modification of varieties for nationalist reasons, in the 18th and 19th centuries was also the preserve of language scholars (grammarians commonly associated with national independence movements) or the language academies established and still powerful in Romance countries and charged

---

① An earlier form of this paper was given at the University of Pennsylvania to present the 16th Annual Nessa Wolfson Colloquium, an occasion marking the thirtieth anniversary of the establishment of the Educational Linguistics Program at the University.

especially with the purity of the national language (Spolsky 2005a). It was Haugen's study of one of these movements (Haugen 1961; 1966) that might be claimed to have launched the scholarly study of language policy as a field. It was also at this time that the involvement of linguists in language planning in the various postwar independent states especially of Africa and Asia helped develop what I have called the American school; their work is obvious in the Ford supported studies of Africa (Bender, Cooper, & Ferguson 1972; Ford Foundation 1975; Ohannessian, Ferguson, & Polomé 1975), in the one comparative international evaluation of lexical elaboration (Rubin, Jernudd, Das Gupta, Fishman, & Ferguson 1977), and in a number of collections such as (Fishman 1968); their work was attacked essentially by the so-called linguistic rights and linguistic imperialism approaches (Phillipson 1992) (which ignored the earlier linguistic totalitarianism of the Arabic conquest or the Spanish in South America to pick on the diffusion of English). More recently, there has been a rapid expansion of the field, with problems being faced with the failures of early planning, the effects of globalization and immigration, the spread of interest to what are called endangered languages on the one hand, and to large state responses to growing multilingualism. In this model, I argue also for a further extension, adding to the earlier concentration on the nation-state as prime focus the importance of language policy at other levels and in other institutions and social groups, which moves the focus closer to education.

I use the term Language Policy for the field as a whole, preferring it to language planning (or language policy and planning). Each social group (or more precisely, speech community) is likely to have a language policy, which may be implicit in the language practices of the members of the group (who speaks what variety of language to whom under what circumstances) or the language beliefs or ideologies of members of the group (what do they believe to be an appropriate policy, and how do they value each of the salient varieties available to the group), or which may be made explicit as a result of language management, namely the effort of someone with or claiming authority to modify the language practices or believe other members of the group.

Language policy exists at many different levels of society. We can study it in the family, noting the actual varieties used in talking to various family members; we can study beliefs at the family level, such as the critical question of what language should be spoken to young children; we can look for examples of management, as in efforts of grandparents or parents to bring up children speaking their heritage language. Beyond the family, another significant level is religion, with the setting of choices of the language to be used for prayer, sermon, sacred text, and teaching: here one can find strict management as in the Catholic church before Vatican II with its insistence on Latin for the mass, or as in the Islamic requirement on the use of Classical Arabic even in parts of the world where it is not understood, or there may be flexibility, as in the Jewish and Christian willingness to authorize translation and in the recent introduction of English into Hindu rituals in the United States (Spolsky 2003).

There is language policy in the neighborhood, reflected in the language of public signs (Backhaus in press; Gorter 2006), the appropriate language to speak in local stores, the acceptability of using foreign languages in public places. Individual institutions commonly have a language policy: the language that workers use with each other, with their employers, and with their customers. There may well be attempts to manage this in regulations set out by local government bodies. Businesses too have policies, often hiring to provide service in specific languages, or encouraging their employees to learn specific languages. Government and civic agencies regularly have policies, reflecting either voluntary adaptation to local language practices or centrally enforced management decisions based on hegemonic monolingual or pluralistic multilingual ideologies, regulations, laws, or constitutions. Of all these institutions, it is no doubt the school that has most chance of influence and managing language practices and ideology.

At the apex, there is the language policy of the nation-state, broken down in some circumstances regionally (the territorial solution adopted by bilingual countries like Belgium and Switzerland or multilingual countries like India). Within any nation, there may be majority or minority ethnic or political or religious groups attempting to persuade the appropriate authority to modify or vary language policy, generally by assigning a higher value and status to the variety they use.

As a result of the complexity of levels involved and the multiplicity of practices and beliefs, the development of a utopian stable language policy remains a major challenge in much of the world. Failure is probably more common than success (Spolsky 2006b). There is regular public debate in much of the world. In spite of its complex territorial management plan, Belgium continues to argue about the status of French and Dutch. Some Swiss cantons are now seeking to replace the teaching of the other national language by English. Malaysia has recently given up on half a century endeavoring to establish Bahasa Melayu by switching to English in language instruction for all school levels. The European Union continues to bicker about the languages used in its institutions, and sets language policy challenges to its new members. The United States, lacking a national language policy, has now developed a National Language Security Initiative to try to encourage the teaching and learning of foreign languages relevant to defense, is slowly implementing a civil rights program to provide access to health and public services for non-English speakers, and continues to struggle with the question of bilingual education and English teaching in schools (Spolsky 2006a).

To have any hope of successful implementation, a national language policy must take into account the full complexity of the sociolinguistic ecology of the society. Unfortunately, data on the language practices of society are commonly sparse. There are number of reasons for this. The first is the nature of the object: I have used the word variety rather than language as a first attempt at this. Commonly, we talk about labeled varieties of language (English, Quebec French, Palestinian Arabic, Argentinean Spanish) as though they were discreet easily identifiable objects rather than complex bundles or clusters of linguistic features—specific pronunciations, lexical items, grammatical patterns, appropriate genres and styles—used in pattern variation by members of the speech community. Some of these variables become salient as methods of identification of group membership, and specific language management policies may be applied—for example, the Spanish Academy has recently ruled that only a handful of the hundreds of names of professions may be used in the feminine form permitted by Spanish morphology and desired by proponents of equality.

Naming a variety is a first step in giving it status, rather than simply a natural action by biological classification. In order to develop an accurate account of the varieties used within a defined speech community, one needs to embark on a long process of careful observation and analysis of an appropriate sample of people and situations. There are such studies, but they are more likely to be found in academic monographs that in published surveys. If there is something more than guesses or estimates, it is likely to be the result of a government census. Censuses, however, have many limitations: the language question is rarely considered very important; it is asked in a number of different ways and it is answered by self-report, often expressing ethnic rather than linguistic claims. But an accurate survey of actual language practices of the various groups constituting a speech community is a critically needed first step.

An additional complicating factor is that language is just one of the many factors relevant to language policy: demography, politics, economics, religion, and culture can all play significant roles in the success of language planning. In Ireland, the failure to coordinate linguistic and economic planning in the Gaeltacht had, it has been shown, serious effects (ó Riágain 1997). In many countries, language revival movements are in fact ethnic mobilization around the language question; once Ireland became independent, the urgency of revival seems to have been lost.

Language beliefs are also difficult to recognize. Various members of social groups are like to have quite distinct attitudes to the salient varieties, and these attitudes may not seem on the surface consistent. Thus, studies of US attitudes to language show general acceptance of the belief that English should be the national official language alongside a general tolerance of other languages and recognition of their importance in education (Robinson, Brecht, & Rivers 2006). Again, a national language policy that ignores popular ideology is unlikely to succeed. In many parts of South America now, native American languages are starting to be recognized in use in education, but their low social status mitigates against the success of language maintenance programs and against their acceptance even by speakers of the language (Hornberger & King 2001).

Among the many beliefs that people hold about language, one of the strongest appears to be a belief in the superiority of one language over another. Another common belief is the existence of some pure correct version of each language, and the acceptance of some authority to rule on it (Fishman 2006). There is commonly a division between those who accept multilingualism as normal and natural and those for whom the ideal is monolingualism.

Especially during the halcyon days of language planning in the 1960s, language management activities were divided in two. The first was called status planning; it involved assignment of some recognized function such as official use or use for education of a named variety of language. This was assumed to be appropriate for government action in constitutional clauses, language laws, or language regulations. Many newly independent nations used the writing of the new constitution to proclaim a national official language. Bilingual nations like Belgium or multilingual nations like India were often involved in long complex struggles over the determination of appropriate status for their competing varieties, each with solid support from a related ethnic group.

The second was called (somewhat confusingly to outsiders) corpus planning; it involved in various modifications to the language itself. There was a relation between the two: a language assigned official status or chosen as the school language of instruction needed of course to have a written variety, and would require standardization, modernization, lexical elaboration, and cultivation. The formal management of these tasks is commonly assigned to the language agency or Academy, or to the Ministry of Education, or in a more laissez-faire approach, left to publishers and schoolteachers.

More recently, Cooper (1989) identified the third significant branch of language management, which he labeled language acquisition planning, which requires, I am arguing, educational linguistics for its implementation. This involves determining which members of the society should be expected to learn which variety of language: it governs in other words language education policy at the various levels of the school system and perhaps even outside it, such as in language teaching programs for immigrants. An important sub-component is called language diffusion management, namely central government or agency activities to teach a national language outside the nation-state where it is official (Ammon 1992; Cooper 1982).

By definition, language management has initiators or actors (a specific agency or person who can be identified), explicit purposes, a plan laying out the steps to be taken, resources to support the agency and its activities, and ideally a method to evaluate the effectiveness of implementation. Like all other planning, there can easily be gaps between plans and implementation.

Educational linguistics and language policy—a personal view

At this point, I propose to think aloud a little about my own academic development, trying to track what I was hoping to understand when I proposed the term "educational linguistics" in Spolsky (1974b; 1978), and how it relates intimately to my own current interest in the field of language policy and management (Spolsky 1977; 2004; Spolsky & Shohamy 1999). The intertwining of the two areas is close: language policy is one of the major areas of educational linguistics, and educational linguistics has come to recognize more and more its social context and responsibilities. Indeed, I will go further and argue that educational linguistics provides the tools that serve language policy and specifically what I call language education management.

The inspiration for my studies in this area came when I began to teach English in a high school on the east coast of New Zealand. Nothing I had learnt in my university studies in English language and literature seemed to have prepared me to understand the problems faced by some of my Maori students, or to help me understand the paradox that those who reported that they still spoke Maori at home proved to be better speakers and writers in English that those who came from homes that had shifted away from the heritage language. In the course of time, I discovered linguistics as an area offering potential solutions, but was continually frustrated by the concern of most linguists for language as an abstract system and later for its instantiation in the brain than for the social context of its users. The structuralists who were my earliest teachers① and the generativists who succeeded them strove to build a science of language protected from the messiness of the real-world-some of the former refused to deal with meaning, and the latter followed Chomsky in his pursuit of the ideal monolingual. Those of us who wanted to teach language were forced to develop intermediate and less prestigious sub-disciplines—contrastive analysis as a cheaper but useful structural grammar that permitted comparisons denied by current theory, second language acquisition that produced data congruent with transformational grammar which had denied relevance to language teaching—to try to influence schools and classrooms, with wasteful and even tragic results. The hope resided, I came to feel, in sociolinguistics and especially in the work of Dell Hymes who refused to accept the artificiality of splitting abstract idealized competence from performance (Hymes 1967; 1974; 1997).

Applied linguistics as it had developed seemed to me to be a fairly soulless attempt to apply irrelevant models to a narrow range of problems, especially teaching foreign languages. It had produced a couple of potential monsters: the deadening drills of the audio-lingual method, and the ungoverned chaos of the early natural approach. I put the challenge in this way:

Many linguists believe that their field should not be corrupted by any suggestion of relevance to practical matters; for them, linguistics is a pure science and its study is motivated only by the desire to increase human knowledge. Others, however, claim that linguistics offers a panacea for any educational problem that arises and quickly offer their services to handle any difficulties in language planning or teaching. Each of these extreme positions is, I believe, quite wrong, for while it is evident that linguistics is often relevant to education, the relation is seldom direct.

---

① While I was at high school, I had read Bodmer's "Loom of language" but Charles Fries was the first modern linguist I read.

(Spolsky 1978).

I proposed rather to start with specific problems and then look to linguistics and other relevant disciplines which could contribute to solution. The other fields were education itself, sociology, economics, politics, and psychology. The relevant sub-fields of linguistics itself were not just language theory and description (including their influence on language acquisition and learning theory) but also the hyphenated fields① of psycholinguistics and sociolinguistics: "Recognition of the complex sociolinguistic forces within a community is essential to the development of a valid and workable language education policy, just as knowledge of the status of the language concerned is vital to a clear understanding of the attitudes and motivations of language learners." (Spolsky 1978: 3)

My appreciation of the social significance of language teaching had in fact, started much earlier: while my earlier work had fitted the current approaches of applied linguistics, by 1971, when I was invited to a conference in Britain, I had already been in the Southwestern United States for long enough to move from talking about the social and political implications of selecting foreign students on the basis of their knowledge of English (Spolsky 1967) to the first of a series of papers dealing with what I called the "language barrier to education" (Spolsky 1971; 1974a; 1986). The situation in the Bureau of Indian Affairs schools that I visited when I moved to New Mexico in 1968 was dramatic: Anglo teachers with little or no knowledge of Navajo were teaching a regular English curriculum to classes full of Navajo children with little or no knowledge of English, dragged away from their homes to boarding schools situated by the US Corps of Engineers for their location close to water rather than to the children's home community. If one could help, one needed an educational linguistics based not on a contrastive or transformational grammar, but on an appreciation of the place of language in society.

The field of sociolinguistics had been born or at least taken its first toddling steps at the Linguistic Institute at Bloomington Indiana in 1964, where a group of young and energetic scholars studied and defined the complementary approaches of sociolinguistics and the sociology of language. A great deal was going on in southern Indiana that summer. Noam Chomsky, the Philadelphia-born son of a distinguished Hebraist, was challenging linguistics and psychology with his theories

---

① This was Carl Voegelin's term.

about the structure of language; Joshua Fishman, brought up on the other side of the street by a committed Yiddishist, was building a sociology of language that would tackle the problems of language minorities everywhere; and elsewhere on campus, Uriel Weinreich, the one scholar who might have bridged the gap between the transformationalists and the sociolinguists was lecturing on semantics. ① Bloomington was where I made my own first contact with big-time linguistics, but I was still confined to an applied linguistics approach, albeit involved in one of the earlier attempts to break into the world of computers (Garvin & Spolsky 1966). It was only a few years later that I became aware of the ground-breaking work of Joshua Fishman, and was persuaded by him of its relevance to education and by Cooper (1968) of its significance for my growing interest in language testing.

Cooper's paper read at a testing meeting in Ann Arbor in fact drew on the pioneering work of Dell Hymes, whose ethnography of speaking was just starting to impress many sociolinguists as a reasonable alternative to the more dehumanized model of what Chomsky called competence (a formal representation of the grammatical knowledge of an idealized monolingual). Trained as an anthropological linguist, Hymes came to Pennsylvania in 1965 and ten years later was persuaded to become dean of the school of education, a position that permitted the instantiation of his views on language into an educational program that became the heart of educational linguistics. It was a year later that Nessa Wolfson joined the faculty, carrying on her own work building bridges between sociolinguistics and second language acquisition, both in theory and an institutional structure.

Against this background, I want in the rest of my talk to describe the closely related fields of educational linguistics and language policy as they have developed into the 21st century.

Educational linguistics

My latest attempt to define the field has been in the preparation of the *Handbook of Educational Linguistics* that Francis Hult and I are currently editing for

---

① His dissertation in 1951 was a pioneering work on bilingualism; he developed his father's work on the history of Yiddish into a major study of dialectology; and he was working on the critical relation between semantics and syntax. His death in 1967 ended the chance of bridging the gap between the theorists and what I like to call the realists.

Blackwell. In a review of a recent Festschrift dealing with applied linguistics, Davies (2006) suggested a distinction between those like Henry Widdowson who argue for a dictionary definition of the field, maintaining that there is "an applied linguistics core which should be required of all those attempting the *rite de passage*" and those who prefer the approach by ostensive definition, "if you want to know about applied linguistics, look around you". He correctly places me somewhere in this latter camp, although in the case of educational linguistics, which I argue is necessarily more focused, I think I have less trouble in finding a core, in the interactions between language and education. It was the very lack of a core in applied linguistics that led me to propose educational linguistics. In planning the *Handbook*, we essentially selected what we considered the core areas and added other areas in which there was relevant research and publication.

We divided the forty or more commissioned chapters into three clusters. The first cluster presents the foundational background, by setting out the neurobiological, the linguistic-theoretical, psychological, sociological, anthropological, and political-ideological knowledge relevant to educational linguistics and the school systems in which it operates. Language, it has come to be realized especially since the work of Chomsky, is embodied in the brain, and growing knowledge of the brain is therefore relevant if not yet directly applicable (Schumann 2006). But, at the same time, all varieties of language and their use are contextualized in social settings, depending on common co-construction and the interplay of social and linguistic structures and patterns. The inevitable effect of code choice on power relationships, the realization that choice of language for school and other functions has major power to include or exclude individuals, has taught many people to take what is often called a "critical" approach and ask who benefits from decisions about choice. Thus, while educational linguistics tries like most other disciplines to achieve a measure of scientific objectivity, it is often committed and regularly interpreted as being on one side or the other in the politics of education. ①

In the central core of the volume, we include 25 chapters dealing with specific themes or sub-areas of educational linguistics. The first group essentially picks up my original language barrier question. One chapter reviews the evidence on choice of language of instruction in schools: all major empirical studies support the

---

① I am starting to wonder again how relevant scientific methods and approaches are to the social sciences.

UNESCO-proclaimed belief in the value of initial instruction in the language that children bring with them from home, and suggest that it takes at least five or six years careful preparation in some model of bilingual education before pupils are ready to benefit fully from instruction in the national official school language. Unfortunately, reality is far different. Other chapters look at this theme. One focuses on cultural as well as linguistic differences between home and school. Another tackles the even more difficult situation where the home language is stigmatized as a dialect or nonstandard. Another considers the relevance of the language barrier to the education of the Deaf, a group now increasingly recognized by some as analogous to a linguistic or ethnic minority. New definitions of literacy are shown to be related to developments of multiple identities in modern societies. A final chapter attempts to analyze causes, looking at the effects of colonization and its aftermaths and the growing pressure of globalization.

The second group deals specifically with language education policy and management. The first chapter describes work in Europe to define common goals for foreign language teaching. The second considers language teaching inside and outside schools. The third presents the theories and practices of language management cultivation initially developed by the Prague School of linguists who were interested in the elaboration of developed literary languages at a time that the American school of language planning was tending to concentrate on the issues faced by previously under-developed languages. The next chapter describes the work continuing with language cultivation in underdeveloped contexts, such as the development of writing systems, the choices involved in adapting vernacular languages to school and other uses, the sharing of functions with standard languages. Another chapter looks at the extreme cases, presenting arguments for the involvement of education systems in the preservation of endangered languages. The final chapter adds a note of realism or sounds the tocsin, presenting evidence of the rapid invasion of primary education throughout the world by English.

In the third group of articles, the central theme is literacy. Thirty years ago, one might have been satisfied with a chapter on the teaching of reading, but now there is separate treatment of literacy in general, vernacular and indigenous literacies, religious and sacred literacies, and the particular approaches to multiliteracies that have developed out of Michael Halliday's alternative view of linguistic theory. (Halliday of course was also at Bloomington, but shortly thereafter moved to Australia.)

The fourth group picks up major themes in Second Language Acquisition, a term coined after the transformational revolution to replace the more obvious language learning is. One chapter tackles the problem of the order of acquisition that started to be studied in the light of Chomsky's claim that language was innate rather than learned. The second takes the opposite view, looking at research encouraged by anthropology into the process of language socialization. The next three return to what have become traditional Second Language Acquisition themes: the nature of interlanguage and the influences one language has on learning another language; the extent to which the language learner is able to reach the proficiency or competence level of the native speaker and whether this is biologically or otherwise determined; and the continuing debate as to whether natural exposure to a new language must be supplemented by explicit teaching and focus on forms.

The last five chapters in this group deal with language assessment, not just as twenty years ago they might have done as simply various topics in language testing, but now in a sociologically anchored and ethically informed discussions of language assessment for inclusion or exclusion (immigrants, asylum seekers, minorities), recent work in diagnostic and formative assessment, ethical approaches to accountability and standards, the potential of scales and frameworks, and the effects of attempts at national standardization particularly in the United States. Again, the recurring concern about policy is evident.

The third and final section of the *Handbook* has a number of sectors exploring the relationship between research and practice. One summarizes recent work in task-based learning. The second outlines developments in instructional approaches that take advantage of current work in corpus linguistics. The third looks at the actual language use inside the classroom. The fourth picks up and describes the field I was working on forty years ago in Bloomington, computer-assisted language learning. It is very different now. The three final chapters present some wider perspectives: an ecological perspective on educational linguistics within the context of semiotics; a classroom agenda which tackles the complex question of what educational linguistics the language teacher should know; and finally, a research agenda of the field itself suggesting the gaps that remain.

The field of educational linguistics has clearly expanded and grown over the years, thanks to the realization by scholars like Nessa Wolfson of the fundamental symbiosis of language and education.

Territoriality or tolerance

Educational linguists are motivated by a desire to understand and improve the relationships between language and education; if we controlled language and language education policy, I suspect/hope that our only goal would be to help pupils build the pluringual proficiency that enables success in the modern world while maintaining connections with their home and heritage. But at all levels (and most of all, at the level of the ethnic groups and nation-states most involved in language management), there is a large range of other motives (Ager 2001). Dominating is the belief in the superiority, importance and power of "my language" to build group or national identity at whatever cost (look at the continued support for an English Only constitutional clause in the USA, while the rest of the world sees English as an untouchable conqueror). As a result, much language management aims to produce monolingual hegemony, and most language education policy aims to homogenize language knowledge. Even the counter-trends, whether a linguistic human right (Skutnabb-Kangas & Phillipson 1995) or a reversing language shift (Fishman 1991) turns out to offer a hegemonous utopian model, tied commonly to an alternative national or ethnic (or religious) choice, equally "imperialistic" or totalitarian in its assumption of being the correct choice.

Indeed, I am starting to suspect that all forms of language management are not just authoritarian (by definition) but totalitarian, as they consist of efforts to force or persuade others to conform to an elitist utopian view of how the world should be. If rather we accept a more liberal or pluralist view, arguing that people should be allowed to choose their own values (and languages) provided they do not harm others, we will see why privileging group authority (ethnic or national or minority) can be seen as interference with liberty. That the effort to impose language (not unlike the effort to impose religion) does not usually work is of course a consideration.

The lessons of sociolinguistic research are surprisingly clear. As another distinguished Penn linguist, William Labov, has recently[1] reminded us graphically, dialect (and analogously language) maintenance is not a problem for the American Black community who are increasingly isolated and ghettoized by social, educational

---

[1] At GURT 2006.

and economic policies. This of course echoed Fishman's finding forty years ago (Fishman 1966) that the American languages being best maintained were those of groups voluntarily (the Amish and the Hassidim) or involuntarily (Native Americans and Spanish speakers) isolated and blocked from intergenerational socioeconomic mobilization. As a result, it is obvious why the main language management solutions proffered in cases of continued conflict is territorial—if you want to live on my side of road (in Flanders rather than Wallonia, in India rather than Pakistan, in Prague rather than Bratislava, in Riga rather than Moscow, in Washington rather than San José,) you better learn my language and forget about yours. Mayall (2006) in a memorial lecture for Dominique Jacquin-Berdal noted that she was one of the few who spoke out clearly against the "cavalier and shallow advocacy of partition as a solution to the problem of ethnic conflict".

I called these "solutions" but as we know, they seldom solve and more usually lead to continued tensions and problems. In fact, I am coming again to realize that looking for utopian solutions to complex social problems may well be, as Isaiah Berlin has reminded us, the wrong approach. It works more or less in science, but in human affairs leads commonly to totalitarian dogmatism and majority dictatorship. Berlin proposes rather than absolute truth acceptance of clusters of probably irreconcilable values. I find this very much in synch with the way the Talmud assumes regularly the continued tension between alternate views, each of which deserves consideration. Of course, a practical mode of conduct must be found if we are to avoid the chaos of "anything goes". In Jewish law, it is generally a practical result permitted within the competing views but often set by a third principle. In Berlin's philosophy, it is the "common decency" which enables us to distinguish totalitarian systems from democratic and genocide from reasonable self-defense. And in language policy, I suggest it should be tolerance ((May 2001) uses the term "tolerability" which he defines a majority acceptance of minority language rights). I would rather expand to majority or minority acceptance of diversity and respect for other languages and varieties. Of course it doesn't make sense to make the claim that all varieties are equal; in social practice, that is clearly not true, and in actual development and state of cultivation, it is equally obvious that every language and variety has developed to fill the functions and niches allocated in its sociolinguistic ecology. And of course it is these differences that linguists so regularly adduce as the motive for maintaining diversity.

Tolerating and respecting other languages and varieties, then, whether in symbolic national constitutions or in civic and commercial language management or in the language policy and practices of educational systems, is a key element in living with the increasingly complex multilingualism of modern cities and states. Perhaps then the ideal form of language management is what we might call accommodation (Cooper & Greenbaum 1987; Giles, Taylor, & Bourhis 1973), by which I mean establishing civic policies that allow individuals the maximum choice of language variety. ① A wise language education policy will accept this, making it possible for all to be educated in their own home language while being offered the choice of acquiring the standard language.

Concluding: the new series

The puzzle raised by my Maori high school pupils half a century ago started to be illuminated by my later study of linguistics. Of all the important views I came to accept, it was the Roman Jakobson vision (Jakobson 1960), interpreted by Dell Hymes, that has provided the broadest framework that underlies the view I take of educational linguistics. As members of the next generation, both Nessa Wolfson and I were engaged in building an institutional structure to support the theory and try to enable and persuade schools to cope better with the language barrier to education that so many pupils throughout the world continue to face, by applying the lessons of educational linguistics to wise and tolerant language policies and cautious language management.

In another completing of the cycle of intellectual endeavor, the decision of Central South University of Forestry and Technology to launch this ambitious series of publications in educational linguistics combines a 2000 year-old Chinese tradition of language policy and management with recent Western develops in the field. The books in the *Foreign Linguistics and Literature Studies Series* already planned by Professors Zhang Huaiyun and Cao Zhixi cover a wide range of relevant fields: dictionaries, language teaching approaches, China's FLT policy studies, translation studies, and international literature and cultural studies. This is an important initiative, and I am deeply honoured to have been invited to offer this introduction.

---

①   For instance, some of the provisions of the European Charters for minority languages, or the provisions of Executive Order 10 in the USA.

References

[1] Ager, Dennis E. (2001). *Motivation in language planning and language policy.* Clevedon England & Buffalo USA: Multilingual Matters Ltd.

[2] Ammon, Ulrich. (1992). The Federal Republic of Germany's policy of spreading German. *International Journal of the Sociology of Language*, 95, 33 - 50.

[3] Backhaus, Peter. (in press). *Linguistic landscape and multilingualism in Tokyo.* Clevedon: Multilingual Matters Ltd.

[4] Bender, M. L., Cooper, Robert L., & Ferguson, Charles A. (1972). Language in Ethiopia: Implications of a survey for sociolinguistic theory and method. *Language in Society*, 1(2), 215 - 233.

[5] Cooper, Robert L. (1968). An elaborated language testing model. *Language Learning* (Special issue No. 7), 57 - 72.

[6] Cooper, Robert L. (1989). *Language planning and social change.* Cambridge: Cambridge University Press.

[7] Cooper, Robert L. (Ed.). (1982). *Language Spread: Studies in diffusion and social change.* Bloomington, IN: Indiana University Press.

[8] Cooper, Robert L., & Greenbaum, Charles. W. (1987). Accommodation as a framework for the study of simplified registers.

[9] Davies, Alan. (2006). Review of Directions in applied linguistics: Essays in honour of Robert B. Kaplan. *Applied Linguistics*, 27(3), 534 - 537.

[10] Fishman, Joshua A. (1991). *Reversing language shift: theoretical and empirical foundations of assistance to threatened languages.* Clevedon, England: Multilingual Matters Ltd.

[11] Fishman, Joshua A. (2006). *Do not leave your language alone: the hidden status agendas within corpus planning in language policy.* Mahwah NJ: Lawrence Erlbaum Associates Publishers.

[12] Fishman, Joshua A. (Ed.). (1966). *Language loyalty in the United States: the maintenance and perpetuation of non-English mother tongues by American ethnic and religious groups.* The Hague: Mouton.

[13] Fishman, Joshua A. (Ed.). (1968). *Advances in the sociology of language.* The Hague: Mouton.

[14] Ford Foundation. (1975). *Language and development: a retrospective survey of Ford Foundation language projects*, 1952 - 1974. New York: Ford Foundation.

[15] Garvin, Paul, & Spolsky, Bernard (Eds.). (1966). *Computation in linguistics:*

　　　　　a case book. Bloomington, IN. : Indiana University Press.

[16] Giles, Howard, Taylor, Donald M. , &. Bourhis, Richard. (1973). Towards a theory of interpersonal accommodation through language: some Canadian data. *Language in Society*, 2(2), 177 – 192.

[17] Gorter, Durk (Ed.). (2006). *Linguistic landscape: a new approach to multilingualism*. Clevedon: Multilingual Matters Ltd.

[18] Haugen, Einar. (1961). Language planning in modern Norway. *Scandinavian Studies*, 33, 68 – 81.

[19] Haugen, Einar. (1966). *Language conflict and language planning: the case of Modern Norwegian. Cambridge*, MA. : Harvard University Press.

[20] Hornberger, Nancy H. , &. King, Kendall A. (2001). Reversing language shift in South America. In Joshua A. Fishman (Ed.), *Can threatened languages be saved?* (pp. 166 – 194). Clevedon, Avon: Multilingual Matters Ltd.

[21] Hymes, Dell. (1967). Models of the interaction of language and social setting. *Journal of Social Issues*, 23(2), 8 – 38.

[22] Hymes, Dell. (1974). *Foundations in sociolinguistics: an ethnographic approach*. Philadelphia: University of Pennsylvania Press.

[23] Hymes, Dell. (1997). History and development of Sociolinguistics. In Christina Bratt Paulston &. G. Richard Tucker (Eds.), *The early days of sociolinguistics: memories and reflections* (pp. 121 – 146). Dallas, TX: The Summer Institute of Linguistics.

[24] Jakobson, Roman. (1960). Closing Statement: Linguistics and Poetics. In Thomas A. Sebeok (Ed.), *Style in Language* (pp. 350 – 377). Cambridge, Mass. : The Technology Press of MIT and John Wiley and Sons.

[25] May, Stephen. (2001). *Language and minority rights : ethnicity, nationalism, and the politics of language*. Harlow, Essex, England &. New York: Longman.

[26] Mayall, James. (2006) .Dominique Jacquin-Berdal Memorial Lecture: Nationalism and Self-determination in Africa. *Nations and Nationalism*, 12 (4), 549 – 558.

[27] P Riágain, Pádraig. (1997). *Language policy and social reproduction: Ireland 1893 – 1993*. Oxford: Clarendon Press.

[28] Ohannessian, Sirarpi, Ferguson, Charles A. , &. Polomé, Edgar C. (Eds.). (1975). *Language surveys in developing nations : papers and reports on sociolinguistic surveys*. Arlington, Va. : Center for Applied Linguistics.

［29］Phillipson, Robert. (1992). *Linguistic imperialism*. Oxford: Oxford University Press.

［30］Robinson, John P., Brecht, Richard D., & Rivers, William P. (2006). Speaking foreign languages in the United States: Correlates, trends, and possible consequences. *Modern Language Journal*, 90(4), 457 - 472.

［31］Rubin, Joan, Jernudd, Bjoern, Das Gupta, Jyotirindra, Fishman, Joshua A., & Ferguson, Charles A. (1977). *Language planning processes*. Mouton Publishers, The Hague.

［32］Schumann, John H. (2006). Summing up: Some themes in the cognitive neuroscience of second language acquisition. *Language Learning Journal*, 56 (s1), 313 - 319.

［33］Skutnabb-Kangas, Tove, & Phillipson, Robert. (1995). Linguistic human rights, past and present. In Tove Skutnabb-Kangas, Robert Phillipson & Mart Rannut (Eds.), *Linguistic human rights: Overcoming linguistic discrimination* (pp. 71 - 110). Berlin & New York: Mouton de Gruyter.

［34］Spolsky, Bernard. (1967). Do they know enough English? In David Wigglesworth (Ed.), *ATESL Selected Conference Papers*. Washington, DC: NAFSA Studies and Papers, English Language Series.

［35］Spolsky, Bernard. (1971). The language barrier to education. In George E. Perren (Ed.), *Interdisciplinary approaches to language* (pp. 8 - 17). London: CILT.

［36］Spolsky, Bernard. (1974a). Linguistics and the language barrier to education. In Thomas A. Sebeok, Arthur S. Abramson, Dell Hymes, Herbert Rubenstein, Edward Stankiewicz & Bernard Spolsky (Eds.), *Current Trends in Linguistics: Linguistics and adjacent arts and sciences* (Vol. 12, pp. 2027 - 2038). The Hague: Mouton.

［37］Spolsky, Bernard. (1974b). The Navajo Reading Study: an illustration of the scope and nature of educational linguistics. In J. Quistgaard, H. Schwarz & H. Spong-Hanssen (Eds.), *Applied Linguistics: Problems and solutions: Proceedings of the Third Congress on Applied Linguistics*, *Copenhagen*, 1972 (Vol. 3, pp. 553 - 565). Heidelberg: Julius Gros Verlag.

［38］Spolsky, Bernard. (1977). The establishment of language education policy in multilingual societies. In Bernard Spolsky & Robert L. Cooper (Eds.), *Frontiers of bilingual education* (pp. 1 - 21). Rowley, MA.: Newbury House Publishers.

[39] Spolsky, Bernard. (1978). *Educational linguistics: an introduction.* Rowley, MA.: Newbury House Publishers.

[40] Spolsky, Bernard. (1986). Overcoming language barriers to education in a multilingual world. In Bernard Spolsky (Ed.), *Language and education in multilingual settings* (pp. 184 – 193). Clevedon: Multilingual Matters Ltd.

[41] Spolsky, Bernard. (1996). Prologemena to an Israeli Language Policy. In Tina Hickey & Jenny Williams (Eds.), *Language, Education and Society in a Changing World* (pp. 45 – 53). Dublin and Clevedon: IRAAL/Multilingual Matters Ltd.

[42] Spolsky, Bernard. (2003). Religion as a site of language contact. *Annual Review of Applied Linguistics*, 23, 81 – 94.

[43] Spolsky, Bernard. (2004). *Language Policy.* Cambridge: Cambridge University Press.

[44] Spolsky, Bernard. (2005a). Is language policy applied linguistics? In Paul Bruthiaux, Dwight Atkinson, William Grabe, William G. Eggington & Vaidehi Ramanathan (Eds.), *Direction in Applied Linguistics: Essays in Honor of Robert B. Kaplan* (pp. 26 – 38). Clevedon England: Multilingual Matters Ltd.

[45] Spolsky, Bernard. (2005b). Language policy. In James Cohen, Kara T. McAlister, Kellie Rolstad & Jeff MacSwan (Eds.), *ISB4: Proceedings of the 4th International Symposium on Bilingualism* (pp. 2152 – 2164). Somerville, MA: Cascadilla Press.

[46] Spolsky, Bernard. (2006a). Does the US need a language policy, or is English enough? Language policies in the US and beyond. In Audrey Heining-Boynton (Ed.), *ACTFL 2005 – 2015: Realizing Our Vision of Languages for All* (pp. 15 – 38). Upper Saddle River NJ: Pearson Education.

[47] Spolsky, Bernard. (2006b). Language policy failures-why won't they listen? In Martin Pütz, Joshua A. Fishman & JoAnne Neff-van Aertselaer (Eds.), *"Along the Routes to Power": Explorations of Empowerment through Language* (pp. 87 – 106). Berlin & New York: Mouton de Gruyter.

[48] Spolsky, Bernard. (in press). Prolegomena to a theory of language policy and management for the 21st century. In Roland Terborg & Laura Garcia Landa (Eds.), *The Challenges of Language Policies in the XXI Century.* Mexico.

[49] Spolsky, Bernard, & Shohamy, Elana. (1998). Language policy in Israel.

New Language Planning Newsletter, 12(4), 1 - 4.

[50] Spolsky, Bernard, & Shohamy, Elana. (1999). *The languages of Israel：policy, ideology and practice*. Clevedon：Multilingual Matters.

Bernard Spolsky

Emeritus, Bar-Ilan University

Israel

PREFACE

Discourse is the most important medium of human verbal communication. For the majority of occasions, we communicate with each other through discourse whether we are exchanging ideas, information, and emotions or across time and space. The study of discourse comprehension (DC hereafter), therefore, is of direct and practical significance to human verbal communication. It also has academic importance, five aspects of which are pointed out by A. C. Graesser et al (1997: 163 – 189). ① The peculiarity of the study of DC: Discourse processing (DP hereafter) is not only limited to language itself in that it is not the mere gathering of sentences or utterances, nor is it only retrieving and constructing the representation of memory. As a matter of fact, the study of DC cannot be replaced by the study from other branches, such as memory psychology, or psycholinguistics. ② The richness of discourse context: Discourse creates such rich contexts that we may limit the interpretation of input like ambiguity in a systematic fashion. ③ Hypotheses testing of psychological theories: Some discourse are microcosmic of events and experiences of the real world and experiments of DP can serve to test the psychological theories regarding human cognitive behavior and emotion through natural or created discourse. ④ The importance of the study of DC: Discourse entails multi-level presentation from phoneme to global message. The fact that humans can coordinate on these levels rapidly shows that DP is a major manifestation of human intelligence. ⑤ The complexity of DC: Discourse is practically interwoven with all-cognitive functions and processes like memory, conception, inferencing, and problem solving.

1. Proposition and proposition analysis

1.1　Idea and schema

During reading, one of the presumptions of DC is to remember the discourse message. Researches (Bransford & Franks 1971; Alan Garnham & Jane Oakhill 1987) show that in language comprehension, what one remembers is not sentences; rather he/she integrates ideas from sentences and forms a mental model. The fundamental characteristic of mental model is that ideas from discourse are reconstructed in the mind of the reader, which is close to Bartlett's (1932) concept of schema.

Schema is a meaningful and organized framework which integrates incoming information. This process is accomplished by making use of present knowledge. When the reader recalls a certain discourse, what he/she uses is the conceptulaized schema which has assimilated the original passage, which means the surface form of the original passage has lost and is replaced by the abstract mental representation. Then, what is the basic unit of organizing ideas in constructing the mental model? The majority of experiments have showed that proposition is the basic meaningful unit in discourse.

1. 2   Text analysis of proposition

Propositions consist of a noun and a verb or an adjective. The richness and complexity of propositions in a discourse affect not only the reading time, but also the recall of discourse contents (G. Underwood et al 1996) . This was supported by Kintsch's (1974) experiments. In his experiments, the subjects were presented with sentences of 16 - 17 words, but the propositions in these sentences vary from 4 to 9. The subjects were required to read a group of sentences and then recall these sentences. The sentence reading time, the time recalling proposition and the accuracy were recorded. The results show that in reading sentences of similar length, reading time increases by 0. 95 second with the increase of a proposition in a sentence; reading time increases by 1. 48 second with one more proposition recalled.

To interpret the role of propositions in DC, Kintsch (1974) proposed a propositional model, which accounts for reader's representation of discourse in terms of textbase consisting of propositions and their relations. The reader needs to construct a representation of the importance or hierachy of each proposition and their relationship in order to maintain meaning.

(1) Turbulance forms at the edge of a wing and grows in strength over its surface, contributing to the lift of a supersonic aircraft.

The explanatory power of Kintsch's model lies in the capture of the complexity of propositions not only in terms of the number of propositions, but also the relationship among them. The formal textbase of this sentence can be written as follows:

① (FORM, TURBULENCE)
② (LOC: AT, 1, EDGE)
③ (PART OF, WING, EDGE)
④ (GROW, TURBULENCE, STRENGTH)
⑤ (LOC: OVER, 4, SURFACE)

⑥ (PART OF, WING, SURFACE)

⑦ (CONTRIBUTE, TURBULENCE, LIFT, AIRCRAFT)

⑧ (SUPERSONIC, AIRCRAFT)

The numbers (1, 4) in propositions ② and ⑤ refer to the propositions they represent. The propositional relationship can be put in the following tree diagram:

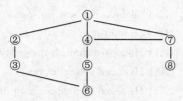

Both ways express the hierarchical relationship among propositions, with P① governing all other propositions, P② ④ ⑦ being the second level propositions, P ③ ⑤ ⑧ being the third level propositions and P ⑥ the fourth level. Each level of propositions is only related to the immediate super-ordinate propositions, as propositions ② ④ ⑦ are only related to proposition ① .

Kintsch et al (1975) also confirmed the importance of the hierarchical level of propositions in the recall of discourse. They presented subjects with reading paragraphs of around 70 words and asked the subjects to recall the contexts after reading. Results show that chances of recalling the first level propositions are twice as high as those at levels 2, 4, and 5. And the recall of higher level propositions facilitates the recall of lower level propositions. If higher level propositions are recalled, the recall probability of their lower propositions raises from 15% to 50%.

2. Inference

Propositional analyses are enough for the understanding of simple sentences. However, under most circumstances, the reader needs to go beyond this level and construct a reader's situation model, in which sentences are interpreted. To go from a purely propositional level of comprehension to an interpretative level, inferences are made by the reader. The major role of inferences in DC is to establish causal and elaborative relationship.

2. 1 Causal inference

Causal inference (CI hereafter) is formed when the reader realizes that there exists a causal relationship between two different events. As the reader identifies these causal relationships among sentences or propositions, their causal dependencies are mapped in a mental representation or network of ideas. To illustrate causal relationships and their network, let's consider example 2 (van Broek & Lorch 1993)

(2) Label

	Label	Statement
①	Setting	(S) There once was a boy named Bob.
②	Initiating event	(E) One day, Bob saw his friend's new 10-speed bike.
③	Goal	(G) Bob wanted to get a 10-speed.
④	Action	(A1) He looked through the yellow pages.
⑤	Action	(A2) He called several stores.
⑥	Action	(A3) He asked them about the prices of bikes.
⑦	Action	(A4) He found the store with the lowest prices on bikes.
⑧	Action	(A5) He went to the bike store.
⑨	Action	(A6) He asked the salesman about several models.
⑩	Action	(A7) The salesman recommended a touring bike.
⑪	Action	(A8) Bob looked at the selection of touring bike.
⑫	Action	(A9) He located some that were his size.
⑬	Action	(A10) He found a bike that was metallic blue.
⑭	Result	(O) Bob bought the beautiful bike.

The mental representation of this story has causal links between the goal and several other sentences like A2, A3, A5, A6 and O. Comprehension problems arise without these links, which are established through inferences. For instance, there is an implicit link between G and A2. In other words, Bob's intention in sentence G led to action in A2. Without this inference, A2 wouldn't make any sense in the story.

2. 2　Elaborative inference

Elaborative inferences (EI hereafter) are different from CI in that the former provide additional information about something already known to exist while the latter establish a relationship between two separate events.

(3) The boy cleared the snow from the stairs. The shovel was heavy.

In this example, the first sentence implies the need of some sort of instrument in clearing snow. Upon reading the second sentence, the reader constructs a mental model by relating "shovel" with "clearing snow" through inference that "shovel" is the tool.

A major question of inference in DC is whether inferences are formed on-line and constitute an integrated part of the reading process, or alternatively, they are made off-line, some time after the reading, perhaps at the time when the subjects are tested. Experimental data from the studies of reading time, verification time, and eye movements during initial reading of sentences show that CIs are made on-line and form part of the reader's situation model, whereas EIs are not essential for comprehension to proceed. Therefore, only when certain conditions are met does the reader make on-line inferences.

In the study of whether EIs are made on-line, discourse psychologists often compare reading or verification time of the implicit and explicit forms of texts. If the time is similar or of no statistical significance, it can be concluded that information provided in the explicit form is also available in the implicit form with an inference made. To illustrate this point, let's compare the above example with a similar yet different one:

(4) a. The boy cleared the snow with a shovel. The shovel was heavy.

b. The boy cleared the snow from the stairs. The shovel was heavy.

Sentence (4) a is the explicit form in that no EI is involved, whereas sentence (4) b is the implicit form and EI is needed. Singer (1979) found that in identical sentence-reading, the second sentence of (4) b takes longer, suggesting that it is at this point that inference is made. If the inference is made upon reading the first sentence (clearing snow), there should not be any time difference reading the sentence of (4) a and (4) b. The extra time required in reading the second sentence of (4) b shows that extra thinking are needed in order to establish links between the sentences. In other words, EIs are not made on initial reading (G. Underwood & V. Batt 1996).

However, research has also shown that the reader may form on-line EIs when certain conditions met.

(5) Sally's diet called for her to eat lots of fresh vegetables. Her favorite vegetable was corn that she could eat right off the cob. This was a diet she didn't mind one bit. She always had plenty of corn with every meal.

O'Brien et al (1988) studied the differences of readers' gaze duration on the target word "corn" by using four versions of this text. Example (5) is the high context, explicit form. To form the implicit version, "corn" is replaced by "one" and to form a low-context version, the second sentence is changed into "Her favorite vegetable was that she should get fresh only in summer". They found that in high contexts, there are no significant difference of gaze duration on the target word, with the explicit form 209 msec., implicit form 211msec, which suggests EIs are

made on-line in high-context discourse. However, the gaze duration are significantly different in low-contexts, with the explicit form 215 msec. and the implicit 234
msec., which suggests that EIs are not made on-line, but rather they are made
when they are required.

3. Local coherence VS global coherence

3. 1　Referring expressions

Referring expressions are nouns, pronouns, and noun phrases that refer to an
entity or proposition in the textbase, situation model, or world. An anaphoric
referring expression refers to a node that was mentioned previously in the text,
whereas cataphoric expressions refer to future text nodes, and deictic expressions
point to the world. As anaphoric expressions have received the most attention by
discourse psychologists (Graesser et al 1994), we will only discuss anaphoric expressions in this section.

3. 1. 1　Typicality effect

Typicality effect shows that the process of inferential reading can run into difficulty if the anaphor is not a typical exemplar of the antecedent and vice versa. Let's
compare example (6) and (7):

(6) a. A bird would sometimes wonder into the house.

b. The robin was attracted by the larder. (typical)

(7) a. A bird would sometimes wonder into the house.

b. The goose was attracted by the larder. (atypical)

Sanford (1977) compared the effect of typical (6a, 6b) and typical (7a, 7b)
antecedent /anaphor on reading and found that it took longer to read sentence (7) b
than (6)b. He also found that when the order of references was reversed, the effect
still exists.

3. 1. 2　Anaphoric island

Anaphoric island refers to the fact that the antecedent is isolated from its anaphor.

(8) They had a feature on violent youngsters, attributing it to drink.

In the example, the anaphor "it" does not agree exactly with the antecedent
"violent". The experiment shows that though readers can comprehend the sentence, almost all of readers will use "violence, the violent behavior or similar structures" when asked to rewrite the sentence. It also suggests that when anaphoric

island phenomenon is encountered in reading, it will take readers longer time (Garham & Oakhill 1987).

3.2 Argument overlap

In DC, if the text is to be regarded as coherent, the explicit statements in a text need to be connected conceptually. And an important dimension for establishing text coherence is referred to as argument overlap (Kintsch & van Dijk 1978; Mckoon & Ratcliff 1992). By argument overlap, it is meant the overlap of the arguments in two recent sentences in the discourse.

(9) Sally Jones got up early this morning. She wanted to clean the house.

Here "She" refers to the argument "Sally Jones" in the first sentence. The two sentences are connected by argument overlap. Research shows that if there is an overlap between the argument with the textbase proposition in WM and that in the recent sentences, continuity is achieved. And if the continuity breaks down, reading time will be increased.

3.3 Minimalist position VS constructivist position

We have already discussed inference and its role. Another important role of inference is mainly to keep the discourse coherent. Here two points of view prevail.

The minimalist position (McKoon & Ratcliff 1992) claims that in normal reading, the only inferences made automatically are those required to establish local coherence and those lexical-level inferences that are based on familiar general knowledge (Fletcher & Bloom 1988). And only under special circumstances may a reader make other EIs and establish global coherence.

McKon & Ratcliff (1992) contrast this minimalist position with a constructivist position in which more EIs including global coherence, are routinely constructed to instantiate a detailed representation of the situation or logic of the narrative or to link disparate parts of the text.

Now let's compare the differences of these two positions in exploring discourse coherence by referring back to example (2) in section 3. In Bob's story, the minimalist position predicts that A6 is only connected with A5, whereas the constructivist position holds that A6 is not only connected with A5, but also with G, the goal statement. Both positions predict the effect of a related adjacent prime upon verification of the targets, but the finding that goal statement predicts the verification of action and outcome statements is only predicted by the constructivist position. If readers only connect adjacent action/ action statements, it is difficult to describe a mechanism for the non-adjacent goal/action and goal/outcome priming in these statements.

The experiments reported by Fincher-Kiefer (1993) , Trabasso & Suh (1993) also support the constructivist position, suggesting that inferences can be formed over distance, not just between adjacent statements, even when the passage is locally coherent.

The apparent conflict between minimalist and constructivist positions may be resolved by considering other determinants of inference-making (besides inference type), such as the salience of the information relevant to the to-be-made inference in a particular context (McKoon & Ratcliff 1992) , the time course of the inferential process (Murray et al 1993) , and its dependence on WM capacity (Whitney et al 1991).

4. The nature of discourse comprehension

Psychological models of DP have specified at length how the multilevel meaning representations are built during comprehension. These complex models are grounded in general theories of cognition. In this section we are going to talk about the psychological mechanisms of DC from the following three aspects: cognitive components, theoretical modeling of the cognitive architecture and resource constraints.

4. 1   Cognitive components

Graesser et al (1997) summarize cognitive components in DP into ten points. ① Knowledge structures: The knowledge in texts and in packages of world knowledge are represented as a network of nodes (i. e. concepts, referents, propositions) that are interconnected by relational arcs. One source of comprehension difficulty lies in the amount of background knowledge of the reader. ② Spreading activation of nodes in knowledge networks: When a node in a network is activated, activation spreads to neighboring nodes, then neighbors of neighbors, and so on. The activation level of a node decreases as a function of the number of arcs between the originally activated node and another node in the network (Anderson 1983) . ③ Memory stores: There are three memory stores in most discourse models: STM, WM, and LTM. Roughly speaking, STM holds the most recent clause being comprehended and WM holds about two sentences. Important information is actively recycled in WM. ④ Discourse focus: Consciousness and focal attention is concentrated on one or two nodes in the discourse representation. ⑤ Resonance: The content that resides in the discourse, STM, and WM may match highly with content that was presented earlier in the text or with other content in LTM. If so, there is resonance with the content in LTM, and the information in LTM gets resonance activated. ⑥ Activation, inhibition, and suppression of nodes: As sentences are comprehended, nodes in the discourse structure and LTM are activated, strengthened, inhibited, and suppressed. The primary goal of some discourse models is to explain the fluctuations in activation values of discourse nodes during the dynamic comprehension. ⑦ Convergence and constraint satisfaction: Discourse nodes receive more strength of encoding so that they are activated by several information sources and that they mesh with the constraints of other information sources. ⑧ Repetition and automaticity: Repetition increases the speed of accessing a knowledge structure and the nodes within the structure. Thus, familiar words are processed faster. The nodes in an automatized package of world knowledge can be accessed as a whole and used with only little cost to the resources in WM (Graesser et al 1997). ⑨ Explanations: Memory or information is enhanced when the reader constructs causal explanations of why events in the situation model occur and why the writer expressed information. Readers actively seek these explanations during reading (Graesser et al 1994). ⑩ Reader goals: The goals of the reader influence text comprehension and memory. For instance, reading a novel for enjoyment is rather different from reading it to take a university exam.

4. 2　Theoretical modeling of the cognitive architectures

In the study of DC, psychologists are all interested in how the language comprehension system can establish correct types and numbers of connections during the DP. Generally speaking, the connections between parts of the text are accommodated by the representations of relevant world knowledge. What is the mechanism, which enables the connections then?

In answering this question, discourse psychologists have developed some sophisticated quantitative and computational models of text comprehension. Two representatives of the models are the CAPS/READER model proposed by Just & Carpenter (1992) and the construction-integrative model proposed by Kintsch (1988).

The CAPS/READER model adopts a production system architecture (Anderson 1983) for creating, updating, and removing nodes in WM and LTM. The production system contains a set of production rules with an "IF (condition C), THEN (action A)" format; if the content of WM matches condition C, then physical action A is performed. Condition C may consist of an arbitrarily complex set of sub-states. There is also a threshold criterion for a condition, such that the condition is satisfied if the aggregate activation value of all its sub-states meets the threshold. Therefore the production rules in the CAPS are hardly brittle, discrete and simple. The set of production rules is evaluated in parallel in each circle of processing. Those rules that meet the threshold of activation will perform various actions, such as scanning explicit input, modifying activation values of nodes in WM, changing the load on WM, strengthening nodes in LTM, and producing output. Kintsch's (1988) construction-integration model adopts a connectionist or neural network architecture of cognition (McClelland & Rumelhart 1986). Two phases are identified in this model. During the construction phase, possible connections between the input propositions are generated undiscriminated and these connections are based on argument overlap, propositional embedding, and highly likely implications, such as the consequences of some event. The integration phase uses a connectionist-like settling algorithm to delete or decrease the irrelevant activation and to converge on a set of connections that define the final inter-propositional connectivity. The final set of activations can predict some performance measures, such as the probability of recall of a given proposition.

4. 3   Resource constraints in discourse processing

In interpreting under what circumstances the reader maintains local and global coherence, the activation level and time in activation spreading, psychologists have gradually come to the agreement that resource constraint in WM is a central concept. Because of the resource limitations, spreading activation can not be undiscriminated or unconstrained. Otherwise there would be computational explosion, for WM is limited in capacity, and reading is a rapidly ongoing process. Normal reading does not allow inferences, which are too time-consuming, and connections, which are too difficult to establish. The central assumption concerning resource constraints in Kintsch's (1988) model is that only propositions that reside in WM simultaneously can be connected. The mechanism that permits connection between different sentences is a limited buffer (typically having a capacity of two propositions) in which propositions from an earlier part of a text can be carried forward. Therefore, whether propositions can be carried forward is critical for them to be integrated. Just & Carpenter (1992) holds similar view. But in their model, resource constraint is described as an overall constraint on available resources, which in turn determines which and how many propositions are carried over to the next cycle (Goldman & Varna 1994).

Conclusion

We have addressed the issue of the process of DC from propositional, inferential, and local and global coherence levels of representation. Then we have analysed the nature of DC in terms of cognitive components, theoretical modeling of the cognitive architectures and resource constraints on DC.

From the above analyses we can conclude that DC should follow several principles that underlie general cognitive mechanisms. One converging principle is that the representation of information is graded, such that it can be in intermediate state other than just being present or absent. Furthermore, a representation's construction and decay may also be gradual. A second related principle concerns the mechanisms of spreading activation and suppression. These mechanisms provide a gradeness of processing to accompany the gradeness of representation. A third principle concerns resource constraint. The very limitations on cognitive resources can account for many types of individual differences and processing strategies in DC.

The empirical and theoretical progress in DP has had some straightforward applications for improving reading, education, text design, and social interaction. For example, Briton & Gulgoz (1991) used Kintsch & van Dijk's (1978) model to guide the revision of technical expository texts. The original texts were naturalistic sample of texts that had problematic referring expressions and coherence gaps. The texts were revised by clarifying referents of referring expressions and by making explicit some critical bridging inferences in the original text. These theory-based revisions dramatically improved memory for the texts when adults were given a delayed-recall test. It was theory that prevailed in improving the memorability of the texts, which confirmed the idea that "There is nothing so practical as a good theory" (Kurt Lewin 1951).

References

[1] Anderson, J. R. 1983. *The Architecture of Cognition*. Cambridge, MA: Harvard University Press.

[2] Bransford, J. D, Franks JJ. 1971. The abstraction of linguistic ideas. *Cognitive Psychology*. 2:331 – 350.

[3] Carpenter, P. A, Miyake, A, Just, MA. 1995. Language comprehension: sen-

tence and discourse processing. *Annual Review of Psychology*. 46: 91 - 120.

[4] Carpenter, P. A, Miyake, A, Just, M. A. 1994. Working memory constraints in comprehension: evidence from individual, aphasia, and aging. In *Handbook of Psycholinguistics*, ed. M. Gernsbacher, pp. 1075 - 1122. San Diego, CA: Academic.

[5] Chafe, W. 1994. Discourse, *Consciousness, and Time*. Chicago: University of Chicago Press Fletcher CR, Bloom CP. 1988. Casual reasoning in the comprehension of simple narrative texts. *Journal of Memory and Language* 19: 70 -80.

[6] Gernsbacher, M. A. 1990. *Language Comprehension as Structure Building*. Hillsdale, Nj: Erbaum.

[7] Gordon PC, Chan D. 1995. Pronoun, passives, and discourse coherence. *Journal of Memory and Language* 34: 216 - 231.

[8] Graesser, A. C, Millis, K. K. , Zwaan R. A. 1997 Discourse comprehension. *Annual Review of Psychology*. 48: 163 - 189.

[9] Graesser, A. C, Singer, M. , Trabasso T. 1994. Constructing inferences during narrative text comprehension. *Psychological Review*. 101: 371 - 395.

[10] Just, M. A. , Carpenter, P. A. 1992. A capacity theory of comprehension: individual differences in working memory. *Psychological Review* 99: 122 - 149.

[11] Kintsch, W. 1998. The role of knowledge in discourse comprehension: a constructive-integration model. *Psychological Review* 95: 163 - 182.

[12] Kintsch, W. 1994. Text comprehension, memory and learning. *American Psychologist* 49: 294 - 303.

[13] Kintsch, W. , van Dijk T. A. 1978. Toward a model of text comprehension and production. *Psychological Review* 85: 363 - 394.

[14] Lorch, R. F, O'Brien J. D. , eds. 1995. *Sources of Coherence in Reading*. Mahwah, NJ: Erbaum.

[15] McKoon, G. , Ratcliff, R. 1998. Memory-based language processing: psycholinguistics research in the 1990s. *Annual Review of Psychology* 49: 25 - 42.

[16] McKoon, G. , Ratcliff, R. 1992. Inference during reading. *Psychological Review*. 99: 440 - 466.

[17] Singer, M. , Graesser, A. C. , Trabasso, T. 1994. Minimal or global inference during reading. *Journal of Memory and Language* 33: 421 - 441.

[18] Singer, M. , Ritchot, K. 1996. The role of working in memory capacity and knowledge access in text inference processing. *Memory. & Cognition* 24: 733 –743.

[19] Stevenson, R. J. 1993. *Language, Thought and Representation*. New York: Wiley.

[20] Suh, S. Y, Trabasso, T. 1993. Inferences during reading: converging evidence from discourse analysis, talk-aloud protocols, and recognition priming. *Journal of Memory and Language* 32:279 – 300.

[21] van den Broek, P. 1990. Casual inferences and the comprehension of narrative texts. In *The Psychology of Learing and Motivation: Inferences and Text Comprehension*, eds. Ac Graesser, GH Bower, 25: 175 – 194, San Diego, CA: Acacdemic.

[22] van den Broek, P, Lorch, R. F. 1993. Network representation of casual relations in memory for narrative texts: evidence from primed recognition. *Discourse Process*. 17:75 – 98.

[23] Underwood, G. , Batt, V. 1996. *Reading and Understanding*. Cambridge, MA: Blackwell.

[24] Whitney, P. , Ritchie, B. G. , Clark, M. B. 1991. Working memory capacity and the use of elaborative inferences in text comprehension. *Discourse Process*. 14:133 –145.

[25] Zwaan, R. A. , Langston, M. C. , Graesser, A. C. 1995a. The construction of situation models in narrative comprehension: an event-indexing model. *Psychological Science* 6:292 – 297.

[26] Zwaan, R. A. , Magliano, J. P. , Graesser, A. C. 1995b. Dimensions of situation models in narrative comprehension. *Journal of Experimental Psychology. Learning. Memory & Cognition* 21:386 – 397.

Yang Zhiqing

Professor of English

Assistant President

Central South University of Forestry & Technology

Phonetic Text in a Universal Phonetic Alphabet

Korea has been known to the outside world as the land of "Morning calm" for centuries. There is nothing really calm about Korea nowadays. In fact she has now turned out to be a highly hustling and bustling society armed with IT industry. Believe it or not she is now a leading country in internet and mobiles phones. "Korea is engaged", as the weekly magazine Time aptly described on the cover page some time ago to dramatize the popularity of mobile phones in Korea.

More than anything else, however, Korea deserves to be known as "The Land of Phonetics and Spoken Language Processing", for it was here in Korea that the most remarkable phonetic alphabet was invented by the King Sejong in 1443. With the promulgation of Hummin Jeongeum (Right sounds for teaching the nation), the Korean alphabet of 28 letters by the king in 1446, Korea was turned into the land of phonetics. The Korean alphabet, now known as "HanGeul" (Unique and great alphabet) was devised on the basis of articulatory and auditory phonetic principles as well as the modern phonological concepts. It is an "Organic Alphabet", consisting of simple and yet versatile letters reflecting the shape of the articulatory organs in action. Therefore HanGeul has rightly earned the reputation of being "the greatest masterpiece of human intellect and a truly universal alphabet". Ladies and gentlemen, you will be literally surrounded by organic phonetic symbols and visible speech sounds whenever and wherever you are in Korea.

1. Earlier Attempts to Devise Universal Phonetic Alphabets

Serious attempts have been made by phoneticians and linguists in the east and west to devise universal phonetic alphabets. Notable among the pioneers are Bell, Sweet, Jespersen etc. Their attempts were highly rewarding and yet their ideas were unfortunately all short-lived. For instance, the Scottish Educationalist, Alexander Melville Bell, father of Alexander Graham Bell the inventor of the telephone.

invented a system of representing the sounds of speech according to the way in which they are articulated, which he called Visible Speech. Henry Sweet, a student of Melville Bell had improved upon this and adapted it to become what he called the Organic Alphabet, "based on a physiological analysis of the actions of the organs of speech".

It is highly interesting to remind ourselves on this occasion that Bell and Sweet appear to have to a large extent used the similar principles that the King Sejong of Korea applied in creating the Korean alphabet over five centuries ago. Just as the King Sejong used the symbol <ㄱ> in Hunmin Jeongeum as a component in the letters for the velar sounds [g] and [k], as resembling the shape of the tongue "blocking the throat", and <ㄴ> as a component in the letters for the linguo-dental sounds [t, d, n] to represent the tongue "touching the upper jaw", and <ㅁ>, representing the shape of the lips, in the labial sounds, so Sweet used a full circle <O> in his Organic Alphabt to represent the open throat in breath, and the symbol <I> to represent the narrowed throat with closed vocal cords, as in the production of voice. Sweet's symbol for the teeth for dental consonants (such as English th in "thin") is <v> based on the shape of teeth. "Open", i. e. fricative, consonants are represented by a broken circle, stopped consonants by the broken circle closed by a bar. A voiced consonant is represented by adding the voiced "bar" to the corresponding voiceless consonant. Notice that the King Sejong used an additional stroke to derive aspirated plosive and affricate consonant graphemes in Korean alphabet:

<ㄱ> [k] → <ㅋ> [kh].

<ㅈ> [c] → <ㅊ> [ch]

According to E. Henderson, Sweet's organic Alphabet lacked, unfortunately, the royal support which ensured the adoption of Hunmin Jeongeum by the Korean nation, and printing difficulties obliged him in his later writings to use in his phonetic transcriptions the adapted forms of the Roman letters that linguists are familiar with today in the alphabet of the International Phonetic Association.

2. International Phonetic Alphabet (IPA)

The IPA is no doubt the most widely used and at the same time, highly successful phonetic alphabet today. However, the IPA symbols, based mainly on Roman and Greek letters, has some serious disadvantages and drawbacks.

Roman: [a, i, e, o, u, p, t, k, s, z, f, x] etc.

Greek : [φ, β, γ, θ, χ] etc.

Modified : [ə, ɛ, œ, ø, ʃ, ɹ, ʁ, ç]

For one thing, the IPA symbols do not represent or reflect the shapes or movements of the organs of speech in the manner that the Korean letters do. Notice the formal resemblance of the shape of the back of the tongue blocking the soft palate to the Korean letter for the velar plosive sound <ㄱ>. Moreover, unlike in Korean alphabet, no formal interrelationship can be found in IPA between the phonetic symbols representing homorganic sounds such as p/b, t/d, k/g, s/z, f/v, etc. They are simply arbitrary and totally unrelated in shape. Notice the formal similarity among the three homorganic consonant letters in Korean in comparison to the formal disimilarity between IPA [k] and [g].

Kor. <ㄱ> [k] → <ㅋ> [kh] → <ㄲ> [k']

IPA. <g> → <k>

Consequently IPA symbols are harder for beginners to learn and use than Korean letters.

3. Advantages of Korean Alphabet

Korean alphabet is unique in many respects and it certainly deserves to be more widely known and understood. The most characteristic features of Korean alphabet are as follows:

3. 1　Phonetically Oriented

(1) Consonant letters: The shape of the basic letters was modelled on the actual shape of the articulatory organs involved in pronouncing the sound represented by the letters. The five basic consonant letters are created as follows:

<ㄱ> [k] represents the velar sound since it resembles the shape of the tongue blocking the throat;

<ㄴ> [n] represents the lingual sound (dental/alveolar sound in modern phonetic terminology) since it resembles the tongue touching "the upper jaw", i. e., upper teeth or teeth ridge;

<ㅁ> [m] represents the labial sound since it resembles the shape of the lips;

<ㅅ> [s] represents the dental sound since it resembles the shape of the teet;

<ㅇ> [ ] represents the throat sound since it resembles the shape of the throat.

As pointed out by Henderson this was exactly what Bell and Sweet had in mind when they tried to devise Organic and Visible Speech about five centuries later. In this manner the five basic letters were established.

(2) Vowel letters: Vowel letters were devised on the traditional oriental philosophical principles of In (negative) and Yang (positive) ... The King devised three basic letters $<\cdot>$, $<->$ and $<|>$, symbolizing respectively "heaven", "earth" and "man" and assigning phonetic values as follows:

Three Basic Vowel Letters

$<\cdot>$ [ɔ] 天 "heaven (round)"

$<->$ [ɯ] 地 "earth (flat)"

$<|>$ [i] 人 "man" (upright)

3. 2 Systematic Derivation

Most Korean graphemes are derived systematically from the basic consonant and vowel letters by addition of extra discritical marks.

For instance the twelve remaining consonant letters were derived by adding to each of the five basic letters one or more additional strokes or symbols which indicated other relevant phonetic features or different manners of articulation at homorganic points of articulation.

e. g. $<ㄴ> \rightarrow <ㄷ> \rightarrow <ㅌ> \rightarrow <ㄸ>$

$[n] \rightarrow [d] \rightarrow <t> \rightarrow <t'>$

It is interesting to note that the basic letter $<ㄴ>$ [n] symbolizing dental/alveolar articulation flows in the derived homorganic letters. Likewise, the remaining eight vowel letters were derived by different combinations of the three basic letters:

$<ㅏ>$ [a] $= <|> + <.>$

$<ㅑ>$ [ja] $= <|> + <.> + <.>$

$<ㅓ>$ [v] $= <.> + <|>$

$<ㅗ>$ [o] $= <.> + <->$

$<ㅜ>$ [u] $= <-> + <.>$ etc.

4. Han Geul: Organic Alphabet of Distinctive Feature

It is worth noting that the Korean alphabet Hangeul has a kind of distinctive theory incorporated in it. In fact one can see that Hunmin Jeongeum of 1446 was created with practically the same kind of distinctive theory that was initiated and developed in twentieth century by Jakobson, Chomsky and Halle.

The notion of distinctive feature and binary opposition is clearly demonstrated by the articulatory and auditory (acoustic) description given in Hunmin Jeongeum of the phonetic value of the three basic vowels, which may be tabulated as follows (table Ⅰ):

Table Ⅰ

Vowel / Features		< l > [i]	< — > [ə~ɯ]	< · > [ɔ~ɒ]
Articulatory (Tongue)	Retraction	—	—	+
Articulatory (Tongue)	Advance	+	—	—
Auditory (Voice)	Shallow	+	—	—
Auditory (Voice)	Deep	—	—	+

Notice that the two distinctive features "tongue retraction", which is articulatory and "voice deep" (dark and dull vocal quality as against bright and acute one), which is auditory (acoustical) are shown to interact to characterize and define the the vocalic quality of each of the three vowels as well as the phonetic relations among them. The interrelationship of the auditory and acoustic

Table Ⅱ

Vowel / Features		< l > [i]	< — > [ə~ɯ]	< · > [ɔ~ɒ]
Articulatory	Tongue Retraction	—	+/− (Slightly Retracted)	+
Auditory (Acoustic)	Voice Deep	—	+/−	+

features of the three Korean vowels may be represented in a somewhat simpler form in table Ⅱ.

5. Limitations of Hangeul (Korean Alphabet) as Phonetic Symbols

Han geul〔hanga? l〕, the Korean alphabet has been widely acclaimed by phoneticians and linguists as an excellent phonetic writing system. Although Hangeul is no doubt a highly successful writing system for the Korean language, it leaves much to be desired before it can be utilized as a truly international phonetic alphabet capable of representing minute phonetic differences of human speech sounds. For instance, there is no way to represent the voiced/voiceless distinction or to distinguish labial and labio-dental articulation in Hangeul writing. Thus the following pairs of English words are indistinguishable in the Hangeul writing.

f/p: fine/pine→파인 [pain] ;

ð/d: they/day→데이 [dei] ;

v/b: vote/boat→보우트 [bout] ;

z/dʒ: zoo/jew →주 [dʒu] ;

l/r: lice/rice→라O [ɾais] ;

ʒ/dʒ: leisure/ledger →레저 [ledʒə].

On the other hand, the Korean alphabet has a definite advantage over IPA in that it has basic letters available for representing the unaspirated, slightly aspirated and strongly aspirated consonants in Korean such as /ㅃ/ (voiceless unaspirated p), /ㅂ/ (voiceless slightly aspirated b) and /ㅍ/ (voiceless strongly aspirated ph). The IPA would need to utilize additional diacritical marks to represent the relevant distinction, i. e., /p/, /p'/, /ph/.

It is necessary, therefore, to implement the current Korean alphabet to make it a really versatile international phonetic alphabet.

6. Principles of International Korean Phonetic Alphabet

The International Korean Phonetic Alphabet, first published in 1971 was devised by the present writer by applying the organic principle much more extensively than King Sejong had done. Accordingly, the IKPA symbols are just as simple and easy to learn and memorize as the Korean alphabet, but at the same time they are much more consistent and logical than the IPA symbols which are unsystematic and arbitrary except in one respect, i. e., retroflex symbols, which are consistently marked by a hook attached to the relevant letters.

The organic principles applied in devising the International Korean Phonetic Alphabet can be summarized as follows:

(1) Mobilizing all HanGeul letters.

All HanGeul letters are mobilized in the making of the Korean Phonetic Alphabet except those representing diphthongs such as <ㅑ> [ja], <ㅕ> [jʌ], <ㅛ>

[(jo] , <ㅠ> [ju] , <ㅖ> [je] , <ㅒ> [jɛ] , <ㅘ> [wa] , <ㅝ> [wʌ] , <ㅞ> [we] , <ㅢ> [ɰi] . In addition, the 4 extinct letters of Hunmin Jeongeum of the 15th century have all been revived and given definite phonetic values. For instance, the triangle is introduced as a symbol representing voiced alveolar fricative [z].

(2) Devising Indispensable Symbols.

New symbols have been devised by adding one or more of the following marks to the relevant letters, consistent with the principles of HunMin JeongEum. Some new symbols are derived by deleting a stroke from relevant HanGeul letters.

① Adding the voice bar [/] , [−] or [\ ] to derive voiced symbols from voiceless ones.

e. g. <ㄱ> [k] + [\ ] → <ㄱ̖> [g].

② Adding a < ∟>−shaped hook symbolizing the front of the tongue bunching up to derive palatalized symbols from non-palatalized ones.

e. g. <∟> [n] + [s] → <∟> [ɲ].

③ Adding <j>−shaped hook symbolizing the tongue tip curling upward to derive retroflex symbols from non-retroflex ones.

e. g. <ㄷ> [t] + [j] = <ㄷ> [ʈ].

④ Adding a small circle under or over a letter to derive fricative symbols from homorganic plosives.

e. g. <ㄱ> [k] + [°] = <ㄱ̊> [x].

⑤ Adding a small hook to derive uvular symbols from velars.

e. g. <ㄱ> [k] + [ɾ] = <ㄱ̖> [q].

⑥ Deleting a stroke from plosives to derive homorganic fricative symbols.

e. g. <ㅂ> [p] − [−] = < ㄐ > [f].

⑦ Adding a stroke to trill symbols to derive homorganic lateral symbols.

e. g. <ㄹ> [r] − [1] = <ㄹ̵> [ɫ].

⑧ Deleting and adding stokes to derive fricative symbols from plosives.

e. g. <ㅂ> [p] − [−] + [\ ] → <ㅄ> [v].

⑨ Vowel symbols are also derived from the basic letters by applying the same principles as shown in the derivation of consonant symbols.

⑩ Two semi-vowel symbols are derived from the relevant vowels by modifying their shape (of IKPA chart) .

(3) Representing Homorganic Sounds Systematically.

The symbols of homorganic sounds that are articulated at the same place of articulation are designed in such a way that they are all marked by a basic articulatory phonetic feature. This will no doubt have mnemonic value for learners and readers.

e. g. ? [k] → ? [kh] → ? [k′]

(4) Devising Diacritical Marks to Enrich the Phonetic Representation.

A number of diacritical marks have been devised to represent various shades of speech sounds such as voicing, palatalization, retroflexion, etc.

7. Advantages of International Korean Phonetic Alphabet.

The advantages of the International Korean Phonetic Alphabet can be summarized as follows :

① IKPA represents the shape and/or articulating action of the organs of speech, just like Hangeul (Korean Alphabet), i. e. , Organic phonetic alphabet;

② IKPA represents the place and manner of articulation in a consistent manner;

③ Homorganic symbols share the common element in IKPA;

④ IKPA is easy to learn, teach and memorize;

⑤ IKPA is capable of serving as a truly universal phonetic alphabet common to all races and nations;

⑥ IKPA is more than a mere phonetic alphabet. It is in reality the articulatory phonetic theory itself which is duly represented by the shape of the letters.

Conclusion

In sum, IKPA is more than a mere phonetic alphabet consisting of arbitrary symbols. The IKPA symbols visualize or mirror the actual speech organs or their action and thus tell us exactly what sort of an articulatory action is involved in producing sounds. IKPA is in reality the articulatory phonetic theory itself, which is self-explanatory for specialists and laymen alike. It is in this sense that the IKPA is rightly called "A Universal Visible Speech" .

References

[1] Bell A. Graham. Historical Notes Concerning the Teaching of Speech to the Deaf. Volta Review, 1900,(2).

[2] Chao, Yuen Ren. *Language and Symbolic Systems*. Cambridge, M. A. : Har-

vard University Press, 1968.

[3] Coulmas, Florian. *Encyclopedia of Writing Systems*. Oxford, Blackwell Publishers, 1996.

[4] Henderson, Gelb, I. J., *A Study of Writing*, 2nd edn. Chicago, London: The University of Chicago Press, 1963.

[5] Kim-Cho Sek Yen. The Korean Alphabet of 1446. Humanity Books & AC Press, 2001.

[6] Kim, Minsu. Juhae Hunmin Jeongeum, Tongmungwan, Seoul, 1957.

[7] Kweon, Jae Seon. An Analytic Understanding of Hunmin Jeongeum (in Korean). Daegu, Ugoltab, 1998.

[8] IPA. *The Principles of IPA*. London, 1949, 51.

[9] IPA. *Handbook of the International Phonetic Association*. Cambridge: Cambridge University Press, 1999.

[10] Ledyard, Gari Keith. *The Korean Language Reform of 1446: The Origin, Background, and Early History of the Korean Alphabet*. Ann Arbor, Michigan University, 1966.

[11] Lee, Hansol H. B. *Korean Grammar*, NewYork: Oxford University Press, 1989.

[12] Lee, H. B. "Preliminary Version of Korean Phonetic Alphabet" (in Korean). HanGeul Haghoe (the Korean Language Society), Seoul, 1949, 51, etc.

[13] Lee, H. B. *IPA and Korean Phonetic Alphabet* (in Korean). Seoul: Gwahagsa, 1981.

[14] Lee, H. B. "International Korean Phonetic Alphabet —Theory and Application—" (in Korean). Malsori No. 21 — 24, The Phonetic Society of Korea, 1992.

[15] Lee, H. B. Korean Phonetic Alphabet for International Use—Its Theory and Application-. Special Lecture delivered at Tokyo University, 1996.

[16] Lee, H. B. Phonetic Symbols and Pronunciation Teaching—Organic Principle of the Korean Phonetic Alphabet-, Keynote Speech delivered at EPSJ Nagoya Conference, English Phonetic Society of Japan, 1999.

[17] Lee, H. B. International Korean Phonetic Alphabet for Computers. *Proceedings of the International Conference on the Computer Processing of Korean Language*. Yanbian, China, 1999.

[18] Lee, H. B. IPA Illustration of Korean, *Handbook of the International Phonetic Association*. Cambridge: Cambridge University Press, 1999.

Appendix 1. IKPA and IPA Consonants and Vowels.

국제한글음성문자
International Korean Phonetic Alphabet

닿소리/Consonants

위치 Place / 방법 Manner	두입술 Bi-la bial	입술-이 Labio-dental	이/잇몸 Dental Alveo lar	혀말음 Retro-flex	뒤잇몸 Post-alveol ar	잇몸-입천장 Alveolo Palatal	센입천장 Palatal	여린입천장 Velar	목젖 Uvular	목구멍 Phar ynge al	소리문 Glot tal
터짐소리 Plosive	ㅂ ƥ ㅃ b ㅍ pʰ ㅃ p		ㄷ ɗ ㄸ d ㅌ tʰ ㄸ t	ㄷ ɗ ㅌ tʰ ㅌ t			ㄱ˺ ᵏɟ	ㄱ ɠ ㄱ g ㄱˠ kʰ ㄲ k	ㄱ ɠ ㄱ ɢ ㄱ qʰ ㄲ q		ㅎ ʔ
터갈소리 Affricate					ㅈ ʥ ㅈ ʤ ㅊ ʧʰ ㅉ ʦ						
갈이소리 Fricative	ㅂ ɸ ㅂ β	ㄴ f ㄴ v	ㅅ z ㅿ z ㅿ θ ㅎ ð	ㅅ ʐ ㅿ ʂ	ㅊ ʃ ㅊ ʒ	ㅅ ɕ ㅿ ʑ ㅆ ʑ	ㄱ ç ㄱ j	ㅈ x ㅈ ɣ	ㅈ χ ㅈ ʁ	ㅈ ħ ㅈ ʕ	ㅎ h ㅎ ɦ
콧소리 Nasal	ㅁ m	ㄱ ɱ	ㄴ n	ㄴ ɳ			ㄴ ɲ	ㅇ ŋ	ㅇ ɴ		
혀옆소리 Lateral			ㄹ l	ㄹ ɭ			ㄹ ʎ				
굴림소리 Rolled			ㄹ r						ㄹ ʀ		
튀김소리 Flapped			ㄹ ɾ	ㄷ ɽ					ㄹ ʀ		
지속/반모음 Approxi-mant	ㅜ w ㅜ ɥ	ㄴ ʋ	ㄷ ɹ	ㄷ ɻ			ㄴ j	ㅜ w ㅜ ɰ	ㅈ ʁ		

홀소리/Vowels

모음 Vowels	원순 Rounded		앞 Front		가온 Central		뒤 Back	
닫힌(Close)	ㅟ y	ㅠ ʉ ㅠ u	ㅣ i	ㅟ y	ㅣ ɨ	ㅠ ʉ	ㅡ ɯ	ㅡ u
반닫힌(Half-close)	ㅚ ø	ㅗ o	ㅔ e	ㅚ ø	ㅓ ə	ㅕ ɤ	ㅗ o
반열린(Half-open)	ㅐ œ	ㅛ ɔ	ㅐ ɛ	ㅐ œ	ㅕ ɜ	ㅓ ʌ	ㅗ ɔ
열린(Open)	ㅐ ɶ	ㅛ ɒ	ㅏ a	ㅐ ɶ		ㅑ ɑ	ㅛ ɒ

Devised by H.B.Lee (1971～　　)

Appendix 2. Illustration of IKPA

Application of International Korean Phonetic Alphabet
국제 한글 음성 문자를 이용한 한국어 및 외국어의 표기

1. 한국어/Korean
1. 아우 [ㅏ ˙ㅜ˙]
2. 애기 [ㅐㄱㅣ]
3. 이발 [ㅣ:ㅂㅏㄹ]
4. 가게 [ㄱㅏ˙:ㄱㅔ]
5. 사람들 [ㅅㅏ˙:ㄹㅏ ˙ㅁㄸㅡ˙ㄹ]
6. 바보야 [ㅂㅏ˙:ㅂㅗ˙ㄴㅏ]
7. 박사님 [ㅂㅏ ˙ㄱㅆㅏ ˙ㄴㄴㅣ˙ㅁ]
8. 다람쥐가 [ㄷㅏㄹㅏㅁㅈㅟ˙ㄱㅏ]
9. 외국인 [ㄷㅞ:ㄱㅜˉㄱㅣㄴ]
10. 짜장면 [ㅉㅏㅈㅏㅇㅣㄴㅕㄴ]
11. 멀리 갔니 [ㅁㅓ:ㄹㄹㅣ ㄱㅏㄴㄴㅣ]
12. 흙 속에 [ㅎㅡㄱㅆㅗㄱㅔ]
13. 대한민국 [ㄷㅐㅎㅏㄴㅁㅣ˙ㄴㄱㅜˉㄱ]
14. 교육헌장 [ㄱㅛ:ㄴㄱㄱㅋㅓ:ㄴㅈㅏ˙ㅇ]
15. 한글음성문자 [ㅎㅏ:ㅇㄱㅡㄹㅡㅁㅅㅓㅇㅁㅜˉㄴㅉㅏ]
16. 아주 착실합니다. [ㅏㅈㅜ ㅊㅏㄱㅆㅣㄹㅏ˙ㅁㄴㅣㄸㅏ]
17. 대단히 좋아요. [ㄷㅐ:ㄸㅏㄴ ㅈㅗ:ㅏㄴㄴ]
18. 정말 감사합니다. [ㅈㅓ:ㅇㅁㅏㄹ ㄱㅏ:ㅁㅅㅏㅎㅏㅁㄴㅣ˙ㄸㅏ]

2. 영어/English
19. Bees fly. [ㅂㅣ:ㅅ ㄴㄹㅏㄴ]
20. small girls [ㅅㅁㅗ:ㄹˉ ㄱㅓ:ㄹˉㅅ]
21. Spanish dance [ㅅㅃㅐㄴㅣ˙ㅊ ㄸㅏㄴㅆ]
22. Comfort in England [ㅋㅏㄱㅁㅓㅌ ㅣ˙ㄴ ㅣ˙ㅇㄹㅓㅋㄴㄸ]
23. English language [ㅏ˙ㅇㄱㅌㅣ˙ㅊ ㄹㅐㅇㄱㄷㅣ˙ㅈ]
24. Very clearly pronounced [ㅂㅔㄹㅣ˙ ㅋㄹㅣ˙ㅋㅌㅣ˙ ㅍㄹㅋㄴㅏㅜㄴㅅㅌ]
25. He's a wonderful singer. [ㅎㅣ:ㅅ ㅋ ㄷㅏㄴㄸㅓㄹㅂ ㅆㅣㅇㅋ]
26. Thank you so much. [ㄷㅐㅇㅋㄴㅜ ㅆㅕㅜ ㅁㅏㅊ]

3. 프랑스어/French
27. Je m'appelle France. [ㅈㅓ ㅁㅏㅃㅔㅌ ㄴㅕㅜ̃ㅆ]
28. Bon jour, ma chérie! [ㅂㅗ̃ ㅈㅜㅈˉ ㅁㅏ ㅊㅔㅖㅣ]
29. Un bon vin blanc [ㅐㅜ̃ ㅂㅗ̃ ㅂㅖㄴ̃ ㅂㄹㅏㅜ̃]

30. C'est très bien. [쌔ㅐ ㅌ ㅌㅐ ㅂ ㄴㅐ]

4. 독일어/German

31. Als ein Wanderer [ㅎ ㅏㄷㅆ ㅎ ㅏ ㄴ ㄴ ㅂ ㅏㄷㅊ ㅗ ㅌ ㅗ]
32. Ich bin ein Mädchen [ㅣ ㄱ ㅂ ㅣ ㄴ ㅏ ㅣ ㄴ ㅁㅐ:ㅌㅓ ㅋㅏ ㄴ]
33. Nur wer die Sehnsucht kennt. [ㄴ ㅜ ㅋ ㅂㅐ:ㅓ ㄷ ㅣ ㅿㅔ:ㄴ ㅿ ㅜ ㄱ ㅌ ㅋㅐ ㄴㅌ]

5. 이탈리아어/Italian

34. Buon giorno. [ㅂ ㅜ ㄴ ㅈ ㅗ ㄹ ㄴ ㅗ]
35. Potrebbe darmi qualche rivista.

   [ㅃ ㅗ ㄸ ㄹ ㅔ ㅂ ㅂ ㅔ ㄸ ㅏ ㄹ ㅁ ㅣ ㄲㅏ ㅌ ㄲㅔ ㄹ ㅣ ㅂ ㅣ ㅅ ㄸ ㅏ]
36. Vorrei cambiare la mia camera.

   [ㅂ ㅗ ㄹ ㄹ ㅔ ㅣ ㄲ ㅏ ㅁ ㅂ ㅣ' ㅏ ㄹ ㅔ ㅌ ㅏ ㅁ ㅣ ㅏ 'ㄲ ㅏ ㅁ ㅔ ㄹ ㅏ]

6. 폴란드어/Polish

37. Przepraszam. [ㅍ ㅊ ㅔ 'ㅃ ㄹ ㅏ ㅊ ㅗ ㅁ]
38. Gdzie jest autobus? [ㄱ ㄸ ㄴ ㅔ ㄴ ㅔ ㅅ ㅍ ㅏ ㄷ 'ㄸ ㅍ ㅂ ㅜ ㅆ]
39. Ile to kosztuje? ['ㅣ:ㅌ ㅐ ㄸ ㅍ ㄲ ㅍ ㅊ 'ㄸ ㅜ:ㄴ ㅐ]

7. 러시아어/Russian

40. Добрый день [ㄸ ㅗ ㅂ ㄷ ㅣ ' ㄸ ㄴ ㅔ ㄴ]
41. Я не понимаю ['ㄴ ㅏ ㄴ ㅣ ㅃ ㅗ ㄴ ㅣ 'ㅁ ㅏ ㄴ ㅜ]
42. Спасибо очень хорошо [ㅅ ㅃ ㅏ 'ㅆ ㅣ ㅂ ㅏ 'ㅗ ㅊ ㅔ ㄴ ㄱ ㅏ ㄹ ㅏ 'ㅊ ㅍ]

8. 일본어/Japanese

43. どうも ありがとう [ㄸ ㅗ:ㅁ ㅗ ㅏ ㄹ ㅣ ㄱ ㅏ ㄷ ㅗ:]
44. ミズオ クダサイ [ㅁ ㅣ ㅿ ㅜ ㅗ ㄱ ㅜ ㄸ ㅏ ㅅ ㅏ ㅣ]
45. ぎせき お かわつても いいですか?

   [ㅿ ㅏ ㅅ ㅔ ㄱ ㅣ ㅗ ㄱ ㅏ ㄷ ㅏ ㄷ ㄸ ㅔ ㅁ ㅗ ㅣ:ㄸ ㅔ ㅅ ㅜ ㄱ ㅏ]

9. 중국어/Chinese

46. Ni hao ma [ㄴ ㅣ ㄱ ㅏ ㅗ ㅁ ㅏ]
47. Mingtian jian [ㅁ ㅣ ㅇ ㄸ ㄴ ㅔ ㄴ ㅉ ㄴ ㅔ ㄴ]
48. Wo xiang huan falong [ㄸ ㅗ ㅅ ㅏ ㅇ ㄱ ㄸ ㅏ ㄴ ㅂ ㅏ ㅌ ㅗ ㅇ]

(Hyun Bok Lee. CBE. Ph. D. Professor Emeritus of Phonetics and Linguistics. Seoul National University)

On Meaning Negotiation Between Teacher and Students in the Foreign Language Classroom

Negotiation of meaning refers to interactional work to achieve a mutual understanding when a communication problem occurs. The study describes an investigation of negotiation-of-meaning processes between teacher and students in an English-as-a-foreign-language (EFL) classroom, focusing on ① the negotiation process through a careful examination of classroom discourse and ② the relationship between linguistic meanings and the social contexts in which interactions take place. A qualitative approach was employed for data collection and data analysis. Data were obtained from a natural class of 23 students and a teacher in an intermediate speaking EFL classroom. The findings revealed ① trouble sources are not restricted to language problems but extend to non-linguistic factors and other context-specific factors; ② the participants' perception of comprehension difficulties is a complex process influenced by the types of problem and the agents who are perceiving; ③ the decision-making process was affected factors like institutional, situational, affective, cultural, and physical factors and receptivity; and ④ the nature of the classroom environment enables negotiation processes to be constructive and productive. In sum, the findings suggest that the teacher-student negotiation process in the EFL classroom is an enormously complex process involving both cognitive and social practices.

1. Introduction

Negotiation of meaning (*NOM*) refers to "the modification and restructuring of interaction that occurs when learners and their interlocutors anticipate, perceive, or experience difficulties in message comprehensibility" (Pica 1994: 494). Since the early 1980s, SLA research has directed considerable attention towards the role of negotiation of meaning as a particular type of interaction. The argument that negotiation of meaning is vital in second language acquisition has been supported by claims that negotiation brings about conditions conducive to language acquisition: ① learners' comprehension of L2 input, ② their production of modified output, and ③ their attention to L2 form (Pica, 1994; Gass, Mackey, & Pica 1998). Many researchers have researched into NOM from a cognitive perspective (Krashen 1985; Long 1983a; Swain 1985; Varonis & Gass, 1985; Gass & Varonis, 1994; Polio & Gass, 1998).

Inspired by these theoretical arguments with regard to the three facilitative conditions bought about by negotiation, comprehensible input, comprehensible output, and attention to L2 form, a large number of empirical studies have been conducted. A great part of the research efforts has been directed towards two issues: ① the causal relationship between negotiation and acquisition; and ② the effect of different kinds of interactional environment, such as task type and participant structure, on the amount of negotiation.

Recently, researchers (Atkinson 2002; Firth & Wagner 1997; Linddicoat 1997) have set out to undertake a critique of what Firth and Wagner (1997) called an *individualistic and cognitive* perspective, a predominant view in SLA research. Pointing out that this research tradition has not represented the social aspects of interaction and language learning, they called for research that is more process-oriented and context-sensitive in order to gain a better understanding of negotiation in the context of SLA. Thus a small, but growing number of research studies that have taken a more social and qualitative approach to the investigation of negotiation. These recent studies are largely characterized by micro-analyses of actual discourse and responsiveness to the situational and social contexts in which negotiation takes place (Aston 1986; Ehrlich, Avery, and Yorio 1989; Nakahama, Tyler, and van Lier 2001; Ko, Schallert, and Walters 2003). They argued that a greater number of meaning negotiations does not necessarily indicate a greater amount of comprehensible input or language improvement. The underlying assumption of this claim is that not all negotiation is equally effective, and thus the mere presence of negotiation does not ensure language improvement. These studies suggest a need for viewing negotiation within its discourse framework and linguistic context to determine the dynamic role of negotiation in L2 language use. Therefore, this study aims to give a comparatively full description of the negotiation process through a careful examination of classroom discourse and attempts to identify the relationship between linguistic meanings and the social context in which interactions take place, attempting to provide answers to the following questions:

① What causes communication breakdowns between the teacher and the students? How are causes for communication breakdown related to the participants' decision-making and resolution processes?

② How are comprehension difficulties anticipated and perceived? How is this process related to negotiation?

③ What factors influence whether the participants decide to negotiate?

④ How are communication problems resolved? What are the roles of the teacher and the students in the resolution process?

2. Method

2. 1 Research Design

To uncover the nature of negotiation of meaning, how negotiation of meaning unfolds among participants and how situational and contextual factors are interrelated with the process of communication are going to be described, using a qualitative approach as its underlying assumptions seemed best suited to the purpose of the present study and the nature of its research questions.

2. 2 Setting and Participants

Data collection occurred during the first semester of 2005 in an intermediate ESL speaking class in the EFL classroom in a university in Hunan Province.

Participants include both the teacher and the students. The teacher, Ms Zhang, had received her master's degree in TESOL, and she has been teaching English in the university for nearly ten years at the time of data collection. There were twenty-three students in her class, with the average age ranging from 19 to 22. They were sophomores in the university and have studied English for at least 8 years as most of them started their formal English learning from the primary school.

2. 3 Data Sources

After obtaining Ms. Zhang's consent, I visited the class at the beginning of the semester, and asked the students for their consent to participate in this study. I briefly introduced myself and explained my study. After obtaining their consent, data was collected from multiple sources, including observations, field notes, video recordings, stimulated recall interviews, participants' notes on communication breakdowns, participant interviews, and artifacts. The purpose of this data gathering was to secure an in-depth understanding of the nature of the phenomenon being studied.

2. 3. 1 Observations

I observed five 45-minute classes during the first two months of the semester. For the first week, I visited the class to become familiar with the setting and the participants and to identify patterns of classroom events. During this period of initial observations, classroom participants also seemed to become familiar with my presence and become less influenced by the knowledge that they were being observed. From the third week on, I observed the class once a week. The main goal of observation in this study was to examine teacher and student interactions firsthand and to gain a better understanding of those interactions within the situational context. I assumed a role as a full observer, rather than as an "observer as participant" (Merriam, 1998).

2. 3. 2 Field Notes

I took field notes while observing the class and shortly after every observation session. Field notes, coupled with video recordings, were my primary data source for reconstructing and analyzing the classroom events. As suggested by Merriam (1998), my field notes included the following information in as much detail as possible:

① Verbal descriptions of the setting, the people, the activities

② Direct quotations or at least the substance of what people say

③ Observer's comments—including the researcher's feelings, reactions, hunches, initial interpretations, and working hypotheses.

2. 3. 3 Video Recording of the Class

All class sessions I observed were videotaped. My purpose for videotaping the sessions was twofold: First, I wanted to get a more complete record of interactions between the teacher and the students. Second, during stimulated recall interviews the videotapes were used as prompts to help participants remember what they had said, heard, thought, and felt in class. The video camera is aimed only at the teacher and blackboard to reduce the obtrusiveness of the camera. Even so, it was necessary to capture students' facial expressions and gestures by supplementing videotaping with other kinds of recording technique, such as taking field notes, because nonverbal cues were effectively and strategically used in classroom interactions, especially between the teacher and the students.

2. 3. 4 Stimulated Recall Interviews

A stimulated recall technique was used to prompt participants to recall thoughts they had had while performing a task or participating in an event. Gass and Mackey (2000) pointed out that stimulated recall may benefit studies in classroom interaction and negotiation in SLA by illuminating issues remaining unresolved through other data alone. They added that "using stimulated recall [...] may be able to move researchers from the realm of speculation to the realm of greater certainty" (p. 128) .

The stimulated recall technique provided me with useful information about the participants' mental processes while they engaged in negotiation of meaning, information that might have passed unnoticed by the interlocutors or me because, in many cases, evidence of communication breakdown and its resolution may have been too subtle and instantaneous to be captured simply through real-time observation.

Furthermore, because an L2 speaker's utterances were often incomplete, it was often difficult to infer his or her intended meaning only from what was said. A stimulated recall procedure sheds light on the participants' mental operations and helps determine whether and how the participant perceived communication difficulty and initiated and pursued negotiation of meaning at a particular moment.

2. 3. 5　Interviews

Participant interviews provided contextualized and self-interpretation of participants' words and actions (Seidman 1998) . My purpose in interviewing the participants was to gain an in-depth understanding of their beliefs and thoughts about English learning and teaching more generally, and about student-teacher negotiation of meaning in the classroom more specifically. I began interviewing the participants when I had become familiar with their classroom behaviors, learning or teaching styles, and participation patterns through observation. Interview topics were selected with respect to working hypotheses, themes, and patterns emerging from a preliminary analysis of the data obtained up to that time.

2. 3. 6　Artifacts

Artifacts, including the textbook, other activity materials, and the course syllabus, were collected and examined. This kind of data source was useful in grounding my understanding of the context of the issue being studied.

2. 4　Data Analysis

Data collection and data analysis were conducted concurrently. Rather than starting analysis after all the data had been collected, I continuously analyzed the multiple sources for emerging themes and patterns while still gathering data. In doing so, I used some analytic techniques generally adopted in qualitative research, such as an inductive strategy and the constant comparative method.

3. Findings and Discussion

Based on the analysis of data obtained mainly from classroom observations, interviews, and stimulated-recall interviews, I adopted a holistic perspective to construct a picture of the nature of negotiation, attempting to understand the negotiation process by focusing on the research questions: ① What causes communication difficulty? ② how are comprehension difficulties anticipated and perceived? ③ what factors influence whether the participants decide to negotiate? and ④ how are communication problems resolved?

3.1 Trouble sources that cause communication problems

The first set of findings I presented involved the identification of various sources of communication difficulty between the teacher and the students in the class as they worked to comprehend each other. Three sources were identified regarding the teacher's comprehension. First, as was expected, the students' linguistic resource deficit was the most salient cause of the teacher's non-understanding or misunderstanding. This deficit was divided into four categories: inaccurate pronunciation, inappropriate word choice, limited overall proficiency, and limited discourse competence. Second, the interaction data showed that general world knowledge was also significantly involved in the teacher's comprehension process. The teacher's lack of prior knowledge of what the students were discussing could activate inappropriate schematic knowledge leading her to build an incorrect interpretation of the students' messages. Third, non-hearing/mishearing was another distinctive factor leading to the teacher's comprehension problems.

The sources of the students' comprehension problems were classified into three categories: students' linguistic resource deficit, background knowledge, and limited attention. First, with regard to linguistic factors, the data showed that the students' limited competence in processing and decoding input inhibited their understanding of the teacher's utterances. Their limited lexical knowledge was another trouble source. Related to this, was *text negotiation*, a unique feature of L2 classroom discourse, negotiation triggered by linguistic forms in written text. Second, the students' lack of background knowledge of given topics and sociocultural norms was associated with their failure to construct correct understandings. Finally, lack of attention provided an explanation for a large part of the students' comprehension problems in the classroom. There were two reasons for the students' lack of attention: limited cognitive resources and selective attention allocation.

Trouble source as a variable has attracted relatively little interest in SLA, although it is of considerable importance in explaining the NOM process. While a large number of studies have investigated the indicator-response elements of the four-part cycle model that Varonis and Gass (1985) proposed, few have examined triggers and trouble sources (Nakahama et al. 2001). Only a few studies (Nakahama et al. 2001; Chun et al. 1982) classified triggers into several categories based on the types of trouble source (such as lexical error, morphosyntactic error, pronunciation error, discourse errors, pragmatic error, content trigger, and task trigger) and studied the relationship between types of trouble source and types of tasks. Those categories, however, have been largely limited to linguistic errors, and few attempts have been made to relate those sources to problem-solving behaviors.

Data analysis showed that trouble sources were not restricted to language problems but also extended to non-linguistic factors and other context-specific factors. In addition, it was found that types of trouble sources were associated with the participants' decision-making processes and their ways of resolving communication problems. In this respect, these major findings can add to our study of the nature of NOM in the language classroom by calling attention to relatively unexplored areas.

In sum, investigating trouble sources may have special importance from both a theoretical and practical point of view. First, it offers a new analytical framework for in-depth NOM analysis. As can be seen from the study, trouble sources are closely connected to the process of deciding whether to pursue negotiation. Language learners are more likely to initiate negotiation when they predict that the trouble source causing the ongoing communication breakdown can be fixed within the scope of their linguistic ability. Perceived causes of breakdown also affect the coping mechanisms they employ to resolve the problems. While the correct identification of trouble sources increases the chance of successful resolution, misperceived trouble sources may not correct the problems and may even worsen the situation. Establishing links among trouble sources, the decision-making process, and the communication problem management may provide us with a more comprehensive framework for analyzing the NOM process.

Second, important practical implications can be drawn from the findings on trouble sources. An awareness of the various types of trouble sources and the interplay between trouble sources and coping mechanisms may enable language teachers to have a better understanding of the communication difficulties they encounter in the classroom. Consequently, they can develop more effective negotiation strategies to resolve the problems. Additionally, language teachers can prepare students to deal with communication breakdowns by making them aware of the importance of identifying trouble sources and adopting resolving strategies accordingly.

3. 2　Perception of communication problems

A second major set of findings was associated with how comprehension difficulties are anticipated and perceived by the classroom participants and how their anticipation and perception are related to the negotiation process. Four distinctive characteristics were identified. First, the classroom participants premodified their language when they anticipated comprehension problems. While the teacher's premodification was determined by her assessment of the students' levels of linguistic competence, the students' attempts were prompted by perception of their own lack of the linguistic knowledge needed to convey their meaning. Anticipating difficulties on the basis of metacognitive evaluations of one's own resources or those of the other led to two contrasting behaviors: the teacher's employing a variety of tactics and the students' withdrawing from turn initiations.

Second, the comprehension process is extremely complex, involving production and interpretation subprocesses. The stimulated recall interviews revealed that the participants were involved in dialogic and social understanding processes through continuous interpretation and re-interpretation of what had been uttered and what had been perceived. At the same time, however, the interpretation process is psychological. Thus, one's interpretation process never becomes completely transparent, so that a possible misunderstanding may remain invisible to both interlocutors and researchers.

Third, different types of comprehension problems are perceived in different ways. I examined two types of comprehension problems, non-understanding and misunderstanding, and analyzed who had initially perceived comprehension problems and how the problems were perceived. The analysis showed that, while comprehension problems that the teacher encountered were more easily detected by her interlocutors primarily because the teacher verbalized what she had understood by utilizing abundant reformulations, the students' problems rarely became known, mainly because they rarely attempted to articulate what they had understood.

Finally, the degree of non-understanding was related to the linguistic realization that signaled the problem. The data revealed that linguistic realizations that fit well with the degree of non-understanding may lead to more successful negotiation, because they enable the message sender to judge how close the recipient's interpretation is to what the sender originally intended and, accordingly, employ effective negotiation mechanisms for the given problems. But the students, who lacked the necessary linguistic resources, often failed to articulate their different levels of comprehension problems, which resulted in less successful negotiation.

Two central findings in this section can be recapitulated here: ① Perception of comprehension difficulties is a considerably complex process influenced by types of problems and the agents of perceiving, and ② the ways and amount of verbalizing one's perceived understanding and non-understanding affect subsequent perceptions and negotiations. Methodological and practical implications can be drawn from these findings.

To date, researchers in SLA have shown little concern with the complicated nature of the comprehension process, probably because one's interpreting and perceiving processes are largely unobservable. The analyses conducted in previous research have relied solely on linguistic realizations of participants' intended meaning without taking into consideration the inherent complexity of the comprehension process. Researchers may have too confidently and naively interpreted the interlocutors' "Yes, I understand" as a sign of successful negotiation, when in fact it did not necessarily reflect their actual understanding. Stimulated recall interviews in this study provided insightful information, information that would otherwise have remained unrevealed. Thus, a research methodology that can shed light on the participants' mental operations in perceiving and interpreting meanings will allow us to make our analyses more reliable and useful.

The findings also have some practical implications. If negotiation is essential not only for language development as proposed in the Interaction Hypothesis, but also for better communication at any given moment, one way of enhancing successful negotiation is to help learners acquire linguistic and strategic skills needed to make their perceptions explicit. Like the teacher's reformulations, the students can be asked to verbalize their understanding so that their interlocutors are able to perceive any non-or misunderstanding and conduct negotiation work more effectively. In addition, knowledge of various linguistic devices for signaling the degree of non-understanding as precisely as possible may allow them to identify and resolve communication problems more successfully. Additionally, when they anticipate comprehension difficulties on the part of their interlocutors, students can be encouraged to make an attempt to negotiate, rather than abandon the topic, by utilizing strategies such as appeals for assistance.

3. 3　Decision making as to whether to pursue negotiation

The third major set of findings related to a variety of factors that affected the classroom participants' decisions on whether to initiate or pursue negotiation. Indeed, negotiating is a juggling act that requires the participants to make moment-by-moment decisions based on their local knowledge of the situation and more general knowledge of the context. Six categories were discussed in particular: institutional factors, situational factors, affective factors, cultural factors, physical factors, and receptivity. These factors, in fact, were intricately involved in the participants' decision-making processes.

The data confirmed the findings of previous studies that students tend to avoid negotiation with their teachers in L2 classrooms. One of the exclusive contributions of this study to research is its penetration into the reasons for the relatively little amount of negotiation in the L2 classroom. Up to now, discussion of this issue has been based on little more than speculation. Thus the suggestions proposed to enhance negotiation in classrooms have not been specific enough for teachers to apply in their own classrooms.

Often, L2 teachers are well aware of their students' unwillingness to negotiate, but ignorant of why. Therefore, they cannot effectively guide their students into more active negotiation even if the teachers believe negotiation can facilitate their students' learning. With respect to this issue, Ms. Zhang made the following comment:

> *I think negotiation is great, I love negotiation, I love the whole class to be that. But, [it's] my bias, and students I think often do not share that, um... they don't want that. [...] I'm sure their non-understanding happened much more frequently than I realized. I think, just like anybody in class, you know, they don't want to raise their hands bidding on saying that they don't understand, that maybe the main thing, um, but I don't know that, because if there is the sole reason, I would expect more people come talk to me outside class, "Ivy [the teacher's first name], I don't really understand," but they don't. So I'm not sure, I mean, that's a big question I have, actually, you know. The main thing I can think of is that they just don't want to be embarrassed, maybe?*

In this light, the findings in this study may provide well-grounded suggestions for classroom interaction. Of course, some of the factors discussed are more inherently a part of classroom context and may be hard to change, even with the participants' conscious efforts, whereas other factors are within the participants' control and can be more flexibly reworked. Thus, any practical suggestion should be based on an understanding of the social context of the classroom and an awareness of the constraints and possibilities within that context.

The related findings and some suggestions associated with each factor can be summarized as follows. First, while the teacher's active negotiation was motivated by her linkage of negotiation to the institutional goal of improving communicative competence, the students did not seem to appreciate that linkage and consequently were not ardently involved in negotiating. Second, the students often did not attempt to negotiate because they were well aware of an implicit ground rule—Do not monopolize classroom talk. Third, whereas the institutionally determined turn-taking system favored the teacher's negotiation work, it deterred the students from initiating negotiation at perceived optimal moments. Additionally, the institutional duty of maintaining classroom interaction led to the teacher's constant negotiation efforts, but the students, who were relatively free from such an obligation, were selective in their negotiation work. As van Lier (2001) noted, this institutional control over the participants' language use is so powerful that any effort to alter it often ends in failure. Some attempts, however, can be made at least at the micro-level. If they believe in the potential of NOM for language development, teachers can explicitly explain it to students, because students tend to embrace a certain activity if they see a connection between the activity and their ultimate learning goal. A possible way teachers can incorporate NOM into the turn-taking system is to monitor their own talk more consciously. For example, by pausing frequently even within a turn, a teacher can allow the students to jump in at optimal points to indicate their nonunderstanding. Calling on students can be another way to give them more responsibility for the flow of ongoing discussions and clarification of meaning. The data also showed that they wanted to be called on and pushed to speak to some extent.

Second, situational factors included three major subcategories. First, in comparison with a whole-class discussion situation, a group setting provided an environment in which the students and the teacher were more inclined to pursue negotiation. Second, the lack of an immediate need to communicate clearly in open-ended conversation in class allowed the students to avoid engaging in negotiation work. In contrast, procedural talk and group-work-reporting activities pushed the students to make an effort to negotiate by creating a strong communicative need at given moments. Lastly, the participants' decision about whether to pursue negotiation depended on their moment-by-moment monitoring of the situation and assessments of the possibility of successful resolution in case of communication problems based on their metacognitive judgment.

Again some implications can be drawn from these findings. First, teachers can take opportunities during group work to engage in one-on-one negotiation with single students in depth, when they are freed to some extent from institutional and social constraints. They may be able to have students take a more active role in interacting and negotiating, for example, by asking the students to reformulate what they understand and waiting until students finish their turn, rather than interrupting and filling the gap immediately after a communication breakdown. Second, tasks requiring immediate communicative purposes need to be designed to motivate students to make an effort to attain successful communication. As shown in this study, a group-work-reporting activity may be a good example. Third, to move beyond their current level of comprehension or production, students should be encouraged and even pushed (Swain 1985) to some extent to make attempts to resolve communication problems, rather than giving up, despite their perceived insufficiency of linguistic resources. Teachers may assist students to overcome their limitation by teaching "compensation strategies" that enable students to use the language for either comprehension or production despite limitations in knowledge.

As for affective factors, the data showed that the teacher's decisions and behaviors regarding negotiation were affected by her concern about the students' emotions and feelings. On the other hand, the students did not consider affective factors significant in their decision-making processes. Nevertheless, this finding may be difficult to generalize because affective factors can influence individuals in different ways. Indeed, many studies on affective factors have suggested their enormous impact on language learning and classroom performance. Teachers' assurances that signaling and repairing non-understanding are appropriate in classrooms may decrease students' negative feelings resulting from their experiences with communication difficulties.

As for cultural factors and physical factors, the analysis revealed that both factors influenced the students' negotiation-related decisions. Most students said that they avoided negotiating as they didn't in other lessons, which confirmed the findings of other studies that Asian students are often shy to speak our their views in class and they are reserved. Physical tiredness was also negatively related to students' participation in negotiation. These two factors are beyond the teacher's influence. More important than any pedagogical suggestion related to these factors may be the suggestion that the teacher simply be aware of their effects on student negotiation. Such awareness will lead teachers to search for better ways of accommodating these factors in classrooms.

Finally, receptivity to classroom components appeared to affect students' participation. For example, students are more likely to participate and negotiate if they are more receptive to classroom-related factors, such as the teacher's way of teaching, the teaching materials, and course content, can be accommodated by teachers. To be successful, a teacher may need to address students' expectations, needs, and complaints first. Although meeting everyone's different needs and expectations may be impossible, the next best solution may be to provide opportunities for each student to benefit in his or her own way, for example, by striving for a variety of activities or teaching methods.

3. 4　Resolution of communication problems

Six salient themes were found that emerged with respect to the resolution process in the classroom. Taken together, these findings may shed light on a new perspective on classroom negotiation. As previously mentioned, research has pointed out that a classroom generally does not provide an optimal environment for negotiation and, more specifically, that teacher-fronted settings are much less favorable for negotiation than group-work situations. Such conclusions, however, have been made based largely on frequency counts of negotiation instances without examining how participants actually engage in the negotiation process. For the conclusions drawn from a comparison of numbers to be meaningful, an assumption is necessary that every negotiation is qualitatively equal, an assumption that simply is not based in fact.

If we look at classroom negotiation from a different angle, there may be room for a reconsideration of the role of classroom interaction. On one hand, Though this study revealed that the number of NOM instances may be smaller in the classroom because the students tended to be reluctant to initiate negotiation with the teacher for social and institutional reasons, the study also showed that the nature of the classroom environment enabled negotiation processes to be more constructive and productive because of the teacher's facilitative and mediating assistance and because of the whole class' collaborative efforts.

The teacher's role was greatly influential in making "scaffolded negotiation" possible in this class. Current pedagogical trends in L2 classroom teaching call for a learner-centered orientation, which is usually interpreted as a call to minimize teacher talk and to increase pair or group activities accomplished by the learners themselves. While I agree with the assertion that learners should be more self-regulated and take more responsibility for their own performance and learning, I would argue that the transferring process should be gradual within the context of scaffolded mediated assistance, as emphasized in a socioconstructivist framework. Within a socioconstructivist perspective, the teacher's scaffolding and intervention become crucial because they enable learners to accomplish work that they may not be able to do on their own.

The teacher's role was critical in enhancing the classroom members' construction of a shared understanding: she was sensitive and responsive to the students' verbal and non-verbal signals of non-understanding; she was continuously checking the students' current levels of comprehension and searching for better ways to resolve the comprehension problems that her students experienced; she provided assistance as the students reconstructed and modified their utterances to resolve communication breakdowns; motivated by her own social and pedagogical concerns, she made an effort to involve the students in the process of co-construction of meaning and understanding; and she offered help by mediating the students' successful communication between each other when they were not able to solve communication problems on their own.

Key to such scaffolded assistance provided by the teacher is the notion of contingency, "the way an adult judges the need and quality of assistance required by the learner on the basis of moment-to-moment understanding" (Gibbons, 2003). In this study, the teacher's scaffolding was accomplished through dialogic exchanges and joint engagement in interaction with the students (Aljaafreh & Lantolf, 1994). To provide appropriate help, she was continuously assessing the students' current level of understanding and their linguistic resources to cope with the ongoing communication problems through *dialogue*, an essential component in scaffolding.

In sum, her scaffolded help enabled the class to engage in more constructive and successful negotiation in the classroom and served to enhance a shared space of understanding among the classroom participants. In this light, classroom negotiation can be considered facilitative and productive. Moreover, such patient and persistent assistance may not be available for students outside the classroom.

The students also played an important role in constructing the scaffolded negotiation. Not only did they cooperate in the negotiation process guided by the teacher, they also actively created a forum in which collaborative negotiation could occur. The students in this study were observed to provide assistance when an individual student had difficulty in comprehending and producing language during negotiation with the teacher.

Taken together, the collaborative nature of the classroom created a social space in which classroom participants were able to provide each other with effective assistance in resolving communication problems. Conceivably, such scaffolded negotiation will eventually develop the students' language learning. Rather than the number of negotiation instances, this unique contribution of a classroom setting to the enhancement of constructive negotiation through reciprocal assistance should be taken into account.

Conclusion

It can be concluded that teacher-student negotiation in the ESL classroom is an enormously complex process involving both cognitive and social practices. At the cognitive dimension, the negotiation process involved constant mental work, such as perception, comprehension, interpretation, and decision making. As this study showed, however, these cognitive processes shaped and were shaped by social interactions with both the situation and interlocutor, so that the negotiation process could not be properly understood apart from its broader context. With respect to the particular social context, this study identified the potential benefits and constraints of the L2 classroom. The findings of this study revealed that, while the classroom could hinder the participants to some extent from engaging in active and extended negotiation due to its social and institutional influence, it could also serve as a site in which the participants collaboratively negotiated with each other toward a shared understanding. An awareness of such benefits and constraints may guide language teachers to employ more effective interactional practices in their own classrooms.

References
[1] Aljaafreh, A., & Lantolf, J. P. (1994). Negative feedback as regulation and

second language learning in the zone of proximal development. *Modern Language Journal*, 78, 465 – 483.

[2] Aston, G. (1986). Trouble-shooting interaction with learners: The more the merrier? *Applied Linguistics*, 7, 128 – 143.

[3] Atkinson, D. (2002). Toward a sociocognitive approach to second language acquisition. *Modern Language Journal*, 86, 525 – 545.

[4] Chun, A. E., Day, R. R., Chenoweth, N. A., & Luppescu, S. (1982). Errors, interaction, and corrections: A study of native-nonnative conversations. *TESOL Quarterly*, 16, 537 – 546.

[5] Ehrlich, S., Avery, P., & Yorio, C. (1989). Discourse structure and the negotiation of comprehensible input. Studies in Second *Language Acquisition*, 11, 397 – 414.

[6] Ellis, R., Tanaka, Y., & Yamazaki. A. (1994). Classroom interaction, comprehension, and the acquisition of L2 word meanings. *Language Learning*, 44, 449 – 491.

[7] Firth, A., & Wagner, J. (1997). On discourse, communication, and (some) fundamental concepts in SLA research. *Modern Language Journal*, 81, 285 – 300.

[8] Gass, S. M., & Mackey, A. (2000). *Stimulated recall methodology in second language research*. Mahwah, NJ: Lawrence Erlbaum Associates.

[9] Gass, S. M., & Mackey, A., & Pica, T. (1998). The role of input and interaction in second language acquisition: Introduction to the special issue. *The Modern Language Journal*, 82, 299 – 305.

[10] Gass, S. M., & Varonis, E. M. (1994). Input, interaction, and second language production. *Studies in Second Language Acquisition*, 16, 283 – 302.

[11] Gibbons, P. (2003). Mediating language learning: Teacher interactions with ESL students in a content-based classroom. *TESOL Quarterly*, 37, 247 – 273.

[12] Ko, J., Schallert, D. L, & Walters, K. (2003). Rethinking scaffolding: Examining negotiation of meaning in an ESL storytelling task. *TESOL Quarterly*, 37, 303 – 324.

[13] Krashen, S. D. (1985). *The input hypothesis: Issues and implications*. London: Longman.

[14] Linddicoat, A. (1997). Interaction, social structure, and second language use: A response to Firth and Wagner. *Modern Language Journal*, 81, 313 – 317.

[15] Long, M. H. (1983a). Native speaker/non-native speaker conversation and

the negotiation of comprehensible input. *Applied Linguistics*, 4, 126 - 141.

[16] Merriam, S. B. (1998). *Qualitative research and case study applications in education*. San Francisco: Jossey-Bass.

[17] Nakahama, Y. , Tyler, A. , & van Lier, L. (2001). Negotiation of meaning in conversational and information gap activities: A comparative discourse analysis. *TESOL Quarterly*, 35, 377 - 405.

[18] Pica, T. (1994). Research on negotiation: What does it reveal about second-language learning conditions, processes, and outcomes? *Language Learning*, 44, 493 - 527.

[19] Polio, C. , & Gass, S. M. (1998). The role of interaction in native speaker comprehension of nonnative speaker speech. *The Modern Language Journal*, 82, 308 - 319.

[20] Seidman, I. (1998). *Interviewing as qualitative research*. New York, NY: Teachers College Press.

[21] Swain, M. (1985). Communicative competence: Some roles of comprehensible input and comprehensible output in its development. In S. M. Gass & C. G. Madden (Eds.), *Input in second language acquisition* (pp. 236 - 244). Rowley, MA: Newbury House.

[22] Van Lier, L. (2001). Constraints and resources in classroom talk: Issues of equality and symmetry. In C. N. Candlin & N. Mercer (Eds.), *English language teaching in its social context: A reader* (pp. 90 - 107). London: Routledge.

[23] Varonis, E. M. , & Gass. S. M. (1985). Non-native/non-native conversations: A model for negotiation of meaning. *Applied Linguistics*, 6, 71 - 90.

(Liu Xiaoling,College of Foreign Languages, Hunan University)

Discourse Analysis of Legal English

1. Introduction

1. 1　The Concept of Legal English

Legal English is one of the important varieties of the English language. It is also the research object of our discourse analysis in this thesis.

"Legal documents refer to those types of texts concerned with guarantee of people's rights, or the enforcement of their obligations, and the terms of punishment for the violation of the law, and the evasion of their obligations". (Zhang Delu, Chen Qigong, & Xu Luzhi 1992: 216)

Legal documents belong to the domain of official documents. The field of legal documents covers a wide range: statutes, decrees, legal provisions, economic contracts, commodity warranty, deeds or trust, insurance policies, wills and testaments, leases and installment plans, etc.

Legal language emerges and develops with the emergence and development of law. In the legislative and judicial activities, legal language obtained uninterrupted growth and gradually became a variant of the national language.

Theoretically speaking, legal language refers to the language used in the legal field, which can be spoken or written. Since it is not easy to gain access to enough data of spoken legal language for systematic study, we define "legal language" as "the written language used for legal documents" in this thesis, with the spoken legal language overlooked. In the English speaking countries, the language used for legal documents is therefore termed "Legal English" .

1. 2　General Purpose of This Study

The general purpose of this thesis is to make a systematical analysis of the significant language features of legal English. Therefore it will be hopeful to enhance the language quality of the personnel in legislative and judicial departments and the legal attainment of the whole people. This thesis aims to help people cultivate a sense of appropriateness, because people have to respond to a given situation with an appropriate variety of languages.

2. Discourse Analysis of Legal English

2. 1　The Concept of Discourse

Discourse is used as a general term of all kinds of speech, lecture, sermon, treatise, etc.

Any use of language displays certain linguistic features, which allow it to be identified with one or more extra-linguistic contexts. That is to say, extra-linguistic factors are relevant to the identification of linguistic features. These situational factors may account for restrictions on the use of a language.

2. 2　Extra-linguistic factors that influence Legal English

2. 2. 1　Medium

Medium refers to graphic signs (visual medium) or sound waves (auditory medium) by means of which a message is conveyed from the addresser to the addressee. The difference in medium results in speech and writing. Essentially, the distinction is non-linguistic, concerning the primary choice of method with which to communicate.

English for legal documents, determined by its visual medium, is written to be read. Therefore it has the characteristics of written language.

As written language, legal English conveys message through visual medium has channel limitation, which means that the transmission of a message is limited to one channel only.

Writers of legal documents spare no efforts to achieve precision and exactness by making special effective use of shapes of type, capitalization, and punctuation, long declarative major sentences and technical terms.

2. 2. 2　Participation

In terms of participation in discourse, the difference between monologue and dialogue should be clarified.

Monologue refers to the utterance of a speaker with no expectation of a response.

Dialogue refers to the utterance with alternating participants, usually, though not necessarily, two in number.

In a monologue the audience has not the opportunity or right to participate. On the contrary, the communication is usually conducted by the cooperation of the speaker and his audience in a dialogue. The speaker continually transmits his message to keep the dialogue going and also asks questions to encourage the active participation of the hearer.

Legal English should be classified in the category of written monologue. Owing to the nature of legal documents (as official documents), legal English used in legal documents as a language carrier to formulate various laws in written form, therefore, is to be read in silence by the public at large. This is just one reason why legal English writers spare no pains to pursue precision and exactness in their writings.

2. 2. 3　Province

In this dimension, we describe the features of language, which identify a discourse with those variables in an extra-linguistic context which are defined with concerns of occupational or professional activity being engaged in. Province features do not give us any information about the people involved in any situation, such as their social status and relationship to each other. These features are found to recur regardless of who the participants are and to relate to the nature of the task they are engaged in. The occupational role of the language-user determines what he may say or write.

It is province, along with other restraints (status and modality) that we will discuss soon, which form the stylistic basis of any variety.

Clear examples of provinces are the "language of" (shorthand for "distinctive set of linguistic features used in") public worship, advertising, science or law. It should be noted that each of these contexts has an intuitive coherence and identity, which may be defined in non-linguistic terms.

The situational variables in the contexts are defined at different levels of generality, depending on the nature of the linguistic features which are being considered. At the most general level, legal English has its own unique characteristics, which are defined by the legal profession and legal activities in which it is used. At other levels, we say "legal English" as opposed to "legal English of business contracts", and so on.

2. 2. 4　Status

Normally, we use different language variations corresponding with the relative social standing of the participants in daily communication. Our audience may be an individual or a group of people. The concept "status" involves a set of factors related to contacts between people from different positions on a social scale. These factors are associated with notions as formality, informality, respect, politeness, intimacy, business relations, and hierarchic relations in general.

2. 2. 5 Formality

The degree of formality is decided by status and some other situational contexts. Formal English is used often in official documents, scientific writings, and business letters. Informal English is used typically in private conversation and personal letters.

Some linguistic features can be seen only in informal English such as simple words, simple sentence structures, minor sentences, and elision, which are rarely found in formal English. Nevertheless, in legal English, that is quite another matter. By contrast, we can find some other features in the five examples of legal documents.

(1) Big words, e. g.

promulgate, supervisory, supplementary··· (Sample 1)

tranquility, qualification, enumeration··· (Sample 2)

interim, application, disclosure··· (Sample 3)

residential, interruption, stipulations··· (Sample 4)

commodity, identical, penalty··· (Sample 5)

(2) Long and complex sentences, e. g.

① Each province, autonomous region, municipal finance bureau and the responsible authorities under the State Council shall administer the accounting affairs relating to enterprises with foreign investment in its own region or under its administration and may, in accordance with these Regulations and the practical circumstances, formulate supplementary provisions, copies of which shall be filled with the Ministry of Finance for reference. (Sample 1)

② We the People of the United States, in order to form a more perfect Union, establish Justice, insure domestic Tranquility, provide for the common defense, promote the general Welfare, and secure the Blessings of Liberty to ourselves and our Posterity, do ordain and establish this Constitution for the United States of America. (Sample 2)

③ Colonial offers Interim Insurance Cover if you and the life to be insured have provided complete and truthful answers to the questions in the Application and Personal Statement and you have satisfied Colonial of your duty of disclosure. (Sample 3)

④ THIS LEASE made the fourth day of December one thousand nine hundred and seventy BETWEEN RESTDENTIAL PROPERTIES LIMITED of Clarendon

Square in the County of London (hereinafter called "the Lessors") of the one part and Stephen Jackson of 25 Potter Street London N16 (hereinafter called "the Tenant") of the other part. (Sample 4)

　　⑤ THE SELLER SHALL ADVISE THE BUYER, ON THE SAME DAY BY TELEX THE DATE OF SHIPMENT, CONTRACT No. ITEMS QUANTITY, TRUCK No. CONSIGNMENT NOTE No. AND THE ESTIMATED DATE OF ARRIVAL AT CUSTOMS. (Sample 5)

Such features as big words, long and complex sentences are heavily used in legal English to reveal its formality.

Still, legal English is typical of its solemn style and tightly-knit structure. In addition, owing to its nature as official documents, legal English is much more formal than other varieties of English.

　　2. 2. 6　Impersonality

Impersonal style refers to the kind of texts which are mainly in written form and absolutely avoid personal feelings, opinions and judgements of both the writers and the readers. Impersonality of language gives people a deep impression of objectivity and impartiality. Such texts as official and scientific writings, especially the legal documents, are typical of impersonal style.

As is known to all, everybody is equal before the law. No one should break the law without being punished. Legal sanctity can not be violated by any individual or group of people. All of the above result in the impersonality of Legal English.

Legal English, as the language of legal documents, possesses some linguistic features, which indicate the degrees of impersonality. In legal English, we seldom see those adjectives with emotional and subjective senses, such as beautiful, wonderful, disgusting, etc. Between the long sentences the only link is the repetition of lexical items instead of pronouns like "he, she, it or they"; furthermore, sentences of passive voice with "shall+be+done" structure are frequently used; all these help to show the impersonal style of legal English.

　　2. 2. 7　Accessibility

Accessibility, interchangeable with readability here, is not to be confused with legibility. When we say something is legible, we mean that the handwriting can be read easily or something is printed clearly enough for the readers to read.

Accessibility involves the quality of content and the ability of readers to comprehend. When we read a piece of writing, it is readable only if we can understand it fully.

When the language is more formal, it becomes less readable. Formal writings usually contain long and hard words, which are difficult for readers to understand. The degree of accessibility is measured by the quantity of hard words in a piece of writing and the length of sentences. There is a formula called "Fog Index" proposed by Robert Gunning in the 1940s:

Fog Index$=0.4 (L+H)$

L—the average sentence length

H—the percentage of hard words (which have three or more syllables excluding inflections and compounds)

Table 1. Accessibility of Legal English

Samples	1	2	3	4	5
Total words	211	372	341	679	513
Average sentence length	35	41	49	113	43
Percentage of hard words	35%	13%	20%	10%	12%
Fog Index	28	21.6	27.6	49.2	22

This table shows that the Fog Indexes of the five samples are all more than 20. The Fog Index of Sample 4 even reaches 49.2 because of the extremely long sentences. The Fog Index of an easily accessible text is between 7 and 12. So we can say legal English is far more inaccessible to common people than other varieties.

2.2.8　Modality

In this part we describe the linguistic features correlated with the specific purpose of an utterance which requires the addresser to choose one feature or set of features instead of others, and finally to produce an overall and conventionalized spoken or written format for his language. Of course, the choice of certain linguistic features should be regardless of a language-user's specific occupational role or relationship to other participants (Crystal & Davy 1969). That is to say, modality is somewhat a question of the suitability of form to the subject matter.

Legal English owns a reputation of having a one-for-one way correlation between content and form. Legal draftsmen and lawyers have been doing basically the same thing day after day—writing property conveyance, drawing up wills, and so on. After a long time, for each kind of transaction there has developed a linguistic formula. Lawyers have a strong desire to turn to a form of words that they can rely on. Therefore, most legal writings are not written spontaneously but are copied directly from 'form book' in which established formulae are collected. There is another reason for developing a model. Leal English, as we know, is unlike normal discourse. The complexity of legal English is not easily grasped, even by experts.

The reliance on forms established in the past and the unwillingness to take risks of using new and unexamined models result in the extreme linguistic conservatism of legal English.

2. 2. 9　Foundation

As we mentioned above, legal English is a variety of English, and like the rest of the other varieties of the English language, it has distinctive features which are different from other varieties, as well as from Standard English. These differences arise from historical, sociological, and jurisprudential processes; each has helped make legal language an unique variety of English (Charrow & Erhardt 1995).

(1) Historical Factors

During the period that English law was evolving, the English language went through a number of linguistic changes. However, legal language had its own processes of change and growth. Therefore, its development did not mirror that of the other varieties of the English language. Legal language has developed a number of its forms and meanings through a legal-historical process which is different from that of the other varieties of the English language. It is the courts, legislatures, and government agencies that decide the meaning of many legal terms, rather than ordinary usage and historical change. The legal definition of *fresh fish*, which has been set by regulations, is *a fish that has never been frozen, no matter when it was caught*. Most legal meanings have certain degree of flexibility, there is a range of meanings for a given word. But in the law the range of meaning is a result of different judicial, statutory, or regulatory interpretations or formal negotiations, not of ordinary linguistic processes.

The English legal system is derived from the legal system of England. Legal proceedings and legal writings in England were first done entirely in Latin, then in a mixture of French, Latin, and finally in English alone. This complicated evolution has left us with some unusual clause and phrase structures and a good deal of terminology that is a combination of Latin, French, and archaic English. In legal language, older words are not always replaced, new words are simply added to the previously used terms. This creates lots of synonymous words, such as terms and conditions, suit and claim, etc.

(2) Sociological Factors

Legal language is the primary tool of the legal professionals. Lawyers have only one way of using their knowledge-through legal language. One important function of legal language is the performative function. Legal language carries the force of the law. Of course, it is not legal language by itself that has that power. Society has granted to certain persons of the authority to make decisions over life and property. A society needs laws, and legal sanctity can help persuade people to follow them. This idea of legal language as carrying the power of law appears to be one reason that lawyers resist even small changes for avoiding the wrong legal result.

(3) Jurisprudential Factors

Common law is usually built first. In the law, terms, phrases, even the whole passage, mean what courts have decided them to mean. Chief Justice Hughes's statement that "a federal statute finally means what the Court says it means" (Charrow, Erhardt 1995) is probably more accurate, as the legal system actually operates. There are numerous instances where a definition decided either by the courts or by statute differs substantially from the common meaning of the term. The interaction between jurisprudence and legal language is nicely illustrated in the often contradictory rules that courts use to interpret the meaning of statutory language. In addition to these rules, the courts have created a host of maxims to take care of specific situations. The purpose of these rules is supposedly to provide objective criteria for resolving statutory ambiguity. Courts often use these rules to support a particular interpretation after they have created a decision. Consequently, different courts have applied the various rules and maxims to the same term and have come up with different meanings.

Conclusion

As indicated by the results of previous studies, the study of legal English cannot be isolated from its context. Legal English, as a variety of English, has its own particular language features concerning contextual restriction.

Extra-linguistic factors relevant to the identification of linguistic features of legal English consist of province, status, modality and foundation. Having considered these dimensions, we got a conclusion: legal English belongs to the category of written monologue; it is the language specially used in the legal profession; legal English is of very formal and impersonal style and the most inaccessible kind of writing; and legal English is typical of its correlation between content and form.

Discourse analysis of legal English is likely to help those people in legal field to cultivate a sense of appropriateness and may also encourage them to learn more professional knowledge so as to be able to speak and write legal English. It is of benefit to sharpening the understanding of legal writings so as to avoid any mistake in judgement and helpful in raising people's ability of correct translation of legal documents.

References

[1] Brown, G. & Yule, G. *Discourse Analysis*[M]. London: Cambridge University Press,1983.

[2] Chomsky, N. *Syntactic Structures*[M]. The Hague and Paris: MoutoN,1957.

[3] Crystal, David, D. Davy, *Investigating English Style*[M]. London: Longman,1969.

[4] Gregory, M., S. Carroll. *Language and Situation* [M]. London: Routledge and Kegan Paul, 1978.

[5] Hu Zhuanglin, Liu Runqing, Li Yanfu. *Linguistics: A Course Book*[M]. Beijing: Peking University Press, 1988.

[6] Hou Weirui. *English Stylistics* [M]. Shanghai: Shanghai Foreign Language Teaching Press, 1988.

[7] Qiu Shi. *Legal Language*[M]. Beijing: Chinese Zhan Wang Press,1990.

[8] Delu, Chen Qigong, XuLuzhi. *Readings of English Styles* [M]. Qingdao: Qingdao Ocean University Press, 1992.

(Jiang Ting,河北科技大学外国语学院)

英汉语辞格的形式、作用和认知意义

1. 引言

修辞（Rhetoric）源于希腊语（rhetorike），意思是"遣词华丽而精湛的演讲艺术"。讲演术或修辞术是古希腊的三大基础学术（含语法和逻辑在内）之一。随着社会的发展，语言和文学的发展步伐也不断加快，因此，修辞的含义也就更丰富了。除了"讲演艺术"以外，它还包括了作品的结构、风格、措辞、韵律等等。在现代英语里，修辞的一般含义是"生动地组合词语之技巧"，甚至有人干脆说成是"写作技巧"。其中有不少修辞方法使用极为频繁，并形成了固定的形式，因而被称为修辞格（figures of speech），即为了追求某一特殊的语言效果而设计的与普通的词句相比在结构和含义上都不相同但又具有比较固定的格式的比较规范的语言表达方法，如比喻和夸张等等。我认为：修辞就是优化措辞（perfection of wording），达到交际的最佳效果。

修辞对语言的表达效果具有独特的作用。所以，其重要性不亚于语法和逻辑：语法是对语言的结构规则而言的；逻辑是对思维的形式及其规律而言的；修辞是对语言表达的质量而言。因此，对于语言学生而言，了解和掌握英语修辞方法（或修辞格）有助于完善自己的英语语言素质、培养自己的英语表达能力、提高自己的英语口语和笔语水平、改善自己的英语思维方法和表达方式从而达到最佳的语言表达效果、实现语言交际的最终目的。

2. 英汉修辞的差异性

英语和汉语都是历史悠久的语种，因而具有丰富的词汇和修辞手法。但是二者之间差异很大。而这些差异恰好对语言表达的效果和语言交际的目标的实现在文字形式和语音方面有着不同的影响方式。首先，从语言及文字形式方面看，英语属于印欧语系，所用的是拼音文字形式；而汉语属于汉藏语系，所用的文字形式是在象形文字基础上发展起来的。其次，从发音及其意义的角度看，汉语是一种声调语言，其严谨的四声系统直接决定着每一个字词的意义；而英语是重音语言，重音在词句中对意义的确定起着决定性的作用。再次，由于文化和社会制度的不同，这两种语言在修辞上也大有不同之处。比如，由于漫长的封建社会给中国留下了特别尊敬长者的传统，所以与"比喻"等修辞手法相比"讽刺"和"幽默"出现得很少；但是这两种手法在英语中却是极为重要的。又如，处于不同文化背景的人在进行比喻时所用的喻体是不大相同的：在英语中不难听到表示羡慕的 You are a lucky dog 之类的句子，但是汉语里几乎没有人会在类似情况下用"狗"来赞美对方。

3. 英汉语辞格的形式、作用及认知意义

英汉修辞虽有差异，但辞格的共同点更多。修辞格（Figures of Speech）到底有多少？阿瑟·翟格尔（Arthur Zeiger）1978 年编写的《英语百科全书》中归纳出了 77 种；日本早稻田大学英文教授增田藤之助所著的《英语修辞学讲义》共收 50 种；中国著名学者陈望道所著并于 1984 年在上海外语教育出版社出版的《修辞学发凡》共收 38 种。其实如果认真细致地总结，可能找到一百多种修辞格甚至上千种。本文根据学生在学习英语修辞格时片面重视其形式、忽视其作用和意义的问题，收集和利用了教材和其他有关资料（见末尾"参考文献"）和对英、汉语的修辞格形式、作用和意义之对比，重点对代表性最强的 43 种英语修辞格的形式、作用及其意义作如下的分析，以此作为英语修辞格的总结，一为初学者之用，二为求得各位批评：

3.1 音韵辞格 **(Phonological figures of speech)**

语言的三要素是语音、语法和词汇。而英语是一种拼音文字，其语音语调在英语修辞中起的作用与汉语相比就要大得多。由于英语句子的词序相当固定，若要想改变或调整句的意思，有时仅仅依靠词序的变化是不行的。何况英语中各种音韵感强的词汇和语调能够极其有效地表达意思和思想感情的微妙变化。音韵修辞格的效果所依靠的不只是词义而是音韵。这类修辞格的应用由于能够使人强烈地感受到语言的音乐美而具有生动、形象、逼真的描述效果。

3.1.1 拟声（Onomatopoeia）

"拟声"实际上是模仿有关事物和动作或行为的声音来造词。拟声词的应用能够使人广泛联想，形成声音与知觉间的共鸣。这样语言表达就会更加直观、生动、形象、传神。这种现象在汉语里也常见，有时还有相互对应的词汇（Mew, miaow 喵；ding dong 钉铛!）例如：

① As you approach the copper-smith's market, a tinkling and banging and clashing begins to impinge on your ear. （你一走近白铁制品市场，就会听到一片叮叮当当、哐哐镗镗的声音。）（from "The Middle Eastern Bazaar"）

②（根据动物的声音而成的）Apes gibber. Asses bray. Bears growl. Beetles drone. Bulls bellow. Camels grunt. Cats mew（purr）. Ducks quack. Eagles scream. Flies buzz. Frogs croak. Geese cackle (gabble). Goats bleat. Horses neigh (snort). Hens cluck. Larks warble. Lions roar. Magpies chatter. Mice squeak. Owls hoot (screech). Pigeons coo. Pigs squeal (grunt). Pugs yelp. Ravens croak. Snakes hiss. Thrushes whistle. Turkeys gobble. Wolves howl.

3. 1. 2 头韵 (Alliteration)

根据希腊文词源，"头韵"的基本意思是"重复使用同一个字母"，但在形式上是指连续重复靠近字词开头的辅音，不一定是重复字词的起首字母。"头韵"是古英语诗歌文体不可缺少的因素，但也常见于现代英语散文、新闻、讲演和广告之中。其作用是利用音谐实现乐感，给人留下深刻的印象。由于汉语里面没有与"头韵"相对应的修辞格，所以翻译这一类的英语句子时只能够尽量做到达意，但难以做到传神。例如：

① It was a splendid population-for all the slow, sleepy, sluggish-brained sloths stayed at home. （那里的人是最优秀的——因为所有的懒虫、睡虫、和反应迟钝的懒东西都还在家里。）—Noel Grove：Mark Twain—Mirror of America

② It was that population that gave to California a name forgetting up astounding enterprises and rushing them through with a magnificent dash and daring and a recklessness of cost and consequences, which she bears unto this day-and when she projects a new surprise, the grave world smiles as usual, and says "Well, that is California all over." （只有那些人才给了加利福尼亚一个至今还享之不尽的美好名声：她不怕牺牲、不惜代价、突飞猛进地建立和发展了震惊世界的事业；每当她在设计新的奇迹时，拘谨的人们只是照常微笑着说："唔，那就是加利福尼亚风格。）—Noel Grove：Mark Twain—Mirror of America

③ The Russian danger is therefore our danger, and the danger of the United States, just as the cause of any Russian fighting for his hearth and home is the cause of free men and free peoples in every quarter of the globe. （所以，俄国的危机就是我们的危机，也是美国的危机，正如俄国人民为幸福和自由而战斗的事业是全世界各地正在享受自由的人民和朋友的伟大事业。）

—Winston S. Churchill：Speech on Hitler's Invasion of the USSR

④ Bye, Bye, Balanced Budget! （平衡的预算，一去不复返了!）

3. 1. 3 半韵 (Assonance)

英语中的"半韵"（根据《牛津现代高级英汉双解词典》）是指两个或两个以上的单词中只有重读的元音相同，而其后的辅音不相同。这种修辞格有利于求得声音的悦耳效果。例如：

① I arise from dreams of thee

In the first sweet sleep of night. —Percy Bysshe Shelley：The Indian Serenade

值得说明的是，在英诗中可见诗行末尾有两词以上的尾音（包括词尾的辅音在内）彼此相同（如：say，day，play 同韵；measure，pleasure 同韵；puff，rough 同韵）。这种情况在英语中常被称为 rhyme，我想在汉语中应该叫做"全韵"，这样正好与刚才提到的"半韵"（assonance）对应起来。下面可见这种"全韵"在诗中的应用：

② One word is too often profaned［有一个被人亵渎太多的词，

    For me to profane it，我无心再来亵渎；

    One feeling too falsely disdained 有一份被人鄙薄太假的情，

    For thee to disdain it. 你也不会再鄙薄。

      —Percy Bysshe Shelley：TO—雪莱：《致——》

所以，严格说来，汉语中的"押韵"虽然与英语中的"半韵"相似，但更接近英语中的"全韵"。例如：

③ 劝君莫惜金缕衣，Fletcher 译：If you will take advice，my friend，

  劝君惜起少年时。   For wealth you will not care.

  花开堪折直须折，   But while fresh youth is in you，

  莫待无花空折枝。   Each precious moment spare.

    ——杜秋娘：《金缕衣》 When flowers are fit for cutting，

                Then pluck them as you may.

                Ah，wait not till the bloom be gone，

                To bear a twig away.

                        —Du Qiuniang：Riches

这种情况在其他的文体中也能看到。例如下面的句子中的 much-touted 和 much-clouted 虽然有人将其划入"半韵"（assonance），但实际上将其划入"全韵"（rhyme）更为合适。

④ The difference between the much-touted Second International（1934）and the much-clouted Third International（1961）is not like the difference between year-ly models but like the difference between the horse and buggy and the automobile.（韦氏字典第二版备受褒奖，而第三版却横遭谩骂。两种版本的遭遇截然不同，他们的区别也绝非能与不同年代生产的不同型号的汽车之间的区别相比。这两个版本之间的区别就像马车和汽车之间的区别一样，具有划时代的意义。）—Bergen Evans：But What's a Dictionary For?

3. 1. 4 谐音（Consonance）

"谐音"是指连续或相近的字词中不同的元音后面出现相同的辅音（有时还有元音）。这种修辞格在英语诗歌和散文中常见，但是在现代汉语里面没有，所以在汉译时难传神，只能是尽量"达意"。例如：

① What would houses and horses be to me without him? (没有他，马和家产对我又有什么用呢？)

② criss-cross (纵横交错) (3) tittle-tattle (搬弄是非) (4) wishy-washy (空洞无物)

3.1.5　同源词并列 (Paregmenon)

英语中的"同源词并列"这种修辞格指的是因几个同源词的连续使用而凭借其类似的音韵增强语气。近距离使用同源词因同音重复而反复撞击读者的心灵，从而加深印象。但是，汉语因没有英语的这种利用词根派生的能力而没有与"同源词并列"相对应的修辞格。所以，我们在学习英语时要细心体会其词意，同时，在翻译时可以考虑用其他的形式来补偿其独特的修辞意义。例如：

① The bride within the bridal dress had withered like the dress, and had no brightness left but the brightness of her sunken eyes. (穿着礼服的新娘身上透出一股死气，那枯槁的形象和她身上的礼服一样，只有那深陷的眼窝中尚存一线活光。) —Charles Dickens

② The flowing water helped her thoughts to flow. (潺潺的流水使她浮想联翩。) —Rumer Godden

3.1.6　重复 (Repetitions)

"重复"作为一种修辞格，常见于演说词、诗歌、散文、小说和议论等较长的篇章之中。形式上，它可分为句首重复、句尾重复、首尾重复和间隔重复等。"重复"的目的是为了表达强烈的感情，表示越来越加剧的紧迫感，强调某一事物或观点的意义。"重复"无论是在汉语还是在英语里都是重要的修辞手段。例如：

① I say to you today, my friends, so even though we face the difficulties of today and tomorrow, I still have a dream. It is a dream deeply rooted in the American dream.

I have a dream that one day this nation will rise up and live out the true meaning of its creed: "We hold these truths to be self-evident; that all men are created equal."

I have a dream that one day on the red hills of Georgia the sons of former slaves and the sons of former slave-owners will be able to sit down together at the table of brotherhood; I have a dream—

That one day even the state of Mississippi, a state sweltering with the heat of injustice, sweltering with the heat of oppression, will be transformed into an oasis of freedom and justice; I have a dream—

That my four little children will one day live in a nation where they will not be judged by the color of their skin but by the content of their character; I have a dream today.

I have a dream that one day down in Alabama, with its vicious racists, with its governor having his lips dripping with the words of interposition and nullification, one day right there in Alabama little black boys and black girls will be able to join hands with little white boys and white girls as sisters and brothers; I have a dream today.

I have a dream that one day every valley shall be exalted, every hill and mountain shall be made low, and rough places will be made plane and crooked places will be made straight, and the glory of the Lord shall be revealed, and all flesh shall see it together.

美国著名黑人运动领袖马丁·路德·金（Martin Luther King）在上面的演说词 "I Have a Dream" 中，先后有九次重复了 I Have a Dream（that...）的句式。他以逐渐加强的情感使得演讲极富感召力，从而把听众带到了一个美好的未来。

从下面的举例可见 "重复" 的各种形式：

② I'll tell you, Governor, if you only let me get a word in, I'm willing to tell you. I'm wanting to tell you. I'm waiting to tell you.（长官，只要你让我说句话，我就会告诉你；我愿意告诉你，我很想告诉你，我正等着要告诉你。）—George Bernard Shaw（句首重复与平行句式重复）

③ You ought to be happy, but you are not happy. You can be happy, though, if you buy what we are making for you!（你本该幸福，但你并不幸福。只要买下我们的产品，你就会幸福。）（句尾重复）

④ Half the time, we cheat the foremen, the foremen cheat the management; the management cheats the customers; the customers are we.（在大半时间里，我们在欺骗监工，监工在欺骗厂主，厂主在欺骗顾客，而顾客正是我们自己。）（首尾重复）

⑤ The American is careless in his manner, his dress and his address; he is careless about his house and his garden, careless in social relationships, shuffling off old and taking on new with utmost carelessness, careless about observing laws, rules and regulations, careless about his food and his drink, and impatient with ceremony, careless about money. He tends to be careless about larger things as well. Perhaps carelessness is the most common and the most pervasive denominators in the American character.（美国人最大的特点是一切都很随便。美国人举止、衣着随便，住房、迁居随便，点缀环境的方式也随便。他们断友、结友、社会

交往也随便。他们在规章制度、法律法规方面，在吃喝礼仪方面，甚至在钱财等大事上面都很随便。）—Henry Steele Commager（间隔重复）

3. 2 意象辞格 (Imagery Figures of Speech)

3. 2. 1 拟人 (Personification)

"拟人"是指把没有生命的东西拟作有生命的东西并赋予它们以人的特性、思想、感情和活动。这种方法在英汉修辞中都常见，其作用主要有二：其一是在童话故事中或科普文体中用形象、生动和寓言般的语言来解释或说明事物或概念，从而使其浅显易懂。例如：

① It was now spring, and all over the country there were little blossoms and little birds. Only in the garden of the selfish Giant it was still winter. The birds did not come to sing as there were no children in it, and the trees forgot to blossom. Only the snow and the frost were pleased. "Spring has forgotten this garden," they said, "So we can lie here all the year round." The snow covered up the grass with her great white cloak and the frost painted all the trees silver. Then they invited the north wind to stay with them, and he came.（春天转眼就到了，到处都有鲜花和小鸟。只有自私的巨人的花园里还是冬天。那里没有小孩，所以小鸟不来唱歌，树木也不发叶、开花。高兴的只有冰霜和白雪："春天遗忘这个花园了，我们可以全年在此常住了。"白雪解开自己的冰衣把大地覆盖，冰霜也给树木披上银装。然后，他们又去请来了北风与他们同住。）—Oscar Wilde

"拟人"能被用来抒发强烈的思想感情，给人留下深刻的印象。例如，Marion Bowland 在《致我的旧旅游鞋》（"To My Old Hiking Shoes"）中就用"拟人"法表达了他对那双鞋子的怀念之情：

② Do you remember the slopes of slippery pine needles that you trod so surely, the great fallen tree trunks and boulders over which you scrambled? All your scars are honorable. You never failed me on the roughest trails; on glistening deck and spray-glazed rocks, you were as steady as on the level beach...（你还记得你曾经自信过人地一踏而过的那些落满了松针的陡坡和那些倒下来的巨大树干和圆石头吗？你身上所有的伤疤都是你的荣誉证书。即使是在崎岖的小路上你也从未让我跌倒过；即使是在船上最滑的甲板上和被海浪冲刷得最滑的岩石上，你也使我如履平坦的沙滩一样稳健而踏实。）

"拟人"法容易理解，但是在把事物比拟成人时要注意英汉语在性别问题上的习惯。一般来说，我们把大自然、祖国、月亮、夜晚、和平、欢乐和船只等比作阴性；把太阳、战争、疾病、时间和恐惧等比作阳性。这种划分的标准一方面是对传统（如史诗和神话）的继承和发扬，另一方面是依据心理因素而定。

3.2.2　夸张（Hyperbole）

"夸张"是指对事物特征过分强调，以便激发人们的想象，从而产生强烈的修辞效果。其作用主要有三：

其一，深刻揭露和批判社会弊病和不良现象，在幽默文体中还带有喜剧的效果。例如：

① His reputation as an authority on Scripture is recognized throughout the world.（作为圣经权威，他已誉满全球。）

—John Scopes：The Trial That Rocked the World

② And at last, as a due and fitting climax to the shameless persecution that party rancor had inflicted upon me, nine little toddling children, of all shades of colors and degrees of raggedness, were taught to rush onto the platform and call me PA!（反对党因为对我怀有深仇大恨而最后给了我一个最恰当、最无耻的报复：他们指使九个肤色不同、衣衫褴褛、蹒跚学步的孩子一齐冲上台来，齐声对我喊："爸爸"。）

—Mark Twain：Running for Governor

其二，渲染喜怒哀乐的情感。例如：

③ Hamlet：I love Ophelia, forty thousand brothers could not, with all their quantity of love, make up my sum.（哈姆雷特说："我爱奥菲莉娅，我的爱已经超过了四百万个兄弟的爱之和。"）

—William Shakespeare

其三，在史诗中体现英雄的气概。例如：

④ Paul was cutting down trees near Whistling River one day. Suddenly the river rose on its hind legs and squirted 4519 gallons of water straight into the middle of Paul's whiskers. Paul let out an angry yell. People heard him from a thousand miles. "I'll tame that river," Paul said, "I'm going to make some changes in it. I'll get rid of its curves..."（一天，保罗正在河边伐木。突然，河水站了起来，一口气把4519加仑的河水喷进了保罗的胡子里。人们在1000里以外的地方都能听到保罗的吼声："我要征服这条河，我要使它改道，我要把河道拷直。"）

—Gladys G. Doty

"夸张"这种修辞格在汉语里也很常用。例如：

⑤ 他们看见那些受人尊敬的小财东，往往垂着一尺长的涎水。

——毛泽东：《中国社会各阶级的分析》

⑥ 这媳妇才算媳妇，要如今的妇女呀，别说守一年，男人眼没闭，她就瞧

上旁人了。

——周立波：《暴风骤雨》

3. 2. 3　顿呼语（Apostrophe）

"顿呼语"是指在文章或说话过程中对不在场之人或事物所作的呼语，或把某种概念或特质拟人化了的谈话。这种修辞格通常与隐喻和拟人法用。例如：

① O Cuckoo! Shall I call thee Bird,　　（啊，布谷！我该叫你鸟，

　　Or but a wandering voice?　　　　　　还是迷了路的人?）

　　—William Wordsworth

② O world! O life! O time!　　　　　　（啊，人世！啊，人生！啊，时光！

　　On whose last steps I climb,　　　　　　　我爬到了您的尾端；

　　Trembling at that where I have stood before;　颤抖着，我站那儿想问：

　　When will return the glory of your prime?　何时您还有正茂风华?

　　No more—Oh, never more!　　　　　　完了——，要这干吗?!）

　　　　（Percy Bysshe Shelley：A Lament）

3. 2. 4　明喻（Simile）

作为一种修辞格，"明喻"通常由 like 或 as 引导，由三个部分组成：本体、喻词和喻体。例如，在下面的例句中，the sky 是本体，like 是喻词，a casque of scorching steel 是喻体。

① And the sky above my head became like a casque of scorching steel.

—Oscar Wilde：The Ballad of Reading Gaol

"明喻"用来表示两个不相似的事物之间的非一般意义上的比较，这种比较的依据通常是某种抽象的品质特性。请看下面的例句：

② Jim looks like his brother.（吉姆兄弟俩相像。）

③ Jim and his brother are as like as two peas.（他兄弟俩长得像双胞胎一样。）

从② 可见，所比较的是两个相似的事物（两者都是人）在一般意义上的比较，故没有"明喻"的修辞格；从③ 可见，所比较的不是相似的事物（两个人与两颗豆子），同时也是在非一般意义上的比较（两兄弟相似的程度与两颗豆子相似的程度之间的比较），故拥有"明喻"的修辞格。

虽然"明喻"在英语和汉语中因语言习惯不同而在喻体的选择上有时有很大的差异，如：汉语里常有"他瘦得像干猴子似的"等说法，而在英语里通常用"He is as thin as a rake（小耙子）。"但是，"明喻"在英汉两种语言中所起的作用基本相同：用来使描写更形象、解释更具体、说明更透彻。例如：

④ The water lay gray and wrinkled like an elephant's skin.

—Nancy Hale（使描写更形象）

⑤ So compared with any ordinary beam of light, the laser beam is a very orderly affair indeed. It is like a military march—everyone in step. In an ordinary beam, the waves are like the people in a crowd going to a football match, jostling and bumping into one another. （和其他光束比起来，激光就像军队齐步走一样——每个人都步调一致；而在普光中，光波就像走在一起去看足球赛的人群——相互碰撞，相互拥挤。）

——Albert Einstein（使抽象繁杂的东西解释得更具体、更易懂）

⑥ He was like a cock who thought the sun had risen for him to crow. （他就像一只骄傲的公鸡，以为太阳每天是为了让它啼鸣而升起来的。）

——George Eliot（为了透彻地说明这个人表现欲太强的特征）

在这里值得补充的是，在英语中，"类比"（Analogy）是"明喻"（Simile）的延伸（extended simile），因为这种明喻所指的是两个不同事物之间在多种抽象品质方面的共性。"类比"修辞格常见于科普文章（有时也出现在文学作品）之中，其作用是使极其复杂的事物更容易地被理解，所用的句式多是由（Just）as...so... 所引导的。例如：

⑦ Just as French people enjoy their wine, so the British enjoy their beer. （正像法国人欣赏葡萄酒一样，英国人最喜欢啤酒。）

——Paul Procter：Longman Dictionary of Contemporary English

3.2.5　隐喻（Metaphor）

"隐喻"的作用与"明喻"相同：使描写更形象、解释更具体、说明更透彻，但是在结构上有所不同：省略了喻词，本体和喻体融合一起，事物比较的共同点被隐含在句子里因而较"明喻"难以理解，需要联想才能体会得到。例如：

① All the world's a stage.

——William Shakespeare（用来生动地描写人世的复杂性）

（cf. All the world is like a stage. ）

② We don't need to spoon-feed the students. （用来具体地解释教学之间的关系）

（cf. We don't need to teach the students like we spoon-feed the babies）

③ The tree of liberty must be refreshed from time to time with the blood of patriots and tyrants. It is natural manure.

——Thomas Jefferson（作者把自由喻为大树，把鲜血喻为肥料，生动形象地说明了文题。）

值得注意的是"隐喻"的另外三种类型："讽喻"或（Allegory）、"寓言"（Fable）和"劝喻"（Parable）。"讽喻"是以人物代表忍耐、纯洁和真诚等各种观念，用隐喻和拟人等有关修辞格，综合组成故事，从而揭示道德意识，给人以教育，典型的例子是班扬（Bunyan）的名作《天路历程》（Pilgrim's Progress）。"寓言"是把各种动物拟人化，当作传说中的人物来讲故事，从而给人以道德教育，最典型的例子有《伊索寓言故事》（Aesop's Fables）。"劝喻"（Parable）与"寓言"一样也是讲故事，但不同的是"劝喻"的故事中的人物不是动物，甚至有时在故事里没有人物出现。看过圣经的人都知道耶稣常常为了劝诫而讲故事，圣经故事大多是有"劝喻"的故事，典型的例子有《浪子的故事》（The Prodigal Son 或 The Lost Son，The Lost Sheep）。

3.2.6　转喻（Metonymy）

"转喻"是指用一个人或事物的名称来替换与其有关的另一事物的名称，从而把几个词的意思凝聚起来注入一个单词或词组中，使比喻的语言即简洁又生动。例如：

① ... but for making money, his pen would prove mightier than his pickax.

—Noel Grove：Mark Twain—Mirror of America（句子中用 pen 代替 writing，用 pickax 代替 digging gold）

② He took to the bottle. （句子中用 bottle 代替了 liquor 和 wine 等）

③ I have never read Li Bai. （句子中用中国诗人李白的名字代替了李白的作品）

下面是些常见的"转喻"例子：

④（用人名于"转喻"中）Uncle Tom 指"逆来顺受、无反抗精神的人"；John Bull 指"英国或英国人"；Uncle Sam 指"美国政府"；Solomon 指"哲人、智者"；Cinderella 指"丑小鸦变成白天鹅"。

⑤（用地名于"转喻"中）The Oval Office 指"美国总统"；Capitol Hill 指"美国国会"；Hollywood 指"美国电影业"；Beijing 指"中国政府"。

⑥（用与职业有关的名词于"转喻"中）blue-collar 指"体力劳动者"；white-collar 指"脑力劳动者"；the veil 指"修女"；the press 指"新闻界"；the throne 指"君王、王位"；the stage 指"演艺业"；the crown 指"王权"。

⑦（用身体部位名于"转喻"中）heart 指"感情、情感、感受"等；head，brain 指"理智、智慧、机敏"等；tongue 指"口才、语言"等；nose 指"直觉、知觉、感觉"等。

汉语中也有类似的修辞格，如：在"枪杆子里面出政权"一句中，毛泽东把枪杆子代替武装斗争。但是不同的语言习惯有不同的表达形式，不能相互全都照搬。

在此必须提出的是不能由于前面的这些常见的"转喻"例词而忘记了另外一种在英语诗歌等文体中常见的修辞格："引喻"（Allusion）。"引喻"即间接提及或暗指历史上或过去的文学作品中，特别是希腊神话、圣经和莎士比亚的作品中所出现的某些意义十分深刻的事物。这种修辞格由于其意义未能直接表明而难于理解。例如：

⑧ It was an astonishing accident followed by an equally astonishing recovery, and many doctors, like doubting Thomas, refused to believe it until they had examined the man themselves. （这的确是个古怪的事故，但其病情的好转和恢复也是一个古怪的事情。所以，即使是医生，也大都像疑心重的托马斯一样，直到亲自考察一番以后才愿承认这是真人真事。）

—Dr. Colin Blakemore: How Brain Research Got Started

这里的"引喻"在 doubting Thomas，暗指了耶稣的 12 大门徒之一托马斯的疑心：听说耶稣死后又从坟墓里出来了一事时，他说他绝对不会相信此事，除非是亲自再看见耶稣手心的钉子痕迹、亲自把手指头再插进耶稣手心的钉子孔、亲自把手插进耶稣的两肋。

3. 2. 7　提喻（Synecdoche）

"提喻"与"转喻"因都是指替代而容易混淆，但是只要把握了关键，区别就不难了："转喻"是用一物代替另外一物，而"提喻"中的替代体现在一体之中。"提喻"是用整体与部分之间、易懂的词与难懂的术语之间、特殊与一般之间、衣物与穿衣物的人之间等等的相互替代。在例① 中，a white skin 代替了 a white person；在例② 中，purse 代替了 money；在例③ 中，souls 代替了 people。所以这三个句子中都有"提喻"。

① All people who work with their hands are partly invisible, and the more important the work they do, the less visible they are. Still a white skin is always fairly conspicuous. （用双手劳动的人总是不显眼：他们的工作越重要就越不显眼；但是白皮肤总是很引人注目。）

—George Orwell: Marrakech

② But neither his vanity nor his purse is any concern of the dictionary's. （但是，无论是虚荣心还是钱袋子都不是这本字典所关心的问题。）

—Bergen Evans: But What's a Dictionary For?

③ I walked, with other souls in pain. （我是走了，但其他很多颗心灵还在痛哭之中。）

—Oscar Wilde: The Ballad of Reading Gaol

但如果比较下面的两个句子中 hand 和 head 两词的意义和用法，我们不难发现例④ 中的 hand 是部分（手）代替整体（人），故用了"提喻"，而例⑤ 中的 head 和 heart 是用一事物（头和心）代替另一个事物（理智和感情），故用了"转喻"。

④ Many hands make light work. （人多力量大。）（Proverb）

⑤ You must let your head rule your heart. （你应该让你的脑子管住你的心。）

3. 3 技巧辞格 (Technical Figures of Speech)

所谓技巧辞格，与音韵修辞格和意象修辞格一样，只是一种分类的方式。我们用它来描写我们在写作过程中所利用的那些虽然没有固定形式、常常重叠交错出现但又的确构成了生动感人而幽默的语言、具有一般写作技巧所未能实现的效果之修辞格。

3. 3. 1 委婉说法（Euphemism）

"委婉说法"作为修辞手法，是指用委婉或温和的词句来表达令人不满意的概念等，即用无害的词句表达讨厌的概念。例如：

①（"发疯了"的委婉说法）

a. He has (got) a slate (或 a screw) loose.

b. He has gone off the rails.

c. He's touched in the head （或：queer; odd; crazy; unhinged; off his head; out of his head; unsound in the mind; not of sound mind; unbalanced; unsettled in the mind; not right in the mind; out of his mind; of unsound mind; soft in mind; not all there; far-gone; not in his right mind; simple-minded; brain-sick; all possessed; not right; not right in his upper story; not quite right upstairs; nuts; nutty; daffy; dotty; goofy; loony; buggy; cuckoo; feeble-minded; innocent; simple; off his chump; off his nut; off his base; off his trolley; off the track; off his rocker; mentally ill 等等。）

②（"死亡"的委婉说法）

a. After life's fitful fever he sleeps well. —W. Shakespeare

b. The dying sun, round and yellow as a pumpkin, was giving up its roseate ghost to the skies.

c. And of course I am anxious to see them married, too—before I go.

d. If I drop let us see what there is for you. —William Makepeace Thackeray

e. If I'm done those two ought to fetch you something. —William Makepeace Thackeray

f. With this sum... and the pension of a widow should she fall, she would be now absolutely independent of the world... —William Makepeace Thackeray

g. And then she fell to thinking what she should do if—if anything happened to poor good Rawdon. —William Makepeace Thackeray

h. It'll be the workhouse, if it's not the other thing. —John Galsworthy

i. It is the less surprising that probability of a transient earthly bliss for other persons when he himself should have entered into glory, had not a potently sweetening effect. —George Eliot：Middlemarch

j. He ceased to be（或：is no more；passed away；is departed from us；closed his life；checked out；took leave of life and bowed himself to the will of Heaven；kicked the bucket；kicked off；gave up the ghost；is gone to his rest；is gone to glory；breathed his last；quitted this world；made his exit；passed on；fell asleep；closed his eyes；went out like the snuff of a candle；took his last sleep；went to his last home；paid the debt of nature；joined his ancestors；went over to（join）the majority；was gathered to his fathers；went west；went off the hook；popped the hook；knocked off；called it a day；piped off；left us；joined his Maker；went to his reward；deceased；bit the dust（i. e. died on the battlefield）；cashed in his chips；took the last count；went to his long account；fired his last shot；made the supreme sacrifice；met an untimely end；received notice to quit；handed in his dinner pail 等）.

③（"醉酒了"的委婉说法）

a. He has had a drop too much.

b. He is fuddled（或：merry；jolly；happy；gay；groggy；in his cups；smelling of the coral；top-heavy；full of Dutch courage；glorious；reeling；far-gone；soaked；boiled；canned；corned；crocked；oiled；fried；lubricated；fresh；loaded；primed；afflicted；organized；polluted；sewed up；lit up；fired up；pie-eyed；out；pickled；plastered 等等）.

④（用形容词的比较级或最高级表示）

a. His coat has seen better days.（i. e. It's old and worn.）

b. I know better.（i. e. I'm not so foolish.）

3. 3. 2 迂回语法（Circumlocution）

"迂回语法"作为一种修辞格，是指用太多的词句来表达很少词句可以表达的思想，常见于幽默的作品中。例如：

① He is a member of the lower social-economic bracket.（cf. He is poor.）

② The lieutenant was irritable；the lieutenant called him a name—well，not a nice sort of name. It referred to his mother.（cf. The lieutenant called him son of a bitch.（军官骂了他一句"狗娘养的"））

3. 3. 3 渐升（Climax）

英语中的"渐升"与汉语中的"层递"法的"阶升"一样，也是根据三项或三项以上事物的内在逻辑关系，由小到大、又少到多、由浅入深、由轻到重、由远到近、由低到高……依次升级，像爬梯子一样，逐渐达到高潮。这种修辞格多用于讲演稿、论说文和散文、诗歌、小说中，从而撞击人们的心弦，达到感人的目的。例如：

① Some books are to be tasted, others to be swallowed, and some few to be chewed and digested. (有些书仅供玩味, 有些书可供浏览, 仅有少数书值得细读和消化。) —Francis Bacon: Of Studies

② We have come to dedicate a portion of that field as a final resting-place for those who here gave their lives that the nation might live. It is altogether fit and proper that we should do this. But in a larger sense we cannot dedicate—we cannot consecrate—we cannot hallow this ground. The brave men, living and dead, who struggled here, have consecrated it far above our poor power to add or detract. . . —Abraham Lincoln: Gettysberg Address

林肯在他的"葛底斯堡演说"中, 按照程度的浅深, 渐渐加强语势, 增强感染力。他所用的三个词 dedicate、consecrate、hallow 在语义上依次上升 (奉献——献祭——使成圣地), 层层加码, 直达顶点。

3.3.4 渐降 (Anti-climax 或 Bathos)

"渐降"与"渐升"相比, 在相关事物的层次方面有所不同, 它可以只要两个层次。在语义结构方面, 它正好与"渐升"相反, 按照由大到小、由远到近、由重到轻的顺序排列语言成分, 形成在语义上虎头蛇尾的不断下降之势头, 达到嘲笑、讽刺或幽默等喜剧性目的。例如:

① Seldom has a city gained such world renown, and I am proud and happy to welcome you to Hiroshima, a town known throughout the world for its—oysters. —Jacques Danvoir: Hiroshima—the "Liveliest" City in Japan

从这个句子可见, 市长本来很可能是要提广岛是因二战中受"原子弹轰炸"而闻名于全世界的事情, 但是他突然想到这一事件并非是光彩的。因此马上改上了"牡蛎"一词。从此我们可见其戏剧性效果之所在。

② Ye Gods! Annihilate but space and time and make two lovers happy. (上帝呀! 请消灭一切吧! 只留下空间和时间! 只让一对相爱的人幸福无边!) —Alexander Pope

3.3.5 矛盾修辞 (Oxymoron)

在英汉语中广为使用的"矛盾修辞"通常把两个意义互相矛盾或不协调的词以"一为修饰语、一为中心词"(在汉语里可能以并列词组)的形式用在一起, 使它们看似违背逻辑但实际上却是运用了同一事物的相互对立的两个因素的交相辉映来表达事物的微妙内涵和寓意, 令人感到意味深长。例如:

① Dudley Field Malone called my conviction a victorious defeat. (D. F. 梅棱说我的败诉是一个胜利。) —John Scopes: The Trial That Rocked the World

② 啊, 祖国, 我亲爱的母亲!

你是那么古老而又年轻;

　　你是那么富饶而又贫穷；

　　你是那么先进而又落后。——刘景林：《祖国啊，母亲》

　　③ It has the poorest millionaire, the littlest great man, the haughtiest beggars, the plainest beauties, the lowest skyscrapers, the dolefulest pleasures of any town I ever saw. （这里有别的城市从未见过的最穷的富翁、最渺小的伟人、最高傲的乞丐、最平凡的美人、最底矮的高楼和最令人悲哀的快乐。）—O. Henry

　　关于"矛盾修辞"构成方法的分析问题，可有不同的出发点。从结构上看，构成方法主要有以下五种：

　　其一，形容词＋名词：a living death （活着的死人）

　　其二，形容词＋形容词：poor rich guys （可怜的阔小子）

　　其三，副词＋形容词：terribly good news （好得可怕的新闻）

　　其四，动词＋副词：hasten slowly （慢腾腾地赶路）

　　其五，名词＋名词：love-hate relationship （爱恨交加的关系）

　　从描述的对象看，构成方法有以下四种：

　　其一，描述主观感受与客观实际之间的矛盾（突出主观感受）：audible stillness （听得到的宁静）

　　其二，描述事物的现象与本质之间的矛盾（突出描述的主观色彩）：grim friendliness （无情的友情）

　　其三，描述内心的矛盾（突出感情的复杂性）：delicious pain （乐趣无穷的痛苦）

　　其四，描述外表与内心的矛盾（突出内心与外情之间的失调）：honorable villain （体面的恶棍）

　　3. 3. 6　"似非而是"的隽语（Paradox）

　　"'似非而是'的隽语"是指表面上看来自相矛盾但却不无道理的修辞手法。这种手法构思巧妙，因而使得很多句子都成为了名言。英、汉语中例句很多：

　　① The child is father of/to the man. （三岁看大，七岁看老。）

　　② 有的人活着，

　　　　他已经死了；

　　　　有的人死了，

　　　　他还活着。——臧克家：《有的人》

　　值得注意的是"'似非而是'的隽语"与"矛盾修辞"有相似之处，但又不完全相同。其主要差别在于："矛盾修辞"依靠意义矛盾词的连续排列来完成（如例③），而"'似非而是'的隽语"依靠句式的结构来完成（如例④）。例句如下：

　　③ No light, only darkness visible. （没有光亮，只看得见黑暗。）—John Milton：Paradise Lost

④ Art is a form of lying in order to tell the truth.（艺术是为讲真理而存在的撒谎形式。）—Pablo Picasso

还要注意的是不可把"'似非而是'的隽语"与"警句"（Epigram）混淆。"警句"作为一种修辞格，指的是具有赞美或讽刺意义的短小、简练、诙谐的格言。例如：

⑤ Knowledge is power.（知识就是力量。）

⑥ Walls have ears.（隔墙有耳。）

⑦ Difficulties are opportunities.（困难就是机会。）

3. 3. 7　轭式搭配（Zeugma）

从修辞实质上讲，英语中的"轭式搭配"与汉语中的"拈连"基本相同：都是将适应于甲项的词语（大多为动词、形容词或介词）顺势拈连乙项，从而达到活泼语言、幽默生活之目的的修辞手法。例如，"人穷志不穷"中的"穷"字，一般来说，与"人"搭配合适，但是与"志"搭配是不当的。然而，这一个字在此句中通过"拈连"，不但不牵强，反而起到了极强的修辞作用。又如，wage war and peace 中的 wage 本来只能与 war 搭配，但被巧妙地用到了 peace 之上，并体现出极强的表现力。

英语中的"轭式搭配"与汉语中的"拈连"之不同之处基本上是一个习惯问题：英语中用来拈连的词通常不必重复（如上面的例词 wage）；而汉语里用来拈连的词通常必须重复（如上面的例句中的"穷"字）。还有很多例子，下面举出几个：

① The businessmen left in high spirits and a Cadillac.（那些商人离开时情绪很高，坐的是卡迪拉克名牌小车。）——《英语美国传统词典》P1489

句子中的 in 同时与 high spirits 和 a Cadillac 拈连。

② I would my horse had the speed of your tongue.（我的马跑路的速度如果能有你的舌头说话的速度那么快就该有多好啊!）—William Shakespeare：Much Ado About Nothing

句子中的 speed 同时与 horse 和 tongue 拈连，使人通过对 horse 和 tongue 的比较而产生联想。

③ 哈西姆跟许多坎尔井匠人一样，替水霸、地主挖了一辈子的水，给自己挖到的只是贫穷和疾病。——袁鹰：《戈壁水长流》

句子中的"挖"字重复使用了一次。

3. 3. 8　转换修饰（Transferred Epithet）

"转换修饰"，或称"移就"，实际上是转换修饰词的位置，使它去修饰它所不该修饰的成分。这种修辞格在英、汉语里都常见。例如：

① Grey peace pervaded the wilderness-ringed Argentia Bay inNewfoundland. (纽芬兰的阿根夏湾四周都是荒芜，只有一片灰色的宁静。) —Herman Wouk：The Winds of War

② Franklin Roosevelt listened with bright-eyed smiling attention. (F. 罗斯福听着，带有一股喜形于色的注意力。) —Herman Wouk：The Winds of War

③ 我将深味这非人间的浓黑的悲凉；以我的最大哀痛显示于非人间，使它们快意于我的痛苦，就将这作为后死者的菲薄的祭品，奉献于逝者的灵前。——鲁迅：《纪念刘和珍君》

④ The Grapes of Wrath（《愤怒的葡萄》）—John Steinbeck

美国作家 J. 斯坦贝克写的小说《愤怒的葡萄》叙述一批受骗去西部当葡萄采摘工移民的艰难困苦，小说以《愤怒的葡萄》为题目，显然是将采摘工的"愤怒"转换到葡萄上来，从而更形象地表现了主题。

从上面的例子可见，"转换修饰"主要用来激发联想、由此及彼、彼此交融、相互映衬、渲染气氛、加深意境。

3. 3. 9 感叹（Exclamation）

"感叹"作为一种修辞格，是指利用感叹号来表达吃惊、气愤、失望和兴奋等感情色彩的修辞方法。"感叹"方式主要有以下几种：

其一，用 What 或 How 开头的感叹句。例如：

① What signs have been wafted after that ship! What prayers offered up at the deserted fireside of home! How often has the mistress, the wife, the mother pored over the daily news, to catch some casual intelligence of this rover of the deep! (那船后漂浮着的痕迹多美啊！家中凄凉炉边的祷告是多么虔诚啊！为了得到点滴的船讯，主妇、妻子和母亲们看报又是多么认真啊！) —Washington Irving

其二，用带有感叹号的省略句。例如：

② She a beauty! I should as soon call her mother a wit! (真是美人！她妈年轻时定是个才女！) —Jane Austen

其三，用带有感叹号的倒装句。例如：

③ Isn't it nice weather today! (今天天气不是很美吗?!)

3. 3. 10 谨慎陈述（Understatement）

"谨慎陈述"作为一种修辞格，正好与"夸张"相反，是种保守或低调的说法。其加强语气的作用不仅是为了使语气委婉，而且含有讽刺意义。例如：

① He has had a drop too much. (他多喝了一杯。) (用小量指大量。) (cf. He's drunk.)

② I'm sort of (kind of) angry at your rashness. (我对你的鲁莽有点儿不高兴。) (用 kind of 或 of sorts 等等。) (cf. I am very angry at your rashness.)

3. 3. 11　双重否定（Double Negation 或 Litotes）

"双重否定"其实也是"谨慎陈述"的另一种形式，即在某些词前加上否定词从而表达极强的肯定意义，或用否定表肯定。例如：

① A：Would you like to come?（甲：你愿意来吗?）

B：Not half.（乙：不止一半，很想来。）（用 not half 指 very much）

② He was not unhappy about his daughter's marriage.（他对女儿的婚事不是不高兴。）（否定词前加否定词）（cf. He was very happy about his daughter's marriage.）

③ No one is free from faults.（没有任何人能够摆脱差错。）（free from 的意义是否定的。）（cf. Every one makes mistakes.）

④ A teacher cannot be too patient with his students.（教师对学生的耐心无论多大都不过分。）（用含有否定词的句型）（cf. Teachers should be as patient as possible with his students.）

3. 4　讽刺与幽默修辞格（Satirical and Humorous Figures of Speech）

"讽刺与幽默修辞格"在英语中的运用比汉语中的运用要多得多。这是因为在中国的历史上，人们对皇帝、权贵、领导、上司、师长、父母和其他任何比自己资格老、年岁长、名望大的人都很敬重。虽然如此，但是我们在日常生活中还是可见各种讽刺和幽默的情境。讽刺和幽默如果运用的及时，就会有利于打击邪恶的行为、维护社会的文明的进步，所以值得学好用好。

3. 4. 1　讽刺（Satire）

"讽刺"虽然有滑稽的味道，但其目的不仅是使人发笑，而且是用来嘲弄愚蠢、罪恶或恶人。"讽刺"按照其尖刻程度（从小到大）可再分为三种类型："影射"（innuendo）、"讽刺"（satire）和"讥讽"（sarcasm）。例如：

① Cool was I and logical. Keen, calculating, perspicacious, acute and astute, —I was all of these. My brain was as powerful as a dynamo, as precise as a chemist's scales, as penetrating as a scalpel and—think of it! —I was only eighteen. —Max Shulman：Love is a Fallacy

作者在这里通过揭露某些人自负的荒谬程度从而达到讽刺（satire）的目的，这种修辞意义体现在上下文之中。因此这种讽刺意义的实现方法是很间接的。

② RODNEY. Ah, Judge Wilson, forgive me—but how can anyone see you if you insist on standing in Mr. Dickinson's shadow? —Peter Stone and Sherman Edwards：1776，（scene 1）

在此句中罗德尼通过对威尔森的"影射"（innuendo）表示他对威尔森的反感，这种修辞方法比较直接地伤害了对方的感情。

③ Since, aside from roaring and admonishing the "gentlemen from Springfield" that "accuracy and brevity are virtues，" the Post's editorial fails to explain what is wrong with the definition，we can only infer from "so simple" a thing that the writer takes the plain，downright，man-in-the-street attitude that a door is a door and any damned fool knows that. —Bergen Evans：But What's a Dictionary For?

在这里，作者通过对反对者的"讥讽"（sarcasm）来肯定自己的词典所给词义的准确性。这种修辞方法的运用很直接地伤害了对方的感情。

④ I do humbly offer it to public consideration that of the 120，000 children already computed，20，000 may be reserved for breed，whereof only one fourth part to be males，which is more than we allow to sheep，black cattle，or swine；... that the remaining 100，000 may at a year old be offered in sale to the persons of quality and fortune through the kingdom，always advising the mother to let them suck plentifully in the last month，so as to render them plump and fat for a good table...

I grant this food will be somewhat dear，and therefore being proper or landlords，who，as they have already devoured most of the parents seem to have the best title to the children. （我斗胆建议大家考虑一下，把在册的 12 万儿童中留下 2 万以供人口繁殖，其中男性留四分之一，这已经比我们留的羊种、马种、牛种、和猪种的比例大多了；……剩下的 10 万可以在一周岁时卖给大英帝国的有钱人家。一定要令其母从婴儿 11 个月开始多给婴儿饭吃，以便使小孩丰满些，供作富人桌上佳肴……

我断言这种食物相当昂贵，所以只有那些把婴儿父母都榨干了的财主们才有品尝这些婴儿的资格。）—Jonathan Swift：A Modest Proposal

这典型的例子，通过这项"庄重的建议"达到了"讽刺"和揭露统治阶级的兽行的目的。这种"讽刺"的方法很间接，但是讽刺意义十分深刻。

3.4.2　双关（Pun）

英语中的"双关"是指用词造句时表面上是一个意思，而暗中隐藏着另一个意思，即利用英语一词多义的特点，使同一个词（大多是同音异义词或同形异义词）在同一个时候传播两种词义，从而写出一词双关的句子，实现幽默或讽刺等目的。英、汉语里都有双关，但几乎不能互译，所以在阅读时要注意，以免不知所云。例如：

① We must all hang together，or we shall hang separately. （我们要么紧紧地团结在一起，要么就会一个个地被绞死。）—Benjamin Franklin

句中的 hang 是同形同音异义词，即表"团结一致"之意，又有"被处绞刑"之义。一词双意，形成双关。

② A：Waiter！（服务员！）B：Yes, sir.（来了，先生。）

A：What's this?（这是什么?）B：It's bean soup, sir.（这是菜豆汤。）

A：No matter what it's been. What is it now?（过去是什么汤我不管。我只问这是什么汤?）

对话中的双关是通过同音异形异义词 been 和 bean 的同音［bi：n］来实现的。对话中的发音［its bi：n su：p］的意义有两种可能：其一是 B 的本义："这是菜豆汤"（It's bean soup）；其二是 A 的误会："这在过去一直是汤"（It has been soup）。一音双义，构成双关。

下面的例子是汉语中通过同音［shi］异义字词"诗"和"尸"来实现双关的。句中的"五马分尸"中的"尸"与"诗"同音，但用意是为了说明自己无法分"身"去做别的事情，如读书等等：

③ 目前忙着写诗、译诗、编诗、教诗、论诗，五马分尸之余，几乎毫无时间读诗，甚至无时间读书了。——余光中（台湾）：《书斋．书灾》

3.4.3 幽默（Humour）

"幽默"是西方人最常用的修辞格之一，主要是通过自贬、自嘲或贬他、嘲他的方式使人发笑（但是有时这种贬低或嘲笑的内容并非全是过失或缺点）或从中取乐。在很多情况下，如果能够恰当运用一些幽默，我们的生活、我们的人际关系等等都将克服好多的窘迫和为难的情境，从而达到批评不伤情、被批不丢面子、道歉和拒绝而不困窘的境地。就其结构而言，"幽默"一般有三种表现形式：

（1）通过巧妙地运用同音异义词（homophones）和同形异义词（homographs）来实现幽默的目的。例如：

① A：What kind of "nese" are you? Are you Chinese, Portuguese or Japanese?（甲：你是什么人? 你是中国人，葡萄牙人还是日本人?）

B：I am Chinese. By the way, what kind of "key" are you? Are you a donkey, a monkey or a Yankee? 乙：我是中国人。你呢? 你是什么仔? 你是驴仔，猴子还是牛仔［美国人］?

这个对话的幽默是通过同音异义词（key—donkey, monkey 和 yankee）而实现的。乙方巧妙地模仿了甲方的思维方式，不卑不亢地回答了对方的挑战。

（2）故意使句法产生歧义从而引出幽默。例如：

② A：I'm in a hurry. Call me a taxi?（甲：我很急。快给我叫一辆出租车。）

B：Sorry, you don't look like a taxi. Would you mind my calling you a buffalo?（乙：对不起! 你不像出租车。我叫你水牛，好吗?）

这个对话的幽默是通过句法产生歧义（call 的两个不同句法结构：甲方把 call 用作带双宾语的及物动词；乙方把 call 用作带复合宾语的及物动词）来实现幽默的，从而使乙方巧妙地帮甲方放松了一下情绪。

（3）故意把不适合眼前语境的文体给用上了，从而导致幽默的产生。例如：

③ I have nothing to declare except my genius. （我所要申报的只有才智）

—Oscar Wilde

这是作者在海关申报纳税品时所说的，而"才智"作为海关纳税品提出来却是令人莫名其妙。因此诙谐幽默。

3. 4. 4　反语（Irony）

"反语"即反话正说或正话反说，是一种微妙的讥讽、谴责、发泄、抨击、蔑视或幽默的方式。例如：

① After a while, it is the setting of man against man and creed against creed until we are marching backwards to the glorious age of the sixteenth century when bigots lighted faggots to burn the men who dared to bring any intelligence and enlightenment and culture to the human mind. —John Scopes： The Trial That Rocked the World

此例是一个"字词式反语"（verbal irony）：用相反意义的字词表达真正的意思。作者在此反话正说（把黑暗的十六世纪说成是"光荣的时代"），目的是使其讥讽和谴责更为尖锐。

② I have been assured by a very knowing American of my acquaintance in London that a young healthy child well nursed is at a year old a most delicious, nourishing and wholesome food, whether stewed, roasted, baked, or boiled, and I make no doubt that it will equally serve in a fricassee （炖肉丁） ...

此例是一个典型的"情境式反语"（situational irony）："反语"的真正意思不是靠句子结构，而是靠整个上下文来体现的。英国十八世纪著名作家 J. 斯威伏特（Jonathan Swift）在他的《一项庄重的建议》（"A Modest Proposal"）中，用的"反语"修辞格是极其巧妙的。为了揭露当时的英国统治者对爱尔兰人民的剥削，为了表现对爱尔兰人民饥寒交迫的悲惨境况的愤慨，他"建议"劳苦大众把自己的亲生骨肉当动物来饲养并卖给有钱人当佳肴食用。作者反话正说、一本正经、沉着镇静、有理有据地论述了他的"建议"。其目的是猛烈鞭打当权者、唤起受压迫者的觉悟。

3. 5　句式修辞格（Syntactical Figures of Speech）

句子是用词和词组构成的、能够表达完整意思的语言单位。在（连续）说话时，每个句子都有一定的语调和语气，句子与句子之间有一个较长的停顿；在书面语上每句子的末尾用句号、问号和感叹号等。按照语气，句子可以分为四类：陈述句、疑问句、祈使句和感叹句。按照结构，句子可以分为三类：简单句、并列句和复合句。根据不同的修辞手段来分类的话，句子可以分为很多的类别，如倒装句、省略句、平行句、散尾句和收尾句等等。句式的各种变化都有利于传达思想、态度和情绪，从而也就构成了修辞的一个重要方面，即句式修辞格。句子就像木匠手上的木头，可以根据各种情况变化万千。下面将主要讨论一些具有特殊功能的句式。

3. 5. 1 平行（Parallelism）与反衬（Antithesis）

"平行"作为一种修辞格，是指把结构相同、意义并重、语气一致的几个词、词组或句子排列成串，形成一个整体，从而凝练句子，使文章条理清楚、论点突出、语言流畅、对称悦耳、表现力强。例如：

① To be or not to be, that is the question. （是生还是死，的确是个难题。）—William Shakespeare：Hamlet（字词平行）

② We will never parley; we will never negotiate with Hitler or any of his gang. （与希特勒讲和？与他的同党谈判？我们不会，绝对不会!）—Winston S. Churchill：Speech on Hitler's Invasion of the U. S. S. R. （句子平行）

③ Then he drank a glass of water, pushed his plate to one side, and doubled the paper down before him between his elbows and read the paragraph over and over again. （然后，他喝了杯水，推盘子到一边，对折报纸放于眼前两肘之间，一遍又一遍地读着那段话。）—James Joyce（字词平行）

④ That is our policy and that is our declaration. （那就是我们的政策，那就是我们的宣言。）—Winston S. Churchill：Speech on Hitler's Invasion of the U. S. S. R. （句子平行）

⑤ They vanish from a world where they were of no consequence; where they achieved nothing; where they were a mistake and a failure and a foolishness; where they have left no sign that they had existed—a world which will lament them a day and forget them forever. （他们在这个世上无足轻重，无所成功，只有错误，只有失败，只有愚蠢；他们最后还得从这个世上消失，从这个对他们痛之一日，忘之永久的世上消失。）—Noel Grove：Mark Twain—Mirror of America（字词平行和句子结构平行的混合）

值得注意的是，在平行句式里，如果有意识地把结构上前后对称和意义上前后对立的两个词、句并列在一起，就形成新的句式修辞格，即反衬（Antithesis）。例如：

① They vanish from a world which will lament them a day and forget them forever. （他们从人世间消失，从这个对他们痛之一日，忘之永久的世上永远消失。）—Noel Grove：Mark Twain—Mirror of America（句中 lament 和 forget 意义相反，句式平行。）

② The Christian believes that man came from above. The evolutionist believes that he must have come from below. （基督教教徒认为人是从天而降；但生物进化论者认为人是自地而出。） —John Scopes：The Trial That Rocked the World（句中的 Christian 与 Evolutionist 意义相对；above 和 below 意义相对；句子结构平行。）

③ The coward does it with a kiss, the brave man with a sword! （懦夫杀爱施亲吻；勇士灭情用利剑。） —Oscar Wilde：The Ballad of Reading Gaol（句中 kiss 与 sword 意义相对；句式平行。）

④ It was the best of times, it was the worst of times; it was the age of wisdom, it was the age of foolishness; it was the epoch of belief, it was the epoch of incredulity; it was the season of Light, it was the season of Darkness; it was the spring of hope, it was the winter of despair; we had everything before us, we had nothing before us; we were all going direct to Heaven, we were all going direct the other way. （这是最美好的时期，也是最恶劣的时期；这是智慧的年代，也是愚蠢的年代；这是信仰的时代，也是怀疑的时代；这是光明的季节，也是黑暗的季节；这是希望的春天，也是绝望的寒冬；我们拥有一切，我们也一无所有；我们在走向天堂，我们也在走向地狱。） —Charles Dickens：A Tale of Two Cities（多组词词义相对；句式平行。）

作者在小说《双城记》的开头用上这一系列的对句修辞格，把那动荡不安、充满矛盾的社会现实生动地展现在读者面前，起到了开宗明义的作用。

"反衬"是一种特殊的"平行"。它特别讲究结构的对称与平衡和反义词的相互衬托，与汉语里的对偶中的"反对句"（如"少壮不努力，老大徒伤悲"）。

3.5.2　散尾句与收尾句（Loose and Periodic Sentences）

"散尾句"与"收尾句"是相反的两种修辞格。前者作为段落和篇章的基础句式，讲究把句子的主体概念放在最前，遵循主句在前、从句在后的原则，使句子的陈述直截了当、客观真实、使句子的内容具有很高的信度；而后者是把句子的主体概念放在最后，把句子的重心调到句尾，形成"高潮"（Climax），使人不到话尾不明白用意。使用"收尾句"能够造成悬念、形成句式高峰、增添语言节奏感、避免文章的单调和乏味、从而达到强调的目的。例如：

① Going to her room at a late hour, he found her in what seemed to him a more composed frame of mind than at any time this difficulty had appeared, a state which surprised him a little, since he had expected to find her in tears. （他深夜去看她，发现她的心态是这场灾难之后最镇定的。这使他感到吃惊，因为他本来以为她会出现泪流满面的样子。） —Theodore Dreiser（散尾句）

② It is a truth universally acknowledged that a single man in possession of a good fortune must be in want of a wife. （有一条真理以被世人广泛承认，那就是：

家产丰厚的单身汉所缺少的一定是妻子。) —Jane Austen: Pride and Prejudice
(收尾句)

③ It comes as a great shock to discover that the country which is your birth-place and to which you owe your life and identity has not, in its whole system of reality, evolved any place for you. (如果有一天发现那生你养你的、那个你认为你是其理所当然的公民的国家，在其整个的现行体系中根本没有你的立锥之地时，你会感到何等地震惊！) —James Baldwin（收尾句）

汉语里也常见这两种句式，这一点从上面的英译汉的例句中可看得清清楚楚，所以不再举例了。

3. 5. 3 修辞问句（Rhetorical Questions）

与普通的问句（期待答复）不同，"修辞问句"（不需答复）是用提问的方式给对方一个答案，即使对方从所给的信息中得出其自己的答案。修辞问句具有极强的说服力和感染力，常用于英、汉语讲演、宣传和广告之中。更具体有些的话，"修辞问句"有两种形式，其一是"提问"（自问自答，以便引人注意下文），如例②；其二是"反诘"（故意发出无疑之问，让对方体会其含义）例如：

① If winter comes, can spring be far behind? （冬天到了，春天还会远吗？）—Percy Bysshe Shelley: Ode To The West Wind

② 谁说中国人不善于改变呢？每一新的事物进来，起初虽然排斥，但看到有些可靠，就自然会改变。不过并非将自己变得合于新事物，乃是将新事物变得合于自己而以。——鲁迅：《华盖集·补白》

此例中的"中国人"系指反动统治者及反动文人。鲁迅以否定形式提问，其实是说这些"中国人"是善于改变自己的面目的。鲁迅用这一个方式表达了他对这些文人投机善变的鄙视和愤怒感情，有力地讽刺了这些变色龙。

3. 5. 4 倒装句（Inversion）

"倒装句"虽然在汉语里用得比英语里少，但是的确是种重要的修辞手段。"倒装句"有两种形式。其一是完全倒装（句子中的谓语动词放到其主语之前），如例①；其二是部分倒装（除完全倒装以外的其他有非正常语序的句中形式）如例②。英语中倒装句的运用是为了更好地表现语气、态度和情绪（当然也不排除个别情况下为了句子的平衡等等语法方面的情况）。例如：

① Black are the brooding clouds. （黑压压的是一团乌云。）—Charles Dickens（正常语序：The brooding clouds are black. ）

② Easily was a man made an infidel, but hardly might he be converted to another faith. 要把某人打成异教徒并不难；难的是怎样改变其信仰。）— T. E. Lawrence（正常语序：A man was easily made an infidel, but he might hardly be converted to another faith. ）

3.5.5　省略句（Ellipsis）

"省略句"是指在一定的语言环境（对话或上下文）里，句子的某些词被略去不说，其目的和作用在于精炼语言、使其活泼新颖、增强其趣味性。这种手法在英、汉语中都常见，其方式可分为承前省（如例①）、蒙后省（如例②）、对话省（如例③）和习惯省（如例④）四种。例如：

① You know the feeling. It's a warm smile.［ ］A relaxed atmosphere.［ ］A lot of caring. You can be yourself.［ ］Just like home.（你懂得这种感受：温馨的微笑、轻松的气氛、周到的关怀、自由自在，就像在家里一样。）

句子的内容正好被省略了（It's）的松散句式表现得恰到好处。

② 我不去喊［ ］，你去喊他来。（［ ］处省略了"他来"）

③ ［你］Stop smoking.（［你］不得抽烟！）（省略了主语"你"［You］）

④ More haste, less speed.（Proverb）（欲速度则不达。）（在成语、套语和名言中多有省略，以求深刻的寓意。这已经成了习惯。）

综上所述，英语修辞格的产生和发展不是在真空中完成的，而是以操英语的各有关民族的政治、经济和文化的不断发展为背景的，同时也是与其他各非英语民族的语言（如汉语）和文化运作的过程中不断发展的修辞手段或修辞格互补的。在学习英语修辞格的过程中，我们必须在注意各修辞格的形式的同时，更多地重视修辞格的作用、目的和意义以及与汉语修辞格的联系和区别，从而让英语更好地为中国服务，让汉语更早地走出中国，走遍全世界，更好地促进人类社会的发展。

参考文献

[1] 王佐良. 英国诗选[M]. 上海：上海译文出版社，1995.

[2] 何自然. 语用学与英语学习[M]. 上海：上海外语教育出版社，1998.

[3] 丁往道，等. 英语写作手册[M]. 北京：外语教学与研究出版社，1996.

[4] 中国英汉语比较研究会. 英汉语比较研究[M]. 长沙：湖南科学技术出版社，1994.

[5] 张培基，等. 英汉翻译教程[M]. 上海：上海外语教育出版社，1998.

[6] 张汉熙. 高级英语[M]. 北京：商务印书馆，1988.

[7] 陆国强. 现代英语词汇学[M]. 上海：上海外语教育出版社，1983.

[8] 胡曙中. 英汉修辞比较研究[M]. 上海：上海外语教育出版社，1994.

[9] Hornby，A. S. 牛津现代高级英汉双解词典[M]. 北京：商务印书馆，1995.

[10] 中国社会科学院语言研究所. 现代汉语词典[M]. 北京：商务印书馆，1995.

[11] 何向明. 现代实用英语写作大全[M]. 北京：中国文史出版社，1995.

[12] 傅新安、袁海君. 英汉语法比较指南[M]. 上海：上海交通大学出版

社，1994.

[13] 张道真. 现代英语用法词典[M]. 上海：上海译文出版社，1983.

[14] 李瑞华. 英汉语言文化对比研究[M]. 上海：上海外语教育出版社，1996.

[15] 曹志希. 高级英语同义词辨析与惯用法[M]. 北京：气象出版社，2000.

[16] Procter, P. 朗文现代英汉双解词典[M]. 北京：现代出版社，1994.

[17] Gillie, C. Langman Companion to English Literature. London：Langman Group Limited，1978.

[18] Morris, W. The American Heritage Dictionary of the English Language. Boston：Houghton Mifflin Company，1980.

（曹耀萍，长沙理工大学；苏秋丹，海南大学；
朱玲，广西南宁师专；曹志希，中南林业科技大学）

韩国语过去时态 "–었었"
和 "–었" 的用法研究

1. 引言

大部分学习韩国语的人认为 "었었" 只是单纯的表示过去的事件，但实际上对 "었었" 的认识只停留在这一层面是不够的。说话者如果只是想单纯的表示事件的先后顺序或因果关系的话，利用过去时制 "었" 就可以充分的表达。"었었" 是以相关联的两个事件为基础，根据两事件之间的相关联性为后盾的。因此本文将对 "었었" 的语法功能是什么以及它同其他时态的关系作详细的分析与论证。本文的写作方法主要是比较法和归纳法，首先从分析 "었었" 同其他时态的关系入手，特别是通过与过去时态 "었" 的比较，分析 "었었" 的基本功能，并以此为基础详细地阐述 "었었" 的基本意义。将其基本意义分成两部分，一部分是表示过去完成时态，另一部分是带有强调和对照的意义，最后从语法构造的角度深层次地分析 "었었" 的功能。

2. "었었" 的用法分析

2.1 "었었" 同其他时态的关系

2.1.1 "었었" 与过去时态 "었"

为了分析 "었었" 的语法功能必然首先把 "었었" 同 "었" 进行比较。在形态上 "었었" 与 "었" 有相重叠的一面，意义上也密切相关。我们可以理解为 "었었" 是与以 "었" 表现的过去情况相比体现更先发生的情况，这种时态经常被称为过去完成时。以下面两个例子为中心，分析 "었었" 和 "었"。

例 1　(1) 코스모스가 피었다. 大波斯菊开了。

(2) 작년에는 코스모스가 피었었다. 去年大波斯菊开了。

这两个句子都是体现大波斯菊过去的行为或状态，在这一层面上来说是有共性的，但也存在差异。例 (2) 与例 (1) 相比给了我们更早发生的事情的感觉，但例 (2) 不是单纯的表示过去的事件，还暗示了那个事件以后所发生的事件。例 (2) 所表达的情况是去年菊花开了，但是今年没开，或者今年其他花开了。即，去年菊花开了的事件之后又产生了其他事件。例 (2) 中体现的 "었었" 的语法构造可以通过以下例句分析。

例 2 (올해는 피지 않았지만) 작년에는 코스모스가 피었었다.

（今年没有开但）去年大波斯菊开了。

（올해는 다른 꽃이 피었지만）작년에는 코스모스가 피었었다.

（今年其他花开了但）去年大波斯菊开了。

在这种情况下"코스모스가피었었다（大波斯菊开了）"的作用是对它以后发生的事件，即今年没开或今年其他花开了的事件有一个暗示作用。所以"었었"与"었"相比表示了在时间上更早的行为或事件，"었었"具备了表示过去完成时态的要素。

2.1.2 "었었" 和其他时态词尾

过去完成时态的意义是用"었었"表示在过去某一动作或状态发生或存在之前就有一个动作或状态发生或存在了。但用"었었"所表现的不只是过去时态，它同现在时态或将来时态也相联系着，通过以下例句来看：

例3 아버지가 오실거라고 했었는데 이제와서 어머님이 오실거라고 한다.

本以为是爸爸要来，现在看来是妈妈要来。

다음주까지 끝난다고 했었는데 다시 물어 보면 월말까지 준다고 할 것이다.

本来说下周之前结束，又一问说是将在月末之前结束。

通过例3我们可以观察到"했었"所表示的过去完成时态不只是同过去事件相关联，也同表示现在的"한다"表示将来的"할것이다"相关联。由此可以看出，即使不体现其他时态的时制词尾，也是同各种时态一一相关联的。但是"었었"所表现出的同现在或未来相关联的关系并不是经常可以看得出来的，也就是说"었었"绝大部分情况是同表示过去时态的"었"相关联而产生的，因此本文主要论述从同过去时态相关联的角度来论证。

2.2 "었었" 的意义

2.2.1 过去完成时态

通过以上内容的阐述，我们可以理解为"었었"是对某一过去事实相比更前一步的事件或状态进行描述，因此叫做过去完成时态。但是不管使用"었"的情况在表面表露出与否，使用"었"的情况与使用"었었"的情况应该是同质的，这是使用"었었"的一大特征，我们通过以下例句看一下。

例4 작년에는 동메달을 땄었다. 去年拿了铜牌。

어제 왔었다. 昨天来了。

여기에 코스모스가 피었었다. 这里的大波斯菊开了。

上述例句中拿铜牌相对于拿金牌，大波斯菊开了相对于其他花开了或者是什么花也没开，来了相对于走了，都是同质的情况。因此我们可以认为"었었"和"었"属于同一系列. 例如，从拿奖牌这个层面上来说内容是一致的，区别在于一次拿了铜牌，一次拿了金牌。使用"었"的情况是不能与使用"었었"的情况

完全断绝的，例如：

例5　（1）나는 중학생일 때도 수학을 전공하려 했었다.

我上中学的时候想学数学专业。

（2）선수는 지난 대회 때도 금메달을 땄었다.

选手在上次运动会上也拿了金牌。

例5（1）里我们可以分析出不管是高中时候还是现在都有想要学数学专业的意思。例5（2）里可以分析得出这次运动会也拿了金牌的意思。总之，通过例句我们可以看出使用"었"的情况很难与使用"었었"的情况断绝开。通过此文的分析我们可以看出用"었었"叙述一件事情时隐含的暗示出那以后这个事件会以一种与之相关联的其他状态或形式出现，或转化为相关联的其他事件。

2.2.2　强调和对照

"었었"不只有表示过去完成概念的功能，同"었"相比较还可以得出它有着强调和对照的语法功能，通过下面的例句我们看一下

例6（1）순이가 예뻤다.

（2）순이는 예뻤었다

小顺以前很漂亮。

例7　（1）순이는 에뻤었지만 지금은 예쁘지 않다.

小顺以前很漂亮，但现在不漂亮了。

（2）순이는 전에 예뻤던 적이 있다. 小顺曾经很漂亮过。

例6的两个句子都是对小顺过去状态的阐述，但是两个句子的意义有着很明显的区别。虽然两个句子都是体现过去的事件或状态但通过例6（2）我们能体会出小顺现在不漂亮了的意思。通过例7的两个句子我们可以看出例7（1）是对小顺漂亮和不漂亮的两个事实进行了对照，例7（2）主要是体现从所经历的角度看这个事件，即小顺有过漂亮的经历。因此，"었었"有体现经验，对照的语法功能。例6（2）中"었었"所具有的强调的功能是通过对照体现出来的。即例6（2）是话者以小顺现在不漂亮的这一现在的事实为前提所阐述的。例7（2）中经验的意义实际上也是通过两个事件的对照为前提，向听者阐述小顺曾经历的形态。

3.　"었었"的语法构造

3.1　"었었"文章的两个解释

不管相关联的两个事件是对照的关系还是顺序先后的关系，两个事件之间总是受到一定的限制的。"었었"所具有的一个不变的功能就是在相关联的两个事

件中，叙述前面的事件的同时，紧密联系后面的事件，向听者叙述它的存在。

例8　그때는 참 좋았었다.

那时非常好。

我们从现实角度分析话者在例文中说话的情况的话，可以分析出两方面意思。一个是想向听者阐述那时之后情况变得不好，另一方面的意思是对"这时虽然不好"但这以前，即"那时非常好的"这个情况向听者阐述。也就是说前者是用"었었"重点对"那时之后的事情"阐述，后者的情况是用"었었"重点对现在以前的情况进行阐述。把这两种情况综合起来看，我们可以看出"었었"的功能是表示对某一过去事件以后或这一事件以前的某一事件的发生或存在进行阐述。这种功能就像是硬币的正反面一样。如同硬币的一面是正面另一面是反面，用"었었"所表达的某一过去事件或状态既可以表示出它以前的某一事件或状态存在，也可以表示出那之后的某一事件或状态的存在。所以我们不能强硬地规定"었었"的功能属于哪一面。因为在语言形式中"었었"所展示的是前一面还是后一面是由它自身的语法构造是什么而决定的。

3. 2　对前面事件的强调

在日常的对话中会出现这种情况：话者对以后发生的事情不予说明，而是通过用"었었"表达出来。在这种情况下"었었"经常用于在日常对话中话者和听者对"었었"以后出现的与之相关联事件已经都知道的情况。也就是说因为是话者和听者都已经知道的事实所以没有必要再进行阐述，只是用"었었"把与之相关联的那个事件表达出来。

例9　작년에는 순이가 1등 했었다.

去年小顺得了第一名。

例句是"었었"单独出现的情况，话者通过对小顺去年得了第一名的事件的阐述，告诉了听者在去年得了第一名之后今年没得第一名，或其他人得了第一名的事实。即表达了与下面例句相同的意思

例10　(1) 순이가 올해는 1등 하지 못했으나 작년에는 1등 했었다.

小顺今年没能得第一名，但去年得了第一名。

(2) 올해는 영이가 1등을 했으나 작년에는 순이가 1등 했었다.

今年小英得了第一名，但去年小顺得了第一名。

通过这几个例句可以看出，在文章构造上话者想表达什么意思的关键在"었었"上。它由有韩国语语序的一般特征决定的，即在一句话中同先表述出来的内容相比，后表述的才是内容的重点。

3. 3　对后面事件的强调

这时与说明前面的事件不同，话者想要表达的重点是后面的事件，在这里通过使用"었었"表达前面的事件的同时，重点放在对后面事件的表达与提示上。

通过例句看一下

例11　(1) 그때는 아파서 잘 못했었다.

那时因为生病没能做好。

(2) 그때는 아파서 잘 못했었지만 지금은 다 나아서 잘한다.

那时因为生病没能做好，而现在病都好了做得很好。

通过例句我们可以看出话者想要表达的内容是"现在病都好了做得很好"的意思。话者用"었었"通过对前面事件表述的同时向听者转达了那之后所体现的不同的情况。例(11-2)中"那时因为生病了没能做好"这个情况听者也有可能是已经知道的。但是即使听者不知道话者想要表达的重点也是"现在病都好了做得很好"。

结语

本文是在比较"었"与"었었"意义的同时阐述了"었었"不只表示过去完成时态，还包含了强调与对照的意义。阐述了"었었"表示过去完成事态，强调，经验对照等语法功能。以及相关联的两个事件中表示前面的事件的同时与后面发生的事件（这个与过去现在还是将来没有关系）密切相关，向听者阐述其存在。在日常对话中，对话者所说的某一事件之后发生的事件话者不向听者阐述，只使用"었었"就可以体现。这种情况下话者说话的重点主要是表述前面的事件。与之相反，用"었었"也可以表述话者说话的重点在后面的情况，即重点放在那之后所发生的事件。这种情况下话者陈述前面的事件的同时重点放在说明那事件之后发生的事件或存在的状态。

参考文献

[1] 李南淳. 时制相叙法[M]. 月印,2001.

[2] 이익섭,채완. 국어문법론강의[M]. 学研社,2002.

[3] 韦旭升,许东振. 한국어 실용 문법[M]. 外语教学与研究出版社,1999.

[4] 서정수. 헌대한국어문법론[M]. 沈阳大学出版社,2000.

[5] 최윤갑. 조선어문법[M]. 辽宁人民出版社,2003.

[6] 남기심. 표준국어문법론[M]. 北京大学出版社,1999.

[7] 권재일. 한국어문법의연구[M]. 辽宁人民出版社,2001.

[8] 崔義秀,俞春喜. 韩国语语法[M]. 延边大学出版社,2001.

[9] 宣德武. 朝鲜语语法[M]. 商务出版社,2003.

[10] 金正熙. 韩国语口语教程[M]. 北京大学出版社,2000.

[11] 李时元. 韩汉语法对比[M]. 外语教学与研究出版社,1999.

（樊强,周禧玲,崔高峰,勾肃,金京姬,中南林业科技大学）

《桃花源记》汉英语篇对比分析

作为语言学的一个重要分支，近年来语篇分析获得了很大的发展。对文本进行语篇分析不仅仅可以帮助读者更透彻地理解文本内容，还可以改善教学方法并评价翻译标准。韩礼德构建系统功能语法目的之一就在于为语篇研究提供一个分析的框架。目前已有众多学者运用此框架对不同语篇进行了分析研究并获得了有价值的成果。但是将功能语篇分析理论用于典籍散文及其英译文的比较研究，到目前为止，在国内外尚不多见。本文试图以系统功能语言学为工具，对《桃花源记》及其两个英译版本进行语篇分析，以探讨汉英语篇的异同，并进一步检验系统功能语法在进行语篇分析时的可应用性。

1. 相关理论

语言学研究中使用的"text"一词，可译为"语篇"、"篇章"或"话语"。任何口头或书面形式的语言片段，无论长短篇幅，只要该片段是一个完整的意义体，即可被称为一个语篇。根据功能语法的观点，语篇是一个语义单位，语篇与句子之间是体现与被体现的关系而不是大小程度的关系，即句子或小句体现语篇，或者说属于语义单位的语篇是由属于语法单位的句子或小句体现[1]。语篇具有语篇特征，这些特征将语篇与非语篇严格区分开来[2]。

语篇分析是对交际中的语言以及语言与语境的关系进行探讨。语篇分析涉及语言使用的方方面面。通常说来，没有哪一种特定的理论或方法是专门用来分析语篇的。在 Approach to Discourse 一书中，美国学者 Schiffrin 提出了六种可用于语篇分析的理论。他们分别是：言语—行为理论、国际社会语言学、交际人种论、语用学、话语分析和语言变体分析[3]。随着语言学研究的发展，研究者们也尝试着将其他不同的理论与语篇分析相结合，如将修辞学、文学批评和文体学理论用于语篇分析。其中功能文体学作为文体学的一个分支，是将系统功能语法与语篇分析相结合，并逐渐成为文体分析的一个重要工具。

在《功能语法导论》一书中，韩礼德提出构建功能语法的目的之一是为语篇分析提供一个框架。他认为语篇分析必须建立在语法分析的基础之上，语法分析必须是功能的并涉及语义。韩礼德曾用功能语法对"Silver"这一语篇进行了分析并探讨了多种语篇特征如：主位结构、及物性、语气、分析过程等，为语篇分析提供了框架和范例。随着语篇分析研究的深入，功能语法被越来越多的研究者用来分析不同体裁的语篇并被证明具有客观性和可操作性。

本文旨在运用系统功能语法的理论从衔接、主位结构和逻辑—语义关系三个角度分析《桃花源记》及其两个英译语篇。所选的例本来自方重和 A. R. Davis 的译文。

2. 衔接

韩礼德和哈桑认为，若包含一个以上完整句子的英语片段被视为一个语篇，那么其中必定存在某些语言特征 [1]。语篇特征（texture features）包括两类：结构性语篇特征和非结构性语篇特征。结构性语篇特征指的是句子本身的结构（如主位结构和信息结构），非结构性语篇特征指的则是在不同的句子中出现的不同成分之间的衔接关系[4]。

衔接是指语篇中意义的关系，韩礼德和哈桑[2]将其定义为：存在于语篇内部的，能使全文成为语篇的各种意义关系。韩礼德将衔接手段分为 5 种类型，分别是：照应、省略、替代、连接和词汇搭配。前四种是语法衔接手段，后一种则是词汇衔接手段。

作为一个语篇，《桃花源记》无疑是很连贯的。虽然语言朴素简洁，是以古文的形式写的，但是其中也运用了大量的衔接手段，使句子、段落之间结构紧凑，语篇连贯。对应于原文中出现的衔接手段，译文也相应的运用该手段。如在："……欲穷其林。林尽水源，便得一山。山有小口，仿佛若有光。"作者重复"林"和"山"字，将段落和句子连接起来，用了词汇衔接的手段。在方重和 Davis 的翻译中，词汇衔接手段也非常明显。在 Davis 的译文中 "The fisherman, in extreme wonder, again went forward, wishing to go to the end of **the grove. The grove** ended at the stream's source, and there he found **a hill**. In the **hill** was a small opening from which a light seemed to come." 其中，"the grove" 和 "a hill" 运用了重复的手段，与原文一致。

在方译中 "He went on further in order to reach the uppermost limits of **the grove**. As **the peaches** came to an end, the headspring of the stream was found to issue from the side of **a mountain**. **A narrow cave**-like opening showed him some light that seemed to emerge from within." 虽然方重没有使用重复的手法，但是 "the grove" 和 "the peaches" 是同义关系，"a mountain" 和 "A narrow cave" 是局部——整体的关系，同样属于词汇衔接的范畴，跟原文基本保持一致。

但是，经分析发现，照应、替代、连接和词汇衔接手段在译文中的使用频率比原文中高很多。如"晋太原中，武陵人捕鱼为业；缘溪行，忘路之远近。"作者省略了本应有的照应手段，而译文中大量使用照应手段，使句子结构完整。Davis 的译文中 "...a man of Wuling, who made his living as a fisherman...forgetful of the distance he traveled." 用了四个指前照应的词。同样在方重的译文中，"...a native of Wuling, who lived on fishing. One day he rowed up a stream, and soon forgot how far he had gone." 用了三个指前照应的词。

省略这一衔接手段是原文语言的一大特点，但是在译文中却很少发现省略这一手段的踪影。如：

（源中人）见渔人，（源中人）乃大惊，（源中人）问所从来，（渔人）具答之。（源中人）便要（渔人）还家，（源中人）设酒杀鸡作食。

（渔人）既出，（渔人）得其船

（渔人）及郡下，（渔人）诣太守说如此

原文中的小句主语都被省略，但通过句序和隐含意思读者完全可以推测出主语。然而在英语中若句子缺少主语，句子结构就不完整，因此译者都将原文省略的主语一一增添上，保证了译文句子结构的完整性。

当代美国著名翻译家奈达在其 Translating Meaning（1983）一书中指出：就汉语和英语而言，也许在语言学上最重要的一个区别就是形合和意合的对比。形合注重语言形式上的接应，意合注重行文意义上的连贯。英语重形合而汉语重意合。英语借助照应、替代、连接词等组成复合句，保持语篇的衔接与连贯。而汉语不借助语言形式手段，而借助词语或句子所含意义的逻辑联系和句序来实现衔接。特别是在古汉语风格的文章中，汉语更多的使用省略这一手段，使句子结构紧凑，韵律一致，从而保证语篇的完整与连贯。

3. 主位结构

主位结构的研究对象是信息的起点和小句中其余成分的关系问题。韩礼德[5]指出：主位"是信息的起点"（point of departure），"是小句关心的成分"（the element with which the clause is concerned）。小句中除了主位之外的其他成分被称为述位。无论是在一个小句中还是在一个完整的语篇中，开头和结尾部分都是很重要的。开头部分通常是题目或者话题，结尾往往是结论。在小句中，通常开头部分是信息的起点而结尾部分是信息中心。韩礼德在《功能语法导论》一书中介绍了三种形式的主位：单项主位（simple theme），复项主位（multiple theme）和句项主位（clause as theme）[6]。

韩礼德认为通常在小句中，主位出现在述位的前面。主位传递已知信息而述位表达未知信息或者新信息。因承载了较少的新信息，主位在语篇构建中起着非常重要的作用。每一个语篇都可以被看成是由相关联的一组主位构成。如果分析出每个小句的主位，则可以得知语篇中信息的起点和主要内容，并对译文进行评价。

通过取原文第三段来进行比较发现，原文是按照时间顺序描写的，主要人物为渔人和村民。在 Davis 和方重的译文中，主位也都反映了故事发展的时间顺序，如 Davis 译文中有十一个小句，主位分别为：① When they saw the fisherman；② When he had answered all their questions；③ When the villagers heard of this man；④ They；⑤ Thus they；⑥ They；⑦ They；⑧ The fisherman；⑨ The others；⑨ He；⑪ The people of this place

在方重的译文中出现了十三个小句，主位分别为：① Seeing the fisherman；② He；③ Others；④ Of their own accord；⑤ After settled down here；⑥ They；⑦ They；⑧ The fisherman；⑨ They；⑩ Then more of them；⑪ It was not until several days；⑫ He；⑬ They

经比较发现，译文中主位表达了已知信息，为读者理解语篇提供了线索。但是 Davis 的译文中用了三个句项主位，而方重的译文中以单项主位为主，与原文的语言风格相比，方重的译文不仅在形式上，更在功能上体现对等。

除此之外，通过对小句的主位结构进行分析，我们发现，原句中若有主语，则译文中的主位和原文的保持一致，但是若原文中将主语省略，译文的主位则往往由省略的那部分主语充当。

如：① 此人——为具言所闻　Theme：此人

Davis 译：they sighed with grief　　Theme：they

方译：they could not help being deeply affected　Theme：they

② 余人各复延至其家 Theme：余人

Davis 译：The others in turn also invited him to their homes. Theme：the others

方译：Then more of them asked him to dine by turns. Theme：then more of them

③ 既出，得其船

句子中"既出"是已知信息，"得其船"是新信息，因此主位是"既出"。

方译：Our fisherman came out, found his boat again

译者将省略的主语增补上并作为句子的主位。

从语法上讲，英语语法是刚性的，形式上要求有的东西，通常不能少。汉语语法是柔性的，一个东西，有它可以，没有也行。刚性就是缺乏变通，说有的不能少，说长的不能短。柔性就是强制性的东西少一点，可伸可缩。因为这个特点，英语的句子结构必须完整，通常主语不能少，因此主位很明显。而汉语讲究形式的对等和韵律，往往省略了主语。因此在译文中补充上的主语通常成为了句子的已知信息即主位。这也进一步证明了英语是主语突出型语言，汉语是话题突出型语言。

4. 逻辑—语义关系

当论及小句和复句中的逻辑—语义关系时，韩礼德[6]认为可以从两方面进行探究：相互依赖关系（interdependency）和逻辑—语义关系（logic-semantic relations）。相互依赖情况包括并列关系（parataxis）和从属关系（hypo-taxis）；逻辑—语义关系包括扩展关系（expansion）和投射关系（projection）。如果两个小句之间存在着互不依存、平等的关系，那这种关系就是并列关系，一般用1、2、3来表示。如果两个小句之间是一个依赖另一个，则是从属关系，一般用 α 和 β 表示。根据韩礼德的观点，扩展由以下三类组成：解释（elaboration，用＝表示）、延伸（extension，用＋表示）、增强（enhancement，用×表示）[1]。经分析原文和译文中句子的逻辑—语义关系，我们发现部分译文保持和原文一致的逻辑—语义关系，如：

缘溪行，忘路之远近。

1 ＋2

两个小句是并列的关系，第二个小句是对第一个小句意义上的延伸，因此可以用1＋2表示其逻辑—语义关系。

方译：One day he rowed up a stream, and soon forgot how far he had gone.

　　　　　　　1　　　　　　　　　　　　　　＋2

两个小句也是并列的关系，第二个小句是对前一个的延伸。

此中人语云：‖"不足为外人道也。"

　　　1　　　　　　　2

根据韩礼德的理论，直接引语和间接引语在传统语法中属于投射的关系。如果被投射的小句是直接引语，那么两个小句就处于并列的关系。反之则处于从属关系。在原句中，第二个小句是直接引语，因此两者的逻辑—语义关系可以表示为：1"2。

Davis 译：The people of this place said to him：‖ "You should not speak of this to those outside."

　　　　　　　　　　　1　　　　　　　　　　　　　　　　　　　2

逻辑—语义关系为：1"2，与原句的一致。

但是经分析发现，原文与译文小句之间逻辑—语义关系最明显的区别就在于原文的句子之间多为并列的关系，而英译小句之间多为从属关系，且从句位于主句之前。

如：见渔人，乃大惊

　　　　1　　　×2

两个小句是并列的关系，第二个小句是对第一个小句意义的增强。因此可以表示为：1×2。

Davis 译：When they saw the fisherman，│ they were greatly surprised.

　　　　　　　　　　　　×β　　　　　　　α

方译：Seeing the fisherman │ they were so eager to find out from whence he came.

　　　　　　×β　　　　　　　　　　　　　　　　　　α

如：及郡下，诣太守说如此。

　　　1　　　　×2

Davis 译：When he reached the commandery，│ he called on the prefect and told him this story.

　　　　　×β　　　　　　　　　　　　　α

方译：As soon as he was back to the city │ he told his adventure to the magistrate.

　　　×β　　　　　　　　　　　　　　α

与上例同理，译文中小句是从属关系，原文中是并列关系。英语是树式结构，句子有一个基本的主干，所有的枝丫都是从主干上分出来，句子的复杂化不影响基本主干，因此小句多有从属关系，通过主从句实现逻辑语义关系。汉语是竹式结构，不存在主干结构，也没有主干和枝丫之分，句子的构造方式像竹子一样一节一节地延伸。因此汉语句子多存在并列关系，如上文所论述的。这也进一步证实了我国语言学界和翻译界的学者对此现象的解释：汉语注重意合而英语注重形合的一个特点[7]、[8]、[9]、[10]。

结语

本文以功能语言学为理论框架，从衔接、主位结构和逻辑—语义关系三个方面对《桃花源记》及其英译文进行了探讨。本文分析表明：在衔接的表现方面，汉语的原文与其英译文之间存在着明显的差别。英译中照应、替代、连接和词汇衔接手段使用频率比在汉语中高，汉语中大量使用了省略这一手段来保持句子结构的紧凑和语言的简洁，这就需要读者在理解时更加仔细品味。其次，对主位结构的分析表明，汉语与英语在信息中心的表达上具有更多的相似之处，均由已知信息推到新信息，这符合人们的认知过程；但主位—述位的内容、表现形式往往不同。最后，在逻辑—语义上，英语更多的利用主从句关系来达到信息的扩展、延伸和传递的特点；而汉语则更多地省略了这些表达主从句关系的关系词，小句之间侧重于建立在并列的关系之上。本文是将功能语言学运用到典籍散文及其英译对比分析的一次尝试，发现了汉英语言的异同，在一定程度上证实了功能语法在语篇分析中的客观性和可操作性。但是结论还需在更多的资料基础上和实践中得到检验。

参考文献

[1] Halliday. M. A. K. & Hasan. R. Cohesion in English [M]. London：Longman，1976.

[2] Schiffrin D. Approaches of Discourse [M]. Oxford：Basil Blackmail，1994.

[3] Halliday，M. A. K. "Dimensions of Discourse Analysis：Grammar". Handbook of Discourse Analysis. Ed. T. A. Van Dijk. [M]. London：Academia Press，1985.

[4] Halliday. M. A. K. An Introduction to Functional Grammar [M]. London：Edward Arnold，2000.

[5] 黄国文. 语篇分析的理论与实践：广告语篇研究 [M]. 上海：上海外语教育出版社，2001.

[6] 朱永生. 主位推进模式与语篇分析 [J]. 外语教学与研究. 北京：北京外国语大学，1995.

[7] 连淑能. 英汉对比研究 [M]. 北京：高等教育出版社，1993：163－173.

[8] 伍雅清. 论英语的形合和意合的差译 [A]. 刘重德主编，1994：152－164.

[9] 刘英凯. 英语形合传统观照下的汉语意合传统 [A]. 刘重德主编，1994：163－178.

[10] 萧立明. 新译学论稿 [M]. 北京：中国对外翻译出版公司，2001：53－54.

（姚尧，长沙理工大学）

《午餐》的人际功能建构

引言

　　作为人类社会活动的产物和交际工具，语言承载着各种不同的功能。韩礼德(1994)把语言的纯理功能分为三种：概念功能、人际功能和语篇功能。语言除了具有表达概念和组织语篇的功能外，还具有一项非常重要的功能，那就是表达讲话者的身份、地位、态度、动机和对事物的推断的人际功能。即语言是做事的手段，是动作，因此它的功能之一必然是反映人与人之间的关系。胡壮麟认为(2000)此功能可以表示与情景有关的交际角色关系，即讲话者和听话者在交际过程中所扮演的角色之间的关系。通过这一功能，讲话者使自己参与到某一情景语境中，以表达他的态度和推断，并试图影响他人的态度和行为。（胡壮麟，朱永生，张德禄 1997）也就是说语言使用者把自己的行为潜势通过语言外化为一种意义潜势来传递给听话者，从而达到交际的目的与意图。

　　系统功能语法认为，在交际的过程中，言语角色可以随时变换，如陈述自己的观点，或者提出问题，下达命令，表示疑惑等。然而言语角色最基本的任务只有两个：给予（giving）和索取（demanding）。交际中的交流物可分为两大类：物品和服务（goods & services）或者是信息（information）。由此，交际角色和交流物这两个变量使言语在交际过程中形成四种主要的功能：提供（offer），命令（command），陈述（statement），提问（question）。而在语言的交流过程中，交际参与者根据自己的言语角色实施一定的言语功能，实现以信息或物品与服务为交流物的意义交换。（苗兴伟 2004）

　　人际功能主要由语气（mood）、情态（modality）和语调（tone）组成。语气由主语（mood）和限定成分（finite）组成，是小句进行交际的关键。小句的其余部分称为剩余成分（residue）。而情态意义被韩礼德分为情态和意态。当言语用以交流物品和服务时，小句以"提议"（proposal）的形式出现，它涉及的是意态。意态的归一度表现为规定和禁止，它通过不同程度的义务（obligation）和不同程度的意愿（inclination）来表现。义务和意愿有两种表达方式：① 限定性情态动词；② 谓语的延伸部分（被动动词词组或形容词词组）。而当言语用以交流信息时，小句以"命题"（proposition）的形式出现，它涉及的是情态。情态的归一度表现为断言或否定，它通过不同量值的"概率"（probability）和不同量值的频率（usuality）来表现。概率和频率有三种表达方式：① 限定性情态动词；② 情态副词；③ 两者并用。详见下表：

交流物 （commodity）	言语角色 （speech role）	言语功能 （speech function）	中介量值 （type of intermediacy）	实现方式 （typical realization）
物品和服务 （goods & services）	给予 （giving） 索取 （demanding）	提供 （offer） 提议 （proposal） 命令 （command）	义务 （obligation） 意态 （modulation） 意愿 （inclination）	限定性情态动词 （finite modal operator） 被动动词词组 （passive verb predicator） 限定性情态动词 （finite modal operator） 形容词词组 （adjective predicator）
信息 （information）	给予 （giving） 索取 （demanding）	陈述 （statement） 命题 （proposition） 提问 （question）	概率 （probability） 情态 （modalization） 频率 （usuality）	限定性情态动词 （finite modal operator） 情态副词 （modal adjunct） 两者并用 （both the above）

（Halliday，1994：91）

1.《午餐》内容简介

毛姆（W. Somerset Maugham）是英国小说家兼剧作家。其短篇小说的题材丰富多样。他文笔简洁流畅，叙事动人，刻画人物鞭辟入里。因此被誉为 20 世纪最杰出的现实主义作家之一。而《午餐》是毛姆最具代表性的短篇小说之一。故事以第一人称倒叙的方式把读者带入 20 世纪初的法国巴黎。故事的叙述者，即男主人公，是位初涉文坛、不谙世事的青年作家。因经不起恭维，不知该如何拒绝一位"热心"女读者的拜访，而不得不打肿脸充胖子，邀请她在法国最气派昂贵的 Foyot's 餐厅吃了一顿午饭。谁料在这位贪吃无厌的女客人步步为营的谋划下，这位青年作家不仅花光了全月·80 法郎的生活费，还险些落入丢尽脸面的尴尬境地。

2. 小说的人际功能

巴赫金的对话理论认为"对话交际是语言的生命的真正所在之处。"语言交际的一个重要目标是进行意义的交流。而我们在进行语言交流的时候总是带着一定的目的，如影响他人的态度或行为，向他人提供信息，将自己的态度或行为向他人做出解释，或使他人为我们提供信息等等。总之，这是一个交际双方共同参与的互动过程。（苗兴伟 2004）

本文将围绕小说男女主人公的对话，在人际功能的理论框架下来探讨双方在交际过程中的言语角色与交际意图。

2.1 "女客人"言语角色与交际意图

小说中的"女客人"是以"热心"的女读者的身份造访青年作家的。而造访的理由也是因为读过作家的一本书，她正好途经巴黎，想亲自见见作家并能聊一聊。读到这里，人人都会认为女客人所要谈论的主题肯定是有关青年作家本人或是其创作的一些情况。然而，这顿午餐确是在一反常态的点菜过程中度过的。从 salmon, caviar, giant asparagus 到 white wine, ice-cream, coffee 和 huge peach，而对作家和他的作品情况却只字未提。由此可见，交际过程中原本将作为主要交流物的"信息"在这里根本没有出现，取而代之的交流物换成了"物品和服务"。而女客人本来应该以提问的方式向作家索取信息的过程却被她不断索取菜品的过程喧宾夺主了。

从语气方面也可看出"女客人"一直是以自我为中心的。在她与青年作家对话的 40 个小句中，有 27 个小句是以"I"作为主语的。与此同时，有 15 个小句的谓语是 eat/have/drink 这类的动词。40 个小句基本都是以直陈语气为主，说明女客人一直在向青年作家提供自己在"吃"的习惯方面的信息而并非询问对方的相关信息。而在与作家的整个对话过程中，女客人仅仅使用了两个问句询问作家的情况：

① What are you going to drink，then?

② Aren't you going to have any?

这显然只关系午餐，无关乎作家的作品。而她也并非真正关心作家要吃什么或喝什么，

因为在 40 个小句中只出现了两个这样的问句，可以看出这只不过是一种敷衍罢了。

以下是就女客人对话中的情态部分来展开分析：

午餐过程中，在每点一个菜之前，女客人总是向作家发出同一类型的信息以降低自己将要带来的威胁：

③ I *never* eat anything for luncheon.

④ I *never* eat more than one thing.

⑤ No. I *never* eat more than one thing. *Unless* you have a little caviar.

⑥ I *never* drink anything for luncheon. *Except* white wine.

⑦ I *never* want more than that.

⑧ I *couldn't* possibly eat anything more unless they had some of those giant asparagus.

⑨ I'm not in the least hungry, *but* If you insist I don't mind having some asparagus.

在这一系列的信息，和③ 同样的小句竟然出现了三次。此类小句使用的都是高量值频率的情态副词 "never"。⑧ 中的高量值否定限定性情态动词 "couldn't" 和低量值概率的情态副词 "possibly" 的连用所形成的矛盾表明了女客人的虚伪。与此同时，在她反复强调 I never eat anything for luncheon. 这一信息时，却不断使用了 "unless"，"except"，"but" 这样的转折语气来一次又一次地点菜，点起菜来可是毫不客气，不断地点当季稀有的菜或名贵的菜。女客人发出的这一系列信息不过是一环扣一环的索取菜品的圈套，让青年作家不断往里钻罢了。

女客人的另外一招是使用委婉、含蓄的试探与磋商性语气来征得作家的同意：

⑩ A little fish，*perhaps*.

⑪ I *wonder if* they have any salmon.

⑫ I *should* be sorry to leave Paris without having some of them.

⑬ Yes，*just* an ice-cream and coffee.

不难看出，女客人在此选择的是低量值概率的情态副词 "perhaps"，"just" 和可行使情态意义的小句 "I wonder if…" 来索取菜品。⑫使用了一个中量值概率的限定性情态动词 "should" 来表示遗憾。然而这一系列小句所表现出的客气与楚楚可怜只是为了博得作家的同情，这实际上是一系列让人无法拒绝的命令，让作家不好意思阻止她继续点菜的行为。

而在女客人点遍各种名贵菜式，大吃特吃的过程中，作家却只为自己点了菜单上最便宜的一道"羊排"和一杯白开水。尽管如此，女客人却不断委婉地暗示作家不该吃得太多：

⑭ I *think* people eat far too much nowadays.

⑮ I *don't* believe in overloading my stomach.

⑯ You know, there's one thing I *thoroughly* believe in, one *should always* get up from a meal feeling one could eat a little more.

此处使用了可行使情态意义的小句 "I think…"，"I don't believe…" 来直陈自己的观点。⑯中出现了高量值概率的情态副词 "thoroughly" 和中量值义务的限定性情态动词 "should" 和高频率的情态副词 "always"。此句囊括的信息不但暗示了作家该少吃点，还为自己能继续点菜找了一个堂而皇之的借口，说明自己还能再吃一点。

非但如此，女客人甚至更进一步地正面指责作家不该吃太多，且看下面这几个小句：

⑰ I *think* you are unwise to eat meat.

⑱ I *don't know* how you can expect to work after eating heavy things like chops.

⑲ I *see that* you're in the habit of eating a heavy luncheon. I'm sure it's a mistake.

⑳ *The fact* is, you ruin your taste by all the meat you eat.

㉑ *You see*, you've filled your stomach with a lot of meat.

从上面的小句可以看出，女客人在此使用的是可以行使情态意义的小句。"I think..."，"I don't know..."，"I see that..."，"I'm sure..."，"The fact is..."，"You see..."都是一系列主观直陈自己意见的句式，并且带有明显的谴责性。此处的主语也毫不客气地换成了第二人称"You"。在自己吃完一顿饕餮大餐之后却毫不顾情面地指责只吃了一块羊排的作家，女客人的大言不惭和伪善自私在此表露无疑。

当午餐进行到最后时，女客人更加肆无忌惮了：

㉒ But I've *just* had a snack and I *shall* enjoy a peach.

㉓中使用低量值概率的情态副词"just"用以再次说明自己吃得少，而紧接着就使用了一个高量值意愿的限定性情态动词"shall"表明自己的肆无忌惮。然而让人匪夷所思的是，在酒足饭饱后与作家告别的时候，女客人非但没有一句感谢的话语，反而扔给作家的是一句义正辞严的劝告：

㉔ Follow my example and *never* eat more than one thing for luncheon.

此处竟然使用了一个祈使句，表达强烈命令的语气。同时使用了一个高量值频率的情态副词"never"，充分显示了女客人的厚颜无耻和冷酷无情，同时也为小说增添了强烈的讽刺效果。

从对女客人对话中的交流物、语气与情态部分的分析可以看出，这位远道而来的客人纯粹就是打着"造访"的幌子来狠"宰"青年作家的。在整个交际过程中，她一直充当的是一个"索取者"的角色，其根本的交际意图不是要与作家交流"信息"，而是能够吃上一顿"免费的午餐"。

2. 2　作家的言语角色与交际意图

在午餐的整个过程中，作家与女客人形成了强烈的对比。他没有像想象中那样在自己的"崇拜者"面前大谈特谈自己的作品与创作。在他所有的对话中，以"I"作为主语的小句极少，说明他没能向女客人交流有关自己的"信息"。作家的直陈语气也很少，疑问语气倒是出现了不少，说明他一直在为女客人提供"物品与服务"。于是像以下这类的小句出现很多：

㉕ What would you like?

㉖ Coffee?

㉗ Are you still hungry?

而作家一边要为女客人提供服务，一边还得为自己的囊中羞涩而算计。于是在眼睁睁看着女客人大吃特吃，而自己垂涎欲滴的同时，还不得不为了节约钱而撒谎：

㉘ My doctor *won't* let me drink anything but champagne.

㉙ *I am going to* eat only one thing.

㉚ No，I *never* eat asparagus.

在自己毫不情愿的情况下使用了否定限定性情态动词"won't"和"be going to"这样的高概率的限定性情态动词以及低量值概率的情态副词"only"和高量值频率的情态副词"never"，表明了作家打肿脸充胖子的尴尬与自己挨饿成全女客人的可怜。

而面对女客人酒足饭饱后扔下的那句无情的劝告，作家只得哭笑不得地回答：

㉛ *I'll* do better than that.

㉜ *I'll* eat nothing for dinner tonight.

事实上作家的晚饭确实已经没有了着落。而此处的高量值意愿的限定性情态动词"will"更加增强了小说的讽刺效果。

由此可见，作家在整个交际过程中所扮演的是一个"提供服务"的角色，而他之所以忍气吞声地承受这样一个角色，也都是因为他碍于面子，以及虚荣心作祟的结果。

结语

近年来，有关话语人际意义的研究与探讨层出不穷。黄雪娥（2003），刘英（2004）等都曾撰文对不同体裁的语篇进行了人际意义的分析。李战子（2002）的《话语的人际意义研究》一书还对这一领域进行了专章的分门别类的研究。

本文在系统功能语法的人际功能的理论框架下对小说《午餐》的人际意义建构进行分析说明，人际功能理论对于解读一些文学作品，尤其是一些对话性较强的文学作品有很大的帮助。把人际功能引入言语角色互动性较强的作品中，可以大大提高读者对作品的鉴赏力。这样可以帮助读者更好地理解交际过程中交际双方的身份、地位、态度、动机以及言语角色的关系与各自的交际意图，从而在很大程度上更有效、更全面地解读文学文本。这也是人际功能在话语分析中的最大优势。

参考文献

[1] Halliday,M. A. K. *Language as Social Semiotics：the Social Int* *of Language and Meaning*[M]. London：Edward Arnold，1978.

[2] Halliday,M. A. K. *An Introduction to Functional Grammar*[M]. London：Edward Arnold，1994.

[3] Maugham，W. Somerset. *Collected Short Stories*［C］. London：Pan Books,1975.

[4] 胡壮麟,朱永生,张德禄. 系统功能语法概论[M]. 长沙：湖南教育出版社，1997.

[5] 胡壮麟. 功能主义纵横谈[M]. 北京：外语教学与研究出版社，2000.

[6] 黄雪娥. 爱米丽的"人际关系"及其悲剧命运[J]. 外语教学，2003，(5).

[7] 李战子. 话语的人际意义研究[M]. 上海：上海外语教育出版社，2002.

[8] 刘英. 英国银行宣传手册的人际意义分析[J]. 外语学刊，2004，(1).

[9] 苗兴伟. 人际意义与语篇的建构[J]. 山东外语教学，2004.

（杨石乔,深圳职业技术学院）

语篇连贯中的转喻机制

随着认知语言学的发展，同隐喻一样，转喻从传统的词格提升为人类概念化的一种心理机制。转喻研究已渐渐从语言的修辞层面深入到认知层面，从它与语言的词法，语法形式的关系等多方面的研究涉及到语篇层面。转喻不仅仅具有较强的修辞功能，可以增加语言的表达效果，而且在语篇层面上制约着语言运用的深层次连贯性，是一种实现语篇连贯的重要深层或隐性衔接手段。本文将主要论述转喻是如何实现和促进语篇连贯的。

1. 语篇衔接与连贯的研究概论

连贯性是语篇的主要特征之一。在过去三十多年的时间里，连贯研究一直是语篇分析的一个重要方面。连贯研究不仅具有理论价值，而且具有较高的应用价值。它有利于我们进一步认识自然语言的结构以及自然语言在语篇层次上如何实现语言的多重功能。连贯研究的历史不长，但对它感兴趣的学者却越来越多。国内外众多学者如 Halliday & Hasan, Widdowson, N. E. Enkvist, 胡壮麟，张德禄，廖美珍等均对语篇的衔接与连贯做了深入系统的研究，虽然他们的观点各异，但一般都把衔接和连贯结合起来处理，努力寻找新的衔接解释手段。最早的研究者 Halliday 和 Hasan 在《英语的衔接》（1976）一书中集中探讨了英语的五种衔接手段：① 指称，② 替代，③ 省略，④ 连接，⑤ 词汇衔接。1985 年，在《语言 语境 语篇》一书中又扩大了衔接概念的涵盖范围，把衔接分为结构衔接和非结构衔接。国内学者胡壮麟在 1994 年出版的《语篇的衔接与连贯》一书中，提出语篇衔接和连贯的多层次的思想，进一步扩大了衔接的范围：① 把及物性结构关系作为一种衔接手段，同时附加了同构关系；② 把语调语音模式纳入衔接范围；③ 把语篇结构作为一种衔接手段；④ 提出了语篇连贯涉及多层次的观点，认为社会符号层对语篇连贯起重要作用。张德禄（2000，2004）对语篇的衔接和连贯进行了系统和深入的研究。先后提出了① 跨类衔接机制概念，② 外指衔接概念，③ 隐性衔接机制的概念，④ 多元意义衔接概念。

上述种种研究极大地丰富了我们对语篇衔接和连贯问题的认识。虽然不同语言学家对衔接与连贯关系有不同看法，如有人认为衔接不能够完全保证连贯；也有人认为衔接与连贯没关系，不能通过形式特征来判断。然而，语篇毕竟是由形式特征来体现的。到目前为止，从形式特征来研究语篇连贯的唯一途径是通过语篇的衔接机制，各种衔接手段对促进语篇连贯性的生成起着极其重要的作用。一个连贯的语篇必定要借助不同的衔接手段来实现，而其中某些深层的衔接手段不过暂未被语言学家发现罢了。通过对认知语言学中的转喻理论的研究，本文认为转喻是一种实现语篇连贯的重要的深层或隐性衔接手段，同隐喻一样，转喻不仅仅具有较强的修辞功能，可以增加语言的表达效果，而且在语篇层面上制约着语言运用的深层次连贯性。在探讨转喻如何促进语篇连贯之前，我们有必要了解一下转喻的概念。

2. 转喻与语篇连贯

2.1 转喻的概念

对转喻的研究已有数千年的历史，但自亚里士多德以来，转喻被认为是一种语言装饰，是一个词对另一个词的替代。较早的认知转喻定义是由 Lakoff & Johnson（1980）提出的。他们认为，转喻指一种实体对另一种相关实体的指称。概念转喻（conceptual metonymy）是我们交谈、思维与行动的一般日常方式，它使我们能够通过相关联的他事物来对该事物进行概念化。换言之，概念转喻不但为语言提供结构，而且也为我们的思想、态度和行动提供结构。Lakoff（1987）进一步指出，转喻选取事物易理解（well-understood）或易感知（easy-to-perceive）的方面代替事物的整体或事物的另一方面或部分。

基于以上认识，同隐喻一样，转喻既是重要的思维方式和认知工具，同时在语言的运用过程中又起着重要的衔接作用。下面本文将从如下几个方面来探讨转喻的语篇衔接作用。

2.2 间接衔接作用

在语篇中起篇章纽带作用的语法手段很多，照应是其中一种。Halliday 和 Hason 认为，照应指用代词等语法手段来表示语义关系。主要有人称照应（personal reference），指示照应（demonstrative reference），比较照应（comparative reference）和分句形照应（clausal reference）等。另外还有外照应，内照应；直接照应，间接照应等等。如：

① Tim is a professor of politics. He lectures at Durham.

② Janet is a lecturer in Arabic. She speaks very good Arabic.

在以上两个例句中，分别用代词 "he" 和 "she" 来指代前文中的 Tim 和 Janet，从而把前后两个分句联系在一起。但当我们面对下列句子时，照应似乎不复存在了。

③ Table 4 is getting impatient. He has been waiting for a long time.

④ John bled so much that it soaked through his bandage and stained his shirt.

在上面的例句中，虽然③、④两个句子不像①、②在语言形式之间具有明显的衔接关系，但它们在转喻的作用下可以构建衔接和连贯性。在例③中，当读者读到第一句时，table 4 与 is getting impatient 之间在字面上形成语义冲突，使读者在大脑中寻找前后相适应的意义，根据语境在相邻性原则的基础上，激活与之相关联的 the person who is sitting at table 4 这一图式，这样才能与 he 构成前后连贯的照应关系。在此，作为参照点的 table 4 被背景化，而作为理想的喻标的 the person who is sitting at table 被前景化。由此可见，table 4 和 he 之间的衔接关系的建立须以转喻机制为基础。关系的建立须以转喻推理为基础。在例（4）中，it 与 bleed 的衔接关系需要依赖于这样的推理，即 bleed（V）→blood（N）→it（PRON），而用 it 直接指代 bleed（V）是一种转喻用法，因为在 it 与 bleed 的关系中，bleed 属于以动作指代其结果 blood（N）。

2.3　省略衔接作用

Widdowson（1979：96）认为，语义上连贯的语篇可以没有形式上的衔接纽带。衔接既不是连贯的必要条件也不是充分条件。例如：

⑤ A：Can you go to Edinburgh tomorrow?

　　B：B. E. A. pilot are on strike.

在这个例子中，并没有衔接的形式，但这个对话是连贯的。从 B 的回答中我们可以推敲出否定的答案。又如：

⑥ A：That's the telephone.

　　B：I'm in the bath.

　　A：O. K.

这几句话乍看起来叫人如坠云雾，但仔细琢磨，在脑海里再现其语言环境，我们就会发现这几句话在语义上是连贯的，只不过是语言使用过程中存在省略而已。句⑤中，B 的回答"B. E. A. pilot are on strike"与其省略部分"I cannot go to Edinburgh."构成了因果转喻关系，说话者以原因代结果。同样，例句⑥中，"I'm in the bath"之后省略的"I can't answer the phone"也是一种以原因代结果的转喻用法，尽管结果被省略了，但读者能够借助于转喻推理迅速激活被省略的成分，建立衔接，营造连贯的语句。由此可见，语言使用过程中存在的许多省略形式与完整形式之间就是一种转喻关系，而这种转喻关系虽然不是一种显性衔接手段，但却是促进语篇连贯的重要隐性衔接手段之一，是语篇中的间接省略衔接。

2.4　事件衔接作用

人类在表征事件的过程中，往往诉诸脚本（script）机制，否则语言材料将显得太匮乏。而对于受话者而言，脚本化过程中被省略的部分可以借助于语境知识而被迅速激活、取回。因此，脚本化事件表述本身也是一种省略类转喻形式。例如：

⑦ John went into a restaurant. He asked the waitress for coq au vin. He paid the bill and left. （Ungerer & Schmid 2001：216）

该语篇在建构过程中考虑到了听话人所具有的有关餐馆用餐的内化脚本（internalized script）知识，所以听话人易于将缺少的部分补充上，如约翰在点菜前大概要看一下菜谱，在付款、离开之前要先用餐等。人们在大脑的长时记忆中一般储备着餐馆脚本的四个场面：进餐馆、点菜、用餐、离开餐馆。该语篇中将用餐这一场面或环节省掉了。该场面处于待激活的缺省（default）状态，随时可以由情景语境激活、提取。（Ungerer & Schmid 2001：214）正常情况下，四个场面组成一个连贯的整体，但在实际语言交际过程中，即使其中一、两个缺少，但在人们的心理中仍然是一个部分环节有待激活、补充的整体，这正如一个圆尽管其部分被擦掉了但仍然是个圆一样——其边界尽管是不完整的，但仍然被视作一个连贯的整体。这种推理性连贯机制得益于人所具有的完形心理。

2. 5 整体部分衔接作用

在人类的思维和语言表达中，事物的整体与其部分之间往往构成转喻关系，这种关系也是建立语篇衔接的一种手段。例如：

⑧ A letter was awaiting Sherlock Holmes.

The envelope was crumbled, the stamp was half off and

the post mark indicated that it had been sent the day before.

［＝the envelope of the letter；the stamp of the letter；the post mark of the letter］

在该例中，envelope、stamp 和 postmark 与 letter 之间是部分与整体之间的关系，在定冠词的协同作用下，建立起前后紧密衔接的关系，从而获得了连贯的意义。

结语

本文从认知思维的角度出发，以认知转喻理论为基础，初步探讨了转喻在构建语篇连贯中的作用，语篇的衔接与连贯可以从多个不同的角度进行研究，作为认知思维的形式之一，转喻可以帮助构建语篇连贯，是语篇的隐性衔接手段之一。虽然转喻理论的研究已受到越来越多的重视，但专门从转喻的角度来研究语篇的衔接性和连贯性才刚刚起步，相信这将为今后的研究开辟一条新的途径。

参考文献

[1] Brown G, & Yule G. *Discourse Analysis* [M]. London: Cambridge Press, 1983.

[2] Halliday, M. A. K. & Hasan. *Cohesion in English* [M]. London: Longman, 1976.

[3] Halliday, M. A. K. & Hasan. *Language, Context and Text: Aspects of Language in a Social-Semiotic Perspective.* [M] Victoria: Deakin University Press, 1985.

[4] Lakoff, George & Johnson, Mark. *Metaphors We Live By* [M]. Chicago and London: The University of Chicago Press, 1980.

[5] Lakoff, George. *Women, Fire, and Dangerous Things* [M]. Chicago and London: The University of Chicago Press, 1987.

[6] Panther & Radden. (eds). *Metonymy in Language and Thought* [C]. Amsterdam/Philadelphin: John Benjamins Publishing Company. 1999.

[7] Ungerer. F. & H. J. Schmid. *An Introduction to Cognitive Linguistics* [M]. Bejing: Beijing Foreign Language Teaching and Research Press, 2001.

[8] Widdowson, H. G. *Teaching Language as Communication* [M]. Oxford: OUP. 1978.

[9] Widdowson, H. G. *Explanations in Applied Linguistics* [M]. Oxford: OUP. 1979.

[10] 胡壮麟. 语篇的连贯与衔接[M]. 上海: 上海外语教育出版社, 1994.

[11] 张德禄. 论语篇连贯[J]. 外语教学与研究, 2000, (2).

[12] 张德禄. 系统功能语言学的新发展[J]. 当代语言学, 2004, (1).

[13] 朱永生. 衔接理论的发展与完善[J]. 外国语, 1995, (3).

（曹斌，中南林业科技大学）

模因复合体与话语含义

引言

模因论（memetics）是基于新达尔文进化论观来解释文化进化规律的，其核心概念是模因（meme）。国外学术界对于这一领域的研究正如火如荼地展开，模因中心、控制论原理等专题网页、模因讨论小组以及模因学期刊相继出现，模因一词已得到广泛传播并进入到了心理学、社会学、文化学、哲学等领域。近年来国内学者也开始积极介入，已有好些文章见诸刊物。从社会语用角度来研究模因论的成果主要有：何自然、何雪林的《模因论与社会语用》（2003），他们对模因作了一个概述，介绍了模因论的由来及模因研究的不同观点，同时对语言使用中的模因现象进行考察，特别分析了汉语语言herg制的四种类型：引用、移植、嫁接和词语变形；陈琳霞和何自然的《语言模因现象探析》（2006）一文以模因学研究成果为依据，探讨语言模因的传播、变异和发展；谢朝群和李冰芸的《礼貌？语言？模因》（2006）将模因概念引入礼貌研究领域。本文在积极吸取这些研究成果的基础上，从模因复合体理论视角探讨模因复合体对话语含义的影响。

1. 模因

模因（meme）最早是在英国牛津大学著名科学家 Richard Dawkins（1976）所著的 The Selfish Gene《自私的基因》一书中出现，是指文化领域内人与人之间相互模仿而散播开来的思想或主意。他在第十一章提出了模因（meme）概念，认为模因是文化进化基本单位，模因为文化进化提供了机制，人类可以利用模因概念来阐释文化进化规律。模因定义的形成经历了两个阶段：前期模因被看作是文化遗传单位或者模仿单位，模因的类型在生活中有曲调旋律、想法思潮、时髦用语、时尚服饰、搭屋建房、器具制造等模式（Dawkins 1976：206）。"一座教堂的建筑，仪式，规则，音乐，艺术，书写方式都是相互协作传播的模因集合"（ibid：212）。至于后期，模因作为大脑里的信息单位，是存在于大脑中的一个复制因子，而在现实世界里，模因的表现型是词语、音乐、图像、服饰格调，甚至手势或脸部表情（Dawkins 1982：109）。模因概念的核心是模仿。模仿理论的奠基者 Gabriel Tarde（Marsden 2000）认定模仿是人类的重要天性，整个人类历史就是一部模仿的历史，是模仿使得某一个人的发明灵感成为大家共有的财富。Tarde 的一句名言就是"Society is imitation（社会就是模仿）"。何自然教授将"meme"译成"模因"，是有意让人们联想它是一种模仿现象，是一种与基因相似的现象。任何字、词、短语、句子、段落乃至篇章只要通过模仿而得到复制和传播、发展，都可以成为模因，模因现象几乎无处不在，任何想法、说法或做法都有可能成为模因。语言本身就是模因存在的一种形式。比如，"生活"这个词看起来普普通通，但实际上是一个十分活跃的模因，具有相当强的复制能力，如"艺术生活"、"支部生活"、"写意生活"、"美容时尚生活馆"、"e 生活"、"点亮我的数字生活"、"生活秀"、"生活视觉"、"生活几何"、"生活海鲜"等。实际上，语言之所以能流传至今就是得益于历代语言使用者不间断地模仿、复制与传播。如果语言不再为人所使用和模仿，那它必然走向消亡。所以，人只要一说话，就在传播模因、复制模因。

2. 模因复合体与话语含义

语言模因在复制、传播的过程中往往与不同的语境相结合，出现新的集合，组成新的模因复合体。模因与模因之间会相互支持，集结在一起形成一种关系密切的模因集合，这就是模因复合体。模因的表现可以是单个的模因，也可以是模因复合体，大脑里的信息内容直接得到复制和传播是模因的基因型，而信息的形式被赋予不同内容而得到横向扩散和传播的，则是无数的模因表现型。所以，语言模因的复制和传播有基因型的"内容相同形式各异"和表现型的"形式相同内容各异"两种方式（何自然 2004）。本文要讨论的属于模因复制和传播的第二种方式：形式相同内容各异的表现型，即同一语言模因在不同语境中的复制和传播。"上网"，在现代社会，指的是通过电子计算机及相关器件访问网站，如"你今天上网了吗"。"上网"还可以在其他语境下复制，如问某渔民："上网的鱼多吗？"这里"上网"的含义已发生改变。从模因的观点看，"上网"就是一个语言模因，它在上述两个语言环境中的出现就是模因的复制和传播过程，从复制和传播方式上说属于表现型。同一语言模因可以在同一文化语境或不同文化语境下进行模因的重组，产生不同的话语含义。

同一模因可以在同一文化语境（如英语或汉语）下复制，由于与语境相关的命题意义、社会意义、情景意义、情感意义、态度意义等相应程度的变化，引起整个话语意义的改变。

表1

语言 场景 模因 意义	I SAW YOU			
	校园 同学-同学 平等	院子里 一群小孩子 平等	考场 学生-老师 不平等	法庭 被告-证人 不平等
命题意义	问候	游戏	考试	出庭作证
情景意义	校园里同学之间聊天问好	院落里孩子们开心玩捉迷藏游戏	考场上教师监考 学生应考	法庭上被告与证人的争辩
感情意义 态度意义	友好	遵守游戏规则 相互配合	严明守纪 有点愠怒	公正严明 实事求是
社会意义	联络感情 实现交际功能	游戏轮的转换	命令、警告	提供证词 伸张正义

表 1 列举了同一语言模因 "I saw you" 的四种表现型。在这里, 每种表现型都是基于情景语境 (主要指交际主体、交际场所) 的变化而产生的。新的语用情景因素的变化组合形成新的模因复合体, 在每个新复合体下, "I saw you" 的命题意义、情景意义、感情态度意义、社会意义都发生较大的改变, 因而整个话语含义发生改变。在校园里, 熟人、朋友之间的问候可以采取非正式的、随意的形式, 如从聊天开始, 提一提昨天在街上 "I saw you" 的事情, 并解释一下 "我" 没来得及向你打招呼的原因, 在日常生活中这是常有的事, 这样有助于联络感情、加强交际。再如, 对于在院落里玩捉迷藏游戏的一群孩子们来说, 必须遵守游戏规则, 相互配合, 一旦找到隐藏起来的伙伴就应该说 "I saw you", 然后立即跑到原来的地点, 开始下一轮的游戏。因此, "I saw you" 就成了一个转换游戏轮的标志。在考场, 监考老师发现平时表现较佳的 Jack 正低声地把答案传给邻桌, 于是大声说出了 "I saw you", 或示警告, 或命令 Jack 停止这一行为, 对于深谙考场纪律的 Jack 来说, 应该能够领会到这一点。在法庭上, 证人出庭作证, 就社会地位来说, 被告处于劣势, 证人处于优势, 其证词 "I saw you" 已经具有了法律效力, 离 "I saw you" 这一语言模因的基本意义更是相去甚远。

对于 "I saw you" 的模因表现型不一而足, 无法穷尽。为何语言会出现如此模因现象? 笔者认为, 可以从分析 "I saw you" 这一语言模因的结构入手。在 "I saw you" 这一语言模因结构中, "I" "you" 的所指可以是任意的, 何时在何地为何原因 "saw" 也是待定的。因此, 没有具体的语用因素我们只能看到 "I saw you" 的基本结构意义, 这种基本结构意义是很不完备的, 具有多维性, 只有具体语用要素俱全才会产生丰满、完整的、确定的话语含义。正是由于它的多维性、很强的适应性，"I saw you"就既创造了多个新的语境模因复合体，同时又依赖这些语境模因复合体产生新的话语含义，即增殖含义。所以，"I saw you"的模因表现型含义就是其基本意义与增殖含义的整合，用公式可表示为，语言模因表现型的含义＝基本意义＋基本含义的增殖含义。借用这一模式，我们可以探讨同一语言模因"Can I help you？"的多种模因表现型的话语含义。

同一语言模因也可以在不同的文化语境下复制和传播，复制后的话语含义可能截然不同。

例如：

表 2

文化　模因	She is a cat	He eats no fish
汉语文化	她嘴馋	他根本不吃鱼
英美文化	她是个包藏祸心的女人	他是个诚实的人

会话 1

A：Hey, Lily. I was told that you knew Mary very well.

B：Maybe. She is a cat.

汉语和英语承载着两种不同的文化。同一语言模因分别融入到两个不同的文化语境后，参与话语的语用因素将被激活，形成新的模因复合体，会话含义相应改变。会话中的两个交际主体如果来自中国，根据中国的文化传统和文化规约，你如果看到 She is a cat 这样一个语言模因，十有八九会联想到这个女人很馋，是个"馋猫"，具有中性意义。如两个交际主体都来自英美国家，此话语就是明显的贬义了，恐怕很难想到英语国家以此说明"她是个包藏祸心的女人"。由于不同的民族往往从不同的思维角度观察事物，开始时只注意到某些事物的某些侧面，而借此作比喻。久而久之，这些比喻便成为该语言的固定组成部分，包含了固定的喻义。人们不再推敲这种事物的其他特征，不再琢磨这个比喻合不合理了。假设交际者 A、B 来自不同国家，作为具有不同文化背景的文化人，对同一语言模因会有相异的表现型，因而很可能就会出现误解。再拿"red eye"来说。在汉语里，"红色"象征着事业的顺利、兴旺、发达、成功等以及受欢迎、受重用等含义，这些含义又引申出羡慕嫉妒等含义，如眼红，红眼病等。英语中的 red eye 没有这种引申含义，倒是指使乘客睡眼惺忪的"夜航班"。从以上事例可以看出，同一语言模因在不同的文化语境中，象"She is a cat"这种隐喻型结构的语言模因表现型的含义是其基本意义与基本意义的喻义的结合。

请看会话 2：

C：How about Tom?

D：Oh, he eats no fish.

根据中国的文化传统和价值观念，如果看到这样" He eats no fish "这样一个语言模因，你肯定以为他们在谈论生活习惯。如果对其产生的历史背景毫无了解，就难以想到"他是个诚实的人"之意义。为什么把吃鱼跟一个人的品德联系在一起呢？原来，这句习语产生于伊丽莎白一世的时代。那时候，信奉天主教的英国人按照罗马人主教会定下的法规，在星期五那天只吃鱼不吃肉。但是，信奉基督教的人却不理会这一套，星期五照样吃肉。这样，某人因为不是罗马天主教徒，就可以得到"He eats no fish"这个评价，公开表明自己不是罗马天主教徒这样诚实的态度。在此话语中，"He eats no fish"陈述了某一历史背景事实，像陈述型结构的语言模因表现型的含义是其基本意义与基本意义的背景意义的结合。在英汉两种语言中，这样的语言模因举不胜举。

结语

模因理论为语用学的研究提供了新的视角。模因即文化信息单位，语言模因在复制、传播的过程中往往与不同的语境相结合，出现新的集合，组成新的模因复合体。在模因理论的框架下，同一语言模因在不同的模因复合体中，产生不同的话语含义。同一语言模因可以在同一文化语境或不同文化语境下进行模因的重组，其话语含义的推导应以其特定的文化语境为条件的。

参考文献

[1] Capone, Alessandro (forthcoming a). "*I saw you*"(*towards a theory of the pragmeme*). RASK：International Journal of Language and Communication.

[2] Dawkins, R. The Selfish Gene[M]. New York：OUP. 1976.

[3] 陈琳霞，何自然. 语言模因现象探析[J]. 外语教学与研究，2006.

[4] 何自然. 语言中的模因 Memes in language[M]. 中国语用学研究会，福州第2届年会，2004.

[5] 谢朝群，李冰芸. 礼貌. 语言. 模因[J]. 福建师范大学学报(哲学社会科学版)，2006.

[6] 王振华. 结构与意义的接口—语用因素[J]. 外语与外语教学，2002.

[7] 朱放成. 语境的分层研究与话语理解[J]. 外语与外语教学，2004.

[8] http://www.google.cn/search 生活

(唐德根，阳兰梅，湘潭大学)

英语演讲语篇的语法隐喻分析

引言

在英语语言世界中，演讲语篇是一种十分重要的语篇形式。演讲又叫演说，讲演，最早见于古希腊的荷马史诗，随后便在西方世界繁荣发展。演讲由演讲者，听众，演讲语言（包括有声语言和无声语言）以及演讲场合四个方面组成。演讲语言又是在叙述、说明、议论、描写和抒情几个基本表达方式上形成的具有独立品格的口语表达方式，以这种表达方式所展开的活动就是演讲活动（陈萍2005）。演讲活动是一种复杂的社会实践，更是一种工具。人们拿起工具总是有目的的，没有目的的演讲是不存在的。演讲者无论是宣传自己的政治主张、观点，或是传播道德伦理情操，还是传授科学文化知识和技艺，从总体上看，其演讲的目的都是与听众取得共识，使听众改变态度，激起行动，推动人类社会向演讲者心目中的理想境界迈进。那么，成功的演讲稿应该具备怎样的语言特点呢？本文以系统功能语言学为理论基础，对比英语日常口语和正式书面语体，从语法隐喻的视角，对英语演讲语篇的特征进行了分析和探讨。

1. 关于语法隐喻

1.1 语法隐喻的概念

韩理德提出的语法隐喻理论为隐喻的研究提供了一个新视角（Halliday 1994）。鉴于传统语言学家多数把隐喻看作词汇层面的隐喻化过程，韩理德认为隐喻还应该发生在词汇语法层面，即语法隐喻（Grammatical Metaphor）。语法隐喻指的是语言在隐喻化过程中词的语法性状发生变化，如动词转化为名词等，而词的意义却没有变化。也就是说，语法隐喻可以理解为一种语法范畴的转换或跨越，从某种过程到其他过程，如从动作过程跨越到事物过程，从事物过程跨越到属性过程等。韩理德以其三大纯理功能思想为理论基础，提出语法隐喻可分为过程之间相互转化的概念隐喻和包括情态隐喻和语气隐喻的人际隐喻。例如：

① a. The driver drove the bus too rapidly down the hill, so the brake failed.

b. The driver's over-rapid down hill driving of the bus resulted in brake failure.

例① b 中的 over-rapid down hill driving 和 brake failure 取代了句（1）a 中的 drove the bus too rapidly down the hill 和 the brake failed，属于典型的名词化现象，即存在于语法层面的隐喻化。广而推之，语法隐喻这一术语不仅包括名词化等现象，还包括许多其他形式的转义现象，如人际隐喻。例如：

② a. He might come.

b. He probably comes.

句子② a 中情态动词 might 在② b 中被副词 probably 隐喻化，即人际隐喻。而对于马丁（James Martin, 1992）提出的语篇隐喻，韩理德的态度是模糊的，本文对此暂且不作讨论。

1. 2　隐喻式和一致式

隐喻式和一致式是判断语法隐喻的一对重要概念（1995 年以后韩理德基本以雅式和土式取代了这一对概念）。在语法范畴的转化中，产生了所要传达意义的隐喻式和一致式。前者指的是一个小句中含有比较多的语义长而复杂的词组和短语，即语法层面上的隐喻；而同样的语义在后者中可以分解为比较多的简明的小句。例如：

③ a. 隐喻式（雅式）：Prolonged exposure will result in rapid deterioration of the item.

b. 一致式（土式）：If the item is exposed for long it will rapidly deteriorate.

比较上面的例子可以看出，隐喻式强调的是事实的严肃性、权威性和科学性，而一致式则更加通俗易懂。两者之间相互转化的过程即打包和拆析。再如：

④ a. 隐喻式：The possibility that he is mad has to be considered.

b. 一致式：We have to consider whether it is possible or not that he is mad.

例④ a 中情态化名词 possibility 将情态意义转化为难以质疑的"事物"，因而掩盖了情态的来源，和一致式④ b 相比，隐喻式在这里更加具有客观取向。

判断语法隐喻的标准是检验语义与语法性状是否保持一致性，即信息的展开是否与展现事件的原始状态相一致，是否与人们惯常的表达方法相一致。胡壮麟等（2005）总结了韩理德和马丁的观点，认为判断标准可以从年龄、难易度、合乎自然度、历时、方式等五个方面着手。但上述标准的可行性至今尚未形成定论。但不可否认的一点是，隐喻式与一致式的边界是模糊的。在语言发展过程中，原本属于隐喻式的表达方法会逐渐成为一致式。因此，本文所阐述的一致式和隐喻式等语言现象更准确地表达应该是"更加接近一致式的语言现象"和"更加接近隐喻式的语言现象"。

2. 英语演讲语篇的一致式分析

一致式是韩理德语法隐喻理论的一个重要支柱。一个隐喻形式必须与一个非隐喻形式对照，而这个非隐喻形式就是一致式，即语言形式直接反映现实世界的结构。因此，措辞中隐喻使用最少的情况意味着语言达到最大限度的简单化，这种"平白的，简单的英语"意味着那是通常的，所谓的一致式（胡壮麟，朱永生等 2005）。

一致式是日常口语的自然形式。韩理德认为"我们的常识世界是用口语构建的，在这里奠定了一致式，建立了语义和语法之间的关系。口语总是优先的，意义由此创立，范畴和经验的关系得以定义。书面语通过脱离这种一致式，经由我所提到的语法隐喻而创建新义"（Halliday 1994）。由此可见，一致式是口语的基础形式。例如下面是一段常见于酒店中的对话：

⑤ A：I'd like a room, please.

B：Single or double，sir?

A：Single, please. Just for one night.

B：All right，sir. Sign here（周刚，牛晓春 1999）.

例⑤ 是最常见的口语对话形式，交际双方为达到交际目的使话轮自然转换。词法上，形容词，代词，动词，名词之间都没有过程的转换；句法上，陈述想法使用陈述语气，提问功能由疑问句完成，命令使用祈使语气。因此，这段对话中不存在概念隐喻和人际隐喻，属于一致式表达法。在这里，说话人没有采用隐喻式而使用一致式是因为交际目的和交际环境要求语言形式应该是通俗简明并且高效率的。

演讲的传播方式使其语言具有口语和书面语的双重特点；而演讲的目的则使语言更多地带有感情色彩和感染力（王佐良，丁往道 1987/2002）。又由于大多数演讲具有转瞬即逝的特点，使得即时效果成为衡量演讲成败的主要标准，并在很大程度上影响着演讲的语言形式。同时演讲的交际对象一般是大量的听众，文化层次不一。这些因素决定了平白易懂的一致式在演讲语篇中不可替代的巨大作用。例如：

⑥ Let us strive on to finish the work we are in. ①

⑦ Like many young people of my age in China, I want to see my country get prosperous and enjoy respect in the international community.

---

① 本文所选美国总统就职演说辞均来自王建华（2001）。

例句⑥ 选自美国总统林肯 1865 年的就职演说，例句⑦ 选自 2002 年全国英语演讲比赛冠军得主的演讲稿。林肯的号召语气选用了典型的祈使句，动词 finish 也没有被名词化的形式诸如 accomplishment 所取代。例句⑦ 用陈述句表达了自己的期望，同时没有进行典型的语法结构的转换。一致式的作用在这里不言而喻，即发挥口语的典型作用—使语言平白清晰，柔和亲切，在适当的时机使用了适当的语言表达形式，赢得听众共鸣。

⑧ Both parties deprecated war, but one of them would make war rather than let the nation survive, and the other would accept war rather than let it perish, and the war came.

例⑧ 同样选自林肯 1865 年的就职演说。对于动词 survive 和 perish，人们在正式语体往往倾向于用其名词化了的隐喻式 survival 和 perishment 用以强调真实性和严肃性。但在此林肯对自己党派进行赞扬，对敌对党派却进行批评，因此使用口语化的一致式适当减轻批评语气，用心良苦可见一斑。

⑨ And there's one thing that only government can and must do.

上句选自撒切尔夫人 1985 年的退职演说。在此句中，情态的表达选取了最典型的一致式，即情态动词传达情态意义。这里的情态动词比较其常用的隐喻式如 we all know, it is the obligation of the government 等更加直白，铿锵有力，表达了一位即将退职的成功首相对新一届政府的殷切希望。

通过调查发现，在演讲语篇中，一致式大量存在，体现了演讲的口语特征，使演讲内容简单直白，易于被听众接受。

3. 英语演讲语篇的隐喻式分析

隐喻式是语言结构不直接反映现实世界，反映出的是一种扭曲的关系，这种不一致的关系就是语言之间的隐喻过程，即在不同的语法域中语言单位发生的转化（胡壮麟，朱永生等 2005）。与词汇隐喻不同，语法隐喻的词语意义没有发生变化，而语法形状却发生了变化，是意义表达方式的变异。例如：

⑩ We enjoy the *fruit* of our labors.

⑪ These apple trees have always *fruited* well. ①

例句⑩ 中的 fruit 是传统意义上的词汇隐喻，而例⑪ 中的 fruit 以转换为动词形式的名词来代替一致式 bear fruits，形式发生变化却表达了相同的意义，这样

---

① 对于例⑥ 的名动转换现象，部分语言学者将其视为语法隐喻的典型之一。朱永生（2006）将其视为似是而非的动词化现象，即这类语言现象并不涉及语法的变化，因而并不属于语法隐喻。

的表达即称为隐喻式。① 韩理德对语法隐喻的分类可简单总结如下：

$$
元功能
\begin{cases}
概念隐喻 \\
人际隐喻
\end{cases}
$$

语法隐喻

$$
层次
\begin{cases}
语义层 \\
词汇语法层 \\
音系层
\end{cases}
$$

图 1　语法隐喻 1996 年模式（转引自胡壮麟 2000）

语法隐喻在各类英语语篇中被广泛应用是不争的事实（朱永生，严世清，2000）。在语言中，名词化，动词化，形容词化以及语气隐喻，情态隐喻等表达方式都属于隐喻式范畴。由于隐喻式多数由长而复杂的词和词组构成，较之一致式更具分量，更加严肃。隐喻式的这一特点决定了这种形式必然多用于书面语体和正式语体中。上一节已经谈过，公众演讲同时具有口语和书面语的双重特点，这决定了公众演讲的语篇表现形式更倾向于正式语体，而隐喻式是体现语篇正式和庄严程度的有效手段之一。请看例句：

⑫ We are led, by events and common sense, to one *conclusion*: The *survival* of liberty in our land *increasingly* depends on the *success* of liberty in other lands.

例⑫ 选自现任美国总统布什 2005 年的就职演说辞。短短一句话就出现了包括三次名词化和一次形容词化的四次语法隐喻（句中斜体部分），都属于概念隐喻形式。而这句话的一致式可以是 According to events and common sense, we can conclude that if we want to let the liberty of our land survive, it's more and more important that the successful liberty in other lands must be firstly achieved. 由此可以看出隐喻式的优势首先体现在经济原则上，即用较少的词来表达尽量多的内容，使语言简练而内容丰富。这恰恰符合了演讲的即时性对语言的要求：用有限的时间来传达尽可能多的信息，阐述观点，传播思想，展示个人魅力。同时，隐喻式不仅可以用来强调所陈述的是一个严肃的已经被证明了的事实，即使用于未发生的事情，也可以用来强调演讲者所倡导的是合理的，可信的，甚至是科学的，其坚定之语气是毋庸置疑，字字珠玑的。请看下例：

⑬ All knew that interest was somehow the cause of the war.

例⑬ 选自林肯 1865 年的就职演说辞，其一致式可以表达为 This interest was surely somehow the cause of the war. 情态意义本应由情态动词或情态副词如 surely 来表达，这里却采用了小句 All knew 形式，属于人际隐喻中的情态隐喻。

---

① 本文所选美国总统就职演说辞均来自王建华（2001）。

这里采取情态隐喻，变主观为客观，从而使演讲者的观点成为大家的共识。在演讲中，演讲者常常采用小句形式来使表达情态隐喻化，如 we all know，it is expected，it is believed that 等形式被大量使用，而其作用就是使自己的演讲不至于过于主观而失信于听众。

⑭ Let every nation know，whether it wishes us well or ill，that we shall pay any price，bear any burden，meet any hardship，support any friend，oppose any foe to assure the *survival and success of liberty*.

例⑭选自肯尼迪 1961 年任美国总统时的就职演说辞。面对国际上复杂的政治局势，年轻的肯尼迪意气风发，自信满满。此句中的斜体部分是连续使用的名词化的语法隐喻。虽然"自由"能否真正成功尚属未知，但此时肯尼迪选择了过程的名词化表达，其用意似乎在于 survival 和 success 能够把过程物化，使原本需要付出极大努力、甚至需要不惜一切代价的过程变为显而易见的不争的事实。又如：

⑮ Now，for decades，we and the Soviets have lived under the threat of mutual assured destruction；if either resorted to the use of nuclear weapons，the other could retaliate and destroy the one who had started it. *Is there either logic or morality in believing that if one side threatens to kill tens of millions of our people，our only recourse is to threaten killing tens of millions of theirs？*

例⑮选自里根 1985 年第二次当选美国总统时的就职演说辞。句中斜体部分是一种修辞问句，这种问句无须回答，只是把本来不言而喻的陈述内容用疑问形式表达出来，加强语气，从而更好地达到交际目的，属于情态隐喻中的语气隐喻，其一致式可以是 It is neither illogical nor immoral in believing that… 对于未来在与前苏联的互相制衡中如何处理核武器的问题上，里根首先否认了传统的冤冤相报的观点。核战争的惨剧尚未发生，里根就以明知故问的口吻唤起听众共鸣，使个人观点成为人所共知的道理。语气隐喻在这里的作用就是强调演讲者所言观点的合理性和可信性，即使所言只是一种预测或推断，也要使听众相信它是不可否认的真理。

4. 英语演讲语篇的语法隐喻特点探讨

本节选用了两个相对完整的英语演讲语篇作为研究对象，全面分析一致式和隐喻式在其中的分布情况和所占比例，并同时对该语篇的语法隐喻特点进行探讨。

附录 1 节选自撒奇尔夫人在 1984 年香港回归签字仪式上的演讲 *This Is A Historic Occasion*，共计 103 个单词。其中比较典型的语法隐喻类型分析如下表：

表1 附录1的语法隐喻类型分析

隐喻式	一致式	意义转换分析		成分转换分析	
a high degree of	highly	性状	个体	adj.	n.
autonomy	autonomous	性状	个体	adj.	n.
enjoyed	customary	性状	过程	adj.	v.
assurances	assure	过程	个体	v.	n.
trading	trade	过程	性状	v.	adj.

通过分析发现，演讲者在演讲过程中会有意无意地使用各种类型的语法隐喻形式。演讲语言作为正式的语言形式，必须做到严肃、可信且不乏文采。因此，演讲者多数会使用语法隐喻甚至变换语法隐喻的类型来达到这一目的。在附录1有限的篇幅内，隐喻式与一致式都占据相当比例并发挥重要作用。在演讲者特意与观众交流时，多数采用一致式的形式，以达到亲切，平和的效果。当演讲者正式阐述自己的观点时，则更倾向于比较多地使用隐喻式。

附录2是美国著名辩论家兼演讲家 George Graham（1830-1904）在其早年作律师时为一位因狗被杀而起诉的人所做的辩护。在辩护中，George Graham 拿出人类兽性的一面与狗人性的一面作对比，引起法官们对狗的感激和同情，以及对杀狗人的强烈憎恶。这不仅仅是一篇辩护词，也是一篇优秀的讲演稿，更是对人性的呼唤，因而成为美国公众演讲的典范之一。本演讲稿共有单词375个，小句复合体16个，隐喻式23处，语篇隐喻度约为1.44，低于一般书面文体（经笔者调查一般书面文体的隐喻度约为2-4），高于口语语体（经调查口语语体隐喻度约为0-1）。由此可见，演讲语言的语法隐喻程度介于口语和书面语之间。而另一方面，在演讲语篇中一致式的应用程度高于书面语体而低于口语语体。

通过上文的探讨，我们发现演讲语言是以口语为传播方式的正式语体，既有口语特点，又有书面语特点。口语表达中一致式出现频率较大，而书面语尤其是科技文体以及文学作品等多以隐喻式形式出现。因此，在英语演讲语篇中，一致式和隐喻式同时发挥着不可或缺的作用。具体来说一篇演讲稿隐喻度的高低，还要受演讲目的、演讲场合、演讲者的语言水平及其对听众认知理解能力的判断等多方面因素的影响。

结语

本文通过对多篇英语演讲真实语料的对比和探析发现，不同于典型的口语以及书面语，英语演讲语篇的语法隐喻特点是一致式和隐喻式并存，二者相互结合又各自发挥优势，缺一不可，这是由演讲语篇同时具备口语和书面语的双重特征而决定的。隐喻式使语言庄重正式且富于文采；一致式直白、通俗，容易被理解和接受。在刻意与听众交流时，演讲者倾向于采用一致式来达到亲切友好的效果；当正式陈述自己观点时，演讲者则更多使用隐喻式来突出演讲的严肃性和合理性。因此，一篇好的演讲稿，在语言策略方面必须做到较好的结合一致式和隐喻式，使语言庄重而不生涩，亲切而不随意，通过对两者的巧妙运用与听众在思想上形成共识，产生共鸣，从而达到获取听众信任，并进一步激励听众采取实际行动的目的。

参考文献

[1] Halliday, M. A. K. *An Introduction to Functional Grammar*[M]. London: Arnold, 1994.

[2] 胡壮麟,朱永生,张德禄,李战子. 系统功能语言学概论[M]. 北京:北京大学出版社,2005.

[3] 王建华(选编). 美国总统就职演说名篇[M]. 北京:世界图书出版公司,2001.

[4] 王佐良,丁往道. 英语文体学引论[M]. 北京:外语教学与研究出版社,1987/2002.

[5] 周刚,牛晓春. 交际英语2000[M]. 大连:大连理工出版社,1999.

[6] 陈萍. 演讲概念界说探讨[J]. 长春师范学院学报(人文社会科学版),2005,(5).

[7] 胡壮麟. 评语法隐喻的韩礼德模式[J]. 外语教学与研究,2000,(2).

[8] 朱永生. 名词化、动词化与语法隐喻[J]. 外语教学与研究,2006,(2).

[9] 朱永生,严世清. 语法隐喻理论的理据和贡献[J]. 外语教学与研究,2000,(2).

附录1

This Is A Historic Occasion（节选）...

It gives *Hong Kong a high degree of autonomy*. Hong Kong people will *administer* Hong Kong and a Special Administrative Region will pass its own legislation. It allows Hong Kong to continue to decide its own economic, financial and trade politics, and to participate as appropriate in international organizations and agreements. It preserves Hong Kong's familiar legal system and the rights and freedoms *enjoyed there*. In short, it provides the *assurances* for the future which Hong Kong needs in order to continue to play its unique role in the world as a trading and financial *center*.

—Margaret Thatcher 1984

附录 2

Tribute to the dog

Gentlemen of the Jury:

The best friend a man has in the world may turn against him and become his enemy. His son or daughter that he has reared with <u>loving care</u> may prove ungrateful. Those who are nearest and dearest to us, those whom we trust with our <u>happiness</u> and our good name may become traitors to their faith. The money that a man has, he may lose. It flies away from him, perhaps when he needs it most. A man's <u>reputation</u> may be sacrificed in a moment <u>of ill-considered action</u>. The people who are prone to fall on their knees to do us honor when <u>success</u> is with us, may be the first to throw the stone of malice when <u>failure</u> settles its cloud upon our heads. The one absolutely unselfish friend that man can have in this selfish world, the one that never deserts him, the one that never proves ungrateful or <u>treacherous</u> is his dog. A man's dog stands by him in <u>prosperity</u> and in <u>poverty</u>, in <u>health</u> and in <u>sickness</u>. He will sleep on the cold ground, where the <u>wintry</u> winds blow and the snow drives fiercely, if only he may be near his master's side. He will kiss the hand that has no food to offer. He will lick the wounds and sores that come in encounters with the <u>roughness</u> of the world. He guards the sleep of his pauper master as if he were a prince. When all other friends desert, he remains. When riches take wings, and reputation falls to pieces, he is as constant in his love as the sun in its journey through the heavens. If fortune drives the master forth, an outcast in the world, <u>friendless</u> and <u>homeless</u>, the <u>faithful</u> dog asks no higher privilege than that of accompanying him, to guard him against <u>danger</u>, to fight against his enemies. And when the last scene of all comes, and death takes his master in its embrace and his body is laid away in the cold ground, no matter if all other friends pursue their way, there by the graveside will the noble dog be found, his head between his paws, his eyes sad, but open in alert <u>watchfulness</u>, <u>faithful</u> and true even in <u>death</u>.

—— George Graham 1855

（注：附录 1 和附录 2 中下划线标注部分为隐喻式，其他部分为一致式）

（叶慧君，刘娲路，河北大学）

语篇分析在司法语境中的应用

1. 概述

语篇指"任何不完全受句子语法约束的在一定语境下表示完整语义的自然语言。"作为广义的"语篇"，"既包括'话语'（discourse），也包括'篇章'（text）。"（胡壮麟 1994：1）本文采用广义的语篇概念。

语篇语言学（也称话语语言学）是一门年轻的学科，它是 50 年代以后才发展起来的；作为独立的学科，它直到 70 年代才有较快的进展。篇章语言学的研究对象是比句子更大的语言单位，包括书面语言和口头语言。语篇的结构、句子的排列、句际关系、会话结构、语篇的指向性、信息度、句子间的语句衔接和语义连贯等等，都是篇章语言学的研究内容。

我国语篇研究有几千年的历史，早在公元前，人们就对语篇结构倾注了有效的思考与探讨。《文心雕龙》云："夫人之立言，因字而生句，积句而成章，积章而成篇。"然而，对语篇学进行独立的系统、科学地研究，是近些年来在西方语言研究的影响下才产生、壮大起来的。"从历史发展的角度看，西方研究语言，无论传统语法学还是现代结构主义语言学，都是到句子为止，而东方研究语言从未局限在句子范围之内。"（王福祥 1994：33）

在法律语境中，无论人们就有关法律或法学问题谈话或写文章，都要表达一定的思想，非一言两语能够了事，因此多数场合要运用好多句子，于是更多的人把语篇看成是大于句子的单位。法学语篇是在特定的法律语境中，研究任何不完全段句子语法约束的在一定语境下，案件当事人所表示的完整语义的言语表达，包括口语和书面语。在法学语境中，大量法学著作、普法教育、法制文学、法庭审判、庭审会议、法律文件、审判中的证人证言、法庭辩论、法官判词等文字和书面材料，为我们研究法律语篇提供了丰富的材料。"总之，法律是可供语篇分析的丰富资源。"（Shuy 2003）

现代意义上的法律语言学（forensic linguistics）是西方语言学研究领域的新兴分支学科，起步于 20 世纪 70 年代末和 80 年代初的西方国家，尤其是英国、美国、德国等。1994 年由国际法律语言协会（The International Association of Forensic Linguists，IAFL）和国际法律语音协会（The International Association of Forensic Phonetics，IAFP）共同创办的会刊—《法律语言学—言语、语言与法律国际杂志》（Forensic Linguistics—The international Journal of Speech, Language and the Law），学术组织和学术刊物的出现，标志着该学科独立存在。十多年来，直接或间接参与法学语言研究的有语言学家、法学家、翻译学家、律师以及法官等。

国内外的法律语言研究起初大都集中在实践方面，重点讨论立法、司法和执法等应用领域的语音、词汇、句法、修辞等微观领域，缺乏整体性。在法庭审理的语言方面，国外许多语言学家（如拉波夫、费尔墨、克鲁克等）提供第一手的语言知识，为解决法律问题作出了独特的贡献。后来，他们从宏观入手，运用语篇分析理论研究法庭中当事人的问话、答话、证人证言、录音真伪识别、话语标记以及男女性别在对待话题上的不同态度等对公正审判的影响；在运用语用学知识的基础上，美国语言学家夏伊和心理学家合作，参与培训司法人员的工作，对司法文告作出了较大的改进。

2. 法学语篇分析在司法语言研究中的应用

早在 20 世纪初，就有人开始使用法律语言的分析方法，解决司法案件中涉案当事人的言语行为，协助法官和律师处理法律诉讼案件，只不过当时没有对其作详细的书面记录。例如美国芝加哥地区法院，就曾经邀请语言学家 McDavid 协助法官参与识别司法案件中被告人的方言特点，最终使案件真相大白。20 世纪 60 年代，美国政府部门及地方政府部门均邀请语言学家参加双语教育、取消种族隔离政策等一系列有关法律问题和案件调查。

就法律语言的性质而言，Shuy 认为 20 世纪 80 年代以前，专家们早期所从事的法律语言研究，被称为应用性语言研究，属于语言学研究的边缘学科。他们被称为方言学家（dialectologist）、音韵学家、句法学家等，从最广义的角度讲，也就是应用语言学家，却没有人称他们为法律语言学家（forensic linguists）。因此，"他们所从事的语言与法律关系的专业性研究工作，却始终名不见经传。"（Deborah Schiffrin 2003：439）.

现代法律语言研究得益于以前用于法庭证据的秘密录音，后者对目前法律语言研究的拓展和组织工作都有不可替代的作用。主要表现在两个方面：其一，20 世纪 70 年代，由于电子技术的广泛发展以及电子侦察（electronic surveillance）在法律案件上的应用，政府部门开始重视白领犯罪（white collar crime）和有组织犯罪（organized crime）等案件的录音材料。其二，语言学家在这一时期拓宽对"超句子、超词汇"（beyond the level of sentence and beyond the level of words）的系统研究，可以说是一种意外收获（serendipitous）。"语篇（话语）分析"、"语用学"、"言语行为"、"意向性（intentionality）"、"推论（inferring）"之类的术语开始进入司空见惯的学术领域。上述两种发展倾向使用语篇分析在录音会话（尤其是执法部门）、指证嫌疑人的犯罪事实等方面，起到了至关重要的作用。

法律语篇（话语）分析不仅仅局限于采用录音证据、会话特点以及其他言语行为研究、刑事法律案件的侦破、书面文本的识别、语音鉴定、嫌疑人的系统语言的侦察等，也可以用于识别民事合同、产品警视标识以及名誉损害所引起的争端等案件。

3. 法学语篇分析方法在美国刑事案件鉴定中的应用

美国早期用于刑事案件语篇分析的录音证据，是 1979 年的 Texas 州诉 Davis 一案：当事人 T. Cullen Davis 是 Fort Worth 市的石油大亨，他被指控教唆他人谋杀其妻子。美国政府采用秘密手段，录下 Davis 和雇用人员的对话，企图以此证明 Davis 确有教唆谋杀妻子的犯罪事实。语言学家根据录音材料分析证明：第一，话题分析证明，Davis 在录音里谈话里根本没有涉及杀人的话题，而公诉机关分析谈话录音后，却认为 Davis 有重大嫌疑。第二，根据 Davis 的答话分析证明：特工人员提出谋杀话题后，Davis 并没有做出相应回答，实际上也没有明确表示对杀人的话题感兴趣。他在答语中改变话题，也没有说任何有关的话，或者只用"嗯，嗯"作为反应。法庭上，双方就"嗯，嗯"的含义展开了争论。公诉机关认为，Davis 是在与特工商定协议，而辩方却认为 Davis 只是在听对方讲话，没有就对方的杀人话题表示认同。

Davis 和特工人员的会话环境也进一步证明，Davis 的语言行为没有蓄意杀人的意思表示。后来法院在审理公诉机关指控 Davis 的"闯入自己家门，头戴溜冰帽，杀害其妻子的男友"后，当庭释放了 Davis。之后，Davis 紧接着向法院提起诉讼，请求法院判决与其妻子离婚。后来 Davis 听说，她妻子离婚时与法官有关系。Davis 为了获取证据，请人跟踪其妻。该雇员向警察告密，说 Davis 要他找人杀死妻子和法官。警方给该雇员带上录音机，派其为警方获取 Davis 的言词证据。整个过程由两次简短的会晤构成，而且均由雇员出面把 Davis 叫出来，两次谈话均在小车上进行。雇员带了枪（这在 Texas 州是常见的情况），扎着空手道用的黑色腰带，身材瘦小的 Davis 从头到尾都显得诚惶诚恐。

公诉机关掌握的所谓"铁的"证据，就是雇员和 Davis 谈话的录音。雇员说，"我把法官给你弄死。"Davis 回答道，"好哇。"雇员接着说，"我把其他人也弄死。"Davis 的谈话确实录在磁带上，但不是回答雇员的。公诉方自己的证言里也清楚地说明了这一点。后经证实，警方让雇员带上麦克风（mike），而且也进行了两次会晤的录音，Davis 和雇员谈话是在一辆停在对面停车场上的敞篷车上录下来的。从录音上发现，Davis 和雇员在谈论 Art 时，Davis 正从车上下来。Davis 一直在说 Art 的事，而急于想得到有罪证据的雇员却一直在强调，要把法官和其他有关人员弄死的事。

庭审时，语言学家同时识别了两次不同的对话，让陪审员阅读 Davis 的所有谈话的书面材料，先是关于 Art 的对话，然后是 Davis 离开小车时所说的话。警方在阅读 Davis 连续谈话过程中"充满火药味（smoking gun word）"的"好哇"这一答语时发现，Davis 本人在谈论有关 Art 的事情的这一段话，成了整个谈话的重要组成部分。分析发现，Davis 所说的"好哇"，根本不是在回答雇员问话。与此同时，语言学家又让陪审员继续读雇员的谈话，同样先阅读两人谈话或有关 Art 的话题，证明 Davis 谈话时与雇员所处的距离。Davis 说"好哇"的时候，与其他不在场的听者身体移动时所能听到录音带上的声音，有着惊人的重合之处。在法庭上，即使有证人证言的录音，人们的关注点乎还是集中在书面材料上。在这种情况下，如果公诉机关只关注书面材料，会极大地影响案件的公证判决。

上述案例为后来若干年的其他刑事案件的语篇分析，开辟了新途径。Davis 一案证明，问话-应答分析是任何会话分析中不可或缺的部分，而且也是刑事案件的录音分析中的重要组成部分。

3.1 言语行为与语用分析

言语行为是语用学的重要理论，研究"在一定语境条件下用于某一特定目的的语言表达形式。"（何自然 冉永平 2002：172）法律语言中，表示承诺、给予、拒绝、赞同、警告和歉意等言语行为，在刑事案件以及合同意向的理解、辨别警示标识以及有关民事案件等其他书面文书的理解有重要作用，类似案例早有记载。（Shuy 1993；Dumas 1990）

美国 Texas 州的 Fort Worth 市就有这样一个案例，记载了民事案件里有关言语行为分析的过程：一位先天耳聋的残疾人企图为买二手车讨价还价时，指控经销商对他实施了非法拘禁、欺诈和情感打击等，违反了 Texas 州政府的颁布《反欺诈性贸易行为法》和《残疾人人力资源保护法》。该残疾人和销售人员之间的书面交易材料，为该指控提供了证据。在长达四个小时的书面交易过程中，该残疾人提供的证据证明，他当天没打算买车，只是承诺考虑考虑，想好了再作答复，而当时销售人员却抢走了他的车钥匙，拒绝交还。市场监管人员证明，残疾人有购买车的意想，而且与售货员进行了长时间的书面"交谈"。在不到一钟头的时间里，他要求对方归还其支票和车钥匙；第二小时的时候，又催促对方，要求索回其车钥匙和支票；第四小时的时候，他占据优势，将书面交谈的材料抓在手中，控制住售货员办公桌，找出了他的支票，径直冲向门口。这时候售货员将其堵在门口，手中摇晃着残疾人的车钥匙。于是残疾人便从售货员手中一把抢过车钥匙，直接奔向他的律师。

经过言语行为分析，残疾人和售货员之间上百轮的书面交谈清楚地说明，他并没有购买小车的意向。残疾人陈述的事实还证明，他曾经七次讲明自己的经济状况，七次要求得到有关小车的资料，三次承诺以后再回去购买，十四次拒绝了售货员的报价，十二次要求归还支票，十一次否定了售货员的开价（say no to offer），而商家在证据面前仍然坚持认为残疾人当天的确钟情于他所看中的那辆小车，甚至认为该顾客同意购买那辆车，最终导致该残疾人长时间滞留在汽车交易市场。

Shuy（1994）认为，这种十分简单的言语行为分析方法，为语言学家提供了更多语言分析机会，而且也有利于该顾客，也为终审判决提供了有力的证据支持。

言语行为分析在贿赂指控案件的侦破方面尤其重要。美国 Texas 州一位政客受贿一案，堪称语篇分析的经典案例。该官员同意收受一笔钱，将该州部分雇员的保险转移到另一家保险公司，以此作为收受贿款的交易。那么，公诉方是如何分析言语行为的呢？

首先，言语行为完全隐含在为了签订更加有效的保险合同和节省 Texas 州政府开支这样的合法语境中。后来，代理人突然再次出价 100，000 万美元，作为竞选捐款（在 Texas 州当时是合法行为）。政客回答说"我们先办这件事，再考虑那件事。"代理人于是便提高赌注，说"每年给你 600，000 万美元，你可以自由支配。"政客回答说，"我们的唯一观点是，我们不能干任何违法的事，也不能让任何人身陷图圄。你们也一样。这件事（指保险方案）合法，因为任何时候有人向我表明，为给州政府节省开支，我都会赞成。"至于竞选捐款，他以合法捐款的方式收下了那笔钱，并清楚告诉对方，他已经如实地向政府报告了此事。代理人叫他不要向 Texas 州政府报告了收款一事。他还是如实地报告了政府。尽管州政府并没有转移保险单，但该政客仍然被指控犯受贿罪。言语行为分析了两种不同的报价（offer），而政客完全否定了两者 之间的联系：一是他自己的言语行为，二是他已经向政府竞选基金委员会报告收款一事。法院最终判该政客无罪。

3. 2　语篇分析的新领域

语篇分析不仅可以应用到刑事案件、民事纠纷案件、合同纠纷案件等众多法律事务，而且在与法律案件有关的语言识别、笔迹鉴定、图像真伪识别以及名誉损害等方面，同样前景广阔。

3. 2. 1　语篇分析在语音识别中的应用

人类声音的识别历史悠久，而且从来就真伪杂糅，难以分辨。《圣经〈创世纪〉》第 27 篇里就可以找到早期有关语音识别的记载：弟弟 Jocob 在其母亲 Rebekah 的唆使和精心装扮下，模仿其哥哥 Esau 说话声，骗取其父亲 Isaac 的信任，最终窃取了其哥哥 Esau 的继承权。

我国古代奴隶制社会统治者制定的是维护其阶级利益的法律，各个王朝的证据制度主要是根据审判的实践经验形成的，比较重视与案情有关的客观材料，要求审判官依据证据推断。夏"作禹刑"，商"作汤刑"，周"作礼刑"，吕侯制"吕刑"。其中都多少包含着证据制度的内容。据《周礼秋官小司寇》和《尚书吕刑》等史书记载：古时办案，须"以五声听狱诉，求民情"。这里说的"听"，就是审问的意思。所谓"五听"，就是要求法官在办案时，应当注意从五个方面观察被讯问人的表情有无变化。这"五听"的具体内容是：一曰辞听："观其出言，不直则烦"；二曰色听："观其颜色，不直则变"；三曰气听："观其气息，不直则喘"；四曰耳听："观其听聆，不直则惑"；五曰目听："观其瞻视，不直则乱"。实际上是要求官吏审案时应当注意受审人的举止言谈、表情心理等。上述"五听"，是我国古代司法经验的总结。当然，这里面有主观唯心主义的色彩，但也包含了一些合理的因素。我国古代在刑事诉讼中，已经注重对被告人心理状态的分析，这是有一定道理的。

当代美国社会，早就有关于语音识别案例的记载，就是 1935 年美国诉 Hamptman 一案。本案的当事人 Charles Lindberg，是一位著名的航海人员。Linberg 在庭审中辩称，他听得出是 Hamptman 给他打的电话，向他索要被绑架孩子的赎金。"本案有关电话声识别真伪一事，直接导致现代语音识别科学新时代的产生。"（Deboot Shiffrin 2003）现在人们对从事该领域研究的工作称为"法律语音学"（forensic phonetics），该学科的产生得益于 Baldwin 和 French 两人合著的《法律语音学》（Forensic Phonetics）（1990）、Hollien's《犯罪声学研究》（The Acoustics of Crime）（1990）以及《法律语言》（Forensic Linguistics）（1996）。这些著作主要解决语音识别（voice identification）中的发音问题，没有涉及说话人语篇形式的识别等问题。

谈话录音识别并不局限于法律语音学家们所分析的种种案件，如录音对话的专案分析，用作指控犯罪嫌疑人的证人证言，每一个讲话人的声音必须记录下来进行识别，而且必须弄清楚每一个讲话人的身份。大多数情况下，做起来并不是太难。尤其是录音带上只有两个人讲话，而且两人讲话的声音不同，就更加不难识别。如果录音里有许多人谈话，识别起来就比较困难。如果几个人说话的声音都低沉，说的都是某一地区的方言，或者讲话声音相同，就应该特别注意其他方面的语音识别特征。令法律语言学家门更加头疼的是准确识别录音带的语音，这时候就要借助声谱仪（acoustic spetrograph）进行分析。这种分析方法不太适用于刑事侦查时的秘密录音，原因是，这种秘密录音的条件通常不如条件优越的实验室。

前面所讲的特定讲话人的声音干扰的录音，在商业会晤中有助于识别某些讲话人的声音，以及讲话人的话语识别特征。比如，三个讲话人的姓氏完全相同，都在不停地谈话，而且讲的又是同一个话题。首先应当弄清谁是答话人，这样做有助于在众多说话人中识别出真正的讲话人。

20 世纪 80 年代初期，在美国政府诉 Harrison A. Williams 一案中，语言学家对著名的 Abscam 一案作了相同的语音识别鉴定。Williams 议员和坎登市市长 Angelo Errichetti 两人的声音都低沉粗犷。办案人员对两人的谈话都进行了秘密录音录像，录像带的效果一片模糊，而且拍摄角度和光线非常差，谁也弄不清楚究竟谁在讲话，在数次关键时候，美国政府的文字记录认为是 Williams 议员为讲话人，而语言学家却认为是 Errichetti 在讲话。由于控辩双方对磁带的声音-图像分析一筹莫展，最重要的语音识别诊断线索，最终还是集中在两位当事人不同的话语习惯上。另外，Errichetti 经常打断其他人的讲话，而 Williams 却没有打断别人讲话的习惯。Williams 经常喜欢使用一些"话语标记"（discourse markers），如"好的"、"而-且-"、"因-此-"，以及"你知道"之类的话语标记，作为他讲话时的发语词；相反，Errichetti 却没有使用这些话语标记的习惯。语言学家注意到上述语言习惯问题，公诉机关却没有弄清两人的话语标记以及讲话时喜欢使用什么样话语标记等习惯问题，案件终于真相大白。

如果说利用语篇分析手段进行语音识别这一潜在的效果在司法领域运用，时至今还得没有得到认可的话，关键问题或许在于使用该手段进行司法案件分析的机会太少。语篇分析的许多问题里面，话语特征分析的重要性与财产损失和争取个人自由相比，也许目前还没有显现出来。另外一个重要原因是，从事法律语言学研究语言学家的人数不多，使用话语分析的语音识别的手段在公正审判各种案件所发挥的重要性，还没有引起广大司法人员和当事人的广泛关注。

3.2.2 语篇分析在名誉损害案件中的应用

近年来，西方国家的语言学家经常应邀作为诽谤或侮辱罪案件的专家证人。美国有关名誉损害的法律特别规定，凡公开散布（无论书面或口头）虚假言论，且证明该言论纯属主观臆断，行为人便构成对他人名誉权的损害。言论的真实性由当事人双方去争论，而该言论的表达方式却是语言学家研究的课题。对言论的分析有许多结构上的解剖措施，可以证明言论的事实根据纯属个人的主观臆断。

所谓"主观臆断"是指某一种观点、判断或评价，是仅存在于某一个人心里的东西，是某人对某一件事的个人主观看法。个人观点的语言结构需要语言专家进行鉴定。还有一些被称为行为性陈述观点，如人们常用表示个人观点的语言有"我想……"、"我相信……"、"对我来说……"或"依我看"等。有些观点性表达，通常有些固定模式：如"我觉得……"、"可以相信……"，或"好像……"等。

有关法律和词典对"名誉损害"一词的表述，在"观点"和"事实"两个方面的定义是一致的，但却没有对该词进行包括语篇在内的语言结构分析。但在处理司法案件时，语言的篇章结构分析是不可或缺的环节。下面是一桩有关名誉损害证据的语篇结构分析。

Roy Harris 起诉某电视台损害他的名誉权。他在起诉书中称，该电视台在两套节目的新闻片段中称他为犯罪嫌疑人。两套节目不断称他为唯一的犯罪嫌疑人或现场只有他一个嫌疑人。实事求是地讲，电视台说他是"唯一嫌疑人"，而且只将其作为怀疑对象，并不构成对他的名誉损害。是不是说他已经实施了犯罪行为呢？对此可得出两种结论：其一，电视台可能辩称，他们这样做是想说明警察的无能。其二是播音员引用警方调查人员的话，说，"他直接走进房屋，然后走入厨房，用枪击中受害人的头部，打死受害人。"在另一套节目里面，说 Harris 是唯一的犯罪嫌疑人。因此公众都知道了是 Roy Harris 杀死了受害人。Harris 本人和辩护律师都没有注意到指称性言语（reference），后来在语言学家的提醒下，才引起了他们的注意。

指称性定义（referential definition）并不是名誉损害赔偿案件中唯一有用的语篇分析程序。语篇框架结构（discourse framing）分析如语篇框架在 Harris 一案中同样发挥了作用。电视新闻节目的典型特征是，其话语既有开头，也有结尾。结论部分特别强调某一特别重要的新闻事件。而在 Harris 一事件中，开场白却没有按照这种框架框架进行。如，

女播音员：几个星期以来，人们也许听说了住在郊外的 Kenmore 的妻子被害一案。

男播音员：一位丈夫与其过去的女友被指控是本案元凶。唔——，今晚的特别节目关注另外一桩凶案，受害人的丈夫正在接受警察调查。

这里有关凶杀案的新闻性框架是进行类比（anology）。"类比"指两个或两个以上的事物在某些方面有些相似，在其他方面可能更相似。因此，通过类比，该丈夫的所作所为与以前发生的 Kenmore 凶杀案和 Harris 一案相比，其语篇框架让人不得不得出这样的结论：尽管 Harris 未受指控，但两个毫无相关案子如出一辙。两者的话语标识（discourse marker）"唔"中的发音拉长了，这一举动说明，接下来要讲的话与 Kenmore 凶杀案在语义上有衔接关系。男播音员所说的"另一桩"词语与此相关联。类比性话语框架让听众推论，Harris 与 Kenmore 丈夫一样，就是凶杀案的嫌疑人。

3.2.3 利用刑事案件说明语言学问题

我们注意到语篇分析方法可以某用于些民事和刑事案件。运用语篇分析的过程是应用语言学研究的范畴。然而，也有人认为可以通过语言分析方法解决来解决现实问题，进一步促进语言学的发展。这就是语篇分析法。

3.2.3.1 语篇分析在刑事侦察中的应用

话题—应答分析为解决与目的性（intentionality）有关的复杂问题打开辟了新途径。无论是语言学家、心理学家还是其他方面的专家，都不可能钻进人们的内心世界，揭示讲话人的内心思想。但录音材料可以帮人们实现把握人们谈话时稍纵即逝的时空，对谈话内容进行反复研究，发现讲话人的话题和回答时的真实意图的种种蛛丝马迹。这样做就像考古学家观察瓷器的一个个碎片去考察逝去的文明史一样。这种考察的实际意图和表达真实意图的线索的差异，有着不可忽视的作用。律师也许会觉得，语言学家提出这样一种考察问题的方法，是在故意揣摩人家的心思。律师的观点和语言学家的观点大相径庭，这也是律师之所以不能像语言学家那样真正体味到对话双方言语行为的潜在意义的真谛所在的原因。

要了解人们的意图就问他们的意图就行了，但在诉讼案件中了解准确而真实的答案的可能性就会大打折扣。人们在日常生活中讲话时，也许不会意识到自己的真正意图，或确切地讲，根本无法清楚地表达自己的真实意图。许多情况下，人们的"自我报道"（self-report）的资料在社会科学领域并没有引起足够重视。由于还没有发明一种能够深入人的内心世界获得真实意图的仪器设备，了解人们所提出的话题，较其他途径而言，很好地把握"自我报道"可能是接近人们的内心世界的有效方法。不能说用上述方法就是能完全了解人们的真实想法的唯一办法，但我们可以通过合理的推理，了解人们的内心世界。

同样，从对他人提出的话题所作出的回应，也可以找到了解其真实意图的线索。我们可能有许多垂手可得的应答方法。我们可以仔细思考是否接收或拒绝，甚至同意或反对别人所提出的话题。无论反对还是赞同，其意图都是合理而清楚的，甚至是可行的。另外，我们也可以改变谈话主题。改变主题的行为有许多可供选择的解答，包括对主题不感兴趣、没办法或不愿意听、或者开小差、采取鲁莽行动，或者害怕卷入话题等等。在上述方法中，很难断定答话人是反对还是赞同对方所提出的话题。尤其在法院，人们很难断定当事人所作出回答，是否承认他真的参加了某种犯罪活动。

3.2.3.2　语篇分析与语言的模糊性

语言使用中的模糊性表达，是语义学研究独特领域（province）。话语的模糊性可以表现在书面语和口头语中。话语序列（discourse sequence）所表现出的模糊性词语和句子，在法律语言里比比皆是。下面以美国政府诉 John Delorean 一案为例，说明模糊性话语分析在司法语言中的运用。

案件的焦点集中在汽车制造商 Delorean 有没有同意购买并销售商品来拯救其公司濒临破产的局面：Delorean 利用英国政府的贷款在爱尔兰新建了一家汽车制造厂。当英国政府发生变化后，工厂陷入困境。（Shuy 1993）检方认为，Delorean 同意"投资"是一件好事，并得到了该谈话的录音证据，以此作为起诉 Delorean 理由。侦察人员几花了个月的时间，想方设法诱导 Delorean 在毒品行业投资。Delorean 没有上圈套，完全拒绝了这笔生意。

　　仔细考察致使 Delorean 同意投资的语言环境，人们清楚地发现，话语序列导致 Delorean 承认"同意投资是一桩好事。"事实证明，侦查人员虽然认定 Delorean 在进行毒品业务，实际上还是对 Delorean 采取了两个步骤：首先是让他成为毒品业务的合伙人，他拒绝了第一套方案。第二步是继续为他寻找合法投资商，向他所经营的汽车行业投资。当侦查人员根据 Delorean 所说的"投资是件好事"这句话进行分析时发现，两种不同语境中"投资"，其意义完全不同。据此，美国政府就认为 Delorean 的意思是愿意在毒品业投资，得到马上转售的机会，以此获得足够的资金，使其公司东山再起。而 Delorean 本人真实意思却是说，有人为他的公司"投资是一件好事"，他的观点得到辩护人及语言学家的支持。检方和 Delorean 双方都使用了"投资"一词，但没有结合特定的语境中去理解和阐释。而"投资"一词须仔细考察具体话语语境和话语系列中才有其具体含义。

　　许多刑事案件话语分析，实际上都集中在当事人的言词上。Shuy 称之为"语言犯罪"（language crime）。（Shuy 1993）所谓语言犯罪就是没有对受害人进行身体上的伤害，如抢劫、谋杀或殴打等，而主要表现在诱导购买或出卖非法财产或具体物品、进行各种形式的教唆、讹诈或密谋获得非法物品等言语行为。当事人彼此之间也不完全清楚上述行为。有的只是含糊其辞，或者用隐语表示。这种方式一方面让犯罪嫌疑人很难理解警方在干什么，另一方面也使执法部门难以确定嫌疑人的真正含义。模糊性言语行为在法庭上是不能作为定罪量刑的根据的。

　　造成语言模糊不清的原因很多，说话人可能故意闪烁其词，也可能无意识地把话说得模棱两可，似是而非。在刑事案件里，控辩双方都企图弄清对方的话语，作出有利于自己的解释。公诉人通常对模糊语穷究其理，认为嫌犯有意掩盖事实真相，而辩方却对同样的话作完或完全相反的解释。例如，1977 年美国 Texas 州发生一起合谋伤害直升机制造商的案件（即美国政府诉 Smith 一案）。Smith 的公司隶属于一家法国制造公司，拥有为以色列生产一批军用直升机的合同。以色列作为美国的同盟国，根据美国涉外军事财政援助计划（该计划是为了帮助联邦成员购买美国生产的直升机软件设备所制定的），该计划必须使用美国政府基金，目的是保证美国国内产业的利益。也就是说，只要直升机是在美国生产的，涉外财政援助计划（FMF）就会在以色列的经费内拨出一大笔款项。如果只是直升机的部分设备在美国生产，FMF 基金会就只能按实际生产的比例部分拨款。

　　美国政府开始怀疑 Smith 的公司在以色列的资金上做假账。检方人员首先找到 Smith 公司负责与以色列签订合同的雇员 Tolfa，说服该人证明 Smith 公司有违法行为，并指派他设法弄到 Smith 与以方人员会晤和讨论此事时的谈话录音。

检方获得了指控 Smith 的唯一证据，而指控 Smith 的证据也仅仅凭该借录音谈话。

法国母公司也可能获悉有关此案的一些信息，或者卷入有关此案的违法行为中。但检方指控 Smith 一案所存在的问题是，Smith 及其公司是否知道此事。检方的起诉书认为，Smith 本人对此事洞若观火。Tolfa 接受指派，诱导 Smith 承认知道造假账一事，并对他的谈话进行了录音。Smith 和 Tolfa 之间的 4 次谈话都录了音，4 个谈话录音均无法提供证据，证明 Smith 知道有关做假账一事；而公诉机关却从几次谈话录音中截取几个片段，认为 Smith 与其母公司有共谋行为或知道该共谋行为，并对他进行指控。显然，公诉方所摘取的信息成了美国政府对 Smith 的指控的焦点是：以色列中间人 Ori Edelsburg 有没有收取从 FMF 基金会支付给他的任何佣金。如果 Ori Edelsburg 真的收了佣金，或者如果 Smith 知道事实真相，就可以证明 Smith 参与了共谋行为。另外，如果 Ori Edelsburg 收取的是法国母公司支付给他的其他交易佣金，且与 FMF 基金无关，就没有证据指控 Smith。

事实证明，此次交易过程非常复杂。Ori Edelsburg 做成了一笔交易，所涉及的不仅仅是向以色列出售了新型的直升机，而且涉及到他所接洽的以色列政府向智利出售设备的交易行为。以色列向智利出售设备一事，只是 Ori Edelsburg 的单方行为，Ori Edelsburgg 的佣金问题，自然成了本案庭审的关键问题。

Tolfa 想尽办法诱导 Smith，让其知道 Ori Edelsburg 所收取的佣金，但不说明该佣金的用途。然而 Tolfa 得到 Smith 的回答，只是"嗯"、"啊"之类的应答之词，而且最终否定了中间人得到了 FMF 基金会支付的佣金。本案经语言学家对 Smith 和 Tolfa 谈话分析提示，Smith 的辩护律师 Dallas，Mark Werbness 等人最终使 Smith 当庭无罪释放。

Tolfa 较早和 Smith 进行谈话时，给他提供了许多次机会，让他自己承认犯罪。Tolfa 的努力没有成功。Tolfa 谨慎地提出，中间人 Ori Edelsburg 收取了 FMF 基金会的佣金。下面是两人的对话（1995 年 4 月 1 日的一次会面）：

Tolfa：Ori 每天都给我们打电话……，我觉得他是在为那笔钱发愁，也就是那笔佣金的事情。

Smith：嗯—嗯。

（Smith 的应答标记）

从 Smith 的"嗯—嗯"答语中，即使 Smith 没有完全承认这是一种不利于自己的回答，公诉机关完仍然相信 Tolfa 有必要再次去试探一下。

一个月过后，Tolfa 再一次对 Tolfa 紧紧围绕 Smith 的公司在接受以色列的一笔重要资金时，支付给 Ori 的一笔佣金这件进行。这次对话如下：

Tolfa：Ori 为了得到那笔钱老是找我的麻烦……他要求支付给他佣金。

Smith：嗯，他是看到我们得到钱，也要得到钱吗？是不是？

这一次会面同样没有给公诉机关提供多少有价值的东西。Tolfa 从 Smith 那里所得到的最有利的材料就是，Smith 听到 Ori 得到了以色列支付给 Smith 公司后所支付给 Ori 的佣金后，感到的很震惊。获得这一线索的理由就是，Smith 在没有得任何信息的情况下所做出的表情，甚至 Ori 给 Tolfa 打电话，实际上也并不清楚。Tolfa 模糊不清（ambiguity）的表达，可能有助于公诉机关为 Smith 在本案中有不打自招的任何共谋行为提供指控证据。但 Smith 没有任何表示。于是，5 个月之后，Tolfa 再次与 Smith 进行了一次谈话。

1996 年 10 月 2 日会面：

Tolfa：ECF（法国母公司）与 Ori 有合同关系。

Smith：噢—嗯……

Tolfa：如果他们插手此事的话，我们会遇到证明书的批准问题。

Smith：我们不想在证明书与主合同书上一样签名。

Tolfa：如果他们弄到文件资料，发现了 Ori 收取佣金……

Smith：AEC（Smith 的公司）合同上没有此事。ECF 会将 Ori 与智利的交易联系起来。

（谈话中 Smith 拒绝承认有牵连）

这一次 Tolfa 的谈话内容更加具体，公诉方认为法国母公司（ECF）与 Ori 的确有合同关系，而且认为 Smith 的公司在美国政府支助给以色列的资金的证明文件上有问题。从 Smith 的回答看，他没有理会到 Tolfa 含糊其辞的真正含义。Smith 觉得，作为董事长，他只负责在主合同上签字，其他人员负责在 FMF 在交给以色列的文件上签字。他只是用较委婉的方式解释"我们的证明文件上有问题"。Tolfa 觉得应该说得更加清楚一点，最终将话说得更明白，企图将法国母公司的文件材料与 Ori 联系起来。Tolfa 的话说得明明白白，Smith 的完全否定 Tolfa 的说法，并证明他的公司与 Ori Edelsburg 没有合同关系，而 Ori 与法国母公司的任何合同关系，只是部分交易涉与以色列向智利军方出售设备有关。

就诱导手段而言，使用模糊语言揭示语言犯罪不失为一种有效的手段。在调查案件的初期阶段尤其如此。使用的语言越模糊，对方就会有更多的机会去澄清其模糊不清的东西，使自己的意思表达更加明白。如果答话人为澄清自己的观点而自证其罪的话，公诉机关就会有效地完成其调查工作。另外，犯罪嫌疑人如果不愿说清楚自己的事，公诉机关就应当考虑以下几个方面的问题：① 对方理解模糊意思，罪证确凿；② 对方另有隐情；③ 对方因恐惧而保持沉默；④ 对方根本无罪，于是对模糊语言的意义毫不领会。前三项对公诉机关的意义在于，可以考虑使用对话录音的措施；最后一种方式说明，继续录音可能没有任何意义了。

公诉机关显然是在作进一步努力，但仍然找不到任何有力证据说明 Smith 知道或者应当知道 Edelsburg 非法收取了从 FMF 基金会支付给中间人的佣金。Tolfa 可能接受了联邦调查局（FBI）负责该的案件特工人员的指令，放弃使用模糊语，直截了当地问：（Smith 拒绝承认与本案有关 1996 年 7 月 26 日）

Tolfa：Ori 是怎么牵扯到本案的？

Smith：Ori 的钱是 ECF（法国母公司）支付的，你知道，即通过"外来途径。"

显而易见，这次所用的方法完全失败，因为 Smith 终于明白了 Tolfa 的意思，并清楚地指出，Ori 所收到的任何一笔经费都由母公司支付，即所谓"外来途径"。"外来途径"指以色列向智利出售淘汰军事设备一事。

我们不能对公诉机关先用模糊语进行引导嫌疑人讲话，然后采用明示的方法，求全责备。这样做就像售货员的工作一样，卖方只是热情地介绍买方所欲购买商品的种种特性，然后才向顾客推销产品。（Shuy 1994）而公诉机关在调查本案时进行卓有成效的情报分析，以防造成时间、资金和嫌疑人情感的浪费。使用模糊语言不失为一种有效的办法，而模糊语言一旦变成了明示语言，起诉的案件也就结束了。

美国联邦调查局之类的执法机关对特工人员有专门规定，其中一条就是针对特工人员使用违法手段诱供的。在上述 Smith 一案中，其违法特征最终水落石出，嫌疑人得到昭雪。而模糊性问题远远没有得到根除。上述案例的嫌疑人所乐意干的事，远远不是特工人员所期望的结果。在这种情况下，公诉机关常常可以从话语环境中的词汇、短语或句子里发现问题。这些词句表面上涉及犯罪，但只从整体语境考察，其含义往往会出乎公诉机关所料。这样的情况在司法实践中屡见不鲜。

3.2.3.3　语篇分析与文体学

"文体分析是考察某一位作者或作者群所使用语言的独特性。"文体分析者对现有的书面和口头材料进行评价，对已知文本与未知文本进行对比分析研究。对比分析写作者和说话人在写作和讲话时的语言以及无意识或很少意识到的语言习惯。（Dehorh Schiffrin 451）例如，写作者在写作过程中对词汇的选择有很高自觉性。但在语法选择、拼写或标点符号的运用上却是无意识的行为。"语篇风格是大多数讲话人和作者很少意识到或难以控制的问题。"（Dehorh Schiffrin 451）

不是说词汇和标点符号的使用习惯对作者不重要。美国 Vassar 大学的 Donald Foster 教授认为："小说《本色》的匿名作者用词习惯表明，作者使用的形容词，大都源于动词词根，且好用 mode，style 等名词，大量使用破折号。"

Genald Mcnamin 的著作《法律文体学》较为全面，对法律文体这一涉及面较广的领域的分析作出了贡献。该书是目前法律文体分析的力作。法律文体学兴起的动力主要来源于对语言形式的研究，如词汇，语法、句法、标点符号、词语或文本的长度，不注重对语篇风格的分析。语篇风格的分析主要用于非法律文本，尤其是书面文本，用于法律语篇分析是最近几年才开始的，且发展迅速，方兴未艾。

4. 法学语篇分析对我国法学语言研究的影响

法学语言（language of the law）指一切有关阐述和解释法律问题所使用的语言，包括立法语言、司法语言、法律科学语言、法律普及语言、法制文学语言、法制新闻语言、法学古文等一切有关法律使用中的日常用语、专业术语。法律语言与其他社会方言一样，是人们根据文化、环境和交际目的、对象等语用因素长期使用中形成的一种具有特殊用途和自身规律的语言功能变体。"广义的法律语言学是 90 年代随着有关法律语言学文章和法庭语言的书籍的陆续面世而兴起的学科"、（Gibbons 1994；Levi and Walker 1990；Rieber & Stewart 1990）"法庭双语以及航空器通讯中断等问题而兴起的研究领域。"（Deborah Schiffrin 2003）法律语篇在分析和研究法学语言、法庭审判、案件调查、证人证言分析等方面起着至关重要的作用。

国外法律语言研究起初从词句开始，逐步转向篇章研究，如 Gerald R. Mcmenamin 的 *Forensic Linguistics：Advances in Forensic Stylistics*；*John Gibbons* 的 *Language and the Law* 和 *Forensic Linguistics：An Introduction to Language in the Justice System*；Peter. Goodrich 的 Legal Discourse，John Olsson 的 Forensic Linguistics，John. M Conley 的 *Just Words—Law，Language and Power*，Frederick Bowers 的 *Liguistic Aspects of Legislative Expression* 等，都专门研究了法律语篇问题。尤其是 Peter. Goodrich 的专著 Legal discourse，从语用、语义、衔接、连贯、语篇内（legalintradiscourse）、语篇外（legal interdiscourse）和社会语境（law as social discourse）等方面，详细地研究了法学语篇的构成、特点、阐释和理解等一系列有关问题。除此之外，我们还可以在英国、美国、加拿大等知名法学杂志里阅读到许多由法学家们撰写的有关法学语言的长篇专论文章，其中包括法学语篇、法学语义、法学语用、法学语言哲学以及法学翻译等。这是国内少有的现象，也是我们的法学家和语言学家应该借鉴和关注的问题。

我国学者研究法律语言始于 20 世纪 70 代年末，虽起步较晚，但研究的深度与广度都直追国外法律语言的研究进程。如宁致远、刘永章的《法律文书的语言运用》、许秋荣等人的《法律语言修辞》、刘愫贞主编的《法律语言：立法与司法的艺术》、潘庆云的《法律语言艺术》、余致纯主编的《法律语言学》、王洁主编的《法律语言学教程》、华尔赓等人的《法律语言概念》、陈炯的《法律语言学概述》、李振宇的《法律语言学初探》、姜剑云的《法律语言与言语研究》、彭京宜主编的《法律语用教程》等等，一大批具有较高理论水平和科学体系的专著、教材出版面世。由于法律语言貌似简单而实则复杂多变的魅力又吸引了不少法学家的参与，更使我国法律语言的研究直接走上独立学科的轨道。诸如吴大英、任允正的《比较立法学》、吴大英、刘瀚等人的《中国社会主义立法问题》、高铭暄的《中华人民共和国刑法孕育与诞生的过程》、谷安梁主编的《立法学》等著作中，都用了一定的篇幅论述了法律语言的问题。（刘愫贞 2005）另外还有潘庆云的《跨世纪的中国法律语言》（1997）和《中国法律语言鉴蘅》（2004）、王道森的《法律语言运用学》（2004），吴伟平的《语言与法律—司法领域的语言学研究》（2002），刘红婴的《法律语言学》（2003）和《语言法导论》（2006）以及王洁、苏金智等主编的《法律·语言·语言的多样性》（2006）等，这些法律语言专著，绝大多数都是从语言识别、文体风格、词语特点、修辞理据、句法特征等微观层面研究法律语言，涉及语篇层面的不多。

曼斯斐尔德曾经说"世界上的大多数纠纷都是由语言所引起的。"研究法学语言的最终目的是为了更好的理解法律以及法律科学研究文本。由于我国社会历史背景、法制体系、法律文化等方面的差异，"法律语言研究的方方面面，与我国法律活动方式的密切联系，受到我国法律制度、法律思维、法律习惯和法律认知的影响，"（李振宇 2006：219）法学语言研究的方法、研究内容、研究范畴、研究手段以及研究水平都有所不同。阅读国内外法律（学）语言专著和和专题研究文章之后，我们对法律（学）语言研究发展脉络的总体印象是：词汇→句法→语篇。

也许是受国外法律（学）语言研究转向的的影响，最近几年出版的几部有关法律（学）语言研究的视野大为拓宽，突破了以往的法律语言研究范围，如杜金榜的《法律语言学》（2004）、刘蔚铭的《法律语言学研究》（2003）、以及李振宇的《法律语言学新说》（2006）等专著，他们在前人研究的基础上，将法律翻译、跨文化法律交流、东西方法律语言对比以及法律语篇（话语）等前沿问题，都纳入法律语言的研究视野。不仅如此，近年来，国内知名的语言学、翻译学、法学刊物也陆续刊登法律语篇（话语）的文章，使我国的法律语言研究走一个向新高潮。

尽管我国的法学语言总的研究方法和趋向和国外大致同步，但就法律语篇研究在司法领域的具体运用而言，国外所取得的成果远远早超过国内。

参考文献

[1] Beaugrande，R. de & W. Dressler. *Introduction to Text Linguistics*[M]. London：Longman，1981.

[2] Halliday，M. A. K. and Hasan，R. *Cohesion in English*[M]. London and New-

york: Longman, 1976.

[3] R. de Beaugrande. *Linguistic Theory: The Discourse of Fundamental Works* [M]. Longman Group UK limited, 1991.

[4] Peter Goodrich. *Legal Discourse*[M]. The Macmillan Press LDT,1987.

[5] Helle Porsdam. *Legally Speaking: Contemporary American Culture and the Law*[M]. University of Massachusetts Press Amherst, 1999.

[6] Janet Cotterill. *Language in the Legal Process*[M]. Palgrave Macmillan, 2002.

[7] Judith N. levi and Anne Graffam Walker. *Language in the Judicial Process*. Plenum Press,New York and London, 1990.

[8] Gerald R. Mcmenamin. *Forensic Linguistics: Advances in Forensic Stylistics*. CRC Press LLC, 2002.

[9] Peter M. Tierama. *Legal Language*. The University of Chicago Press. Chicago and London, 1999.

[10] Marshall Morris. *Translation and the Law*[J]. *American Translators Association Scholarly Monograph Series(Volume VIII)*. John Benjamins Publishing Company, 1995.

[11] John Gibbons. *Language and the Law* [M]. Longman. London and New York, 1994.

[12] John Gibbons. *Forensic Linguistics: An Introduction to Language in the Justice System*[M]. Blackwell Publishing, 2003.

[13] David Mellinkoff. *The Language of the Law*[M]. Little, Brown and Company. Boston and Toronto, 1963.

[14] Roger Shuy. *Linguistic Battle in Trademark Disputes*[M]. Palgrave Macmillan, 2002.

[15] Roger W. Shuy. *Language Crimes: The Use and Abuse of Language Evidence in the Courtroom*. Blackwell, 1993.

[16] Alfred Phillips. *Lawyers'Language: How and Why Legal Language is Different*[M]. Routledge, 2003.

[17] Susan Berk-Seligson. *The Bilingual Courtroom: Court Interpreters in the Judicial Process*[M]. The University of Chicago Press, 1990.

[18] Enrique Alcaraz Varo and Brian Hughes. *Legal Translation Explained* [M]. St. Jerome Publishing, 2002.

[19] Lawrence M. Solan. *The Language of Judges*[M]. The University of Chicago Press. Chicago and London, 1993.

[20] William C. Robinson. *Forensic Oratory: A Manual for Advocates*[M]. Fred

B. Rothman & Co. Littleton, Colorado, 1993.

[21] John Olsson. *Forensic Linguistics*：*An Introduction to Language*，*Crime and the Law*[M]. Continuum. London and New York, 2004.

[22] Bryan A. Garner. *The Elements of Legal Style*[M]. Oxford University Press. New York and Oxford, 1991.

[23] 胡壮麟. 语篇的衔接与连贯[M]. 上海：上海外语教育出版社,1994.

[24] 王福祥. 话语语言学概论[M]. 北京：外语教学与研究出版社,1994.

[25] 鲁忠义,彭聃龄. 语篇理解研究[M]. 北京：北京语言文化大学出版社,2003.

[26] 潘文国. 汉英对比纲要[M]. 北京：北京语言文化大学出版社,1997.

[27] 刘蔚铭. 法律语言学研究[M]. 北京：中国经济出版社,2003.

[28] 陆文慧. 法律翻译:从实践出发[M]. 香港：中华书局,2002.

[29] 孙万彪. 英汉法律翻译教程[M]. 上海：上海外语教育出版社,2004.

[30] 张志铭. 法律解释操作分析[M]. 北京：中国政法大学出版社,1998.

[31] 李振宇. 法律语言学初探[M]. 北京：法律出版社,1998.

[32] 姜剑云. 法律语言与言语研究[M]. 北京：群众出版社,1995.

[33] 邱实. 法律语言[M]. 北京：中国展望出版社,1990.

[34] 刘愫贞. 法律语言:立法与司法的艺术[M]. 陕西人民出版社,1990.

[35] 杜金榜. 法律语言学[M]. 上海：上海外语教育出版社,2004.

[36] 潘庆云. 中国法律语言鉴衡[M]. 汉语大词典出版社,2004.

[37] 宁致远. 法制语文[M]. 北京：中国法制出版社,1996.

[38] 刘红婴. 法律语言学[M]. 北京：北京大学出版社,2003.

[39] 吴伟平. 语言与法律:司法领域的语言学研究[M]. 上海：上海外语教育出版社,2002.

[40] 王道森. 法律语言运用学[M]. 北京：中国法制出版社,2003.

[41] 潘庆云. 跨世纪的中国法律语言[M]. 上海：华东理工大学出版社,1997.

[42] 陈炯. 法律语言学概论[M]. 陕西人民教育出版社,1997.

[43] 王洁. 法律语言研究[M]. 广州：广东教育出版社,1999.

[44] 李振宇. 法律语言学新说[M]. 北京：中国检察出版社,2006.

（熊德米,湖南师范大学,西南政法大学）

西方语言学发展轨迹

任何科学的发展都有规律，但不是所有科学发展的轨迹都相同，这是因为各种科学研究都有自己的目标、方法和具体的过程。当今的语言学涵盖了大量的子学科及相关活动，所有这些都以语言学为名致力于各类语言的研究。近来语言学涵义的扩展意味着我们需要聚焦于语言学科的核心及其自 19 世纪起源的"语言的科学"的发展。"语言的科学"至今仍被用来解释现代语言学，尽管语言学家们对此莫衷一是。

1. 语言学的起源

人类的出现意味着语言的产生，但是语言学的出现是后来的事了，尽管语言研究的起源却要追溯至很远的过去。语言书写体系（例如后象形文字）的充分发展不仅需要清楚地知道语言的发展过程，还应了解语言发展过程的重要作用。如此才能使知识得以世代传承，据此可知语言学的研究源于那些出现文字的文明古国——美索不达米亚、北印度、中国、埃及等。而印度作为最早致力于语言学传播的国家之一，导致了公元前第一个千年中潘尼尼的梵文语法的诞生。几乎在同一时期，希腊人在从事他们的语言法典编纂，这一系列的工作以狄俄尼索斯·斯拉克思的《语法科学》为标志达到了高潮。

古代希腊人为历史语言学打下了良好的基础（刘润清，封宗信 2004）。虽然当时的"语法"情况多而复杂，难以尽述，但希腊语法一直是西方学术的基础，直至 18 世纪，出于日益增长的文化普及的需要，在启蒙运动中，教育与宗教相分离，也催生了西方各国自己的语法。拉丁语法创立之初旨在将其作为一门外语教授，因此高度规范。而这种规范的生搬硬套导致了母语教学的过于简单化：以拉丁语为基础的经院语法，这在某种意义上玷污了传统语法作为一个整体的地位及其发展。

19 世纪开始，现代语言学研究有了明确的发展目标。欧洲 19 世纪早期对语言学研究重新定位的原因之一是改进语言教学，同时也是与其他语言学传统恢复联系的原因：尤其是与梵文学者的联系。他们在语言研究方面的客观性和敏锐性符合当时深受自然科学研究方法和步骤影响的学术潮流，例如瑞典植物学家卡尔·里纳俄斯对植物界的分类在 18 世纪产生过巨大影响。地质学作为另一门科学为语言研究提供了合适的模式。事实上，19 世纪严谨的科学研究展现了当时的现实要求及其不切实际的"落叶归根"愿望之间的辩证联系。这种愿望来自美、法科学界及古典传统在艺术和科学之间的分歧。

当时语言科学讲究严谨的研究方法：包括仔细观察、细心收集"事实"、精准记录、客观判断、公示研究结果、积极承担责任等。然而更具意义的是语言研究中坚持了自然科学"普遍法则"的学术理念。随着19世纪20年代早期以来的新兴学科转入对比研究，此类竞争日渐增多，新兴学科在研究语系的过程中使用的音的转换概念以及"语言谱系"等一系列研究都受到了生物学研究的影响，特别是1859年达尔文所著《物种起源》的影响。

因此，19世纪70年代的语言学界十分活跃。一些莱比锡的德国年轻学者质疑当时语言学理论的科学性，认为当时的音变规则，除非没有例外，否则都是不科学的。他们认为语言研究的证据不只是文字材料而应源于口语。这些观点之中充满浪漫主义色彩，得到了费迪南·德·索绪尔的重视。作为当时莱比锡新语法学派活动一名积极的青年学生，他认为，甚至在他死后才出版的《普通语言学教程》一书中也重复写道：语言不应被视为一种自身和谐发展的机制，而是一种语言群体集体心智的产物。

1876年，索绪尔成为了当时最受尊敬的语言学者。1906～1907年，由于其学术背景，他在家乡的日内瓦大学开设了一系列的语言学讲座，他在巴黎担任十年教授之后于1891年回到日内瓦。到1911年他又讲了两门教程。出版的这些讲座将19世纪的"历史语言学和对比语言学"有效地转化为20世纪当代语言学学科。这是索绪尔最后的学术贡献。两年之后他死于癌症，时年56岁，没有留下讲稿或讲课笔记。他在日内瓦的同事和学生共同合作，经过复杂的编辑整理，于1916年在巴黎出版了《教程》一书并使其著作公之于世。这一系列的特殊事件使索绪尔获得了"现代语言学之父"的美誉，当然也是当之无愧的。

2. 现代语言学轨迹

20世纪的西方现代语言学研究可分为两个主要阶段：其一阶段持续至20世纪20年代末或30年代初，其二是1960年后由高等教育的发展所引起的扩展和分化阶段。两阶段之间有一过渡期，对欧洲和美国的语言学研究产生了不同的影响。

2.1　阶段一：现代语言学的开端（1911～1933）

2.1.1　现代语言学的五大原则

现代语言学是由索绪尔在其学术生涯末期建立的。他在开始打破传统模式时不是年幼的顽童，而是资深的政治家，他的伟大之处不仅是他在19世纪取得伟大成就的那种能力，而且是他为未来的研究建立了一门崭新的学科。虽然并非他的每一个观点都很正确，但他经手的语言学研究的确有了极大的突破和发展。

① 语言学是对语言自己的科学研究

强调科学并不新鲜，尽管在不同时期不同语境中有不同的表述方式。而索绪尔观点的重要之处在于对语言本身（philology 从未放弃过与篇章研究的关系）的关注。

② 语言学不具规定性特征

这是语言科学定义的一个明显的开端。或许对于美国语言学来说，由于其更为实用的定位，这更为重要。

③ 口语是研究的基本目标

口语原则在语音学界和语言学界已得到了大力支持，但索绪尔对其重要性的阐述十分明确：现实地看来，文本或许是唯一可获得的材料。

④ 语言学是一门自发的学科

作为一门新学科，语言学需竭力摆脱其他强势学科的影响，例如心理学，哲学及人类学。

⑤ 具体时间点上的共时语言研究优于其历时研究

索绪尔的这些原则对语言学进行了彻底的革命——"这一点是绝对的，没有任何条件可讲"。可以这样说，这是语文学无法越过的界限，也是他的理论之核心，即："语言学家必须首要考虑语言结构的研究，然后再将其余的语言现象与之相联系"。

2.1.2 美国语言学的开端

纯属巧合，语言学在大西洋两岸可以说是同年出现。1911 年，索绪尔在日内瓦讲授了最后的课程系列；而就在同年正式的《美洲印第安语言手册》的第一部分在华盛顿出版。由佛兰斯·博厄斯（1859～1942）所作的前言被认为是美国语言学的里程碑。

与注重理论的欧洲语言学不同，美国语言学首先考虑的是应用。美国印第安语言项目是个大规模的研究，旨在及早涵盖包括即将消亡的大量语种的研究范围，这项研究由自称已有语言科学新知的人类学家牵头。他认为：研究数据和有关结论如果想得到认可，就必须严格遵循正确的步骤去研究。

当时，这类项目成了所有主要语言学家的惯例，它也为区分语言学家与语文学家提供了明确的标准——尽管也有像列昂纳德·布龙菲尔德一样在两方面都精通的大师，但是布龙菲尔德在去德国研究访问之后出版的第一本书中仍显示出对语文学的强烈兴趣，尽管他把自己的学科称为"语言学"，并很容易地就被美国学者们接受了。尽管博厄斯和布龙菲尔德早期著作的发表先于索绪尔，但他们有意追随惠特尼，而且使用的方法与上文所列的五个原则却是一致的。布龙菲尔德在自己论文的引言中所言具有指导意义："我希望此书能让学习哲学、心理学、人种学、语文学及其他相关学科的学生更为公正客观地了解语言的问题。"

　　美国另一位重要的年轻学者是爱德华·萨丕尔，他同博厄斯一样是一位对语言有着强烈兴趣的人类学家。在 1921 年出版的典型散文体的《论语言》一书中，萨丕尔对语言研究的新方法作了扩展性陈述，第一次介绍了如形式语言学行为模式等重要概念，这些概念的影响日渐深远。他也强调了形式与功能的独立性："语言形式只可能当作句型模式来研究，脱离其相关的功能分析。"

　　很快就有了各种研究机构。1924 年 12 月美国语言学协会成立，第二年其机构刊物《语言》面世，在欧洲，索绪尔的追随者于 1926 年建立了布拉格学派，其成员包括了后来在该学科历史上占有一席之地的许多重要人物：例如雅克布逊和特鲁别茨柯依。1928 年，第一届国际语言学代表大会在海牙举行，而第一届国际语音学代表大会于 1932 年在阿姆斯特丹举行。最终随着布龙菲尔德第二部著作《语言论》的问世，语言学的确立已无疑问，尽管说出来有点令人吃惊：在 1924 年成立的美国语言学协会的 264 名发起成员中，只有两人的学术方向与这门学科有着明确的联系。

　　英国的语言学发展当然也不容忽视。几个世纪以来英国人在语言学的两个方面一直都很擅长：语音学和词典编纂，而且两者在 19 世纪末都成绩显赫。举例来说，宣布语音学的科学地位并不难，而且它还具有可观的实用潜力，主要表现在语言教学、医疗或声音记录等新技术方面。词典学受益于 19 世纪对历史的迷恋，这为《牛津英语词典》打下了基础。这些造就了英国的优势地位，正如《美洲印第安语言手册》计划造就了美国的优势地位一样。若语音学从广义上可归于语言学范畴，那么词典学就得再考虑了，因为这本质上是一项语文学的活动。新语言学科的新颖之处在于对方言学的兴趣，在 19 世纪 40 年代前期的《语文学学会议事录》中方言学占了很大的比重。但英国没有像惠特尼一样的人物来引导语文学向现代语言学的转变。在英国，主要的角色都由语音学来扮演，因此主导的担子也就落在了"教会欧洲人语音学"的亨利·斯威特肩上。但他对自己享有盛名的传统语文学研究极力保护。他将语音学的火炬传给了丹尼尔·琼斯，而这门学科早在 1912 年就在伦敦大学成立了专门的院系。至 1921 年设立了系主任一职，琼斯是当之无愧的人选。普通语言学则在 23 年之后才能享受类似的荣誉。"语言学"一词在英国的历史在此篇中是具有指导意义的。斯威特回避了"语言学"一词，而宁愿用他自己创造的"话语文学"，琼斯几乎不需要"语言学"一词，因为他的大多数工作都与语音学数据密切相关，普通"语言学"的问题并未被注意到也不紧迫，尽管他的语言教学同事哈洛德·帕默将其用作东方研究学院教授的课程名称。牛津和剑桥则根本不愿承认"语言学"一词的存在：例如奥格登，大概是牛津剑桥在 1945 年之前最接近语言学家的一位学者，在《意义的意义》一书中只有在翻译其他文字或介绍作过著名补充马林诺夫斯基时才使用"语言学"一词。英国的学者还对美国学者说过"语文学"一词才是正确的称谓，但是惠特尼在美国的早期基础工作已经取得了成果。

2.2 阶段二：过渡时期（1925～1960）

现代语言学研究在欧洲和美国几乎同时出现，而且两者的战后复兴都始于大约 1960 年；但其间的研究在两个大陆上之间却有很大的不同。美国的结构语言学或后来所知的描写语言学的规模在整个战争期间也都有发展，直至 20 世纪 60 年代又有乔姆斯基的"生成语法"占据中心地位。另一方面，索绪尔的语言学理论在一战后的欧洲被理解和吸收之后便再没有什么变化了。

由于停滞，索绪尔的《教程》几乎没有涉及到对特定语言应用的描写，但是创建于 1926 年的布拉格学派部分填补了这段空白。音系学是布拉格学派第一个但并不是唯一的研究重点。对功能主义语言学加以吸收后，布拉格学派很快有了自己的特点，功能主义也是 20 世纪 30 年代末巴黎的马丁内在战时拘禁前和十年美国生活后的标志。从不同的意义上讲，功能是路易斯·叶姆斯列夫于 1943 年在哥本哈根发表的语符学理论的核心，尽管在 1953 年英译本出现之前几乎不为人知。最终，由于马林诺夫斯基做出的贡献，语言学开始小规模地发展。尽管曾简单提到博厄斯和萨丕尔在美国的作用，马林诺夫斯基的研究将这门学科引入了一个截然不同的方向——远离句子和句子成分的结构特性而转向篇章的功能价值以及社会作用。20 世纪 40 年代和 50 年代在伦敦出现了一个新型的语言研究综合模式，即弗斯等人把传统的英语语音学/语系学"微观"研究与马林诺夫斯基的篇章研究传统有机结合以及后来的布拉格学派在马林诺夫斯基人类学框架之内的"情境语境"研究。这种分类或许相当混杂，但在弗斯的学生韩礼德的影响下融成了一个影响强大的模式：语言的社会环境和普遍理论框架内真正形成了一种形式与功能的有效联合。可以说是韩礼德完成了从索绪尔结构主义开始的长期过渡。

美国的语言学研究经历了更多痛苦。经过了战争期间一段长期的发展，结构/描写语言学的所有主要创始人在几年内都去世了。萨丕尔 1939 年 55 岁时死于心脏病；沃尔夫 1941 年死于癌症，年仅 44 岁；博厄斯死于 1942 年；布龙菲尔德 1947 年 60 岁时中风，虽然幸存下来却已不能再从事学术研究。下一代学者由于战争的耽搁不足以继承前人的事业，布龙菲尔德的同事和追随者们并没有预料到领导的重担会落到他们肩上，因此可以理解地退缩了，没有接替布龙菲尔德的使命。在如此环境下，新的主动权从主流被迫转向弱势学科，20 世纪 50 年代美国社会的巨变促成了语言教学和外交工作中的应用语言学。

1950 年，这些滞后的语言学家因接替了布龙菲尔德创始的研究工作而被公认为"后布龙菲尔德"学者，但实际上，他们不是重新思考其研究方法，而是不可避免地拓展了结构分析的领域。在某种程度上，当时最有影响力的哈里斯提出了"转换语法"的观点，从而结束了这个过渡期。到 20 世纪 60 年代，哈里斯的这一观点被他以前的学生乔姆斯基变成了"转换生成语法"，从而再现了战时语言学研究的生机与活力。

2.3　阶段三：语言学的扩展与分化

从大约 1960 年起，欧洲和美国的语言学都受益于战后经济复苏和高等教育的发展。大学里新的院系和新的研究项目提供了好多的职位。在这个活跃时期，这门学科吸引了大批年轻人，包括在美、英等国持有崭新观点的乔姆斯基和韩礼德等学者。

表 1 中只提供了少部分当前标题下的内容，但这并不意味着他们活动不够。正是由于活动太多以至于很少能独树一帜，而且，自 1960 年以来的所有重要著作在语言学书刊中都有讨论。

战前大西洋两岸保持一致的结构主义理论和主题在 20 世纪 60 年代初到 70 年代迅速消失，留下的两种相对的研究方法都来自结构主义"谱系"中不同分支。一种直接传承于乔姆斯基的结构主义，另一种有着较复杂的起源，但无疑最终还是回归至索绪尔。

这两种方法均有着典型的特征。生成主义典型地把数据理想化，并且常用数据来进行影响日益扩大的语言习得研究及其在人脑研究中的作用研究。这里关注的并不是"现实世界"；语言成了认知的王国。然而对许多人来说，这个世界因不断产生新的知识领域而充满魅力。功能主义者则拒绝这种语言理想化：语言位于现实的事件中，以不同方式影响着每个人生活。这对他们最具吸引力，因为他们想要了解、影响和控制语言对日常行为的作用。这是一种高度注重真实语言数据的研究方法，而且近几年来，通过使用计算机扩充了大量的资料并以资料为基础判断语言学普遍化的情况，功能主义者已经能够在一度为生成主义者所垄断的技术手段方面与之一争高低。功能主义者不像他们的生成主义对手那样经常使用"科学的""个体的""认知的"这些词，而是经常使用的是"人类""社会""关系"这类词。即使是在未来，这两方也不可能达成一致；但最终将会出现双方的综合体，因为他们都身处同一现实世界。

两种研究途径的对立不会改变这样的事实：定义现代语言学不仅靠"主流"，而且也要考虑其覆盖面的广度。三个首创于 20 世纪 60 年代的分支理应占据特别显著的地位，但无疑另外还有很多其他分支。

描写主义传统重视语言的多样性，对合理数据认真收集和分类，并将语言置于现实生活中。其主流地位虽在 20 世纪 60 年代失去了但还继续存在。例如在与约瑟夫·格林伯格等学者合作的研究中。这类研究所关注的是，不同的语言之间既有句式的相似之处也有一种形成普遍理论的数据联系；但他们讨论的不是"所有的语言中都有的某种共同特征"，而是其窄于表面现象的变化范围。

美国另一个主要的发展是对生成主义主流的直接挑战。20 世纪 50 年代出现的社会语言学在 60 年代形成了气候。他们从某种程度上以萨丕尔和温瑞哥的理论为基础，但也为现代语言学研究引入了全新的研究领域：例如语言的转变及其过程与人类交际的语言学推理一起成为重要的主题。要确认具体的领导者不太可能，但威廉·拉波夫，约翰·刚柏兹，戴尔·海默斯及约书亚·菲舍曼都是重要贡献者。

如果说社会语言学充实了生成主义，那么 1960 年后语言学研究的心理语言学作为第三个主要发展方向对有关语言学习和习得的理论在功能主义背景下所处的劣势地位给予了补充。然而，这种对称的努力可能受到了误导，因为，心理学（在 19 世纪后期，常被认为是对新学科产生具有巨大威胁）对语言学而言从未有过"中立"态度。它披着行为主义外衣，加强了布龙菲尔德的结构主义，它的认知主义表现成了生成主义的主题：乔姆斯基也因此而至少一次公开表示承认认知心理学的霸主地位。事实上，其支持者都认为现代心理语言学的魅力就在于它与新兴的认知科学紧密相连。

示意图 1 显示了 20 世纪语言学研究的三种主要途径：结构主义，功能主义和生成主义，但并没有显示交叉衔接的例子，也没有包括主流之外的社会语言学或心理语言学等子学科。但是功能主义和生成主义的确都是从结构主义演变过来的。其不同点在于功能主义把语言看成社会结构的成分，而生成主义更多地把语言看成人的生理和心理结构的成分。因此，交叉衔接是隐性的，例子是显性的，交叉状态显示与否就无所谓了。

［示意图 1］(Malmkjær 2004)：

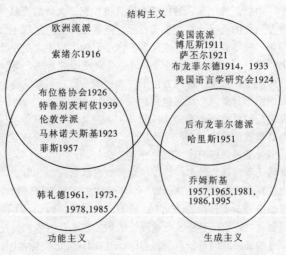

　　根据这个推理，可知未来的语言学研究会越来越具有交叉性，也就是前面的示意图基础上的进一步交叉，具体学科分支得看研究者的心理在自然和社会发展中的演变状态。如下图（示意图 2）的中间和交叉范围，这样将有不少的语言学家的出现：

［示意图 2］

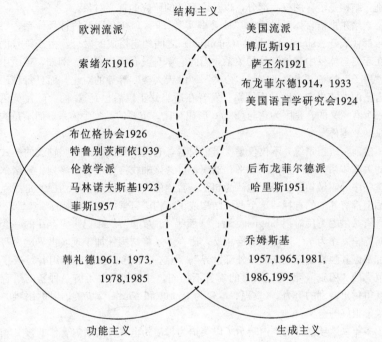

2.3.1　结构主义

　　语言学的结构主义流派可以有两种解读方式：一种是源于索绪尔，另一种源于博厄斯创立的美国结构主义流派。

　　（1）索绪尔模式

　　在他的《普通语言学教程》中，索绪尔恰当地把语言比作国际象棋，指出各"棋子"的设计与它们的名字在结构上是不相关的：它们可以采用参与双方一致认可的任何形式，只要每方都以分成相对照的六类的十六枚棋子开局，且各类中的棋子数目正确。这样比赛就可以按照棋手一致认同的规则进行。这种类比说明了共同构成一盘"象棋""比赛"的表面现象及比赛进行的基本规则之间的差异。或许索绪尔想指出的最重要的一点是系统中各有关成分是根据它在系统中不同的位置来定义的：牵发而动全身，例如拿走象会破坏"象棋"，但如果这种缺少象的比赛规则被参赛选手一致接受，那么一种新的游戏或许会产生。同样，语言是一套范畴任意的规则系统，语言的运作遵循了某种约定俗成的类似于全社会都把玫瑰一致叫做"玫瑰"的"社会合同"。

象棋的类比有利于理解为什么索绪尔关于语言理论的第一步是引出言语（或所运用的语言）（parole）的具体实例与基本的语言或语言体系（langue）之间的区别：结构是语言的核心部分，也是语言学的研究的首要对象。

索绪尔把语言体系描述为"社会事实"，即一套社会认可的符号体系，每个符号都代表音（signifier）与义（signified）之间约定俗成的融合。由于符号的意义在于它与体系中其他符号的关系，因此它本身没有任何意义。例如，英语中能指"房子"的意义来自于它与"公寓"、"摩天大楼"等等的对比，而且每种语言用自己的方式决定这种对比体系。发音在适当修正以后也是这样：/p/在英语中是一个有意义的音是因为它与/b/ /t/形成对比。重要的是整个体系，而不是构成体系的"零件"。

然而，语言系统并不仅仅是大量的符号，它是一套按两条对照轴线的模式排列的关系体系。第一条是"水平"轴线，沿着该轴线符号组合成序列。索绪尔不把这些序号叫做句子，因为他认为句子是言语的实例。而且，序列中的每一点在纵轴上都有其他的选择。这个两维结构成了结构语言学的核心的特征。

索绪尔竭力反对把language语言（那些"现实世界"中已事先存在的一套套范畴标记）作为学术用语；恰恰相反，语言体系将结构施加于现实世界，而每种语言都以其独特的方式来"看外部世界"。但这并不意味着语言使用者是成了语言范畴的"囚犯"，而是说语言的确各不相同，并且如果要了解一种新的语言范畴就得付出特别的努力。《教程》本身为langue和parole译成英语时的困难方面提供了很好的范例。

多年来这项翻译的空白暗示了以英语为母语的世界对索绪尔著作的接受相当缓慢，尽管布龙菲尔德本人作为美国的早期书评作者，也承认索绪尔"为我们人类的语言科学提供了理论基础"；但他也指出他与索绪尔的"语言分析不是把词语而是把句子作为基础"的观点有所不同。这后来成为索绪尔语言学派与包括乔姆斯基在内的美国语言学界的主要区别。

（2）美国结构主义

弗朗兹·博厄斯在为《美洲印第安语言手册》作序时提出其目标是开始一项尽可能屏弃歧视与偏见的科学研究并致力于对手头实际工作的客观而现实的研究方法。

作为人类学家，博厄斯首先提出对语言、种族和文化的关联不要抱有过于单纯的想法，而应在建立联系之前先对它们进行独立研究；接着他转向语言及结构主义中第一个最具标志性的主题：尊重数据，让数据为自己辩护。他在抨击当时

"原始种族发音不准确"的偏见时指出：听话人是在把自己的语音系统强加于人后再去抱怨听不懂；语言学的首要任务是基于"每种语言都有自己确定而有限的音群"的原则去客观而准确地描写语音。这一点后来便成了"音位原则"。其基本原则包括：

① 所有的语言都是不同的："在讨论不同语言的特征时就会发现不同的基本范畴"。

② "每种语言都有合适的定位"不要将先入为主的范畴强加给数据——包括源于其他印第安语种的范畴。

③ 句子是语言的基本单位："既然所有的言语活动都旨在服务于思想交流，句子就成了思想表达的自然语言单位"。

美国结构主义的以数据为先的实证主义规则早已存在，但后来的布龙菲尔德在一段著名的结构主义名言中又提到了"语言研究中唯一有效的结论来自归纳。"

萨丕尔的《语言论》一书中提到了另一重要举措：书中第一次用结构术语讨论问题，也引进了形式句型的概念，并在后来的著作中进一步阐述了这个概念。

萨丕尔对语言、文化及社会生活完全综合的研究方法后来被本杰明·李·沃尔夫在其"萨丕尔—沃尔夫假说"中得到修正。根据这一假说，人脑摆脱不了语言系统的认知约束，但也有相对缓和或许更令人信服的说法。这个观点真正需要的是一个长期的研究计划，但萨丕尔和沃尔夫两人的早逝给后人留下了太多的任务。

最后，布龙菲尔德的《语言论》到来了，很有可能是这一时期最为经典的著作，然而却因主题不一而难以评价。正如马修斯所说："布龙菲尔德的《语言论》令人叹为观止的原因之一在于其学科中众多的既定智慧与众多的崭新知识达到了和谐统一。"

这本语言学书跑遍了整个美国，标志着一个重要的分水岭：如果没有《语言论》，美洲印第安语项目的完成定会使语言学吸收到传统的学术界；而《语言论》的出现使得这门学科已经赢得了其该有的独立地位。

《语言论》绝不是一本描写主义手册，它对整个传统的和现代的语言学领域的描述极为广博、详细，但它现在更为人所知的是后来的反对者所批判的而不是它刚面世时试图想解决的，尤为明显的是意义研究方面。众所周知，布龙菲尔德接受行为主义的观点，包括科学调查需要明显可见的证据等原则。这使他着手于意义的情景理论，他以一则关于"杰克和吉尔"的趣闻为例说明了这个理论。简要地说，吉尔对杰克说了之后杰克从树上摘了一个苹果给吉尔。很长一段时期内，研究意义的这种方法对外语教学产生了极大的影响。但它没对语言学理论做出什么重大贡献，甚至在巧妙处理后的杰克和吉尔的故事中也不知道吉尔到底说了些什么，尽管这个故事将情景研究法解释得很清楚。布龙菲尔德对科学的连贯性需求使他进入了智力的困境，因此他尝试不同的办法。这一次他主张得到意义的科学定义的唯一方式就是要拥有相关的科学知识（例如盐的定义必须与化学有关）。最终，他放弃了，说道："任何话语都可以用词汇和语法的形式得到充分描述；我们唯一必须记住的是意义的界定无法用上科学的思维办法"。不幸的是，这种缺陷的长期影响使得他的追随者们对此感到过敏，以致促成了一种迷信：意义必须脱离语言学的科学常规。

有趣的是，布龙菲尔德如果没有在 1949 年仓促去世，他是否会修正其意义理论的机械观？（当然不是不可能，他在过去就改变过主意；）然而，他的继承者实际上更加坚定地努力去拓深描写主义语言学的实际解析步骤。布龙菲尔德的学说强调形式特征和机械技巧的重要性，其主要产物就是"分布分析"方法。这种方法禁止使用意义和"混合层次分析"，只准通过在所有可能的结构环境中利用替换等手段去系统地测试数据来建立范畴体系。这种"自下而上"的认识方法有它自己的长处，但最终将寸步难行。以这种方式决不会"发现"更高层次的语法单位，正如战后的乔姆斯基等人所批评地一样。

（3）生成主义

生成主义与乔姆斯基联系密切，所以经常被说成"乔姆斯基革命"。然而，正如里昂和其他一些人所强调的，划清转换生成语法与所谓"生成公司"的更广义的理念之间的界限是非常重要的，然而，接受前者并不意味着一定要服从于后者。

转换语法最早出现于 20 世纪 50 年代初"后布龙菲尔德学派"的领导人物哈里斯的著作中。哈里斯是乔姆斯基在宾西法尼亚大学时的导师。转换语法也是哈里斯博士论文"转换分析"的主攻方向，其基本概念就是句子类型，例如主动句和被动句之间的系统相联。这一点与传统语法是相同的，但由于意义独立性却为结构主义所摒弃。乔姆斯基根据这些雏形创立了"核心句"理论，这个理论可以解释为一套短语结构规则加一套转换规则来"生成"非核心句。"生成"即提供结构描述。这个模式是他第一本专著《句法结构》的基础。

乔姆斯基再次提出"规则"概念，其争论性是可以预见的。结构主义者在对传统语法的批判中专门使用与数据密切相关的"模式"和"结构"来代替"规则"。"规则"一词会使人想起古老的学院语法，但言语并不具有规定性，例如英语句子由名词短语跟动词短语构成。乔姆斯基的这种形式为 S→NP VP 的规则是在应用过程中受到经验挑战的英语句子结构理论。概括地说，乔姆斯基主张科学的语言学应像其他任何科学一样先从理论开始，他认为结构主义提供的数据处理的程序不可取。这些过程也没有想象的那样实用。他们的最终目标就是通过分析"发现"语言的语法——这个目标被乔姆斯基当作实现不了的梦想而抛弃。乔姆斯基认为语言学理论应当指定更加有限而符合惯例的目标：即在可选描述之间提供选择方式（例如以下的三种分析：the dog/chased the cat 或 the dog chased/the cat 或 the dog/chased/the cat）。

1957 年，乔姆斯基的语言学和心理学观点保持相对独立，但在 1959 年当他对行为主义领导人物、当时心理学家斯金纳的《言语行为》发表了具有对抗性观点后，事态的发展就比较明朗了。乔姆斯基观点的言外之意是对结构语言学的方法与步骤进行进一步批判。正如我们所见，结构语言学的方法与步骤受到了行为主义思维的严重影响，尤其是在意义的关键领域。

1965 年，乔姆斯基在修正他的模式时抛弃了"核心句"概念，而为句法学理论引入了革命性的新概念：深层结构与表层结构的区别，两者通过转换相互联系起来，例如，使主动句与被动句具有相同的深层结构，但不同的转换过程生成了两种不同的表层结构，出版的《句法理论若干问题》作为"标准理论"而为人所知。然而，这种模式在实践中很快就显示出它处理英语以外的语言时的困难和笨拙。对此，乔姆斯基及他的同事在 20 世纪 70 年代做出了修正与充实，创立了"扩充式标准理论"。原来的短语结构规则大部分都被更为灵活的句法方式即"X-阶理论"所替代。深层和表层的区别与转换一起被保留下来，但由于作了重大修改，也有新特征，一切都趋向于更加简明。修正后的模式（称作《管约论》），后来的《原理与参数》于 1981 年问世，给整个"生成公司"提供了新的研究方向。自那时起，不断有精简的改动，直至 20 世纪 90 年代出现的《极简程序》为止。

乔姆斯基的研究一直以来以同一目标为动力：解释人类语言习得。上面提到的很多改动都是专门为了帮助描述语言习得过程，通过提供与语言习得者天生能力相符合的简化的程序。"天赋观念"的再次提出是乔姆斯基影响最深远也是争议最大的观点。其核心概念是人类语言习得不能由社会学习理论解释：太大、太普遍，没有什么解释不了。乔姆斯基认为每个人脑中都存在一种叫做"普遍语法"的东西：一套天赋的界定语言本质及决定习得过程的原则，它具体语言的特征无关。具体语言的习得是通过与具体环境中的数据切触而实现的。

习得过程的产物是一套社会交往、个人思考、表达情绪等活动所需的知识/能力体系/（competence）。乔姆斯基把活动归类于"语言行为"（performance）。"语言能力"与"语言行为"的区别让人联想到索绪尔的"语言系统"（langue）与"语言运用"（parole）的对照，但这两个术语的选择是从心理学的角度，而不是语言学的角度。"语言能力"似乎是"知识"的一个奇怪的同义词，但"语言行为"却是合适的称号，尽管典型地以否定形式描述，由于记忆来源的限制、分心、注意力的转移以及各种障碍对深层语言能力做出真实反映的错误，就像语言对索绪尔一样，语言能力是乔姆斯基语言学理论的终极焦点，他本人对语言能力的解释有一段著名的的话"与之相关的是一个理想化的说话人———听话人，在一个完全同质的言语社团当中，社团中的每个人都能完美地掌握语言并不受语言运用限制的影响。"自 1965 年以来，理想化的语言使用者如何与实际语言习得者之间的交际是乔姆斯基学派研究的核心问题。

　　(4) 功能主义

　　生成主义重新系统地阐述了结构主义，但并没有改变其基本原理，例如句子的向心性。而功能主义对结构主义进行了改进在于恢复了因片面注重语言形式而忽视的另一方面。形式与功能传统上在描述语言及其运用时就不可以分割。形式与范畴的建立相关联，而功能则与它们之间的联系相关联。例如，在猫抓老鼠的英语句子 The cat caught the mouse 中，"猫"和"老鼠"都是名词（词组），但功能却不同："猫"是句子的主语而"老鼠"却是动词的宾语。"功能"（function）可以扩充从而涵盖概念上的区别：猫有生命，可以充当"抓"这个动作的执行者（agent），而老鼠却是"受抓"动作的受事（patient）。

　　然而，功能主义甚至比这范围还要广，它可以说是具有两个源头，都来自欧洲：其一是布拉格学派，包括马泰修斯，雅克布森及克鲁别茨柯依；（其二是由马林诺夫斯基创于 1923 年的"伦敦学派"的语言学家。

　　布拉格学派（1926～1939）的首要目标是探索索绪尔学派的结构主义及为它的拓展提出建议。他们最著名的著作是特鲁别茨柯依的《音位学理论》，一部描述音位的著作，在 1939 年特鲁别茨柯依去世后经雅克布森的大力协助在布拉格出版。继索绪尔之后，特鲁别茨柯依第一个系统地区分了语音学与音位学，将区分置于功能环境中："音位学的必要性在于语言中语音的语言学功能，而语音学关注的是现象，并非功能。"该原则最有名的例子则体现在音位以及音位在区分不同单词的功能上，如英文中的"pin"和"tin"。音位本身作为一种具有区别性特征的系列源于布拉格学派，并在 1942 年被雅克布森介绍到美国。在与莫里森，哈勒以及其他人的合著中，音位的这一特征被灌输其中，如他们合著的作品《语言的基本准则》（1956）。

　　要提的另一方面则是卡尔布勒提出的对文本所采用的功能分析法。他归纳了三个方向：即以关注文本内容的表达能力为中心，外加一对对比性功能，即与说话者/作者相关联的"表达性"功能和与听话者/读者相关的意动功能。布勒的观点开创了该领域研究的先河，其影响波及到后来的雅克布森和韩礼德。谈到对于前者的影响，在 20 世纪 50 年代末举行的文体学的研讨会上，雅克布森所作的贡献便足以说明，使得布勒提出的框架大篇幅地在大会上得以展现。

　　布拉格学派在介于句子成分的微观功能和文本设计的宏观功能之间创建了一个非常重要的研究领域，即后来被人们所熟知的"功能句子观"，该观点用于区分语言单位和文本结构特征之间的系统关系。功能句子观特别关注文本中有连续性的句子在反映信息的发展模式方面是如何构建的，例如，一个句子中的"新信息"（述位）在另一个句子中变成了"已知信息"（主位），并且，每种语言在表明这些关系的过程中都有自己独特的形式。

英国的功能语言学功不可没。英国对于语言的科学研究所做出的主要贡献体现在语音学方向。这一点在 1912 年得到了伦敦大学学院（UCL）的普遍认同。1916 年东方学院（SOS）的成立极大地扩大了语言科学的专门研究，人们期望该学派能秉承美国人为美国印第安语言所做的贡献，为大英帝国的语言发展做出了贡献，从某种程度上将这在过去确属事实。再者，马林诺夫斯基作为来自伦敦经济学院的人类学家，对语言研究颇感兴趣，从而与弗斯建立了学术联系。弗斯自20 世纪 20 年代末便是该学派的一位高级研究员，同时，他是英国的第一位普通语言学教授。

马林诺夫斯基在 Trobriand 岛上所作研究的基础上建立了一种文本类型的功能性语料库，该语库特别关注了学前群体的口语特征。他在这方面所作的主要理论贡献在于他所提出的"语言环境"这个与伦敦语言学紧密相关的理念。他提出，倘若不具备语言环境方面的常识，口语意义的连贯表达是不可能的。在一个描述小舟靠岸的例子中，倘若我们知道在靠岸的浅水中人们会用短桨代替长桨，那么，一个直译为"我们用短桨各就各位划动小舟"的句子只能被理解为"我们快靠岸了"，也就是说：语言环境赋予文本一种意义，如果不存在这种语境，意义也不复存在了。对于马林诺夫斯基作为弗斯学说的推崇者，自然会认为语境意义和语言形式之间相互依赖是至关重要的。

在 1950 年的著作中，弗斯把"语言环境"这个概念拓展成一种模式结构。这正如他本人所说，他从中得到的重要方面便是语境中语言变体的重要性，该概念即后来人们所熟知的"语域"。事实上弗斯研究的中心是对"意义"在其所有表现形式中的研究；但是，直到韩礼德登上研究舞台之后，意义和其语言实现形式之间相互依赖的重要关系才有了系统的基础。

韩礼德对 20 世纪末语言学的贡献尤为巨大，他的著述涵盖整个语言研究领域，从形式句法学到阅读的教学，他在这些著述中所展现出的个人才能以及给读者带来的灵感是该领域研究中前所未有的。因此，要全面地总结他个人所作的贡献是不可能的，除非重点强调一、两个方面。首先，他继承了弗斯的观点，坚持认为语言研究必须是综合的，整体统一的，而不是受"语言系统/言语行为之间的区别"的干涉；相反，语言学研究必须将语言看作"社会进程的一部分"，或者视之为一种"社会符号"，更具体地讲，语言学家必须清系统而楚地陈述人们为了满足其社交需要（interpersonal function）和认知需要（ideational function）而在所支配的语言系统（textual function）内做出选择。这三种功能（metafunctions）提供了基本的理论框架，其关键概念是选择的网络系统。这些特征说明了为什么韩礼德用"系统功能语言学"作为其研究方法的原因。

正如韩礼德在《功能语法导论》中所讲到的一样：他早期的著作集中讨论语

言中意义的重要性，因为他觉得形式句法学研究低估了意义的重要性。但后来他转移了研究的重点，因为他发觉语言在形式上的特征也被忽略了：人们只是盲目地寻求意义上的表达。二者相互依赖，这才是他的著作的基本原理，在这里特别值得一提的是他与哈森合著的《英语中的连贯》，及其对辛克莱，库尔达的话语分析传统的支持。

值得再提出的是在过去约 150 年的时间里有两大宏观主题对语言学的历史发展起到了巨大的作用，这两个方面都离不开对方法论做出重大决策的理论意义。

第一个主题是语言体系与使用中的语言之间的基本区别：索绪尔对"语言（系统）/言语"的区别是最初始的；但是乔姆斯基对"语言能力/语言运用"的对比与其旗鼓相当；而布龙菲尔德的结构主义在寻求"类型"的过程当中心照不宣地注意到了"系统/使用"之间的区别。从表面上看来这是一种处理材料范围的便捷方式，但不久（langue，competence，system 等）这些抽象而理性的同义词被"移"到最重要的位置，从而忽视了它们那些平淡的、日常的"现实世界"所需的对应词。我们可以说，语言是主观和客观互动的最佳产物：如果不是说话者的主观愿望，现存语言中就没有东西会说出来，倘若不是因为人类的需求、爱好和经济发展等各种原因导致的主观愿望，就不会有任何言语产生，也不会有过去产生或习得的任何语言之类的东西。

最后，有必要重述索绪尔提出的语言学研究的基本目标，因为它反映了语言学发展的第二个主题："多元性"与"普遍性"之间的鲜明对照。这一点在 1921年就被萨丕尔认同："语言的诸多特点当中没有哪一种比其普遍性更突出、更有概括性了；而语言几乎令人难以置信的多元化也绝对不比言语的普遍性逊色。"1926 年索绪尔所提出的，尽管从具体细节上可能过时了，但与语言学的主旨是完全一致的。语言学的目标是：① 描述所有已知语言，记录它们的发展史，这就包括追溯各大语系的发展史，并且追溯得越远越好，同时重建各语系的起源语。② 确定各语言中永恒不变的动因，从而构建语言规律来揭示历史已证明的特定语言现象之普遍规律。③ 界定语言学范围从而科学地定义语言学。

尽管如此，洪堡特认为语言学的重要任务是：① 探发人类语言结构的差异，描述这种差异的本质属性。② 从适当的角度出发，并以更简单的方式，对表面看来无穷的多样性加以梳理。③ 寻索这种差异的起源，特别是它对说话者的思维力量、感觉和性情的影响。④ 最后，通过语言来考察人类精神的发展过程，因为在整个人类历史上，语言都深深地卷入了精神的发展，伴随着精神走过一个又一个阶段。

也就是说，语言研究主要在以下四个方面，其一是个体语言的本质特征；其二是所有语言的普遍规律；其三是寻求语言个体与其使用者之间的联系；其四是寻求语言与人性的关系。

基金项目：(1) 全国教育科学十一五规划课题，项目名称：教育语言学学科体系构建研究，课题代码：课题批准号 FAB070441；(2) 湖南省哲学社会科学成果评审委员会项目，项目名称：教育语言学研究，代码：0606037B

参考文献

[1] Bloomfield, L. *An Introduction to the Study of Language* (Amsterdam and Studies in the Theory and History of Linguistic Science, Series II. 3. Classics in Psycholinguistics); facsimile reprint K. Koerner (ed.), introduction by J. F. Kress, Amsterdam and Philadelphia: John Benjamins; 1st edition 1914, London and New York: Bell and Holt, 1983.

[2] Bloomfield, L. Review of Ferdinand de Saussure's *Cours de Linguistique Generale*[J]. *Modern Language Journal*, 1923, (8): 317 - 319.

[3] Bloomfield, L. *Language*[M], New York, Holt. Rinehart and Winston; revised edition 1935, London: George Allen and Unwin, 1935.

[4] Boas. F. *Handbook of American Indian Languages*[M]. Washington, D C: Smithsonian Institution, Bureau of American Ethnology,1911, Bulletin 40.

[5] Chomsky, N. *Syntactic Structures*[M]. The Hague: Mouton, 1957.

[6] Chomsky, N. *Aspects of the Theory of Syntax*[M]. Cambridge, MA: MIT Press, 1965.

[7] Chomsky, N. *Lectures on Government and Binding* [M].Dordrecht: Foris, 1981.

[8] Chomsky, N. *Knowledge of language: Its Nature, Origin and use*[M]. New York: Praeger, 1986.

[9] Chomsky, N. *The Minimalist Program* [M].Cambridge, MA: MIT Press, 1995.

[10] Greenberg, J. H. (ed.) *Universals of Language* [M]. 2nd edition, Cambridge. MA. and London: MIT Press, 1966.

[11] Halliday, M. A. K. Categories of the theory of grammar[J]. *Word*, 1961, (17): 241 - 292.

[12] Halliday, M. A. K. *Explorations in the Functions of Language*[M]. London: Edward Arnold, 1973.

[13] Halliday, M. A. K. *Language as Social Semiotic*[M]. London: Edward Arnold, 1978.

[14] Halliday, M. A. K. *An Introduction to Functional Grammar* [M].London:

Edward Arnold;2nd edition, 1994.

[15] Harris, Z. *Methods in Structural Linguistics*[M]. Chicago：University of Chicago Press, 1951.

[16] Jones, D. The theory of phonemes and its importance in practical linguistics [J]. *in Proceedings of the First International Congress of Phonetic Sciences*. Amsterdam, 1932.

[17] Labov, W. *The Social Stratification of English in New York City*[M]. Washington, DC：Center for Applied Linguistics, and Oxford：Basil Blackwell,1966.

[18] Malmkjær, K. (ed) *The Linguistic Encyclopedia (2nd edition)*[K]. London and New York：Routledge, Taylor and Francis Group, 2004：xxv‑xli.

[19] Malinowski, B. The problem of meaning in primitive languages[J]. supplement to C. K. Ogden and I. A. Richards. *The Meaning of Meaning：A study of the Influence of Language Upon Thought and the Science of Symbolism*, London：Kegan Paul, Trench, Trubner,1923.

[20] Sapir, E. *Language：An Introduction to the Study of Speech*[M]. Oxford：Oxford University Press, 1921.

[21] Saussure, F. de. *Cours de linguistique generale*[M]. Lausanne and Paris：Payot, reprinted 1974 as Course in General Linguistics. Glasgow：Fontana/Collins,1983；Oxford：Duckworth. annotated by R. Harris, 1983.

[22] Trubetzkoy, N. S. *Grundzuge der Phonologie：Travaux du Cercle Linguistique de Prague*[M]. published in English 1969 as Principles of Phonology, trans. C. A. M. Baltaxe. Berkeley and Los Angeles：University of California Press,1969.

[23] Weinreich, U. *Languages in Contact*[M]. The Hague：Mouton；revised edition, 1968.

[24] 刘润清,封宗信. 语言学理论与流派[M]. 南京:南京师范大学出版社,2004：69-93.

[25] 威廉．冯．洪堡特.(姚小平译注)洪堡特语言哲学文集[M]. 长沙:湖南教育出版社,2001:226.

(曾灿涛,湖南第一师范学院;曹志希,中南林业科技大学;

刘伟,山东外国语职业学院;王晓丽,湖南涉外经济学院)

奥斯卡颁奖晚会演讲的文体分析

引言

奥斯卡颁奖晚会的文体特征，笔者曾从音位，词汇，句法层进行分析[1]，本文将从修辞和语篇层对奥斯卡颁奖晚会的文体特征进行进一步分析。文体分析不仅能够使我们深入领会文本的意义，而且可以为我们挖掘文本的美学价值提供比较客观的依据[2]。

1. 修辞特征

奥斯卡演讲中的修辞手法的使用也不同于正式演讲，体现了文体的非正式性。

1.1 排比

排比是最常用的修辞手法之一。它是将相似的结构排列在一起，名词与名词，代词与代词，句子与句子，甚至段落与段落。排比成分形式相似，意义紧密联系，用来表达强烈的情感，增强语势和节奏。

在奥斯卡演讲中，排比是最常用的修辞手法。在宣读候选人的名单时常使用排比。

From the film *Conair*，"How Do I Live" sung By Trisha Yearwood and written by Diane Warren. From the film *Good Will Hunting*，"Miss Misery" sung by Eliot Smith who also wrote the music and lyrics. And from the film *Titanic*，"My Heart Will Go On" sung by Celine Dion and written by James Horner and Will Jennings.

（Madonna Ciccone，第70届奥斯卡颁奖晚会）

获奖者也常用排比来列出自己所要感谢的人。

I would like to thank Emily Watson and Fernanda Montenegro and my friend Kate Blanchett and the greatest one who ever was Meryl Streep.

（Gwyneth Paltrow，第71届奥斯卡颁奖晚会）

上述排比的使用强调了内容的重要性，也更容易吸引观众的注意力。

在奥斯卡演讲中，排比也被用来制造幽默气氛。

And then Tom said to Gwyneth that he loved *Shakespeare in Love* and then Gwyneth said to Tom that she loved *Cast Away*, and then Julia said to Mel that she love *What Women Want*, and Mel said to Julia that he loved *Erin Brockovtch*. And then it was late and they all went home.

这是第 73 届奥斯卡颁奖晚会的主持人在说到作为一个好莱坞演员，他也可以像一般人过日子。在这句话中，演员们在相互吹捧着说喜欢对方拍的影片，并且被主持人说成是"谈论艺术"。当然说话人本意不是如此。在这里，他只是开玩笑，而排比的使用使得幽默气氛更浓。

这些都与排比在正式演讲中的功能不同，在正式演讲中，排比主要用来增强语言的说服力。

1.2 重复

重复也是一种重要的修辞手法，通过句子，词汇或意义的重复来进行强调，增强语势和节奏感。

在奥斯卡演讲中，重复主要出现在获奖者的演讲词中，使用频率仅次于排比。

I would like to thank the Academy from the bottom of my heart. I would like to thank Emily Watson and... I would like to thank Harvey Weinstein and everybody at Miramax films for their undying support of me... I thank you, thank you so much everybody.

(Gwyneth Paltrow, 第 71 届奥斯卡颁奖晚会)

该例中，既使用了间接重复，又使用了直接重复，更能表达说话者的感谢之情，使语句更有力。

在奥斯卡晚会中重复最多的是"Thank you"。

Jack Lemmon, wherever you are, thank you, thank you, thank you... because I am proud of you and I love you and thank you, thank you, thank you.

(Kevin Spacey, 第 72 届奥斯卡颁奖晚会)

由于激动和准备不充分，获奖者好像无法更好地表达心中的感激之情，而只是反复说着"Thank you"。事实上，这句简单的话就足以有效地表达他们的心意了。

1.3 双关，拟人，隐喻和突降

奥斯卡演讲中还使用了其他的修辞手法，它们的使用更说明了其文体的非正式性。

双关巧妙利用英语许多词谐音、多义的特点，在同一句话里同时表达两层不同意思，以造成语言活泼、幽默或嘲讽的修辞效果。在奥斯卡演讲中，演讲者常用这种修辞法来制造幽默的效果。

So I am the last "twentieth century fox".

(Whoopy Goldberg，第 71 届奥斯卡颁奖晚会主持人)

句中，"fox" 有两层意思：第一层是指那些性感有魅力的女性；第二层是指 20 世纪福克斯公司。因此，观众听到这句话立即哄堂大笑。

I am the original sexy beast.

(Whoopy Goldberg，第 74 届奥斯卡颁奖晚会主持人)

这例是名词型隐喻。像这样的句子是不会使用在正式演讲中的，因为它的使用会降低演讲的正式程度。而奥斯卡颁奖晚会的主持人为了活跃气氛，较多地使用了这种幽默的句子。

拟人是将物当作人来描写的修辞手法，以使语言生动。

在奥斯卡演讲中，当颁奖者宣布获奖者时，用的是 "the Oscar goes to " 而不是 "the winner is "，说话者把奥斯卡金像比作人能够走向获奖者，生动而形象。

正式演讲中，层递常用来增强语势和感染力。与此相反，在奥斯卡演讲中突降却被使用。突降指在说话或写作时内容急转直下，突然从庄严崇高降至平庸可笑，藉以取得嘲弄讥讽或幽默滑稽的修辞效果。

And everyone of them is thinking the exact same thought—that we are all gay... You have black people, white people, Asians, Hispanics, Jews, Christians, all working together, all because of a single common love：publicity.

(Steve Martin，第 73 届奥斯卡颁奖晚会主持人)

由以上分析可知，历届奥斯卡主持人常用这四种修辞手法来制造幽默风趣的气氛，从而缓和观众的紧张情绪。

2. 语篇分析

我们主要从照应手段来分析其语篇特征。

谈到照应手段，我们肯定要讨论衔接与连贯。衔接强调形式而连贯强调意义。本文着重分析衔接。语篇衔接可以通过运用各种照应手段实现。英语中有五种主要的照应手段：参照关系，替换关系，省略关系，连接关系和词汇照应[3]。这里我们主要分析省略关系和连接关系。

2.1 省略关系

省略可以加强语言的结构联系，可以使语言多变，不枯燥，简洁，活泼。省略可分为三种：名词性省略，动词性省略，从句省略。

This is the biggest party in Hollywood. Probably the second biggest if you count the Democrats.

·

(Whoopy Goldberg，第 71 届奥斯卡颁奖晚会)

另外两例我们在前面列举过，这里我们再列出来。

The White-Hot Trail of Jaws, I was over in Kentucky. Senior year New Jersey, Apocalypse now. Valley Forge, Pennsylvania, Raging Bull.

Should we celebrate the joy and magic that movies bring? Well, dare I say it? More than ever!

(Tom Cruise，第 74 届奥斯卡颁奖晚会)

省略使句子更简洁，因为省略的句子成份往往是已知信息，省略使我们把注意力放在新信息或更重要的信息上[4]。如果我们把省略恢复成完整的句式，会发现句子变得冗长，乏味。

总之，省略主要用于口语和非正式文体中。因此它的使用使奥斯卡演讲文体趋于非正式化。

2. 2 连接关系

连接关系是通过词或词组来体现句子与句子之间的关系。连接成分的照应作用是间接的，它们本身不能直接影响前一句或下一句的结构〔4〕。

连接成分可分四类：时间顺序，递进，转折和因果。对连接成分的分析将有助于我们分析奥斯卡颁奖晚会演讲的文体特征。首先，连接成分的正式程度不同，一部分多用于口语，一部分多用于书面语。第二，一般说来，在口语中连接成分多放在句首，或者说，一旦出现连接成分，我们就把它听成是句子界限。而在书面语中，连接成分则不局限于句首，常出现在句中。因此，我们可以通过把连接成分放在句中或句末来增加语篇的正式程度。

(1) 时间顺序连接

奥斯卡演讲中表时间的连词是 "then"。

And then last September came an event that would change us.

(Tom Cruise，第 74 届奥斯卡颁奖晚会)

(2) 递进连接

奥斯卡演讲中表递进的连词只有 "and"，使用频率很高，而且常用在句首。

And now here is the hottest working mom in show business, the one, the only Madonna!

(Billy Crystal，第 70 届奥斯卡颁奖晚会)

(3) 转折连接

"but" 是奥斯卡演讲中用来表转折的连词。

But all the Oscars and all of the stars are here tonight and we're ready for our annual celebration.

(第 72 届奥斯卡颁奖晚会主持人)

（4）因果连接

奥斯卡演讲中表因果的连词有 "because"，"so"，且用在句首。

And if ever there was a category where the Oscar goes to someone without there being a winner, it's this one. Because I do not fell like the winner.

（Michael Caine，第 72 届奥斯卡颁奖晚会）

Oscar is 71, honey. So welcome to the early bird special.

（Whoopy Goldberg，第 71 届奥斯卡颁奖晚会）

由上可知，奥斯卡演讲使用的连词多用在句首，而且这些连词词不达意多用于口语等非正式文体中。鞠玉梅曾指出 "and, but, because, so, then" 这五个连词是非正式文体的标志[5]。因此，我们可以更进一步说明奥斯卡演讲的非正式性。

在作者前三篇的分析之上，通过本文以上的分析，我们可以说奥斯卡演讲虽然属于公众演讲，但却是非正式文体，它具有随意性的文体特征。

参考文献

[1] 廖丽琼. The Stylistic Analysis on Phonological Features of Oscar Speeches[J]. 语言与文学研究,2004,(3).

[2] 奥斯卡颁奖晚会演讲的文体分析——词汇特征[J]. 外语教学与翻译,2005,(9).

[3] 奥斯卡颁奖晚会演讲的文体分析——句法特征[J]. 中南林学院学报,2007,(2).

[4] 秦秀白. 英语体裁和文体要略[M]. 上海:上海外语教育出版社,2002.

[5] Halliday, M. A. K & R. Hasan. Cohesion in English[M]. London:Longman,1976

[6] 王佐良,丁往道. 英语文体学引论[M]. 北京:外语教学与研究出版社,2000.

[7] 鞠玉梅. 英语文体学[M]. 青岛:青岛海洋大学出版社,1999.

（廖丽琼,王小宁,中南林业科技大学）

从语篇角度解析电影《天下无贼》台词

1. 引言

语言学家韩礼德，凭借自己对语言的独特见解，在借鉴前人理论成果的基础上发展了功能语言学，历经几个阶段的发展，其语言学理论已经趋于成熟。M. A. K. Halliday，作为系统功能语法的创始人在其书 *An Introduction to Functional Grammar* 一书中明确指出构建功能语法的目的是为语篇分析提供一个理论框架。这个框架可以用来分析英语中任何口头语篇或书面语篇。目前这个框架被广泛而成功地用于分析各种文体，比如新闻语篇、广告语篇、医学语篇等。但运用功能语言学对电影台词进行分析的文章则为数不多。

根据 Halliday（1994）的观点，语言系统中有三个用于表示功能意义的纯理功能，也就是大多数人熟知的人际功能、概念功能和语篇功能。本文从这三个纯理功能的角度尤其是概念功能下的人类活动与自然界的六大过程，对电影《天下无贼》经典台词以及较具代表意义的话语进行语篇分析。

该影片讲述的是一个关于灵魂净化的理想主义故事：小伙子傻根在西北打工五年要回家过年娶媳妇，他带着五年工钱六万元上路，他单纯朴素，相信"天下无贼"，连他内心的喜悦也是如此阳光明媚，他的单纯明亮感动了一对惯盗，为让"天下无贼"成为现实，这段"危险之旅"使盗贼成为英雄，其中也穿插了以黎叔为代表的另一伙贼的故事，十分喜剧，也发人深省。

2. 理论背景及台词分析

2.1　韩礼德的三大纯理功能

三大纯理功能（人际功能，概念功能，语篇功能）是韩礼德系统功能语法的重要组成部分，是进行语篇分析的重要理论依据。下面，本文将分别介绍这三大纯理功能以及这些理论在本片台词中的体现。

2.1.1　概念功能（ideational function）

语言可以用来表现语言使用者对主客观世界的认识和反应，就是概念功能。概念功能又可以分为经验功能（experiential）和逻辑功能（logical）。语言在日常生活中，往往被用于跟别人交谈，也可以用来谈论主客观世界的事务、情态、时间以及对世界的认识，包括情感、信息、思想等。语言的这种功能在语法中称为"经验功能"。在韩礼德的系统功能语法中，经验纯理功能是三大纯理功能中的一个重要的组成部分。"人们可以通过及物性系统把人类的经验功能分为：① 物质（material）过程，② 心理（mental）过程，③ 关系（relational）过程，④ 行为（behavioural）过程，⑤ 言语（verbal）过程，和⑥ 存在（existential）过程。"（胡壮麟，朱永生等 2005）

（1）物质过程（material process）：这个过程表示做某事的过程（Process of doing），至少有一个参与者（动作者）也可能涉及到另外一个参与者（或者目标），还可以涉及到环境成分。

例如：The mayor dissolved the committee.

这个例句中，the mayor 就是 actor，dissolved 就是过程。

（2）心理过程（mental process）：这是表示"感觉"（perception）、"反应"（reaction）、"认知"（cognition）、"情感"（affection）等心理过程的活动。心理过程一般有两个参加者，一个是心理活动的主体即"感觉者"（sensor），另一个是客体即被感知的"现象"（phenomenon）。

例如：I love this cup.

这个句子表示一个心理过程，发生心理变化的是 I；this cup 是现象，被感知的客体。类似于这样表示心理过程的句子在本片台词里体现的非常多：

片段一：

背景：在临上车前，盗贼集团的老二，为了自己能多掌握点权利，批评李冰冰扮演的女贼小叶，不许她去打扰黎叔，其实他的目的在于不让小叶得到黎叔的重用。而小叶则不同意他的说法，因此起了一点小争执，此刻的黎叔按捺不住发话了：

黎叔：说了多少回了，要团结，这次出来一是锻炼队伍，二是考察形势，在这里我特别要表扬两个同志，小叶和四眼。他们不仅超越了自己，也超越了前辈。希望你们在今后的工作中百尺竿头，更上一步！

Gee（2000）在其书 *An Introduction to Discourse Analysis：Theory and Method* 中指出："话语分析有必要研究人们如何在具体语境中使用语言来进行社会活动，建立社会身份。"黎叔的这段话，貌似冠冕堂皇，但是里面的内涵很有寓意。黎叔是个老手，大家之所以怕他，就是因为他的老奸巨猾，老谋深算。他的话是话中有话。他的话也反应了他的心理过程，其实是将自己的态度或者命令传达下去。

片段二：

背景：刘德华扮演的王薄试图打探傻根是否真傻决定去试探一下。

下面看一下他们在那个场景中的对话：

傻根：大哥，你怎么了，大哥。你为什么事这么伤心呢？你说话呀，你到底怎么了？你有啥难事你跟我说啊！（急得跺脚）怎么了，大哥？

王薄：你大姐她是……大好人是吧？（流眼泪）

傻根：嗯。

王薄：她一天都高高兴兴的是吧？

傻根：啊。（马上要哭了！）

王薄：可是她不知道……她活不了几天了……（泣不成声）

傻根：大姐得的什么病啊？怎么不给她治啊？

王薄：（叹一口气）她得了绝症！

傻根：绝……绝症是什么病啊？（开始流泪）

王薄：就是你眼看着她咽气……没办法呀！（河南话）

傻根：没办法……就不管啦？

王薄：我这次就是要带她去北京治病，可是，可是我钱不够……

傻根：那得需要多少钱呀？（泣不成声）

王薄：很多……我一辈子也赚不了那么多钱……是你大哥没用，我想把自己给卖了……（拍傻根肩膀）我告诉你，不可以给她知道，你要答应我，让她开开心心的，能过几天就几天，你懂吗？嗯？男子汉不能哭！

以上的对话中，当傻根得知自己的好姐姐得了绝症而且无法治愈的时候，心理很着急，他的话语完全体现了他的内心世界。比如"没办法……就不管啦？"他的言外之意就是说没有办法也得想办法啊，怎么能不管她呢？他们的对话，完全显示了傻根心理的矛盾情绪。一方面自己辛辛苦苦工作五年赚到的六万块，等着回家娶媳妇，还有很多梦想需要这六万块去实现，而另一方面又被王薄编的悲惨故事而感动，心理又有个声音在告诉他，要把钱拿出来给王丽治病，因为王丽是对他很好的干姐姐。这样，王薄就可以继续下一步的行骗活动了，因为他已经掌握了善良的傻根的内心真实想法。果然，没多久善良的傻根就把王薄拉到车厢外，二人展开了以下对话：

傻根：大哥，这五千块钱你拿去给俺大姐治病。

（王双手举起来，表示不能接受，然后双手扶住傻根肩膀）

王薄：你干什么？你不要娶媳妇了？

傻根：俺算了算，盖房子要三万，买两头牲口套上一架车要一万，剩下一万办酒席，买个电视机，还有床上铺的盖的。

王薄：（惊讶的放下双手）"不是都没了？"

傻根：俺寻思着，电视机俺先不买了。

（王薄做出激动状，双手握住傻根的手及其手里的钱）

王薄：你的心大哥心领了，你的钱大哥不能要。（边说边往怀里揣钱）

傻根：大哥你不要说了，是俺跟大姐有缘。

（王薄转头）

王薄：不要，不要，不要……

（傻根硬塞给他）

傻根：这五千块钱，你一定拿上，不要嫌少。

这段对话算是正与邪之间的经典对白了，因为面对傻根这么单纯又善良的人，任何一个有良心的人都会于心不忍，都无法再下手欺骗。但是王薄这个内心比较复杂的人物，在此时此刻还没有打算改邪归正。他们的对话不时有喜剧成分在里面，在加上二位的演技高超，虽然二位人物都掉眼泪了，观众会忍俊不禁。然而笑后又不免被傻根的纯朴感动，同时也感觉到傻根几乎与世隔绝的心理状态值得观众为他捏把汗。

（3）关系过程（relational process）指的是一个物体、人、物、情形、事件等，与另一个处于何种关系的过程，或者指一个物体的性质，特征，情形等。关系过程分为两类，即"修饰型"（attributive）关系过程和认同型（identifying）关系过程。修饰关系型中的两个参与者分别是"载体"（carrier）和"属性"（attribute），认同型的两个参与者分别是"被认同者"（identified）和"认同者"（identifier）。

片段一：

背景：刚上火车的时候，黎叔假装是个瘸腿花眼的老人家，故意接近傻根想去偷了他身上的六万块。但是老套的王薄立马把他阻止了，然后硬生生的把他拖到了车厢外，二人展开下面的对话：

王薄：你演的还挺像的，我告诉你，我们都是一样的，都是狼。那只羊我吃定了。

黎叔：你说什么，我不明白？

王薄：别骗我了，你演的还挺像的。（转身走，并模仿黎叔刚才瘸腿走路的样子）怎么瘸来着？这样？……这样？

黎叔：（看着王薄的模仿加以评价道）：恩，恩，恩腿再拖点地。

上面的对话中，王薄的一句话挑明了他跟黎叔的关系"我们都是一样的，都是狼"，这句话属于上述理论中的修饰型的，"我们"是载体，"是"是过程，"狼"是属性。

经典之处在于黎叔的最后一句话"腿再拖点地"，这句"指导性"的话实际上就等于承认了自己是装出来的，也是对王薄挑明了身份，在这里导演安排双方都挑明了身份，为下面的明争暗斗做了很好的铺垫。

片段二：贼团老二在卧铺车厢内劝黎叔下令去偷了傻根的钱，而黎叔在跟王薄一轮回的较量后发现王薄和王丽并不是简单人物，就满心城府的说：

黎叔：(傻根) 闻着是肉味，吃到嘴里就是毒药！传我的话下去："这趟车，不打猎。"

老二：现在是一个没有心眼的羊，身边趴着两个有贼心的狼。

黎叔的话体现了认同型的关系过程。将傻根的钱定义为"毒药"，老二的话则将傻根定义为"没心眼的羊"；将王薄二人视为"有贼心的狼"。

(4) 行为过程 (relational process) 指的是诸如呼吸，咳嗽，叹息，做梦，哭等生理活动过程。这个过程一般只有一个参与者，即"行为者" (behaver) 而且行为者一般是人。

(5) 言语过程 (verbal process) 指人们通过讲话进行交流的过程。它涉及的参与者是"讲话人" (sayer)，"听话人" (receiver) 和讲话内容。

例如，He told me that he loves me. 这个句子就是一个言语过程。其中，he 是讲话人 me 是听话人，that he loves me 是讲话内容。

片断一：傻根被王薄骗到手五千块的时候，被王丽发现，二人展开下列对话：

王丽：你搞什么鬼啊？这孩子刚才还好好的。

(王薄掏出钱)

王薄：可不是我偷的，是你那傻弟弟硬要塞给我的！

王丽：他为什么要给你钱？

王薄：没说什么，我说你得了绝症。

王丽：(发怒) 太缺德了你！

王薄：你不要以为我骗他五千块啊，我告诉你，我就是想试试看他是真傻还是假傻，看来他真是傻。

王丽：那我也实话告诉你：打从我第一眼看到傻根，我就喜欢这傻弟弟，他可不是一凡人。(走远，然后转身对正在数钱的王薄说) 我再告诉你，这弟弟我是认下了。这是缘分，谁要想动他就得先过我这关！

在这段对话中，就体现了言语过程，"我告诉你"中，"我"是讲话人，"你"就是听话人．后面的都是讲话内容！

(6) 存在过程 (existential process) 指的是某物或者某人的存在情况。这个过程只涉及一个参与者，即"存在物" (existent)。

例如：There is a little boy in the office. (a little boy 是存在物 in the office 是环境成分)

片段：傻根的钱差点被贼团老二得手，幸好得王薄所救，被他救回来之后傻根一点察觉都没有，还乐滋滋的问："大哥，大姐，你们饿了吧？俺包里有俺老乡给俺煮的鸡蛋。"傻根的这句话中"鸡蛋"是"存在物"，这句话虽然简短，但是是存在过程的体现。

2. 1. 2　人际功能（interpersonal function）

人际功能包括：语气（mood）系统，情态（modality）系统，基调（key）系统。语言的人际功能是指讲话者作为参与者的"意义潜势"，是语言的参与功能。人们在日常生活中通过语言来建立和保持社会关系；在实际交往中人们不断交换交际角色，但是，无论角色怎么样交换，主要的交际角色只有两个，即"给"（Giving），和"需求"（Demanding）。Halliday（2000）认为人们在日常交际中所交换的既可以是信息（information）也可以是货物和劳务（goods and service）人们可以通过语言，比如使用陈述句来给予信息，也可以使用语言，比如疑问句，包括一般疑问句和特殊疑问句，来表示对信息的需求。如果我们把言语角色和两种交换物组合起来，便构成了"提供"（offer），"陈述"（statement），"命令"（command），"提问"（question）这四个言语功能通过语法上的语气来体现。例如陈述句（declarative clause）通常用来表示陈述，疑问句（interrogative clause）通常用来提问，而祈使句（imperative clause）则用来表示命令。

语气和情态是人际功能的重要组成部分。从语法的角度看，语气由"主语"（subject）和"限定成分"（finite element）构成。它们的出现顺序决定对语气的选择。但是有些小句的语气部分还含有情态状语（modal adjunct）。

人际功能在本片体现之处很多，因为只有通过这些人际功能才能将这些本不相干的人联系起来，建立起各自的关系，然后开展故事。

片断一：

背景：刘若英扮演的王丽在跟刘德华扮演的王薄吵架之后，被抛弃在人烟稀少的砂土路上，恰巧，傻根以及同村来的大叔们骑车路过此，好心的傻根停下来给王丽提供水喝，然后还载她一程，二人展开了下面的对话：

王丽：喂，你叫什么名字？

傻根：俺没大名，村里人都叫俺傻根。

王丽：你不是本地人啊？

傻根：俺是河北的，来这修庙的。

王丽：那你可积了大德了啊！

傻根：俺是个孤儿，打记事来就跟着村里的大人修庙讨生活，修庙是俺村祖上传下来的手艺。

以上的对话，虽然王丽没有将自己的身份和家世告诉傻根，但是傻根却提供了一些关于自己身份的信息"information"，每个句子都是陈述句，回答简单利落，语气也只是陈述语气没有夹杂任何感情色彩，只是在向一个陌生人提供自己的情况。

看下面一段对话：

片段二：

背景：傻根要会计把他五年修庙的钱提出来带回家盖房子娶媳妇，会计和傻根的一些大叔劝他最好把钱邮寄回家，免得被偷，而傻根却不肯。

大叔 A：傻根，过来，钱给你取回来了。

（傻根端着碗走过去）

大叔 A：傻根，你看，六万吧？让会计给你寄回去吧。

会计：我跟你说，这寄回去了，六万块就变成五万九千四了。得交邮费。

傻根：六万块钱……，六万块钱就交六百块的邮费啊？

会计：国家规定的！

傻根：六百块钱在俺家都能买头驴了。

大叔 A：省六百，你丢六万？（对会计）还是给他寄回去。

大叔 B：这贼可多着呢！

会计：再给你偷了！

大叔 B：别说偷，给你抢咯！

傻根：哪有这么多贼？

大叔 A：听叔一句话，还是让会计给你寄回去。

傻根：六万块钱，还没一块砖重呢，俺还带不回去它？

大叔 A：（对傻根）……还犟的很呢！

以上的对话中，各人物都在交换信息。最典型的是会计在跟傻根解释，邮寄六万要交六百的邮费是国家规定的。大叔 A 对会计说"还是给他寄回去"这是一句祈使句，表示命令。他毕竟是村子里这群人的带头人，而傻根的那句话"六百快钱在俺家都能买头驴了"则更直白的表达了他心里的真实想法，他很珍惜这六百块钱，并将其以信息的形式传递给了面前的几位大叔。

2.1.3 语篇功能（textual function）

主位—述位结构（Theme-Rheme），信息结构（information）和语篇衔接（cohesion）三个部分构成了语言的语篇功能。Halliday（2000）认为，主位是信息的起始点，是小句的开始点；述位是围绕主位所发展的话语，往往是话语的核心内容。作为一个信息结构，一个小句可以分为主位（Theme）和述位（Rheme），并且依照顺序排列—主位总是置于小句的开头。

根据 Halliday（2002）的观点，主位有标记性（markedness）与无标记性（unmarkedness）之分。在陈述句中，主语充当主位是无标记的，其他成分充当主位是有标记的。在 WH-疑问句中，WH-成分充当主位是无标记的，其他成分充当主位则是有标记的。在 yes/no 疑问句中，操作词和主语构成的主位是无标记的。在祈使句中，通常是句首的动词充当主位。如果不是上述这些形式，则该小句的主位是有标记的。

我们再看分析傻根在车上的一段震撼观众心灵的话。

背景：葛优扮演的黎叔假装是一个瘸腿的瞎眼老头去接近傻根，善良的傻根要给他让座，被王薄阻止了。事后，王丽和王薄对傻根进行教育。

王丽：（对傻根）你刚才当着那么多人的面喊你身上有钱，说不定真把贼给招来了。

傻根：你们说那老人是贼？

王薄：说你缺心眼你还不承认，贼会把字刻脑门上吗？

傻根：（边看王丽和王薄边说）你们怎么跟俺老乡似的，把人想的那么坏！

王丽：人心隔肚皮，害人之心不可有，防人之心不可无。你就小心点嘛！

······

傻根：俺家住在大山里，在俺村，有人在大道上看见摊牛粪，没（mo）带筐，就捡了个石头片，围着牛粪画了个圈，过几天想去捡，那牛粪还在。别人看到那个圈就知道牛粪有主了。

俺在高原，逢年过节都是俺一个人在那看工地。没人跟俺讲话，俺跟狼说话，俺不怕狼，狼也没伤害过俺。

俺走出高原，这么多人在一起跟俺说话。俺就不信，狼没伤过俺，人，他会害俺？人怎么比狼还坏呢？

导演安排这段台词是有他的目的的，傻根这段话，那么真挚，打动了所有的观众，确实发人深省。从语篇功能的角度看，"俺家住在大山里……"，"俺在高原……"，"俺走出高原……"这些开头，就是三段信息的起始点，后面的内容都是围绕这些展开的，分别描述了在大山、高原和走出高原的事情。

结语

韩礼德给我们提供了三大纯功能的理论，尤其是概念功能中的六大过程，成为分析本部经典电影的理论工具，通过这样的解读，不难看出这部电影台词的意义和价值。

Halliday 在其书 *Language as Social Semiotic：The Social Interpretation of Language and Meaning* 中认为："人类交流信息的方式是多样的，其中语言只是其中的一种。但是从系统的复杂性和功能的多重性来看，语言是任何其他方式不可比拟的。"电影就是用有限的语言来表达深奥的主题，否则就不能称其为一部好的电影！希望类似的分析能够运用到其他的经典电影台词中。

参考文献

[1] Halliday, M. A. K *An Introduction to Functional Grammar* [M]. Beijing: For-

eign Language Teaching and Research Press & London: Edward Arnold. 2000.

[2] Halliday, M. A. K *Language as Social Semiotic: The Social Interpretation of Language and Meaning* [M]. Beijing: Foreign Language Teaching and Research Press & London: Edward Arnold. 2001.

[3] James. Paul. Gee *An Introduction to Discourse Analysis: Theory and Method* [M]. Beijing: Foreign Language Teaching and Research Press, 2000.

[4] 胡壮麟,朱永生等. 系统功能语言学概论 [M]. 北京:北京大学出版社,2005.

[5] http://zhidao. baidu. com/question/1784608. html

（王青,上海大学外国语学院）

广播新闻话语分析之数词视角

引言

对于广播新闻话语的分析一直都是众多社会科学学科的研究对象：语言学家们研究新闻话语是为了揭示新闻话语的语言学特点，并同时为新闻工作者提供一定的原则；社会学家们致力于发现广播新闻话语与社会之间的关系；教育家们则把新闻话语看作是一种课堂教学的教学材料，从而期待学生既学会语言同时又了解社会。因为大众传媒在今天这样的时代已经成了我们生活中必不可少的一部分；大众传媒在今天这样的时代已经越来越体现出了它的广泛性和重要性；大众传媒话语，比如像电视节目、报刊文章和广播节目，是语言学、文化和社会学研究的主要的题材来源。而且这些大众传媒话语就是社会过程和变化的反应灵敏的晴雨表；同是又起着娱乐大众和让大众了解他们所处的时代的重要作用；再者传媒也是外语学习者获取语言知识和信息的一个主要的渠道。所以对于大众传媒话语的研究既可以丰富语言学的研究，又可以发掘人们在态度、观念、意识形态和权利关系等等方面的变化，还可以在一定的程度上促进外语教学。

话语的语言特点可以从多个层次进行，而广播新闻话语的词汇特点也纷繁多样，而本文试从数词的角度去做进一步的探讨和研究。

1. 话语分析

1.1 话语分析的界定

"话语分析"（discourse analysis）这一术语是由美国结构主义语言学家哈里斯（Z. S. Harris）在他发表于 1952 年美国《语言》（language）杂志第 28 卷的一篇题为"话语分析"的文章中首次使用的。可自从其诞生之日起至今都一直处在形形色色，林林总总的分争当中，而我们也必须首先把"话语"（discourse）和"篇章"（text）两个概念区分开来。一般来讲，人们认为话语是大于句子的单位，这样的理解不很精确，因为它的范围很广，可以是词、短语、小句（包括告示、标牌、广告等），也可以是一首诗歌、一篇日记、一次对话、一场演讲、一部小说等等。克拉申（Caire Kransch 1998）从社会语言学的角度把话语定义为讲话方式、阅读方式和写作方式，同时也是某一话语社区的行为方式、交际方式、思维方式和价值观念。有些语言学家从话语分析的研究对象内容上来定义它。如斯塔布斯（Stubbs 1983）认为话语分析是对"自然发生的连贯的口头或书面话语的语言分析"。还有一些语言学家从话语功能角度定义话语。威多森（1979）认为话语分析是对"句子用于交际以完成社会行为的研究"，强调话语的交际功能；布朗和尤尔认为话语分析是对使用中的语言的分析，它不仅仅是探索语言的形式特征，更是对语言使用功能的研究。

由此可见，话语结构形式、话语规则、话语模式等等都是话语分析这一新的研究领域的不同侧面。话语分析学者由于各自不同的语言观念及理论侧重，对话语进行了不同侧面的观察和分析。综合而言，所有对话语分析的定义无外乎两个层次，一、话语分析是对超句单位结构的静态描写；二、话语分析是对交际过程意义传递的动态分析。

1.2 广播新闻话语分析

新闻报道作为现代生活中一个愈来愈不可缺少的部分，对于新闻的理解学者还是颇为一致的；其中王佐良认为："新闻报道文体指报纸、杂志、广播电台、电视台等大众传媒工具在消息报道中使用的文体"（王佐良 1997）。那么其中报道的内容就是新闻话语了。《牛津现代高级英汉词典》（1995）把新闻定义为"新的或新鲜的信息；对于最近发生的事情的报道"（new or fresh information；reports of what has most recently happened）。新闻话语作为一种话语类型，具有了我们所定义的话语的所有特征：首先新闻话语无论是在语义上还是在语用上都是非常连贯的；其次该话语是一种交际形式，而且这种交际是发生在广播电台和听众之间的一种动态过程；再次该话语同时具有口头话语和书面话语的特点，这也正是广播新闻话语的独特之处。

2. 广播新闻话语中的数词

2.1 数词的使用

数字通常都能够给听众一种科学和令人信服的印象。但是广播新闻话语当中数字的使用却是个矛盾的问题。支持使用数字的人认为数字通史让听众觉得所报道的新闻真实可靠，更具有说服力和权威性；反对使用数字的人认为数字往往能给听众，尤其是外语学习者的收听造成一定的困难和障碍。从目前的研究看来，广播新闻话语当中既有数字的使用也有模糊词的应用。下面就是一个典型的使用数字的新闻报道：

A quick move to the financial markets. The Don Jones share index closed **36** higher at **7928**，while earlier the **100，18** ended up **33** at **6046**. The dollar is at **1**

German Mark **77. 8** and at **122** Japanese Yen. The Pound stands **1** dollar **69** cents.

在这条短短的新闻报道当中就使用了九个数字，其实这种现象也只出现在经济新闻和体育新闻话语当中。请看下面的体育新闻：

Sabathia improved to **7 - 1** in **10** career starts against the Devil Rays and hasn't lost to them since **2004**. He retired **12** of the first **13** he faced until yielding three hits and **two** runs in the **fifth**—snapping Tampa Bay's scoreless streak against the left-hander at Jacobs Field at **31** innings.

2.2 模糊词和模糊限制语的使用

美国数学家罗夫蒂·扎德（Lofti A. Zadeh）在他的《模糊集合》中建立的模糊理论在得到了科学界的认同之后，逐渐被应用到了众多的科学领域，语言学也不例外。世界上的定义和概念是以两种形式存在的——清晰概念和模糊概念；清晰概念指那些有明确的内涵和外延的概念，而模糊概念指那些没有明确的内涵和外延的概念。模糊限制语（Hedges）是指一些"把事情弄得模模糊糊的词语（Lakoff，1972）。这些词语就话语的真实程度或涉及范围，对话语的内容进行修正或限定，表明说话人对话语内容没有充分的把握，介于肯定和不肯定之间，体现了说话人的主观认识与评价。模糊限制语是模糊语言家族中的一员，已经引起了国内外许多语言学家的注意，如 Lakoff（1972）从模糊角度，Schiffrin & Channel 从话语分析的角度，何自然（1988）从语用的角度分别对模糊限制语进行了探讨和研究。

根据全铁平先生的分类，我们可以把模糊词和模糊限制语分成三大类（1986）：第一类外延没有明确的下限，但是却有明确的上限，比如说"开水"；第二类外延没有明确的上限，但是却有明确的下限，比如说"婴儿"；第三类外延既没有明确的上限也没有明确的下限，比如说"温水"。

通常说来新闻话语讲究的是报道内容的准确，那么为什么还要使用模糊和模糊限制语呢？首先我们要明白的是准确并不等于精确，所以模糊词和模糊限制语的使用并没有和新闻写作和报道的原则背道而驰！其次广播新闻话语中的模糊词和模糊限制语的使用也与自然语言的特征相符合，因为自然语言本身就包含有为数众多的模糊词和模糊限制语，不然的话新闻话语当中的模糊词和模糊限制语有时从哪里来的呢？再次模糊词和模糊限制语的使用也符合我们的言语交际的规律，其实人类交际和思维的提高不仅表现在精确思维上，同时也表现在模糊思维上。下面让我们通过一个具体的广播新闻话语来看一看模糊词和模糊限制语在新闻话语当中的使用：

The United States say it will send *a team of* experts to North Korea to *assess how severely* the communist stage has been affected by chronicle *food shortage*. Washington said *the team* would check the donated food was reaching *the most needed* and examine how ***future shortage*** be avoided. North Korea is suffering its third consecutive year of ***poor*** harvest. ***Since last month*** the United States warned it faces wide spread famine.

从上面这条新闻我们就可以看出来模糊词和模糊限制语在新闻话语中的使用频率有多么高!

2.3 数词与模糊词的结合使用

上面我们分别提到了数词与模糊词在新闻中的使用情况,可在实际操作中,我们往往会把两者结合起来使用。请看下文:

Estimated 1600 children gain the right to live in Hong Kong as a result. . . ***The large majority of more than one hundred*** countries will send representatives have approved its attempts.

从上述例子不难发现,为了保持与客观事实基本一致,当我们对某个交通事故中的死伤人数不大清楚时,也就只能用模糊词或模糊限制语了。

理论上来讲,数词与模糊词的结合使用是为了尊重事实,更好体现出新闻的准确性,可笔者在实际的广播话语中却发现了些蹊跷:同样的一件事实报道,有的媒体给出了几乎精确的数字,有的媒体给出了模糊的数字,有的媒体却把两者结合起来报道。而结果如何呢?笔者调查发现,大众往往更愿意相信给出精确数字的媒体,并由衷地认为他们的报道更专业,更精确。事实又是怎样?请看下面的例子分析。

下面两段是讲述南非约翰内斯堡动物园内山羊跳过栅栏误入狮栏而发生的一件有惊无险的事:

I

One morning a small incident took place in the Johannesburg Zoo. A mountain goat leapt over the wall of the goats' reserve into the lions' enclosure. A lion named Satan began to stalk it. But before the lion attacked the goat, the keepers arrived and one of them shouted " Get inside, Satan. " The lion obeyed and went into its cave. The keepers shut the door of the cave and rescued the goat, which was vainly attempting to climb the perpendicular wall.

II

Apparently exhilarated by this morning's spring like weather, one of the mountain goats at the Zoo decided to see what was over the next wall. He took a running jump and landed on the lions' terraces.

A Johannesburg man, Mr. H. A Rose-Innes, spending a quiet morning on leave at the Zoo, saw the whole episode, which was as exciting to watch as any Game Reserve drama-and far safer.

In no time about **100** people had assembled, **mostly** children on **holiday**, and excitement rose as Satan, after recovering from his first surprise at this unexpected gift from heaven, began to stalk the goat. But lions, long fed on meat which they do not need to hunt, lose a little of their cunning and their agility.

笔者通过调查问卷的形式对两则新闻作了统计分析。本次问卷总数为100份，回收答卷100份，全部为有效意见。

下表是对两则新闻的意见统计分析：

问　　题	所 占 比 例		
你认为新闻Ⅱ比新闻Ⅰ更可信吗?	1. 是	55. 8%	
	2. 否	25. 6%	
	3. 不确定	18. 6%	
你认为新闻Ⅱ比新闻Ⅰ更专业吗?	1. 是	61. 5%	
	2. 否	18. 4%	
	3. 不确定	20. 1%	
你认为新闻Ⅱ比新闻Ⅰ更具可读性吗?	1. 是	73. 9%	
	2. 否	11. 6%	
	3. 不确定	14. 5%	

从上表可以清楚地看出，对于描写更具体，也就是说如果哪家媒体在报道中给出了更为准确的数的话，大多数听者或读者便会追随哪家媒体。而实际上，笔者给出的例子Ⅰ是纽约时报的报道，而例子Ⅱ却是随便添油加醋，不符合事实，或者说严重失实的报道。如果听者或读者能仔细想想句中的疑点，也就可以得出正确的结论了。可为什么得出的结论却截然相反呢? 这也许正是因为对于新闻话语我们向来都是从正面的角度去理解和引导，久而久之便对它没了防线，没了辨别的能力，而某些不良的媒体正是抓住了我们这些心理来进行欺骗性的写作。

2. 4　如何辨别广播新闻话语中数词的真伪

绝大多数时候我们都认可新闻的准确与真实性。可当冲突和矛盾出现时，我们不得不用一些方法加以鉴别和分辨，力求找出事实的真相，还原事件的本来面貌。笔者以为以下几点有助于我们提高分辨率：

（1）加强对背景知识的了解。

（2）多比较，多分析。

（3）勿夸大数词作用，不盲目迷信数词。

结语

　　以上从分析广播新闻话语的词汇特点入手，我们看到了数词在广播新闻话语中的使用，以及模糊词和数词结合的意义所在，也质疑了它的真伪。值得提出的是，数词的使用仅仅只是其词汇的特点之一，我们还必须将其他的特点合并起来才能更好地，更进一步地对广播新闻话语进行分析，使它为我们所用，为我们服务，而不是我们被它牵着走。

参考文献

[1] James Paul Gee. *An Introduction to Discourse Analysis*：*Theory and Method* [M]. 上海外语教育出版社,2000.

[2] 李悦娥. 话语分析[M]. 上海外语教育出版社,2002.

[3] 周学艺. 美英报刊导读[M]. 北京大学出版社,2003.

[4] 李佐文. 试论模糊限制语的人际功能[M]. 北京第二外国语学院学报,2005.

[5] http//:sports. yahoo. com

[6] 谢荣镇. 新闻写作[M]. 北京大学出版社,1987.

[7] 张健. 新闻英语文体与范文评析[M]. 上海外语教育出版社,1994.

[8] 何自然. 语用学概论[M]. 湖南教育出版社,1988.

（曾志江,中南林业科技大学）

谎言的认知语用解读

引言

谎言是人类社会生活当中的常见的语言现象。人们交际中的话语随时随地或多或少都会带有谎言的成分。谎言是言语交际中的极端现象，对其深入地认识和研究能够揭示语言交际的真实面貌，而对谎言的认知语用分析能够对人们产生和理解谎言的深层原因进行深度剖析。关联论作为言语交际的解释理论，侧重于对话语生成和理解的认知过程的描述。运用关联论，从言语的生成与理解两方面探讨交际中谎言的认知机制，从认知语用的角度，揭示谎言的生成和理解的原因。

1. 谎言及其特性

很多故事教导儿童做人要诚实，不得骗人。家长在教育子女时常常会说到这样一句话："做人要诚实，不可以撒谎"。古今中外，名人雅士也把诚实作为最重要的品格之一加以颂扬，认为撒谎是小人之举。但是在现实生活当中，又有多少人没有过说谎记录？成人们常常为了教育儿童，喜欢把诚实挂在嘴边，而谎言却经常出现在他们的日常交际当中。有一句口头禅：人不说谎话，办不成大事，这真的极具讽刺意义。与此相反，倒是那些被教育的孩子们，却极少撒谎。被教育者反倒是教育者的楷模，原因何在？

《周易·系辞上》所说的"书不尽言，言不尽意"被看作是言意之辩的最早论述，言首先不能尽意，从动态上看，转化为由文字表达的意也已经发生了变化，经过一层一层的递减，情由隐而显，却因显有隐。当我们专注于语言去发掘文本的意义时，这意义已经和原始意义隔了许多层了。语言与意义，或者说语言与作者意欲表达的意义之间具有固有的不可弥合性。一切语言都有修辞的特性，因而一切语言都有不可靠性与欺骗性。倘言、意分离之言被称为"谎言"，文学语言也就是所谓的"谎言"。柏拉图和亚里士多德论诗时所谓的"谎言"各有侧重地隐含着以上诸种含义。总之，谎言具有言意之间的不可弥和性，无论善意或者恶意，它都具有不可靠性和欺骗性。

谎言是多门学科如哲学、语言学、逻辑学、符号学等的研究对象（樊明亚，

1999）。人们很早就开始了对它们的研究，并越来越深刻、全面地认识它们。根据约翰·塞尔（John Searle 1998）的观点，谎言属于断言式的言语行为，它们"在真和假的范围内是可以评价的"，其结构可以区分为话语的语言行事力量或语旨用意（illocationary force）、话语的命题内容两个部分，一般可用符号 F（p）来表示其形式。谎言在真和假的范围内也是可以评价的，但它与其所陈述命题之真假的关系却是不确定的。李先焜（1998）认为，意向性是判定谎言的一个标准，即明知为假而有意言之的话是谎言。对于真假，亚里士多德有过著名的表述："说非者是，或是者非，即为假，说是者是，或非者非，即为真。"因为谎言与其所陈述命题之真假没有必然的联系，我们不能根据话语所陈述命题的真假去判定其是否为谎言，应该如何理解谎言与说话者的意图呢？谎言表现为信念与断言的不一致。无论是知道为假而有意言之，还是相信或认为是假而有意言之，其意向没有质的差别，都是言不由衷，并都希望听话者相信，接受他所说的话———谎言。说谎言者不希望听话者知道其信念与断言的不一致，或者说希望听话者相信、接受其断言，以达到欺骗的目的，谎言与所陈述命题的真假之间没有必然联系。

美国语言哲学家格赖斯（1975）于 1967 在哈佛大学所作的演讲中提出了"合作原则"和"会话含义"理论。格赖斯紧紧抓住了言语交际行为的一个非常重要的方面，即交际过程总是和交际意图分不开的。任何交际过程都涉及交际意图，任何成功的交际都取决于听话人对说话人交际意图的准确理解。格赖斯提出的四条"合作原则"中的第二条质的准则，即：所说的话力求真实，尤其是不要说自知虚假、缺乏足够证据的话。他认为遵守了这些准则就是遵守了"合作原则"。在现实生活中，说话人悄悄地违反"质"的准则（或者说是说谎）的例子比比皆是，如医生或病人家属对一个癌症病人故意隐瞒病情，就是违反了"质"的准则的例子。故意违反或利用质的准则来向听话人传递一种会话含义——故意说谎。

谎言是一种语言现象，并且是人类自语言诞生以来就普遍存在的语言现象。谎言的产生和理解有其心理和社会的基础。如此看来，说谎是人类生活的一个重要特征；对谎言的认识和研究是语言研究中的独特视角，又是具有重要意义的研究课题。有人把谎言分为善意和恶意两大类。大多数人认为说谎是一件坏事，但探究产生和识破谎言的社会以及心理原因却会给我们以出乎意料的启示——人际关系中谎言随时随地都会发生；善意与否，不是每个谎言都会被揭穿，每个谎言又都没有必要去揭穿，有些谎言一旦被揭穿，会引来麻烦，甚至严重后果。

2. 言语交际中谎言的认知过程分析

Sperber & Wilson 把认知与语用学结合起来对言语交际进行研究，于 1986

年提出"关联论"（Relevance Theory），在 1995 年又对其中的部分内容作了补充和修改，后来许多学者相继发表论著发展并完善关联论（Blakemore 1992；Carston 1995；Verschueren 1999；Marmaridou 2000）。关联论开拓了语用学研究的新领域，对言语交际做出了许多独到的阐述，尤其从认知心理的角度深度探索言语交际中的规律与特性，开创了语言本体研究的新学科：认知语用学。它从认知的角度揭示了人类交际中话语的重要特征：关联性。

根据关联论（Sperber & Wilson 1995），发话者发出话语，要经历确立话语意图、语码编制（确定指称）、确定命题态度、话语态度等明示过程。发话者发出连续的语音组合，使命题信息向受话者明示（包括命题内容和命题态度），同时话语也承载着发话者的交际意图。发话者依其心理需求和语境作用而发出话语传达给受话者，目的是为了改变受话者的认知环境。受话者依据发话者的明示行为进行一系列推理活动。关联论提出了最佳相关原则（Sperber & Wilson，1995）：如果话语既能产生足够的语境效果，又只须为此付出最小的努力，那它就具有了最佳相关性，在正常交际行为中，任何话语理解都必须符合这条最佳相关原则。

Sperber 和 Wilson 认为：一次交际的成功是双方语用努力的结果，只有双方相互配合，真诚合作并且以交际关联性统辖整个交际过程。双方都认为自己的交际意图是达到最佳相关度，通过命题确定和语境推理，由互信达到互明，做到互相交替理解对方发出的话语，从而使交际获得成功。交际失败一般是交际中某一方的失败致使整个交际过程中断或完全失败，而交际成功是双方的成功，是双方的话语推理获得了最佳的语境效果。在 Sperber 和 Wilson 看来，语境效果就是语境含义，它是新信息与旧信息相互作用的结果，并因此而形成新的语境，通过这一语境化过程（contextualization），旧的语境不断地得到修正、充实和优化，形成更便于信息处理或话语推导的基础。

在《狼来了》这篇寓言故事中，谎言始终贯穿整个故事情节。本文就以这篇寓言故事为材料，以关联论为理论框架，从发话者和受话者两个方面讨论谎言的生成和理解过程，分析言语交际中失误与成功的原因，揭示谎言生成的心理机制和理解谎言的心理过程。这则寓言故事出现了几次交际失败与成功的现象。一次言语交际行为中包括参与者双方。由于各自的交际意图的不同可以导致某一方的交际失误，即：没有正确识别对方话语背后真实的交际意图。下面我们从参与者各自认知语境的变化和语用推理的机制两个方面来说明言语交际中谎言的产生与理解的真实过程。

故事有三个交际场面，且都以失败而告终。从故事中，牧童两次说谎，成功地骗了村民，从牧童的角度他是取得了交际的成功，而村民进行了合理的推理却没有推理出牧童的真实意图，最后上当受骗，交际失败。这两次交际行为的失败主要由于牧童虽然使用正确的言语形式，并不是真诚地使用这种形式。虽然这种言语形式与相关语境是最佳相关，但他说谎的真实意图与村民由于听到这些话语所得出的语境假设却毫不相关。牧童的话语中具有两个意图层面：话语本身所具有的常规意图（表层意图）和话语背后的隐含意图（深层意图，即说谎意图）。他的谎言所具有的话语相关性是他意图的意图的相关，而村民的理解中的该话语的相关性到仅是由话语得出的牧童的意图的相关。因此导致牧童的交际意图即说谎意图的实现，村民的交际意图没有实现。下面分别从牧童作为发话者和村民作为受话者两个方面揭示话语生成与理解的认知过程，以及交际失误的原因。

2.1 发话者的谎言生成过程

故事中的牧童在设计第一次骗局时首先要有产生谎言的意图，并设想如何利用谎言来获得骗局的成功。根据关联论，发话者向受话者明示的话语行为只是线索或证据，仅仅被用来改变受话者的认知语境，引导受话者利用这则话语和认知语境的相关信息生成一组语境假设，进行语用推理。

发话者要实现自己真正的谎言意图，需要从其认知环境中寻找实现这个意图的证据。这故事中牧童为了实现自己欺骗的意图，本能地选择了最大关联性的话语："狼来了！"，并且附加上具有最大关联性的话语情态。此话语具有最大关联性是由于它在当时语境中具有的违实性。要生成这则话语，牧童首先要从他的认知语境中筛选出具有关联性的证据支持他的欺骗意图的实现，这样的证据可称作语境假设。为了实现欺骗村民上山救助的意图，他利用一系列与此意图最为相关的语境假设，并生成了同这个意图最为相关的谎言话语："狼来了"。

假设图式（一）：

① 当地常有狼群出没。
② 当地曾发生过狼群威胁羊群和牧羊人的事例。
③ 当地村民曾听到过类似的呼救声。
④ 当地村民曾救助过牧羊人。
⑤ 只要发出呼救"狼来了"，村民一定会前来救助。

我们知道，在正常交际活动当中，绝对不相关的言语几乎没有（Grice，1975），相关只是程度的问题。最佳相关原则一般认为，强度高的假设具有较大的语境效果。牧童设想这一系列谎言假设同他的意图最为相关，并且明白当地经常有狼群出没，经常威胁牧羊人和羊。牧童选择此话语是由于此话语与他的欺骗意图最为相关。他知道村民一旦听到呼救声，就会意识到有人受到野兽的威胁，就会前来救助。牧童的认知环境储存着以往类似的或经验性的信息，也属于语境假设，还有类似话语确定的命题形式，与村民共有的语言系统，因而他知道村民会理解他发出的话语。他也知道他们发出的话语的句式和附加情态是呼救时最为相关的形式。村民听到这种形式的呼救后，会认为有人在呼救，而不是游戏，更不会认为是欺骗。假如当地从未有过狼群出没，他就不会发出这则呼救话语，也许会发出"老虎来了"或"狮子来了"（如果有老虎或狮子出没于此的话）的呼救话语。总之，他所发出的呼救话语，无论从词语句式、情态、和语音特点都符合呼救话语的标准。他相信当村民听到这则呼救话语时一定会相信牧童是在求救而会前来救助他，而不会相信他是虚假呼救，是在说谎，或是在欺骗。

上述与谎言有密切关联的语境假设对于牧童的欺骗意图，与其他相关语境假设相比，是具有最强的假设力度的语境假设。他相信村民听到他的呼救话语会识别出他请求救助的意图是真正的意图。这是他的真正的谎言意图得以实现的关键因素。

上述分析是从牧童发出话语之前的认知环境改变的过程而得出他的谎言意图实现的可能性。假如村民的认知环境中包含下列语境假设：当地根据没有狼群出没，或者经常听到这个男孩子喊叫"狼来了"是在唱一首当地民谣，或者知道男孩一贯撒谎等，他们就不大会相信"狼来了"是真正的呼救，牧童的真正的谎言意图就不可能实现，村民也不可能做出虚假判断而上当受骗。

2.2　受话者的谎言理解过程

下面从受话者的角度分析村民听到"狼来了"话语后的理解过程。

任意一个现象都会引申出一组假设，但实际上人们并不是对每一个现象都作出积极的反应，或去构建该现象所明示的或暗示的假设。只有具有一定相关性的现象才会引起人们的注意。当首次听到话语"狼来了"之后，村民的认知环境会因这一序列声音刺激而得到某种程度的改变。如果他们认为这串声音符号与他们是相关的，是值得注意的，那么这串声音符号对于他们的认知环境来讲是新的信息，于是就开始对这种信息进行处理而不会考虑该话语的真假，因为他们相信这则话语是具有最大相关性的话语。相关的声音刺激都会在受话者的感知系统中得到突显的地位，于是对语音的处理便开始了。当听到这则话语，村民可能因为该言语刺激而产生一系列语境假设：

假设图式（二）：

① 它是一组声音符号。

② 它是某人发出的一组声音符号。

③ 它是男孩子发现的一组声音符号。

④ 有人在山上。

如果这一组声音符号如同其他许多声音一样进入村民的听觉器官，他们可能不会对之加以注意，因为他们在当时的自然环境中，会接收到来自外界的各种声音，并且大多是非言语声音。但人们常常本能地对他们可以解读的并且有意义的声音最为敏感，即一组语音与他们的认知环境最为相关，或者说，这种语言形式传达的新信息一般是值得处理的信息。村民听到的是属于人的语言中的具有意义的一组声音符号，这组语音符号马上会当作语言信号被自动分析，并赋予其意义。这是对该话语解码的开始。这个过程通常经过消除歧义、确定指称和语义充实得出话语的命题形式。

如果村民相信牧童的话语的命题意义为真并有足够的证据证明他们相信其为真，他们确信上述命题形式为真而非假，因而他们不会识别牧童的谎言话语。根据这则话语的附加情态，他们便推理出下面一系列假设：

假设图式（三）：

① 这个话语与村民最为关联。

② 一个男孩喊出这句子："狼来了"。

③ 这个男孩先相信"狼来了"才喊出这句话。

④ 他还相信他和羊群遇到了危险。

⑤ 狼来了要对他和羊群造成伤害。

⑥ 因此他在呼救。

上述系列语境假设中，首先村民相信这则话语与他们最为相关，因为他们听到带有呼救情态的话语便会立刻确定其命题意义及命题态度。他们相信附近有狼群出没，还相信牧童呼喊狼来了不是谎言，还相信牧童和羊群会有危险，还相信牧童遭遇狼群时不能逃脱，会有生命危险，因此他们就可以推理出这则话语的语境隐含："牧童在呼救"。这个明示意图并不是牧童的真实意图，而是他谎言的外衣或者假象，但是为什么村民根据上述言语刺激形式，调用认知环境相关假设，进而推理出"牧童在呼救"这一虚假的语境隐含的呢？

根据关联论，受话者接受语言刺激，会马上以此为线索，展开一个语境假设图式。图式中所有的语境假设都被看作是相关的信息，与新信息结合会产生最大的认知效果，并且处理新旧两种信息时所付出的心理投入也最少，上述假设图式与推理出的发话者意图便取得了最佳关联，推理中止。他们因此而相信"牧童在求救"。

村民没有推理出牧童的谎言意图上当受骗，可以从两方面进行分析。话语"狼来了"是确定的明示行为，它仅仅是一组语音序列，具有命题意义并附带着发话者的话语情态。它对不同受话者有着不同的作用，对受话者的认知环境的改变也因人而异。一方面，村民听到这则话语后，结合认知语境得出了假设图式。这则话语以最少的精力和加工时间得到足够的认知效果（Carston1988），因而同该假设图式发生了最佳关联，并且对该假设图式进行了强化，导致村民推导出了"有人在呼救"的意图。另一方面，村民的认知环境一定包含有关"撒谎"的假设。所以，这则话语也可能对他们明示了下面的假设。

假设图式（四）：

① 牧童常常进行恶作剧。

② 牧童呼救是恶作剧。

③ 牧童欺骗村民上山救助。

④ 牧童是在撒谎。

⑤ "狼来了!"是一则谎言。

在村民看来,这组语境假设与牧童的呼救话语也具有关联性。根据关联原则所揭示的人们的认知对最佳关联的认知取向(Sperber & Wilson 1995:58),这一组假设与新信息结合没有产生语境效果或者产生的语境效果较小,并且处理起来要花费较大心理努力,因为他们要处理假设图式(四),须要绕过最可及的假设图式(三),(正像走路一样,绕道而行,舍近求远),所以假设图式(四)并没有得到强化,反而因假设(三)的强化而进一步削弱。假设图式(三)得到了强关联,假设图式(四)得到了弱关联。这便是村民未能推理出牧童的欺骗意图的真正原因,最后导致牧童的谎言话语被村民接受,达到了欺骗村民的目的。

牧童第二次骗局与第一次骗局类似。相比较而言,牧童第二次谎言话语的生成过程有所不同之处,但话语理解方式基本相同,这里不再赘述。

结语

关联论揭示了交际中的话语特性——关联性,并指出了交际双方认知语境的互明性和动态性。运用关联论的基本理论观点不仅可以解释谎言话语的理解过程,还可以揭示交际中谎言话语的生成过程。通过对谎言话语产生和理解的认知过程进行细致地描述,我们更清楚地认识谎言背后的深层次的认知机制,更好地揭示言语交际过程中的语用推理的实质。关联论的语用观为我们重新认识言语交际中的语用问题提供了新的视角,而运用关联论对谎言这一极端而又常见的语言现象进行认知语用分析为探索语言与认知的相互关系和作用提供了有利的途径。

参考文献

[1] Best J. B. *Cognitive Psychology International* [M]. Thomas Publishing Inc. , 1998.

[2] Blackmore, D. *Understanding Utterances* [M]. Oxford:Blackwell, 1992.

[3] Carroll D. W. *Psychology of Language* [M]. 外语教学与研究出版社,2000.

[4] Grice, H. P. Logic and Conversation[A]. In Cole P. & J. Morgan (eds.) Syntax and Semantics[C] , vol. 3. Academic Press,1975.

[5] J. R 塞尔. 间接言语行为[C].A.P. 马蒂尼奇编. 牟博等译. 语言哲学. 北京:商务印书馆,1998.

[5] Sperber D. & D. Wilson. *Relevance:Communication and Cognition* [M].

Oxford：Blackwell，1995.

[6] 樊明亚. 假话、谎话与反话的逻辑分析[J]. 上饶师专学报,1999,(19).

[7] 何自然. 语用与认知——关联论研究[M]. 外语教学与研究出版社，2001.

[8] 李先焜. 谎言—一种典型的符号学现象[J]. 哲学译丛，1998 增刊.

[9] 冉永平. 认知语用学的焦点问题探索[J]. 现代外语，2002,(1).

（刘长青,廊坊师范学院外国语学院）

《宿建德江》五种英译本
的语篇功能分析

引言

　　国内对古诗词英译的研究有很多，无论在理论还是在实践方面都取得了丰硕的成果。从翻译实践上来看就有早期的翁显良的《古诗英译》、许渊冲的《唐诗三百首新译》和《唐诗三百首》，近期的有唐一鹤《英译唐诗三百首》，但就其研究的理论角度来看，大多数从文学的角度出发，如许渊冲先生提出的古诗词英译的"三美"原则，即"音美"、"意美"和"形美"，再有顾正阳教授的古诗词研究的美学视角，或是按照中国近代的著名翻译家严复提出的"信、达、雅"标准，张培基等提出的"忠实通顺"原则，但是对于古诗词英译到底应该采用什么样的标准，就目前来看，翻译界还无法有普遍认可的标准。（黄国文 2006：18）本文在系统功能语法的框架下，从语篇功能角度探讨古诗英译，试图为古诗词英翻译方法带来一些启示。

1. 关于语篇功能

　　韩礼德（1970，1973，1985，1994，2004）把语言的纯理论功能分为三种：概念元功能、人际元功能和语篇功能。语篇功能是指人们在使用语言时怎样把信息组织好，同时表明一条信息与其他信息之间的关系。该功能主要由三个语义系统构成：主位-述位系统，即主位结构，已知信息-新信息系统，即信息结构和衔接系统。（黄国文 2006：53）

1.1　主位结构

　　从语篇章功能角度看，一个小句可以切分为主位（theme）和述位（rheme）两个部分；主位是信息的出发点，是句子的开端。就主位结构而言，一个小句划出主位后，剩下的部位就是述位，即围绕主位加以叙述发展的部分。根据韩礼德对主位的划分，胡壮麟、朱永生等（2006）将主位分为"单项主位"（Simple Theme）和"复项主位"（Multiple Theme）。只由经验成分（如：过程、参与者、环境成分）充当的主位属于单项主位，它在语法常表现为名词词组、副词词组或介词短语，或是小句。由经验成分与人际成分和（或）语篇成分构成的主位属复项主位。它在形式上包含连续成分（continuative）和结构成分（structural）和连接成分（conjunctive）等语篇成分。主位有标记主位（Marked Theme）和无标记主语之分（Unmarked Theme）。由主语充当的主位是无标记主语，如果主位不是小句的主语，这样主位就是有标记主位。

1.2　信息结构

信息结构是把语言组织成为"信息单位"的结构。信息单位是信息交流的基本成分。所谓信息交流就是言语活动过程中已知内容与新内容之间的相互作用。可见信息结构就是已知信息与新信息相互作用而构成的信息单位的结构。（胡壮麟、朱永生等 2006：172-173）信息单位结构构成的形式有：（已知信息）＋新信息。其中最常见的信息单位结构是：已知信息＋新信息。因信息结构由声调重音突出（tonic prominence）来体现，而不是通过语言单位的排列表示，所以一般情况下书面语篇不进行信息结构分析，如果必需的话，也要由受过正规教育的专业人员进行朗读。（黄国文 2002：100）这里我们在分析古诗时也只从已知信息和新信息的角度做简单的分析。

1.3　衔接系统

衔接是一个语义系统，它是一种谋篇意义，是指语篇中语言成分之间的语言联系。当话语中的某个成分的解释取决于话语中另一个成分的解释时，就出现了衔接。衔接是语言系统的一个部分，衔接的潜力在于语言本身所具有的系统手段。（Halliday & Hanson 1976：4-5）衔接的手段有很多，韩礼德（1976，1985，1994，2004）把衔接分为语法衔接（grammatical cohesion）和词汇衔接两种（lexical cohesion）两种。语法衔接有：照应（reference），省略（ellipsis），替代（substitution）和连接（conjunction）。词汇衔接也有四种：重复（repetition），同义/反义（synonymy/antonymy），上下义/局部-整体关系（hyponymy/metonymy）和搭配（collocation）。

在下面的分析中，笔者将对照上述的理论，具体分析古诗英译本《宿建德江》中三个语义系统的具体体现。

2.《宿建德江》源语语篇的主位结构分析

孟浩然的原诗是这样的：

宿建德江

移舟泊烟渚，日暮客愁新。

野旷天低树，江清月近人。

从主位结构的角度看,《宿建德江》一诗的主位和述位的划分是这样的。以下分别用 T 代表主位（theme），R 代表述位（rheme）。

宿建德江（R）

主位 T	述位 R
移舟	泊烟渚
日暮	客愁新
野旷	天低树
江清	月近人

原诗的标题是省略了主位的一个主位结构，它点明了全诗的主旨，可以看作是全诗的宏观主位，也就是全诗信息的出发点，而该诗的每一行都有自己的信息出发点，即主位，都用来传递新的信息，这种主位传递新信息的信息结构在诗歌中是十分常见的。从上面的表可以看出，原诗的四行主位都是单项主位。其中第一行是动词短语，是省略了动作参与者的过程主位；第二、三、四行则由表达环境成分的小句充当，也就是韩礼德所提到的句项主位，它是单项主位的一种。就全诗的述位而言，第一行是短语，而其余的三行都是小句。其中第一行述位是一个重复题目的已经信息，它表明了事情发生的地点，第二行是主人公的心理活动描写，三、四行是江面自然景观的描写。全诗眼是一"暮"字，表达了主人公的心绪，水迷茫，在迷茫中行进的小船，又使作者联想到身世的飘忽不定，更增加惆怅。无际的旷野，小树与天衔接，平静的江面皎洁的明月与人相伴。日暮给了诗人愁绪，也给了读者以充分的想象空间。

3.《宿建德江》五个英译文的语篇功能分析

笔者收集了《宿建德江》的分别是由 W. J. B. Fletcher、Bynner、张廷琛 & 魏博思、许渊冲、唐一鹤等翻译五种英译版本，为了方便起见，下面分别以 Fletcher 译 Bynner 译、张魏译 许译和唐译代表五种不同的英译文。

3.1 主位结构

《宿建德江》英语译本的主位结构分析。下面就不同的五种英译文进行逐行的主位结构分析：

第一行：

译者	主位	述位
Fletcher 译	Our boat by the mist-covered islet	we tied.
Bynner 译	While my little boat	moves on its mooring of mist
张魏译		Mooring the boat among the mists
许译	My boat	is moored near an isle in mist grey
唐译	By the misty islet	The traveler's boat was mooring

第一行的五种不同的译文主位结构可以分为三类：一是参与者充当主位：Our boat by the mist-covered islet（Fletcher 译），而 While my little boat（Bynner 译）、My boat（许译）是物质过程的动作者充当主位；二是主位空缺的：（张魏译）；三是环境成分充当主位：By the misty islet（唐译）。其中 Bynner 和许的译文的主位是无标记主位，Fletcher 译和唐译为有标记主位。该四种译文都是单项主位的译法与原文一致，而 Fletcher 把 Our boat by the mist-covered isle 放在句首，当作有标记主位，多少有点头重脚轻，这样安排可能是考虑到要让 tied 置于句末，与第四行 The river is bright with the moon at our side 押韵。唐的译文把环境成分做主位，也是出于这样的考虑吧！相比之下许的无标记主位显得清楚明了。

第二行：

译者	主位	述位
Fletcher 译	The sorrows of absence	the sunset brings back.
Bynner 译	And daylight wanes	old memories begin
张魏译	Day	wanes
	A wanderer's	ache persists
许译	I	am grieved anew to see the parting day
唐译	His sorrows	came up again In the dusk of the evening

第二行的五种译文有四种都采用参与者做主位：The sorrows of absence （Fletcher 译）、Day、A wanderer's（张魏译）、I（许译）和 His sorrows（唐译），其中许和张魏译文是动作者做主位，该四种主位单项主位。Bynner 译的则是带有语篇成分 and 和句项主位的复项主位。在这五种译文中，张魏、许和唐的译文都是无标记主位，而其余的则是有标记主位。值得一提的是张魏的翻译与其他四种译文不同，在形式上采用了两个并列复句，把原文的一句翻译成两句，这里似乎有违原文的意思，也许译者是为了考虑到句末的［s］押韵吧。显而易见 Fletcher 的译文还是有上面提到的头重脚轻的问题，这样做也是为了把"back"放到句尾，保持与第三行的押韵。

第三行：

译者	主位	述位
Fletcher 译	Low breasting the foliage	the sky loomed black
Bynner 译	How wide	the world was
	how close	the tress to heaven
张魏译	In the vast wilds	the sky descends to touch the trees
许译	On boundless plain	trees seem to scrape the sky
唐译	The sky	stooped lower than trees in the vast wilderness.

这五种译文可以分为三类不同的主位结构，且都是单项主位。一类是过程主位：Low breasting the foliage（Fletcher 译）；二是参与者做主位：Thy sky（唐译）；三类是环境成分做主位：In the vast wilds（张魏译）、On the boundless plain（许译）和表示程度的环境成分 how wide 和 how close（Bynner 译）。五种译文都采用与原文相同的单项主位，其中只有唐的译文是无标记主位，而其余四句都采用有标记主位。与众不同的是，Bynner 把原诗的一句译成了两个小句，而且各自都有自己的主位，而且是有标记的，这样的翻译显然与原文有一定出入。许的译文可能是出于与下一行的末字"nigh"押韵的考虑，而采用了有标记主位。也许是出于同样的考虑，Fletcher 也用 Low breasting the foliage 有标记主位，句子的平衡性似乎遭到一定程度上的破坏。

第四行：

译者	主位	述位
Fletcher 译	The river	is bright with the moon at our side.
Bynner 译	And how clear in the water	the nearness of the moon (is)
张魏译	As brightening waters	bear the moon to be
许译	In water clear	the moon appears so nigh
唐译	Near the shadow of the moon on the clear stream	The man on his boat was standing

第四行的五种译文有四种都是单项主位：The river（Fletcher 译）、As brightening waters（张魏译）、In water clear（许译）和 Near the shadow of the moon on the clear stream（唐译）。其中 Fletcher 与张魏的译文是参与者做主位，许和唐的译文采用环境成分做主位，这与原文的差异交大。Bynner 的译文是一个语篇成分与环境成分一起构成的复项主位。除了 Fletcher 的译文以外，其余的四句都是无标记主位。许的译文处于押韵考虑，同时保持了与第二句译文在句式上的一直，采用有标记主位；而唐的译文 Near the shadow of the moon on the clear stream 长长的有标记主语，有头重脚轻，且完全相同的句式，第二、三行都用有无标记主位，有为了押韵而押韵之嫌。

上面的分析表明，分析每行诗的主位结构，对于整首诗的语篇功能的分析起着及其重要的作用，同时通过分析，在古诗的意境传达方面，采用有标记的主位似乎没有其他相应的采用无标记的主位好，且过分的强调押韵也可能会破坏句子的平衡性。

3.2 信息结构

以上是从主位结构角度对《宿建德江》五种不同的英译本进行了分析，考虑到书面语篇特点，在此对其信息结构作简要的探讨。

从原诗来看，因为该诗的题目是一个主位缺省，只有述位的主位结构，所以该诗的每一行的主位都是新的信息，除了第一行的述位重复了诗的题目，是一个已知信息以外，其余的都是新信息，这符合胡壮麟、朱永生等（2006：172-173）提出的信息单位结构构成的形式一（已知信息）＋新信息。就每一个小句而言，小句有一个内容重点，原诗的第一行"泊烟渚"、第二行的"客愁新"、第三行的"天低树"、第四行的"月近人"都可以看着是原诗的内容重点。英语语言的特点"尾部负重"，即通常情况下信息中心都是在小句的句末。而在对几种英译文的分析过程中，在该首诗的翻译中译者有为了诗的"音美"即押韵而改变原诗的信息中心的倾向。Fletcher 的译文采用的是 abba 的韵律，但是这种押韵影响了他对信息结构的处理。他将第一行"移舟泊烟渚"与第二行"日暮客愁新"分别翻译成 Our boat by the mist-covered islet we tied 与 The sorrows of absence the sunset brings back，分别为了与第一行的 "side" 和第三行形成句尾 "black" 押韵。而完全改变了该两行诗的信息中心。还有唐的对第二行与第三行的翻译：His sorrows came up again In the dusk of the evening（第三行）；The sky stooped lower than trees In the vast wilderness（第四行），显然第三行是为了与第一、四行句末压 "ing" 尾韵。这样放置信息中心的位置于不顾的做，没有遵从英语从旧信息过渡到新信息的习惯。因为一味的考虑韵律而改变英语语言的信息结构有点顾此失彼。

相比之下，许的译文则较好的处理好信息中心与韵律的关系。一方面实现了译文的 aabb 的韵律特征，同时很好的表达了每句的信息中心。在保证了译文与原文的诗行的数量保持一致情况下，全诗除了第二行以外，使得每行的信息中心都落到了尾部：

行	原诗	许译文
第一行	泊烟渚	moored near an isle in mist grey
第三行	天低树	trees seem to scrape the sky
第四行	月近人	the moon appears so nigh

许对第二句的处理是考虑押韵为先，而舍弃了信息中心的要求，这种处理正说明了古诗英译的语言学视角的可行性。在多数情况下以信息中心为指导，但是在必要的情况下也要做一些韵律方面的调整，这是否也说明了古诗英译的语言学与美学的角度是可以贯通相容，相互补充的。

3.3 衔接系统

根据 Halliday & Hanson 对衔接的定义，原诗并没有任何衔接现象。即没有出现体现衔接意义的语法和词汇手段。但是其译文在不同的程度上使用了各种衔接手段，这也体现了汉英语言的差异，汉语重意合，很少使用衔接手段；英语则重形合，一段话要想表达一个完整连贯的语义，往往要用到多种衔接的手段，在这五种英译文中运用了照应、同义、省略、连接和等三种衔接手段。

这里所说的照应是人称照应，如唐的译文的 the traveler 与下文的 his，his 和 the man 分别构成照应。同时 the traveler 又与 the man 是同义，这就使得全文在词汇层面上衔接连贯。Fletcher 的译文上也使用了 our 与 we 的照应手段。许的译文第一行的 "my" 与第二行的 "I" 相照应。在五种译文中，Bynner 使用了省略衔接手段，在诗的第二 "how close the trees to heaven" 与第四行的 "And how clear in the water the nearest of the moon"中省略了"is"。说省略了"is",是因为全诗采用的是完整的小句。再看在几种译文的连接手段的应用。张的译文在最后一行用了时间表达连词"as"衔接上文的"A wanderer's ache persists"这一心理过程,保持了行文的流畅。相比其他四种译文 Bynner 的译文中使用较多的连接词,用 while 表示"移舟泊烟渚"这样的过程,用连词"and"连接"日暮"作"客愁新"的时间状语,形成逻辑照应;后两句的,"how","how","and how",引导的排比结构,这些衔接手段的使用符合译文的语篇衔接。但也不能忽视语义层的衔接,如英文中的"how+adj"j给人更多以欢快的感情,不能很好的表达原来诗的"愁"丝。

结语

本文在系统功能语法的框架下,从语篇章功能角度分析古诗词英译,列举了现有的《宿建德江》一诗的五种英译版本,从主-述位结构、信息结构和衔接系统等三个角度对五种版本进行比较分析。以往对古诗词翻译的研究注重从美学和文学的角度,而本文是对古诗的功能语篇分析,所以重点在于语言分析和语篇分析,而没有很少涉及到文学、美学的意境传达。这也说明了对同一首诗的英译本的分析可以是多方位、多角度的。从语言学角度对古诗译本分析是一种新的尝试。通过此实践,笔者试图论证语言学理论在语篇分析中应用的可能性及其不足,同时希望能给古诗的英译方法论与实践提供一些启示。并希望能从文学、美学和语言学的角度为古诗英译找到一个很好的结合点,使古诗词原意得到更好的传达。

附:《宿建德江》的五种英译本
Fletcher 译文:
Mooring on the River at Jiande
By Meng Haoran
Our boat by the mist-covered islet we tied.
The sorrows of absence the sunset brings back.
Low breasting the foliage the sky loomed black.
The river is bright with the moon at our side.

Bynner 译文:
A Night-Mooring on the Jiande River
By Meng Haoran

While my little boat moves on its mooring of mist,
And daylight wanes, old memories begin…
How wide the world was, how close the tress to heaven,
And how clear in the water the nearness of the moon

张廷琛 & 魏博思译文：
Spending the Night on the Jiande River
By Meng Hao-ran
Mooring the boat among the mists-
Day wanes
A wanderer's ache persists
In the vast wilds the sky descends to touch the trees
As brightening waters bear the moon to be

许渊冲译文：
Mooring on the River at Jiande
By Meng Haoran
My boat is moored near an isle in mist grey;
I'm grieved anew to see the parting day.
On boundless plain trees seem to scrape the sky;
In water clear the moon appears so nigh.

唐一鹤译文：
Put Up for the Night at Jiande River
By Meng Haoran
By the misty islet,
The traveler's boat was mooring.
His sorrows came up again
In the dusk of the evening.
The sky stooped lower than trees
In the vast wilderness.
Near the shadow of the moon on the clear stream,
The man on his boat was standing.

参考文献

[1] Halliday, M. A. K. Language Structure and Language Function [A]. In John Lyons (ed.). *New Horizons in Linguistics* [C]. Harmondsworth：Penguin Books, 1970：140-165.

[2] Halliday, M. A. K. *Explorations in the Functions of Language* [M]. London：Edward Arnold, 1973.

[3] Halliday, M. A. K. & R. Hasan. *Cohesion in English* [M]. London：Longman, 1976.

[4] Halliday, M. A. K. *Introduction to Functional Grammar* [M]. London：Arnold. 1985/ 1994/ 2004.

[5] 胡壮麟. 朱永生, 等. 系统功能语言学概论[M]. 北京：北京大学出版社, 2006, 172-173.

[6] 黄国文. 语篇分析的理论与实践[M]. 上海：上海外语教育出版社, 2002, 100.

[7] 黄国文. 翻译研究的语言学视角探索-古诗词英译本的语言学分析[M]. 上海：上海外语教育出版社, 2006, 7.

[8] 唐一鹤. 英译唐诗三百首[M]. 天津：天津人民出版社, 2006, 237.

[9] 许渊冲. 唐诗三百首[M]. 北京：高等教育出版社, 2001, 68-69.

[10] 张德禄, 刘汝山. 语篇连贯与衔接理论的发展及应用[M]. 上海：上海外语教育出版社, 2003, 8.

[11] 张廷琛, 魏博思. 唐诗一百首[M]. 北京：中国对外翻译出版公司, 商务印书馆(香港)有限公司合作出版, 1991, 24-25

[12] 吕叔湘. 英译唐人绝句百首[M]. 湖南：湖南人民出版社, 1980, 25.

（章凤花,上海大学）

英语政治语篇中指称词语的顺应性分析

——美国总统大选辩论例析

引言

关于指称问题，古今中外的学者曾从语义、句法、语用、和认知等角度做过十分有益的探讨。但是，这些研究大都侧重于对指称的形式特征、分类、文体分布、语篇中的衔接和连贯等方面的描述和解释，而有关指称深层机制的研究还不多见。当今社会竞争日益激烈，而美国总统大选辩论具有典型的竞争特点，对社会及受众群的影响巨大，对政治辩论乃至一般辩论均具有指导作用，因此具有研究价值。本文专门针对近两届美国总统大选辩论中总统候选人称呼对方时使用的指称词语进行顺应性分析，从数据分析中找规律，试图发现一些政治语篇中指称表达的特点。

之所以将 2000 与 2004 美国总统大选辩论作为我们的研究对象不仅是因为时间最近，而且含有大量灵活多变的指称词语，其影响力巨大。

1. 理论基础

语言顺应论是比利时语用学家维索尔伦（Verschueren 1999）在其著作《语言学新解》中提出的。他认为，语言使用实际上是人们不断地对语言做出选择的过程。语言选择有很多特点，发生在语言的各个层面，除语言形式，还涉及语言使用策略。语言选择由语言使用的三大特点为前提组成，即语言的变异性、协商性与顺应性。语言顺应涉及四个方面：语境关系顺应，指语言选择中要考虑的各种语境因素；语言结构顺应，指顺应涉及各语言层面和语言结构原则；顺应性的动态，指语言选择和协商过程中不断变化的顺应过程；顺应中的意识突显，指交际者对语言选择的意识程度。这些关系是相互依存、相互制约的。

Verschueren（1999）把语境分为交际语境和语言语境。前者由语言使用者及其心理世界、社交世界和物理世界组成，语言使用者即说话人和听话人，是整个语境的中心，因为语境构成成分都要靠他们去激活；后者也称语言信息通道，即信道（linguistic channel），指语言在使用过程中根据语境因素而选择的各种语言手段。

Verschueren 的语言顺应理论以"综观"为主导，较为全面地阐释了人类使用语言的各种现象，深入探究了人类语言交际的心理机制及其过程以及社会、文化的作用，揭示出语言运用的实质。

2. 英语指称词语对交际语境的顺应

交际语境包括交际者；心理世界，如认知及情感因素等；社会文化世界，指各种社会文化因素、人际关系等；物理世界，如时间、空间、外貌、体语等。

2.1 英语指称词语对说话者的顺应

在现实交际中，说话者并不总是他们所说的话语的直接来源。语言的使用并不是那么简单的。让我们先看一个 1999 年戈尔的采访片段：

① (Excerpt from an interview of Gore on CNN's Late Edition on March 9, 1999)

During my service in the United States Congress, *I took the initiative in creating the Internet*. I took the initiative in moving forward a whole range of initiatives that have proven to be important to our country's economic growth and environmental protection, improvements in our educational system.

许多政治评论家与媒体批评戈尔"创造了因特网"这一说法，下面我们来看一下布什在 2000 年第一场辩论中的一段话。

② (Bush at the first presidential debate, October 3, 2000) ①

Look. This is a man who's got great numbers. He talks about numbers. I'm beginning to think not only did *he invent the Internet* but he invented the calculator. It's fuzzy math. It's a scaring—trying to scare people in the voting booth. .

在这里布什引用戈尔在一次访问中的原话称呼对方，并对其进行讽刺，不用提到其姓名观众便知道布什指称的对象，因为有共有的知识背景。

2.2 英语指称词语对说话者的心理世界的顺应

心理世界包括交际双方的个性、情绪、愿望、意图等认知和情感方面的因素。

2.2.1 英语指称词语对说话者的意图的顺应

③ (September 30, 2004 The First Bush-Kerry presidential Debate)

Kerry: But we also have to be smart, Jim. And smart means not diverting

---

① All the extracted materials from the 2000 and 2004 American presidential debates in this thesis are selected from http://www.debates.org/pages/debtrans.html.

your attention from the real war on terror in Afghanistan against Osama bin Laden and taking it off to Iraq where the 9/11 Commission confirms there was no connection to 9/11 itself and Saddam Hussein, and where the reason for going to war was weapons of mass destruction, not the removal of Saddam Hussein.

This president has made, I regret to say, a colossal error of judgment. And judgment is what we look for in the president of the United States of America.

以上这段话谈论的是布什在美国 911 事件后采取的措施。克里很明显地表达了他的愤慨。"The president of the United States of America" 的使用表达了其认为布什没有采取正确而明智的措施去应对此次恐怖袭击的内心世界。因此他使用了总统的全称目的是想向观众传达布什不称职，不适合这个神圣的职位。挑战者倾向于对在任者使用含有头衔的称呼以强调对手政务上的不足。

2.2.2 英语指称词语对说话者的情绪的顺应

④ (October 13，2004 the Third Bush-Kerry presidential Debate)

Kerry：President Bush has taken—he's the only president in history to do this. He's also the only president in 72 years to lose jobs—1.6 million jobs lost. He's the only president to have incomes of families go down for the last three years; the only president to see exports go down; the only president to see the lowest level of business investment in our country as it is today.

这里克里采用排比句谴责布什的不称职，顺应了说话者克里的情绪。当时克里情绪激动，强烈的表达了他的愤慨。他希望观众也产生共鸣，以达到自己的目的。

2.2.3 英语指称词语对说话者的动机的顺应

⑤ (October 3，2000 The first Gore-Bush debate)

Bush：If we don't trust younger workers to manage some of their own money with the Social Security surplus, to grow from $1 trillion to $3 trillion, it will be impossible to bridge the gap without it. What *Mr. Gore*'s plan will do causing huge payroll taxes or major benefit reductions?

⑥ (October 13，2004 the Third Bush-Kerry presidential Debate)

Kerry：And we start—we don't do it exclusively-but we start by rolling back *George Bush*'s unaffordable tax cut for the wealthiest people, people earning more than $200，000 a year, and we pass, hopefully, the McCain-Kerry Commission which identified some $60 billion that we can get.

上述两例中，在 2000 年，戈尔是副总统，布什是州长，2004 年，布什是总统，克里是州长，挑战者。作为挑战者，尽管职务比在任者低，但由于争夺的是同一职位—总统，因此他们把对手看作是平等的竞争者，称呼对方用 Mr. 加上姓或者仅仅用名加上姓。这顺应了说话者的心理动机。

2. 3 英语指称词语对物理世界的顺应

物理世界中最重要的因素是时间和空间的指称关系。总统候选人通常要依据观众的类型构成来决定他们对竞争者的指称词语的使用。一名候选人可以在自己的竞选活动中用"our opponent"来称呼其对手，因为可能所有的观众都是自己的支持者。但是在总统大选辩论中，观众的组成是混合的，是由持不同政治观点的人构成的，因此这里"my opponent"要比"our opponent"更加适合。以下例子就是顺应了观众构成这一物理世界因素的需要。

⑦ (October 8，2004 The Second Bush-Kerry presidential Debate)

Bush：You remember the last debate? *My opponent* said that America must pass a global test before we used force to protect ourselves. That's the kind of mindset that says sanctions were working. That's the kind of mindset that said，"Let's keep it at the United Nations and hope things go well."

2. 4 英语指称词语对社交世界的顺应

社交世界指社交场合、社会环境对交际者的言语行为所规范的原则和准则。为了顺应释话人的社会地位及职务，说话人采用的指称词语往往采用符合对方的头衔。

⑧ (October 13，2004 the Third Bush-Kerry presidential Debate)

Kerry：This really underscores the problem with the American health-care system. It's not working for the American family. And it's gotten worse under President Bush over the course of the last years.

⑨ (October 3，2000 the first Presidential Debates)

Bush：Well，I would first say he should have been tackling it for the last seven years. The difference is we need to explore at home. And the vice president doesn't believe in exploration，for example，in Alaska...

3. 英语指称词语对语言语境的顺应

语言语境指上下文，包括语言的连贯、语段关系、话语顺次等。衔接一般指一个语篇或文本内部关系的公开标记形式（这里的文本通常又叫做语篇的上下文或有关的文本片段）。我们一起来看一下句际衔接的两个例子。

⑩ (The first Gore-Bush debate, October 3，2000)

Bush：The man loves his wife and I appreciate that a lot. And I love mine. The man loves his family a lot，and I appreciate that，because I love my family. I think the thing that discourages me about the vice president was uttering those famous words，"No controlling legal authority." I felt like there needed to be a better sense of responsibility of what was going on in the White House...

　　这里布什本意并不是强调戈尔爱自己的妻子家庭，而是想让观众更加注意后面所要提到的内容。转换到新的话题时，采用的指称词语由反复使用 the man 变为 the vice president。

　　下面这个例子同样如此开始反复使用 Governor Bush 形成呼语，接下来 Gore 想着重指出的他与布什不同的地方以及布什应该做而没做到的地方通过转换指称词语为 the governor，来形成对照。

　　⑪（The first Gore-Bush debate，October 3，2000）

　　Gore：We agree on a couple of things on education. I strongly support new accountability, so does Governor Bush. I strongly support local control, so does Governor Bush. I'm in favor of testing as a way of measuring performance. Every school and every school district, have every state test the children. I've also proposed a voluntary national test in the fourth grade and eighth grade, and a form of testing the governor has not endorsed. I think that all new teachers ought to be tested, including in the subjects that they teach.

结语

　　美国总统大选辩论中指称词语有其特点。既然是一场辩论，难免会有争锋相对的地方。但是辩论双方仍然试图避免给亿万观众造成攻击者的形象。他们竭力维护自己的政治形象，这一点对竞选总统来说尤为突出和重要。因此双方尽可能少地采用直接指称词语，而用间接指称词语，因而美国总统大选辩论中指称词语灵活多变。在辩论动态的进行过程中，双方为了顺应各方面的因素不断转换指称词语。指称现象本质上是交际者实现顺应，最终实现交际目的的一种语言策略，是动态地顺应各种语境因素的语言选择的结果。顺应论对政治语篇中的指称词语有较强的解释力。

附：2000 与 2004 美国总统大选辩论中指称词语使用统计表

2000 Gore-Bush Debate ♯1①

How Gore referred to Bush	
Variety of referring expression	Frequency
1. my opponent	2
2. the governor	19
3. Governor Bush	17
4. The Bush	1
Total	39
How Bush referred to Gore	
Variety of referring expression	Frequency
1. the vice president	11
2. the man	6
3. Mr. Vice President	5
4. this	5
5. my opponent	3
6. Vice President Gore	3
7. this man	3
8. the administration	2
9. The Gore and Clinton folks	2
10. Vice President	1
11. this administration	1
12. Mr. Gore	1
13. my worthy opponent	1
14. the past administration	1
15. somebody	1
16. big exploding federal government	1
Total	47

2000 Gore-Bush Debate ♯2

How Gore referred to Bush	

---

① Tables of referring expressions used in the 2000 American presidential debates come from Wen-Chia Hu. 2004. Televised Presidential Debates—A Study of Reference in Cohesive Discourse [DA]. Submitted in partial fulfillment of the requirements for the Degree of Doctor of Education in Teachers College，Columbia University.

Variety of referring expression	Frequency
1. Governor	2
2. the governor	11
3. Governor Bush	1
Total	14
How Bush referred to Gore	
Variety of referring expression	Frequency
1. the vice president	9
2 the administration	8
3. Mr. Vice President	8
4. the horse	2
5. this administration	1
6. these folks	1
7. Vice President Gore	1
8. then-Senator Gore	1
Total	31

2000 Gore-Bush Debate #3

How Gore referred to Bush	
Variety of referring expression	Frequency
1. Governor	4
2. the governor	13
3. Governor Bush	10
4. this	1
5. here	1
Total	29
How Bush referred to Gore	
Variety of referring expression	Frequency
1. the vice president	4
2. the administration	1

3. Mr. Vice President	5
4. big federal government	1
5. this	1
6. the federal government	6
7. Vice President	2
8. somebody	1
9. one of my opponents	1
10. my opponent	1
Total	23

2004 Bush-Kerry Debate #1

How Gore referred to Bush	
Variety of referring expression	Frequency
1. my opponent	20
2. he	33
3. you	8
4. some	1
5. Senator Kerry	1
6. the senator	1
7. Senator	1
Total	65
How Kerry referred to Bush	
Variety of referring expression	Frequency
1. President Bush	4
2. the president	50
3. this administration	1
4. this president	13
5. the administration	1
6. he	47
7. you	12

8. Mr. President	1
9. thePresidentoftheunitedStatesofAmerica	1
10. a president of the United States	1
Total	129

2004 Bush-Kerry Debate ♯2

How Gore referred to Bush	
Variety of referring expression	Frequency
1. my opponent	11
2. he	81
3. Senator	1
Total	93
How Kerry referred to Bush	
Variety of referring expression	Frequency
1. President Bush	2
2. the president	58
3. this administration	2
4. this president	10
5. his administration	1
6. he	66
7. you	2
8. Mr. President	6
9. the first President in 72 years to lose jobs	1
10. a president of the United States	1
11. this	1
12. sir	1
13. his administration	1
Total	152

2004 Bush-Kerry Debate ♯3

How Gore referred to Bush	

Variety of referring expression	Frequency
1. my opponent	17
2. he	31
3. you	2
4. the senator	4
5. Senator	1
Total	55

How Kerry referred to Bush

Variety of referring expression	Frequency
1. President Bush	8
2. the president	43
3. this administration	2
4. this president	11
5. the administration	1
6. he	37
7. you	2
8. Mr. President	2
9. the first President	2
10. George Bush	1
11. the only president	4
12. The government	1
13. the republican leadership of the house and Senate	1
14. this	2
Total	117

参考文献

[1] Ariel，Mira. Interpreting anaphoric expressions：A cognitive versus a pragmatic approach [J]. *Journal of Linguistics*，1994，(30)．

[2] Halliday, M. A. K. Introduction to functional grammar [M]. London：Edward Arnold. 1985.

［3］Moore. Meaning and Reference［C］. Oxford University Press,1993. 160,156.

［4］Peccei,J. S. Pragmatics［M］. London:Taylor & FrancisLimited,1999.

［5］Verschueren,J. *Understanding Pragmatics*［M］. London:Arnold,1999.

［6］Wen-Chia Hu. Televised Presidential Debates—A Study of Reference in Cohesive Discourse［DA］. Submitted in partial fulfillment of the requirements for the Degree of Doctor of Education in Teachers College, Columbia University. 2004.

［7］Yule, George. *Pragmatics*［M］. Shanghai:ShanghaiForeignLanguageEducationPress,2000.

［8］何自然,于国栋.《语用学的理解》—Verschueren 的新作评价[J]. 现代外语,1999,（4）.

［9］康啸. 角逐布什——克里传略[M]. 北京:中共党史出版社,2004.

［10］刘植荣. 美国历届总统辩论精选[M]. 南昌:江西人民出版社,2005.

［11］李丹. 中英文指称的对比分析[D]. 上海师范大学,2005.

［12］李富民,李晓丽. 美国总统全传（下）［M］. 北京:中国社会科学出版社,2004.

［13］麦迪. 悲喜美国新总统—2000 年美国大选纷争内幕[M]. 北京:时事出版社,2000.

［14］钱冠连,霍永寿. 语用学新解[M]. 北京:清华大学出版社,2003.

［15］许保芳.《英汉叙事语篇人称指称对比分析》. 中国海洋大学硕士论文. 2005

［16］许余龙. 英汉指称词语表达的可及性[J]. 外语教学与研究,2000,（5）.

［17］张举栋.《不同文体中英汉指称词语可及性的对比研究》. 上海海事大学硕士论文. 2005

［18］http://www. debates. org/pages/debtrans. html

（张帆,中南林业科技大学）

语境真实性之文化思考

引言

语境是一个很广泛的概念，从语言学角度来看，指社会文化语境，也就是语言形式赖以生存的社会文化形态，它涉及人类生活的各个方面，从衣食住行、风俗习惯到价值观念等等。狭义的语境是指语言形式出现的具体语境，又称情景语境。语境这一概念最初由英国人类学家 B. Mali-nowski 提出，他使用的是一种比喻的说法，认为讲话人所处的情境也像上下文一样对语义的解释具有可参照性，因此提醒人们在理解词义时要考虑情境上下文（context of situation）。B. Malinowski 把情景语境分为三部分：一、参与者的有关特征，包括参与者的语言行为和非语言行为；二、有关的事物；三、语言行为的效果。

伦敦学派创始人 J. R. Firth 将 Malinowski 的观点纳入语言学研究领域对语境作了重新界定进一步指出语境是语义分析平面上一套彼此相关的抽象的概念类别。他选择"话语"作为观察语境的立足点。以 Hallidy 为代表的系统语言学家，继承了 Malinowski 和 Firth 的语境思想，对语境和语言系统的选择和作用作了大量深入研究，他认为情景语境包括话语范围即语场（Field of discourse）、话语基调即语旨（Tenor of discourse）和话语方式即语式（Mode of discourse）。语场指的是话题及与话题有关的交际场景；语旨指的是交际双方的社会关系及角色；语式是指交际媒介的形式如书面语、口语等。从上世纪 80 年代中期开始，语言学界对语境的研究出现了一种令人瞩目的新趋势，即更侧重于对语境的特征、类型、作用和功能的探讨，对语境真实性的研究也出现了不同视角上的观点。例如，Sperber & Wilson 从心理角度的语境真实性进行研究，认为语境不仅是客观的场景，还是认知的心理产物。于有交际任务的真实环境里，不同社会身份成员选择合适交际方式参与言语活动，语境的基本特征之真实性（truth value）才会得以体现出来。本文主要以 Halliday 的语境理论为基础，从文化方面对语境真实性做出一些思考。

1. 文化对语境的影响

文化是一个笼统的概念，在分析语场、语旨、语式的影响时，需要对 Edward Hall 的语境理论进行简单介绍。人类学家 Edward Hall 将语境划分为 "低语境文化"（low context culture）和"高语境文化"（high-context culture）。在低语境文化中，环境所蕴涵的信息较少，大多数信息需明确表达出来，人们的交流遵循直接的原则。在高语境文化中许多信息都储存在收讯者身上和背景之中，需要直接用语言表达的信息较少，人们的交流也显得较为间接。例如，中国人写文章喜欢用典故和成语，这使得语言更加精炼和丰富多彩，就是高语境文化起作用。Gidykunst 将十二个不同文化的国家按"低语境"到"高语境"的方式排列，排在第一的是瑞士，排在最后一位的是日本。美国和中国分别排在第四位和倒数第二位。

1. 1 不同文化中语式对语境真实性的影响

高一虹（1999）曾对两篇作文《回忆 xx 中学》作出对比，分别是由已移民美国三年以母语为西班牙语的奥斯瓦尔多和在美国读某大学的中国青年周某写的。综合两篇作文的话语方式，话语基调，话语范围，便能揭示奥斯瓦尔多和周某所处的"情景语境"是大不相同的。虽然他们当时处于相同的社会环境和语言环境，但由于都深深受到了自己本族文化的影响，奥文行文流利过于口语化，情感流露于字里行间，周文语法 错误较多，情感表达含蓄、深沉。从文化方面看，奥斯瓦尔多的母语为西班牙语，而西班牙语是拼音语言为基础的，属于曲折语系，而周某的母语是汉语，属孤立语系。另外，两人从小所接受的教育思想，文化陶冶和宗教信仰等都不一样。正因为如此，中国教师和外国教师对两作文的评价也截然相反。这就表明了受本民族文化影响，不同民族的人在相同社会环境中所表达的话语方式也很不一样。

1. 2 不同文化中语旨对语境真实性的影响

Ronald Scollon & Suzanne Wong Scollon（1995）指出，理解语境语旨时，需要考虑交际参与者的两个方面：他们是谁，即他们的身份，以及他们在该语言事件中的地位和职责。这一点在"高语境"的日本文化中体现尤为明显，在使用日语过程中，要依据说话对象选择敬语、尊他语或自谦语等不同的语言表达方式。例如，日本人在日常生活中多使用简体，但对上司和长辈必须使用敬体。而美国人喜欢开门见山，直来直往，而把拐弯抹角当成是思路不清或缺乏诚意。从日本人看来，直截了当会认为对对方的感情不予考虑，只有上级对下级才能直来直去，讲话类似下命令。因此为促进跨文化交际，要入乡随俗，不同民族在不同地区表达同样的交际目的时，要注意在交际语境中使用不同的话语基调，也就是依据不同文化采用不同的交际方式在真实语境中实现交际目的。不同语境文化造成的冲突，很大程度是由于两者几乎截然相反的特征引起。中国人喜欢讲情面，不愿意明确表达自己的意愿，尤其是否定意味，美国人则相反，喜欢"就事论事"，以便统一认识。

在 Halliday 的语境理论中，情景语境的话语方式，包括口语、书面语、打电话、发 E-mail 等等。高语境文化国家和低语境文化国家在真实语境中话语表达方式也会表现出很大差异。在中国有一对恋人，小伙子在情人节那天给远方的女朋友拍了一封电报，三个字："我爱你"，这种古老而浪漫的方式给女友一个惊喜，也使他们的感情得到了进一步的发展。而在美国恋人之间相互说："I love you!"是很正常也很频繁的事。那么美国人就会难以理解中国小伙子发电报的行为，甚至会觉得荒唐可笑。这是因为中国人情感表达方式含蓄，而美国人更喜欢情感表达方式直白。于是在跨文化交际中便会出现不同的话语表达方式。

1.3　语境的建立过程受文化影响

Sperber & Wilson 在 Revelance 一书中指出，话语的理解是语境的建立过程，语境的选择是按照与言语交际是否相关的原则进行的。他们（1986）指出，一个回合的交际结束时，这一回合的话语意义组成一个即刻语境（the immediately given context），构成下一回合释义所需语境的一个结成部分。这即告诉我们，语境是动态变化的，要把语境置于发展变化的言语交际过程中进行研究，交际过程也便是语境的构造过程。在顾及语境真实性时，交际者必须依照双方不同的文化思想来建立语境。

结语

早期的语境研究，往往限于对语境概念的界定，对语境要素的归纳，说明和对语境研究意义的阐释。由于语境研究的蓬勃发展，使得目前语境研究中同时出现了一些问题，这主要表现在两个方面，第一，虽然大家都认识到语境是动态变化发展的，但是许多语境研究都还停留在静态的分析描写上，缺乏相应的动态方法。第二，对语境的本质缺乏全面统一的认识。由于认识平面不一样，有的学者认为，语言学家设定的，一个用于分析言语事件的抽象理论概念。有的则认为语境是客观存在的具体事物（上下文、言语环境等）。Firth 辩证的提出"语境最好用作一种适用于语言事件的纲要式具体构造物，……它是一组相关的范畴，跟语法范畴不同，但同样具有抽象性"。在此指导下，本文针对语境真实性，从文化角度作出一些思考，这可谓是跨文化交际过程中的沧海一粟，但对促进交际不无指导意义。

参考文献

［1］Sperber，D.，and D. Wilson. *Relevance*［M］. Oxford：Basil Blackwell Ltd.，1986.

［2］Ronald Scollon and Suzanne Wong Scollon. *Intercultural Communication：A Discourse Approach*［M］. 社会科学文献出版社，1995.

［3］高一虹. 语言文化差异的认知与超越［M］. 上海：上海外语教学与研究出版社，1999.

［4］苏新春. 文化语言学教程［M］. 上海：上海外语教学与研究出版社，2006.

［5］谢琴丽."交际教学法和系统功能语法"复旦外国语言学论丛［J］. 05秋季号.

［6］刘焕辉."语境与语言交际"语境研究论文集［J］. 北京：北京语言学院出版社，1992.

［7］何兆熊，蒋艳梅."语境的动态研究"外国语［J］. 1997,(6).

（潘衡跃,长沙理工大学;曹志希,中南林业科技大学）

跨文化交际中的中日两国寒暄语分析

引言

在中日两国语言文化生活中，有关使用频率很高的あいさつ语（寒暄语），它们的表现结构、本来的意义、文体上的特色等诸多因素，往往不被人们所重视。对于这些司空见惯的寒暄语表现，它们一般失去了本来的意思，而仅仅作为一种间投语、感叹语或是惯用表现。例如「おはよう」（你早）、「こんにちは」「こんばんは」（你好）、「おやすみ」（晚安）、「さようなら」（再见）、「ありがとう」（谢谢）等，在这些不胜枚举的寒暄语背后，隐含着丰富的价值内容。

日本的文字来源于汉字，日本文化与中国文化有着千丝万缕的联系。但日语毕竟是日语，日本文化更不等同于中国文化。在言语交际中为了确保话语在运用上取得成功，我们不但要懂得语言结构的规约力量和语言运用的策略，而且更应该懂得语言运用的社会文化因素。对中日两国寒暄语的惯用表现进行比较研究，分析寒暄语背后的语言文化、生活习惯、思维方式等，可以揭示两者的差异。而这些有时明朗、有时微妙的异同之处，对于学习日语的中国人以及学习中文的日本人而言，都是比较难以理解的问题。基于上述原因，本文通过对中日两国寒暄语进行考察，包括一些必要的对比研究，探讨中日寒暄语的共性和差异，并对这些共性和差异进行解释。对中日寒暄语进行研究将有助于提高日语和汉语学习者的跨文化交际能力。

1. 对寒暄语进一步的定位

既然寒暄语用于交际之中，我们就有必要在会话结构中对寒暄语进行更准确的定位。钱厚生（1996）对会话的总体结构进行了分析，并提出了一个寒暄语作为会话结构成分的框架；总的说来，对于一个完整的会话，其总体结构包括寒暄语、会话主体和告别语；会话主体是指会话的话题，会话主体以外的部分都被视为寒暄语；完整的寒暄语中可能包括 1 个寒暄语，开始接触包含在寒暄语之中；告别语之中可能包括 n 个寒暄语，结束接触作为第 n 个寒暄语包含在告别语之中；会话主体则可能包括 m 个话题，而每个话题可能包括打开话题、话题主体和中止话题三个部分。

（1）① 田中：今日は。佐藤さん。大丈夫ですか。

② 佐藤：あ、田中さん。今日は。おかげさまで、だいぶよくなりました。

③ 田中：そうですか。安心しました。あ、これ、近くで買ってきたおかゆですが、よかったらどうぞ。

④ 佐藤：わあ、いいにおいですね。ありがとうございます。そうだ。このあいだのコンサートの時は、怒ってすみませんでした。

⑤ 田中：いいえ。電話をしなかったわたしのほうが悪かったんです。

⑥ 佐藤：いいえ。気にしないでください。

⑦ 田中：ごめんなさい。佐藤さん、わたしはこれで…。ゆっくり休んでくださいね。じゃあ、また。

⑧ 佐藤：じゃあ、また。本当にいろいろどうもありがとう。

以上是田中去探望正生病的同班同学佐藤的会话。在这一段话中，① 为寒暄语（开始接触）以及打开话题，② 为对① 的应答及打开话题，③ 以下为话题的主体，⑦ 为结束语题及告别语，⑧ 为⑦ 的应答（结束接触）。

会话的结构尽管比较复杂，但正如钱厚生（1996）所指出的那样，一个完整的会话必定包括寒暄语，会话主体和告别语三个部分，所以，我们可以把上面的框架作为一个理想的模型去考虑交际中的寒暄语。另外，从以上的会话例子可以看出，日本人即使是比较熟悉的人在交谈时，也习惯于使用许多的寒暄语，由此可见，寒暄语在日本人的交际生活中的重要性。

为了更准确地区分寒暄语和会话的主体，这就需要研究寒暄语的语用功能。

2. 寒暄语的语用功能

Austin 的言语行为理论认为"说话就是做事"。即，话语是具体说话人在具体场合为了具体目的说出的词句。它们并不是目的，而是借以达到目的的手段，即以某种方式影响听话人的手段。他把言语行为分成三个次行为：言内行为、言外行为、言后行为。通过对寒暄语的分析，可以发现寒暄语属于表述行为，用于向听话人表达某种感情。具体说来，寒暄语主要表达说话人对听话人的亲近、敬意、告别语主要表达希望维持友好关系的愿望（小林 1987 等）。所以，寒暄语不能简单地完全按照字面意义理解。比如，问候「お元気ですか」的时候并不是说话人担心对方的健康情况，而是在表达说话人对听话人的关心。

值得注意的是，寒暄语在实现其语用功能时，语境起着至关重要的作用。也就是说某一言内行为因语境不同，其言外行为可能具有不同的意义。

（2）（社員研修教室の入り口で偶然に会ったAとB）；AとBは日本人。

A：久しぶり、元気?

B：うん。これから中に入ろうと思って。

A：そうか、僕は今はもう帰るから。じゃ、頑張ってね。

(3)「そうですか。大変ですね…。でも、あまり難しく考えないで、頑張って…」

(4)「家の玄関でA（夫）とB（妻）」；A是中国人，B是日本人。

A：いってきます。

B：いってらっしゃい。今日も頑張ってね。

A：どうしておれだけ頑張らなきゃ行かんのか。

B：ええ、どうしたんの。

　　(2)中的「頑張ってね」是寒暄语，即处于会话话题之外。然而，而(3)中的「頑張って」则是表示自己同情的鼓励的话。即(3)重视的是该话语的内容，用前面的框架来说，它处于会话话题之中。

汉语的"吃了吗?"常用作寒暄语，然而它也可作为"询问"：

(5) A：吃了吗?

B：还没呢。

A：那我们一起吃饭去吧。

这个例子中的"吃了吗?"不是寒暄语，而是说话人真心求得听话人的回答。

　　所以，很多时候被用作寒暄语的话语，在另一语境可能不再具有寒暄语的功能。

　　如果我们把语境的概念扩大为某一文化，这一结论仍然适用。在某一文化中用作寒暄语的话语，在另一文化之中却不适用，因此而导致文化误读的例子很多。例如，以上的(4)的对话就证明了这一点，作为日本人的妻子出于关心用日本人惯用的寒暄语「頑張って」问候了中国人的丈夫，但是，中国人的丈夫不理解这一习惯，误解了其妻子的意思，按照中国人的思维方式，认为妻子总是要求他工作要努力「頑張って这句话中文直译是努力加油的意思」，所以，他就生气地问妻子为什么每天总是要他一个人必须努力呢? 他妻子被他这一问，弄得莫名其妙，就问他到底出了什么事呢? 诸如此类因语言背后所隐藏的文化因素引起的跨文化交际的误读现象还有很多。

　　由上述可知，使用寒暄语进行寒暄的人关心的是其语用功能，即言外行为的实现，但这并不是说其字面意义，或者说其言内行为无足轻重。另一方面，从整体上来看，日汉寒暄语在信息性上是存在一定差异的，汉语文化中倾向于使用信息性强的寒暄语，而日语中却未必如此，在语境并不清晰的情况下，信息性强的寒暄语容易被误读为会话的话题，在跨文化交际中更是如此。

3. 中日寒暄语对比和分析

限于本文篇幅，我们无法在这里全面地对比中日寒暄语，从有助于跨文化交际的角度出发，我们发现中日寒暄语主要存在以下一些异同。

根据表达内容（字面含义）的有无把寒暄语分为"命题性寒暄语"和"非命题性寒暄语"两类。还可进一步将命题性寒暄语分为"指人性寒暄语"（直接或间接性地与被

寒暄的人有关）和"非指人性寒暄语"（以天气等与对方无关的寒暄内容）两类。对于告别语，日语和汉语中的非命题性寒暄语都比较简单；而命题性寒暄语有较多相似之处。

(1) じゃね。

(2) さよなら。

(3) バイバイ

(4) いっていらっしゃい。

(5) 再见。

对于寒暄语，日语中存在系统的非命题性的日常寒暄语，而汉语则没有；而命题性的寒暄语，值得重视的是，中国人更倾向于使用交谈性寒暄语，而且汉语寒暄语说涉及的内容比日语更广。如陈指出，在特定的语境下，几乎所有的话语皆可用于问候。

彭曾指出，中国人与熟人见面时，不用"こんにちは"（你好），而代之以"だいぶ痩せてきたな"（你变瘦了），"ちょっと太ってきたな"（你发福了），"背がだいぶ伸びたな"（你长高了），其实中国人是把这些话当作寒暄语的，但在日本文化中是避讳谈及此类内容的。他还指出：中国人常问对方"在什么地方买的?""这个多少钱买的""您买的不贵啊。"然后对此加以"称赞"——"您买的不贵呀"。在中国人看来，此类话多数无非是些旨在增进双方的亲近感的寒暄语罢了，但在日本社会，"询问价钱"是失礼的，一般应该换说成「いいものを持っていますね」（您的这个东西真是好）「すてきですね」（很漂亮）之类。以上这些例子可以看出中日寒暄语使用习惯的不同。

4. 跨文化交际中的文化误读

在日本的生活中，有几个特定场合的整齐划一的寒暄方式。例如，日本人进家门之后要用"ただいま（我回来了）"和家人打招呼。家里的人要回应"おかえり（回来了）"。出门要说"行って来ます（我走了）"，对方应回答"いってら

っしゃい（你去吧）"。日语里约定俗成的寒暄方式比较多。因这些话语形式意义单一，使用场合固定，所以并不难掌握。不过，有些情况就需要仔细分辨，否则会误读。

"一个冬天的早上，我在教学楼门口遇见一位熟悉的日本朋友。朋友跟我打招呼，'寒いですね（真冷啊）'。我根据自己的感觉，一本正经地回答，'いいえ，寒くないですよ（不冷啊）'。我当时特纳闷，朋友的表情有一丝尴尬。现在明白，'寒いですね（真冷啊）'是日本人常用的寒暄语。并不是要你回答冷不冷"（中国留学生，1998 年）。

"有一天中午，我骑着自行车回学校。在校园门口附近，遇到了一个中国朋友，他问我'吃饭了吗?'，我回答说'还没吃呢'。我本以为对方会邀请我跟他一起吃饭，于是下了自行车，满心欢喜地等待着他的邀请。可是对方却简单地说了一句'啊，是吗?'，转身骑上自行车就走了。我呆呆地愣在那儿，看着他远去的背影，心里真不是滋味，'他也未免太冷淡了吧'。后来才知道，'吃饭了吗'不过是中国人一般打招呼时的用语"（日本留学生，1998 年）。

上面的两个例子形象地说明了中日两国的招呼语是各具特色的。日本人的寒暄内容经常涉及季节、天气。日本列岛位于中纬度，气候湿润温暖，四季分明，更受到有规律的季风影响，因此气候多变。台风、梅雨、暴雪、樱花、红叶、雨汛，大自然培养了日本人敏锐的"季节感"。日本人十分喜欢谈论与季节、气候有关的话题，并将其发展为一种寒暄方式。交流一下彼此对季节天气的感想，能让人们之间产生连带感与一体感。值得一提的是，日本人无论自己的真实感想如何，都不会反驳否定对方，而是不断地随声附和，以保证交际的继续进行。日本人在书信的"前文"部分，也常常把有关季节的话语作为开场白。谈天气这种社交文化，由于双方共同感知阴晴冷暖，会生出同一屋檐下的共同意识吧。

有时，日本人的寒暄里隐含着弦外之音，必须细细品味，否则可能闹出笑话。20 世纪 80 年代一位中国学者赴日研修，在各方面都得到指导教师 K 先生的关照。有一次，和 K 先生一同参加一个学术会议。其间的一个晚上，K 先生打来热情的电话："コーヒーでものみに行きませんか"（不去喝点咖啡什么的吗）。他不假思索地回答说："夜コーヒーをのんだら眠れませんから、失礼します"（对不起，我晚上喝咖啡睡不着觉）。当时，他并没有觉得这个回答有什么不得体之处，事隔十几年，他在研究日本语言中的间接表达方式时，想起了这个例子，进行了反思。其实当时 K 先生的真正意图是邀请他去聊天。

此外，中日两国过年时的寒暄语也有差异。当代一部分中国人喜欢用"恭喜发财"来拜年，门口贴着的对联也常常有"恭喜发财"、"财源滚滚"的字眼。这个习俗恐怕是中国改革开放以来，从经济起飞先行一步的南方传播开来的，但仍有许多人继续使用"恭贺新禧"的传统用语。但不管怎么说，直言"发财"对日本人来说有点不可思议。特别是在贺年片上，或新年的早晨对别人说"祝你发大财"，一定会被认为头脑有问题。日本新年的寒暄语和传统中国相同，通常是"恭贺新禧！"日本也有自己特色的贺辞，如"恭贺新禧！今年也请多多关照！""多谢您的关照，祝您健康、多福！"

结语

如上所述，跨文化交流过程中出现的误读，常常是由隐藏在语言背后的文化因素引起的。非本族人与本族人用语法没有错误的句子进行交际时仍然会发生误解的原因，正是由于忽略了交际中的文化因素，因而产生误会。对外语学习者来说，单单掌握语法知识是远远不够的，还应认真体会、领悟语言中所蕴含的文化规约。

另外，在跨文化交际中，外语学习者不应期待把母语中的寒暄语译成外语便会产生相同的效果。而且，外语中的寒暄语也不能简单地按字面意思去解释。但研究结果表明，对外语学习者来说，母语对外语的干扰难以避免。因此，有必要对寒暄语深入加以研究。在教学时，仅仅在句子层面上讲讲授寒暄语是不够的，还要意识到它是整个会话结构的一部分，它对成功完成交际具有不可轻视的作用，这样将有助于提高外语学习者的交际能力。

参考文献

[1] 钱厚生．Greetings and Partings in English and Chinese[C]．北京：商务印书馆，1996．

[2] 野元菊雄．挨拶言葉の原理[J]．日本語学 9 所収，1983．

[3] 比嘉正範．挨拶と挨拶言葉[J]．日本語学 9 所収，1983．

[4] 小林佑子．挨拶行動の日米比較研究[J]．日本語学 1 所収，1986．

[5] 许昌华，李奇楠．现代日语间接言语行为详解[M]．北京：北京大学出版社，2001．

[6] 朱永生．PHATIC COMMUNITION [A]．王福祥，文化与语言[C]．北京：外语教学与研究出版社，1994．

[7] 顾日国．礼貌、语用与文化[C]．载胡文仲编文化与交际，北京：外语教学与研究出版社，1994．

[8] 王秀文．日本语言与跨文化交际[C]．北京：世界知识出版社，2003．

[9] 王南．通过寒暄语透视日本文化[J]．日语知识，2004．

[10] 刘剑波．日常の挨拶についての日中对照研究[J]，日语学习与研究，1986，(6)．

（林春，中南林业科技大学外语学院）

Discourse Analysis in Foreign Language Teaching

Introduction

Discourse analysis is a term which has come to have different interpretations for us working in different fields. In the field of foreign language teaching, it involves a practical approach to language use, which demands, in belief, a straightforward practice of language in the classroom rather than an insightful analysis of making discourse. Therefore, we have no wish to show how a discourse is worked in nature, but try to demonstrate how a pre-programmed discourse is structured in foreign language teaching, and interested in its content and context in class for the purpose of improving our foreign language teaching and making students use language effectively.

1. Discourse in the classroom

There exist two kinds of discourse: the first is an exchange of ideas and emotions through language. This kind is carried actually out of the classroom. The second is an instructional discourse in which forms are practiced mostly in the classroom (Claire Kramasch 1999) . This kind is usually embodied as a teaching program, and it happens and ends with the process of teaching.

As a discourse in the first kind is concerned, each produce of a discourse has its meaning and purpose. It characterizes in a succession of starting and ending in a certain time and place. Comparatively, the discourse in the second kind is pre-programmed one or being produced by students' imitating. It has its limitations from the forms of written and spoken language in the textbook. To a large degree, the discourse in class could be regarded as an "unreal" one in terms of discourse analysis in general. It does not bear meaning and purpose as it has in the first kind, nor is it important to when and where the discourse is happened. Much of it is impregnated with learning values.

Here we do not mean to say that the discourse happened in the classroom is "unreal", we mean that the discourse, as far as classroom treatment is concerned, can be unrealistic; but we have real English which, as far as language is concerned, is frequently handled in the realistic ways. On the other hand, the discourse in the second kind is generally referred to classroom-centered research and is motivated by an attempt to look at the classroom as a setting for classroom language acquisition and learning in terms of the language input provided by the teacher's talk (Jack C. Richards 2001) . Therefore, the discourse in class is generally related to knowledge of language itself, such as the words, sentence structures, and so on. In that case, the discourse yields only to a sense of language being learned from the textbook.

Given discourse in the classroom, we would like to demonstrate the fact of a discourse by examining its content and context during the course of foreign language teaching.

2. Discourse Content in the Classroom

Discourse analysis involves the data, and the data studied in discourse analysis is always a fragment of discourse (Gillian Brown, George Yule 2000) , especially in foreign language teaching, where the discourse usually appears both in a written and a spoken piece from the textbook. These are two forms of discourse in terms of teaching. The former will include a study of content development and cohesion across the sentences; and the latter will focus on those aspects, plus turn-taking practices, and opening and closing sequences of a piece of a discourse. Whatever forms a discourse is appeared in class; its content is always decided and arranged in a teaching way.

This provides foreign language teaching with a way of using discourse analytic techniques to look into the discourse content signified by the forms of words, phrases or structures which is not usually identified or be aware of in a natural discourse. It is largely related, as mentioned above, to a teaching program of which students are required to understand the discourse content. Here is one of the examples of analyzing discourse content in the classroom.

A: Good morning, why are you in such a hurry?

B: Well, what time is it, please?

A: It's 9, but why?

B: Oh, I'll be later for class again.

It is worth noting here, before discussing this short piece of written conversation, we would like to inform, in terms of discourse analysis in geranial, that the conversation happens between speaker A and B. The speaker is one of the important elements for discourse analysis, in other words, without the attendance of the speaker, discourse analysis might find no way to go.

While in language teaching, as Claire Kramasch once argued that in the foreign language classroom teacher and learners are both participants and observers of a cross grammatical exercises, communicative activities, and the discussion of texts (Claire Kramasch 1999). This argument shows us a fact that in the classroom the original speaker of a discourse in the textbook will be probably turned out to be a part of the discourse content, as words or phrases are used as parts of the content to be learned by students in class.

As far as teaching is concerned, the discourse, either in spoken or in written piece, can be very effectively exploited for purposes of developing students' using of language. Let's come directly to that example discourse presented above to see how its content is managed to teach in class.

This is, of course, a pre-programmed discourse from the textbook. The point of where and when the discourse starts and ends is indicated, and the content is also set well. From that discourse, we first recognize the connection of the content between the first two lines, it shows that there are two references revealed between speaker A and B, one is "in such a hurry", and the other is "what time". We have also noticed that speaker A felt strange as he saw speaker B, so he wants to know "why are you in such a hurry?" Commonly, he expects that speaker B would answer: "I'm late." or some words like that. Unfortunately and unexpectedly, speaker B asks instead of answers "what time is it?" In a sense of discourse analysis, the expression in speaker B does not refer to anything that speaker A wants to know.

It seems unreasonable in a way of shifting that content in a discourse so unexpectedly. As a matter of fact, there is no way that one participant can place absolute constraints on what the other can say. Yet this does not mean that one utterance can be followed by any other utterance (Amy B. M. Tsui 2000). This is not the point that teaching should consider, but it will make one of a good content possible for teaching, because teaching pays close attention to what students will learn from it's the discourse in the textbook, not what discourse will appear to be in analysis.

Along with discourse analysis, that situation, however, is based on rational, sometimes overtly logical, sequence to a discourse in nature (Gillian Brown, 2000). This situation is also existed in the first two lines of the example discourse above. Although both speakers talk about different things, the content of the discourse goes along naturally, validly and effectively. But all that will be unconsciously neglected with the participating of teacher and students, because this piece of discourse, including the speaker A and B in the original discourse, is already served as the whole content for the classroom teaching.

What teaching will do is to make students understand what content the discourse bears or what words the speakers are used. For instance, speaker A's responding "it's 9, but why?". In teaching, it might be explained directly to the students, by saying, "it is an omitted sentence, and it is often used in the spoken language." Likely, we may also tell students that this omitted sentence refers to "but why do you want to know the time?" and so on. Students thus have no alternative ways of uttering their own discourses, as they will do in a natural discourse, which will normally present optional ways of content concerning any topics.

Taking content in foreign language teaching into account, the content of a discourse hinges on the context which will affect discourse attributes. The presence of that discourse is probably not related to the general discourse because teaching is investigating the use of language in class. It is more concerned with the potential relationship of content, or relationship of one word or one sentence to anther, on the particular occasion of language use, than with the relationship between the students and the students' exchanging their ideas. In fact, we view discourse in class as a developing language ability process rather than a finished product; and this, above all, corresponds with how the participants handle the content in the discourse context of foreign language teaching.

3. Discourse Context of Foreign Language Teaching

Discourse context of foreign language teaching could be characterized as a language use in a special time and space. We call it "special" because the discourse produced is usually based on a pre-programmed discourse from the textbook which is of course for language teaching. So, what meaning indicated or what purpose presented of a discourse, as it is usually concerned in common situations, will be paid a insignificant attention in the classroom context. It needs to be recognized too that one fact of discourse context of teaching is that there is no practicable discourse correlated to the language used in common. It has in common with language knowledge itself, as is mentioned above, the words, sentence structures, and so on, which is often dependent on the discourse or transactional context of language teaching (Jack C. Richards 2001). In other words, in discourse context of foreign language teaching we stress more on the relationship of one word or one sentence to anther than on the relationship between the students and the discourse content on the particular teaching occasion of language use.

It is because making a discourse in the context of foreign language teaching is imitating or practicing the use of language, rather than one produced by speakers for a communicative purpose. To some extent, the content is restricted in a context of teaching, and context, therefore, will decide when and how the discourse happens and sometimes will inference students' way of using language in that specific time and place.

There is some contextual information for teaching to interpret when a piece of discourse is dealt with in class, for example, words or sentence structures that are applied as a content of discourse. In order to interpret these in a piece of discourse in class, analyzing the discourse in the contextual ways will become a practical approach to fulfill the teaching purposes. This could be probably explained by a figure of the discourse context of foreign language teaching bellow:

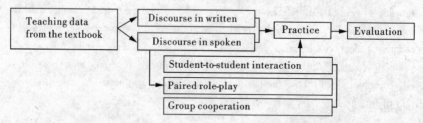

The Discourse Context of Foreign Language Teaching

Here, we would like to serve the discourse context of teaching as a supposed context for discourse produce, because in that context, the speakers and hearers are all students who are learning to use language, not to communicate. Although language teaching in the classroom is also a kind of communication, there has no reference of the discourse as we usually have in nature. What happens between the students (speakers) is less important than what words or sentences are used in a discourse for students to acquire. Therefore, students will be promoted to utter something like a conversation under the discourse context of foreign language teaching.

According to the figure above, when we teach a piece of discourse in class, we can make full use of the data from the textbook, both a written and a spoken piece of discourse, to show some information in the teaching context for students to practice. Based on a discourse in written or in spoken, students are required to imitate by practice with the ways of student-to-student interaction; a paired role-play and a group cooperative activity through discourse context during the course of teaching. To help students to make their own discourse, the explanations of the discourse content is necessary to raise students' recognitions of effective use of language.

Given that discourse context of foreign language teaching, the discourse produced among students will be evaluated by their practice. Thus, a better understanding of the influence of the discourse context of foreign language teaching could be simply illustrated as: teaching data from the textbook are a basement of the discourse content according to which students' practices are performed, regardless of its discourse context, by the activities of student-to-student interaction; a paired role-play task and group cooperation, and then the results of discourse will be evaluated in the classroom to respect the language teaching.

Generally, the discourse analysis is describing what speaker and hearers are doing, not the relationship which exists between sentences (Gillian Brown, George Yule 2000). On the other hand, discourse in nature will probably have some references which are treated as an action on the part of the speaker (Gillian Brown, George Yule 2000). These might not be included in making a discourse in the context of teaching, so students often do not provide such explicit guidelines to help the other side following the topic.

The question of what a discourse is intended to count can often be an important part of a participant's perception of what is going on in a conversation (David Brazil 2000). Otherwise the teacher would consider the use of language properly in context where discourse is used to communicate specific messages and to manage the organization of knowledge that students will understand what is said or written.

Accordingly, language used in that case can gain insight into the effect of the activities of students' discourse production and their language development. It is also possible that students make different discourses in response to some contents of a pre-programmed one from the textbook in the discourse context of teaching.

Conclusion

In sum, what teaching is actually concerned with the discourse analysis is to examine how language is used whether it is a spoken or written piece. So, it cannot be restricted to the description of linguistic forms independent of the purposes or functions which those forms are designed to serve in human affairs (Gillian Brown, George Yule, 2000). Since foreign language teaching is a certain way of the language use, discourse analysis will help foreign language teaching to provide not only as a teaching method for investigating foreign language interactions among students in the classroom but also can benefit students whenever they use that language out of the classroom.

References

[1] Claire Kramasch. *Context and Culture in Language Teaching* [M]. Shanghai: Shanghai Foreign Language Education Press. 1999:29.

[2] Jack C. Richards. *The Context of Language Teaching*, [M]. Foreign Language Teaching and Research Press, 2000: 71,102.

[3] Gillian Brown, George Yule. *Discourse Analysis*, [M]. Foreign Language Teaching and Research Press, 2000:1, 27, 28, 69.

[4] Amy B. M. Tsui, *English Conversation* [M]. Shanghai: Shanghai Foreign Language Education Press, 2000:217.

[5] Gillian Brown. *Language and Understanding*, [M]. Shanghai: Shanghai Foreign Language Education Press, 2000:18.

[6] David Brazil. *A Grammar of Speech* [M]. Shanghai: Shanghai Foreign Language Education Press, 2000:168.

(Ren Xiping, Wang Bei, Han Xiaohong, 河海大学)

Structuring in Teacher-initiated Text-based Questioning Discourse in Classrooms

1. Significance of structuring analysis

Everything that occurs in the classroom goes through a process of live person-to-person interaction (Ellis 1994: 565). Allright (1984: 156) sees interaction as "the fundamental fact of classroom pedagogy". Classroom process research views language lessons as "socially constructed events" (Ellis1994: 573), the interactional events that take place in a classroom, which is similar to what Hymes called "speech events".

Mclaughlin (1985: 149, cited in Ellis1994: 567) points out that, in the existing proliferation of studies, the behavior of the teacher and the learners is often treated separately and consequently information is lost about the sequential flow of classroom activities. Hence, it is of great importance to establish a framework to systematically act out for what happens between the teacher and learners. The study of discourse structure just keeps to the point.

Classroom discourse has an identifiable structure (Ellis 1994: 574). Bellack et al. (1966, cited in Meighan 1986: 157 - 158) suggested that the language interaction in classrooms can be broken down into four basic moves or categories related to the recognizable functions of language being used and to how instances of talk are structurally related. There are structuring moves (utterances working to create and direct the setting for talk and activity in a lesson), soliciting moves (designed to elicit some kind of response), responding moves (which are directly tied to structuring moves) and reacting moves (talk designed to clarify, expand or evaluate a prior move without being directly elicited by the prior move). Soliciting—responding—reacting is similar to question—answer—evaluation. When addressing the issue of what is the unit of classroom discourse, Ellis puts forward "interactional sequences", loosely defined as "a unit of discourse with a unitary topic and purpose" (1994: 578). Given the complexity of classroom discourse, Goffman (1996, cited in Hu 1994) contends that interactional unit is more appropriate than discourse unit because interaction can be both verbal and nonverbal (e. g. silence). The analysis of discourse interaction is aimed at disclosing how the exchange between the teacher and learners propel the learning activities to move forward (Sinclair & Coulthard 1975; Coulthard & Montgomery 1981; Sinclair & Brazil 1982, cited in Li & Fan 2002).

2. Related studies of questioning structuring in language pedagogy

Structuring in questioning refers to the systematic and dynamic features of a question-and-answer exchange with a definite topic which is realized by one or two teacher questions. Also, a question may be answered by one student or be responded by the chorus response. The teacher may direct the same question to several students. Besides, the teacher may request the respondent to clarify his/her response. The process of a questioning sequence may be very short and simple. But sometimes it might be long and complex. All this depends upon the patterns of structures in questioning, that is, the structuring of questioning.

A classic study in questioning structuring in the west was conducted by Sinclair & Coulthard (1974, see Meighan 1986, also Ellis 1994), who developed a hierarchical model consisting of lesson, transaction, exchange, move and act. Burton (1980; 1981, cited in Hu 1994: 218) exchanges "lesson" with "interaction" thus establishing a system made up of "act—move—transaction—interaction". The most clearly defined element is the exchange part which is also known as the "IRF" pattern typically having three phases involving three moves: initiating, responding, and follow-up. Each move is realized by means of various kinds of act. Questioning represents the typical structure of classroom teacher-student interaction: teacher question—student response—evaluation.

In China, Li & Fan (2002) reported their study of the structuring of questioning at the university level. The data was collected from 20-hour EFL majors' oral classes. Based on the analysis of the data collected, they identified the following four patterns of questioning structures:

Pattern I: IRF

It refers to the initiation—response—feedback structure. In this structure the teacher solicits a student, who gives the response before the teacher provides the feedback.

e. g. T: What's the meaning of this word?

Ss: 饺子

T: Yeah. You are right.

Pattern Ⅱ: *IRFR*

This is realized by the structure "initiation—response—feedback—response". It indicates that sometimes in the move of feedback the teacher makes correction of the student's error in responding, thus generally leading the student to reacting to the teacher's repair.

e. g. T: What do you do every morning?

P: I clean my teeth.

T: You clean your teeth every morning.

P: I clean my teeth every morning.

Pattern Ⅲ. *IR (IaRa (IbRb)) F*

This structure shows that when the student reacts to the teacher's question, the teacher does not give the respondent an immediate response. Instead, the teacher makes further inquiries regarding the uncertainty about or incompleteness of the learner's prior reply which the student needs to react.

e. g. T: Everybody prepared? Have you got prepared?

S: Have a little.

T: Oh?

S: Have a little.

T: A little is enough.

Pattern IV. IRaFaRbFb

In this structure, the teacher poses a question, invites several responses. The teacher does not acknowledge every student response until s/he has heard a few replies. Then the teacher comments on the merits of the answers. Sometimes the teacher may offer a non-committal response to a student's reply such as repetition or rephrasing of the student's answer, but is advised not using too frequently (Holden 1989: 26).

e. g. T: Uhm, 如果你表示不同意呢?

S1: I disagree with you.

T: Yeah, uh, I disagree with you.

S2: I'm not sure.

S3: I don't think so.

T: I'm not sure, right. I don't know. I don't think so.

Pattern I reflects the "transmission style of education" (Barnes 1976, cited in Ellis 1994) and the biggest teacher control over teacher-learner interaction. It is a one-to-one one-way interaction. Pattern II emphasizes input in language learning. It is still an unilateral exchange in language classrooms. Pattern III is added up in the structure by echoic questions such as clarification requests or confirmation checks (Long & Sato 1983, cited in Ellis 1994 and Chaudron 1988), thereby establishing interactional meaning negotiation in the teacher's perspective and ensuring the increase in more participation by individual students. Pattern IV is essentially a questioning structure for redirection, which provides opportunity for more students to play the game. Therefore, the teacher controls lessons and in the meanwhile student participation is widening in scope. In Li et al. 's view, Patter II, III and IV are varieties of the basic Pattern I. If Patterns III and IV are frequently used, which shows that the teacher reduces the control over classroom discourse, more opportunities will become available to students. As a corollary, students will become more active in and responsible for classroom language learning and thereby improve their communicative ability.

It should be pointed out that Li et al. 's investigation, though a good attempt in this respect, is to a large extent confined to an analysis of the structure between a teacher and a student, which does not really reflect the comprehensive yet complicated classroom questioning structuring that may consist of prompting, probing, peer repair, student-initiated question and others which might be embedded in teacher-initiated questioning. For instance, Huang (1988) acknowledges that classroom [questioning] structure is distinctive from that outside school (1988: 178 – 179). In some cases, the teacher might make interruptions/interjections while a student is uttering. Wang (1998) also illustrates how the respondent becomes the initiator in the questioning process thus establishing a genuine teacher-student meaning negotiation and interactional conversation exchange. Therefore, structuring in questioning should be further explored by investigating classroom questioning activities.

3. The structuring of teacher-initiated text-based questioning

3. 1　Why text-based questioning

So far, the focus of existing studies in terms of classroom English teacher questioning is too general, in other words, the description and analysis in those studies are concerned with depicting the general picture of classroom teacher-initiated questioning, addressing not only teachers' procedural questions, but also their language-orientation questions as well as meaning-orientation questions.

With the increasing attention in text studies and text instruction in language classrooms, text-based questioning by classroom teachers should never be ignored when classroom questioning is concerned, because there is a close link between text instruction and the questioning method. The essence of classroom instruction is basically a text-based interaction/dialogue between the teacher and learners. Text teaching is an activity or a process of understanding and even recreating texts. Reading or listening to texts in textbooks in the form of dialogues/conversations or short passages are good samples of the target language in use for students, which present them with models of texts. For non-native students who learn the target language mainly by means of textbooks, texts provide them with both linguistic elements and living language.

Text instruction is a goal-driven process: obtaining and interpreting text meaning, analyzing and studying linguistic features of texts. Text-based EFL teaching and learning has dual orientations: studying and using language. As for the use of language, it indicates comprehension and production of utterances in the target language. Text-based questioning is an ideal technique that integrates text understanding and meaning expression: questions guide students to make sense of texts and elicit their understanding of texts by way of oral production. In other words, text-driven questions require students to express what they know about the texts they contact and deal with. In turn, students' responses to text-based questions reflect to a large extent whether and to what extent they comprehend the given texts. Students' responses also help both the teacher and students themselves perceive the linguistic competence of learners.

With regard to texts and questions, Richards and Divesta (cited in Sun 1999) first proposed that questions be attached to texts and students are required to read texts and answer those text-based questions. Text-based questions and questioning have some advantages: text-based questions guide students and focus their attention on certain text information; they instruct students to choose appropriate cognitive processing strategies to tackle with text information. In addition, studies by Boker and other researchers (cited in Pi 1997: 261: 262) provide evidence of the relationship between text learning effects and text-based questions: when dealing with texts with attached questions, learners achieve better grades in intentional learning than when dealing with texts without any attached questions. This manifests that text-based questions are used as a form of learning tasks and the result of text learning with questions as tasks is significantly different from that without questions in terms of intentional learning.

In EFL classroom text instruction is an intentional pedagogic activity guided by teachers. Therefore, the significance of text-based questions to text learning, just as Ur puts it, lies in that a text-based question as a learning task is useful for two reasons: first, it can provide the learners with a purpose in text contact and make the whole activity more interesting and effective; second, we need to know how well our learners are learning, and we can get this information conveniently through the results of comprehension tasks (Ur 1996: 143 - 145). In effect, it is possible that text-based questions and questioning shifts the classroom style from focusing on teacher to focusing on students, which formally provide opportunities at which students can speak in a few seconds what otherwise will have been spoken by the teacher in the lecture method. Meanwhile, text-based questions are brought to students as purposeful tasks for them to accomplish, which can motivate students to a great extent. For teachers, text-based questions are used as tasks for text instruction and also as a kind of effective teaching strategy that, as an external condition, assists learners in text learning.

Since text-based questions and questioning by teachers are so important in EFL classrooms, empirical research should be carried out in this respect. The latest related study is Pei (2002), which investigated several senior EFL teachers' text-based questioning in reading classes. The limitations of that study lie in that: firstly, the method of data collection is the use of questionnaires, which cannot reflect the real situation of teacher text-based questioning; secondly, the study only examined types of teacher questions in terms of cognition as well as wait time. So, Pei's study, though a good attempt, fails to achieve good results of getting an authentic picture of teacher text-based questioning. Therefore, the present study focuses on the structuring of text-based questioning initiated by teachers in classrooms. The research questions in this study are: *What patterns of structuring of questioning are there in each teacher's text-based questioning activities? What are the similarities and differences between the subject teachers in their initiated text-based questioning?*

3. 2   Research design

In this study, three junior EFL teachers (A, B and C) who graduated from the same teacher college in different years and now work at the same junior middle school were examined in their classroom text-based questioning. The general information about the three subject teachers are as follows：

Teachers	Gender	Years of teaching	Grade level of their students	Class size
Teacher A	female	3	Junior 2	65
Teacher B	female	5	Junior 2	66
Teacher C	female	2	Junior 1	67

The subject teachers and their students used the following materials： *Junior English For China 1B and 2B* (*published by People's Education Press*) ; *New Concept English：First Things First* (as supplementary material). Teachers A and B had for each unit every week seven lessons with two extra lessons on Sundays. They usually finished one unit within a week. Teacher C had five lessons for each unit each week. Four complete units of lessons given by each teacher were observed in their classrooms. In order to collect the relevant data on the teachers' text-based questioning, all their lessons were observed by the researcher using techniques such as tape-recording and field note-taking and then were transcripted after observation.

3. 3　Data presentation and analysis

3. 3. 1　Structuring in Teacher A's text-based questioning

In Teacher A's lessons, altogether four patterns of structuring have been identified in her text-based questioning. They are：IRF, I1R1F1I2R2F2, IR1/R2/.../ F, and IRI'R'F.

Pattern I：IRF

In **Teacher A's** text comprehension questioning, the majority of the questioning exchanges follow the basic IRF pattern：the teacher initiates a question, students respond to it, and then the teacher evaluates the response.

e. g.　T：What's the weather like on that day?

S：very cold.

T：Yes. It's very cold. Thank you.

Pattern II：I1R2F1I2R2F2

But in some cases when she used **probing questions** after the student's response to the initial question, the questioning structuring becomes I1R1F1I2R2F2. In Teacher A's text comprehension questioning, this pattern emerged 12 times as there were 12 follow-up questions in the data.

e. g. T: Jiang Shuai. Did Roy sleep well at night?

S: No.

T: Yeah. No, he didn't. Do you know why? Why?

S: Because he always er because er he always dreams about hard work.

T: Yeah. He always dreams about hard work. (to Ss) Yes? (to S) Sit down please.

Pattern III: IR1/R2/.../F

It is found that Teacher A occasionally (10 times) used the strategy of redirection in question distribution. If a question is redirected to several students, the teacher receives responses from different students. In such case, the teacher invites several students to offer responses to the same question. Thus, the pattern of questioning structuring "IR1/R2/.../F" is established.

e. g. T: Why did people not go to him any more? 为什么大家都不去这个医生那儿呢? 谁听明白了? (S1) Zhang Xiaoliang.

S1: have a young doctor.

T: a young doctor to help the people. OK. (to S2) Liang Jie, 你呢?

S2: because the doctor began to forget something.

T: Yeah. (to S3) Xie Jialiang.

S3: He began to forget something.

T: 有没有不同答案呢? (to S4) Zhang Xiaofeng.

S4: He began to forgets something.

T: 好, 都坐下吧。 The answer the answer is, the doctor began to forget things.

Pattern IV: IRI'R'F

There is no system that ensures that the class keeps silent and attentive while a respondent is answering a question. As a result, the teacher sometimes might find it difficult to hear clearly the respondent. Therefore, the teacher can **make requests for the student to repeat** his/her response (e. g. 1) or ask him/her to make clarifications of the responses (e. g. 2).

e. g. 1 T: Guo Kai. This question. Why did the children pull the boat out of the water?

S: Er—they're afraid they can't find their boat.

T: Pardon?

S: They're afraid, they can't find their boat.

T: Uh, they're afraid they they couldn't find their boat. (to Ss) Yes? (to S) you are right. Sit down, please.

e. g. 2 T: Tian Lei. Which island are the children going to? Which island are the children going to?

S: first.

T: the farther one or the farthest one?

S: the farther one.

T: Yes, the farther one.

It is found that Teacher A used such expressions as "Pardon?", "I beg your pardon?", "Mmm?", "嗯" to show her requests for students to repeat their answers. This kind of insertion sequences in the teacher's questioning exchanges has emerged 3 times.

3. 3. 2　Structuring in Teacher B's text-based questioning

In Teacher B's text-based questioning, four patterns of structuring of questioning have also emerged, which are: IRF, I1R1F1I2R1F2, IR1/R2/../F, and IRI'R'F.

Pattern I: IRF

In Teacher B's text-based questioning, most questioning exchanges take the IRF pattern. The teacher raises a question, a student gives a reply and then the teacher gives comments on the response.

e. g. T: Who invites Helen and Jim for lunch? Who? Who? Shi Ruyi.

S: Pat and Tom.

T: Pat and Tom. Yes. Very good. Sit down, please.

As most of the text-based questions are display questions easy to answer, the pattern of IRF is most prevalent in the classroom.

Pattern II: I1R1F1I2R2F2

When *follow-up questions* are used in a questioning exchange, the structure of questioning becomes complex. In Teacher B's lessons, there are 15 probes. They are all why questions. It is observed that in five questioning exchanges initiated by yes/no questions. Teacher B insists using why questions to probe her students when they answer "Yes" or "No".

e. g. T: Did the Smiles have many friends when they moves there? Did they? Liu Xing.

S: No, no, they didn't.

T: Yeah. No. Why?

S: (silent)

T: Why? Tell me why.

S: Because it is a new town.

T: Mmm.

S: they didn't meet many people. . . .

Pattern III: IR1/R2/. . . /F

In Teacher B's text-based questioning, *redirection* is much used by her in three types of text-based questioning. She wants to involve more students in speaking in class and therefore she uses this technique in her questioning 39 times. Consequently, 39 questioning exchanges take the form of IR1/R2/. . . /F. It is found that more students are involved in her lead-in questioning exchanges than in reading/listening comprehension questioning ones. In one case, fourteen students are engaged in answering the same question. This is because lead-in questions are referential/open-ended. Also, in listening-text comprehension questioning, she exploits this structure of questioning, which helps students grasp ideas on the tape. This structuring of questioning is sometimes used in reading-text comprehension questioning. The following excerpt is an episode from the listening-text comprehension questioning work:

e. g.　T: Why did people not to go to him not to go to him any more? 为什么后来人们不去呢? (to S1) Liu Xiawen.

S1: because there was young doctor.

T: there was a young doctor. Sit down please. (to S2) Zhang Ming.

S2: because he is old, and, he is 医术落后了。

T: No. (to S3) Wu Haiwei.

S3: because, er, the doctor, forgot things.

T: (to Ss) Yes or No? Yes, because he forgot things. Ok. Good. Sit down please.

Pattern IV: IRI'R'F

In this pattern there is usually a meaningful negotiation between the teacher and the respondent. As the questions are all initiated by the teacher, it is often the teacher who *requests her students to make clarifications*. As said before, no system has been established in her lessons to ensure all the class to keep quiet when some student is answering a question and the class is sometimes noisy when questioning is happening. As a result, the teacher in such cases has to use clarification requests in questioning exchanges at times.

e. g. T: Next one. Now, why did the woman come to see the doctor ? Why? Why? Zhang Shaohua.

S: Her knees * * *

T: Again, please.

S: Her knees hurt badly.

T: Yes. Very good. Sit down, please.

It is observed that when making requests for her students to clarify their answers, the teacher often uses "Pardon?", "Mmm?", "Again, please" . However, it should be pointed out that if the teacher can require the class to attend to the respondent when answering a question, then there is no need to use such structuring of questioning because it is a waste of time.

3. 3. 3 Structuring in Teacher C's text-based questioning

In Teacher C's text-based questioning, only two patterns of structuring of questioning have been identified, which are: IRF and IRI'R'F.

Pattern I : IRF

In Teacher C's lessons, 75% questioning exchanges are formed in this pattern. She directs a question to an individual student or the entire class, the student (s) answer (s) and she gives feedback.

e. g. T: Why do some people like their bedrooms? 喜欢卧室，为什么呀？ Why? Why? (to a volunteer) Shen Ke.

S: because they like sleeping.

T: Why? Because they like 什么呀, sleeping. Yes. Sit down.

During the class observation, it is found that she tends to start and end a questioning sequence at a fast speed. It seems that she does not want to spend much time on the questioning work. This can also be seen in her treatment of the textbook. To her the questioning work is only a ritual job she must do with her students. Therefore, the pattern of IRF as the basic questioning structuring is frequently used in her class questioning.

Pattern II : IRI'R'F

As evidenced in class observation, Teacher C *stresses the accuracy of students' linguistic production*. So, in the process of students' answering to her questions, she keeps a close eye on the respondent's linguistic performance. In cases when the students make mistakes in answering, she will immediately make intervention. Thus, in the basic IRF pattern, another ask-and-answer sequence is inserted.

e. g. T: Li Meng. 下面这个问题。How do they work? How do they work? 他

们怎么工作呀？

S：They worker hard.

T：嗯？they worker hard? worker hard?

S：Er，they work，work hard.

T：哎，记住了，work hard，不是 worker。worker 是什么意思？

Ss：工—人—

T：Li Meng, sit down, please.

Sometimes she uses the expressions such as "Pardon?", "Again", Mmm " or" 你刚才说的啥？大家听她/他再说一遍 " to imply to the respondents that they have said something wrong and should make correction. When interrupting, she usually just repeats the respondent's words in a rising intonation. "

Conclusion

(1) Findings from this study

The major findings from the present study can be summarized as follows: a) Similarities in structuring of each teacher's initiated text-based questioning. The pattern most frequently adopted by the subject teachers is the IRF and other patterns such as IR1/R2/.../F, IRI'R'F and I1R1I2R2F are occasionally used by them because of lack of or less occurrence of redirection, probing, clarification requests for learners in the process of classroom questioning. b) Differences in structuring of each teacher's initiated text-based questioning. There are obvious differences between the three teachers in the structuring of text-based questioning. Both Teachers A and B adopt four patterns of structuring in their initiated text-based questioning, which are IRF, I1R1F1R2I2F2, IR1/R2/.../F, IRI'R'F. However, there exist big differences between the two subject teachers—IR1. R2/.../F is much used by Teacher B because of her frequent use of redirection strategy and 15 times the pattern of I1R1F1I2R2F2 occurs because of the introduction of probing questions; the IRI'R'F pattern is sometimes adopted by the teacher when she can not hear the respondent clearly. However, other patterns as varieties of the basic questioning structure IRF, though used, were less frequently observed in Teacher A's classrooms. Teacher C does not use the techniques of probing or redirection in her classroom text-based questioning, so the patterns of IR1/R2/.../F and I1R1F1I2R2F2 have been rarely found in her data and only the patterns of IRF and IRI'R'F have been frequently adopted by her.

(2) Implications for professional training

It should be acknowledged that varied patterns of questioning structuring based on IRF have positive influence on students' classroom learning both motivationally and linguistically: a) The pattern "I1R1F1I1R2F2" is used mainly for a questioning exchange consisting of an initial and a probing question. If it is frequently used, this questioning structuring increases the amount of individual student's classroom thinking and language production. b) The structure "IR1/R2/.../F" is essentially a useful pattern emerging in redirection. It provides opportunities for more individual students to participate in responding to the same question and for students to share different responses. By exploiting such structuring pattern in the questioning activity, the teacher involves more students in the questioning work, thus the scope of student involvement is enlarged. c) As for the structure of "IRI'R'F", some interactive meaningful negotiation devices are introduced in the questioning process, such as clarification requests and confirmation checks. This pattern of questioning structuring helps the teacher negotiate interactively with the respondent even though the student remains passive in the whole questioning process.

What patterns of questioning structuring there are and how frequently those patterns are exploited in teachers' questioning reflect how teachers and students interact in the questioning course. As indicated in this study, the teachers do not know how to make meaningful negotiation with their students, how to involve more students in answering questions, how to help students make successful responses or and how to explore and extend students' thinking. Consequently, the teachers simply follow the initiation-reaction-follow-up procedure (IRF) in most cases of their initiated text-based questioning. In some sense, whether the structuring of questioning is complicated or not can be regarded as an indicator of teachers' effective and positive questioning. If teachers can learn to use various patterns of structuring in questioning work, the process of questioning will become more flexible, interactive and effective. However, all the three teachers in this study report in the informal interviews that they know little about classroom questioning and they are not clear about what options they have in dealing with text-based questioning. They admit that what they are doing in questioning work is simply based on their own intuition, previous learning experience, their peer teachers' teaching practice, and understanding of what should be done in teaching, instead of on any theoretical guidance. They also express that current TEFL methodology courses provided at teacher colleges do not offer student teachers any practical help in classroom questioning. All the subject teachers expect to improve their questioning skills but they do not get access to the effective approaches

Texts are samples of real language in use. There are many approaches to tackle texts and the question-and-answer method is considered as one effective way that can be adopted in text instruction. Text-based questions can be used as tasks for students to perform in their text learning. Unfortunately, there have been so far few TEFL courses that integrate questioning strategies into text instruction (text listening/reading comprehension). Gruenewald & Pollark (1990: 49 – 50) point out that questioning can be classified as processes but does not receive much attention. It is reported that most teachers are unaware of their questioning patterns and they are unable to analyze or change them because they are not trained in asking questions (Good & Brophy 1991: 26; Gruenewald & Pollark 1990: 49). In other words, most teachers do not know how to make a good question, nor do they know how to utilize questions appropriately. Therefore, it is expected that in the near future TEFL courses containing text-based questioning strategies can reach practical teachers so that teachers can be theoretically guided in the course of their text instruction. Practice without any effective theoretical guidance is thought to be blind attempts. Unless teachers are aware of how, why and when they should ask questions, they are unlikely to be effective in their questioning behaviors. Teachers will become more competent in their text-based questioning through professional training.

References

[1] Allwright, R. The importance of interaction in classroom language learning [J]. *Applied Linguistics*, 1984(5): 156 – 171.

[2] Chaudron, C. *Second Language Classrooms: Research on Teaching and Learning* [M]. Cambridge: CUP, 1988.

[3] Ellis, R. 1994. *The Study of Second Language Acquisition* [M]. Oxford: OUP.

[4] Good, T. L. & Brophy, J. E. *Looking in classrooms (5th. ed.)* [M]. New York: Harper Collins Publishers, 1991.

[5] Gruenewald, L. J. & S. A. Pollak. *Language Interaction in Curriculum and Instruction (2nd ed.)* [M]. Austin: Pro-ed, Inc. 1990.

[6] 胡壮麟. 语篇的衔接与连贯 [M]. 上海：上海外语教育出版社,1994.

[7] 黄国文. 语篇分析概要 [M]. 长沙：湖南教育出版社, 1988.

[8] 李悦娥,范宏雅. 话语分析[M]. 上海:上海外语教育出版社,2002.

[9] Meighan, Roland. 1986. *A Sociology of Educating*（*2nded.*）[M]. London: Holt, Rineheart and Winston Ltd.

[10] 裴军. 高中英语阅读课问答情况的调查研究[J]. 中小学英语教学与研究, 2002,(7):40－42.

[11] 皮连生. 学与教的心理学[M]. 上海:华东师范大学出版社,1997.

[12] 孙华. 阅读教学中提问的心理学分析[J]. 江西教育,1999,(4):21.

[13] Ur, P.. *A Course in Language Teaching*:Practice and Theory[M]. Cambridge:CUP,1996.

[14] 王得杏. 英语话语分析与跨文化交际[M]. 北京:北京语言文化大学出版社,1998.

＊注:本文根据笔者硕士论文"基于语篇的语言教师课堂提问研究" (BNU2004)的部分资料整理而成。

（刘炜,吉首大学）

英语词汇教学与认知发展模式

引言

　　词汇是语言的核心；是交际的基础，因而英语词汇教学在整个英语教学中的作用是不容忽视的。对于学生来说，要想学好英语，首先就得掌握相当大的词汇量。对于教师来说，要想让学生记住更多的词汇，并能在他们的言语交际中灵活运用，教师就必须采取一些措施，传授行之有效的记忆方法和技巧，从而帮助学生提高词汇的习得效率。本文主要探讨了目前英语词汇教学的现状以及认知发展模式。在认知发展模式中，主要涉及了认知发展模式的成因及基础。与此同时，本文还探讨了认知发展模式对英语词汇教学的重要启示，指出图式理论在很大程度上对英语认知词汇的激活以及词汇教学方法的改进起着重要的指导作用，从而有助于提高英语词汇教学效果。

1. 目前英语词汇教学的现状

　　当学生的英语语法知识、阅读和写作能力等都有一定的基础之后，词汇量的大小实际上已成为影响他们英语水平的重要因素，而在现行的传统词汇教学的框架下，英语教师一般按照传统的套路进行词汇教学，学生根本不能透彻理解和掌握单词的确切意义与文化内涵，从而导致很难达到用英语进行交际的目的。因此，我国目前英语词汇教学还存在很多问题，主要表现在以下两个方面：

1.1 缺乏系统的理论作支撑

　　目前，虽然教师和学生都认识到词汇能力的重要性，但是对于什么是词汇能力，如何提高词汇能力这样的问题却没有系统的理论作指导。在英语词汇教学中，许多教师只是在课堂上把词义和用法等从词典中抄下来讲一遍，再让学生在课内或课外背一下。这样的教学方法也使学生误以为词汇学习毫无方法可言，只需靠死记硬背就行了，并且把词汇能力差只是归咎为努力不够。实际上，词汇能力包含多种能力，如理解性词汇能力、使用性词汇能力、词义扩展的逻辑想象能力等。因此，要想提高英语词汇教学的效果，教师就必须从理论出发，以相关的理论为指导来进行词汇教学。在实际的英语词汇教学中，教师可根据学生个人的实际情况并就相关的理论，制定因人而异的词汇教学方案，从而有效提高英语词汇教学效果。

1.2　英语词汇教学的输入、输出形式单一

由于缺乏传统的理论知识作指导，教师的词汇教学方法和学生的词汇习得方式都存在一些问题，主要表现在词汇的输入和输出方面。目前，在应试压力的影响下，大部分学生仍采用死记硬背的方法进行词汇的习得；而教师基本上也只是讲解生词或课文里遇到的生词，给学生提供一些同义词或反义词，或举出一些例句。这种单一的输入方法很难使学生对词汇之间的联系有深入的了解，也无法激活对新词的认知。与此同时，这样的教学方法也无法使学生的词汇输出能力得到好的锻炼。因此，我国目前的英语词汇教学迫切需要从旧的教学模式中走出来，找到相关的理论作指导，从而达到提高英语词汇教学的目的。

2. 认知发展模式

认知发展模式是认知心理学中的一个概念。认知既是大脑的产物，而大脑又是生物进化的结果，因而，一般认为认知的发展阶段是和人类进化阶段基本相一致的。美国麦克莱恩（P. MacLean）曾把认知结构的发展分为三个阶段，而布朗（J. Brown）则认为要增加一个阶段（Brown 1977：10-24），其基本模式为这四个阶段：① 感觉—肌动（sensori-motor）阶段。这是认知产生的初始阶段，认知的形式实现为躯体活动。知觉、动作、空间一起围绕身体的空间进行。感情是本能性的，如生物在这个阶段已有饥饿、睡眠、性的本能。② 边缘系统—表征性（limbic-presentational）阶段。在这个阶段，物体可以形成心理表象。临床和实验的结果表明，边缘系统的下部与吃饭、发怒、尖叫、自我保护等功能有联系。③ 皮质—表征性（cortical-representational）阶段。新皮质的大脑见于高级哺乳动物和人类，可称为认知大脑，但因为它仍与边缘系统和次皮质保持联系，故又是一个情感的大脑。④ 不对称—符号（asymmetric-symbolic）阶段。语言的产生是这个阶段的最重要成果，因为有了语言，人类的思维也就越来越精细。（转引自桂诗春 2001：64-65）维戈茨基（L. Vygotsky）就说过，"一个词就是人类意识的一个缩影。"（Vygotsky，1970）因此，词汇的习得过程也应该同认知发展模式的四个阶段一样，是一个从低级到高级，从简单到复杂，从具体到抽象的不断发展的过程。

下面主要从认知发展模式的成因和基础两方面来阐述。

2.1　认知发展模式的成因

关于认知的发展模式的成因已有很多学者对此进行过研究。他们主要从两方面进行了分析。一方面，从神经学的角度来分析。哈特利（David Hartley，

1705—1757)认为，经验引起神经振颤，经验的顺序就是振颤的顺序，当刺激再次呈现时，接受过刺激信号的脑区与第二脑区都会被唤醒。例如，一系列感觉A、B、C、D形成一定模式后，如果唤醒A，也就会唤醒B、C、D（Murphy and Kovach 1972：34 - 5）。另一方面，从心理学的角度来分析，综合反应是过去的经验经过整合而产生的一种整体作用。正如巴甫洛夫（I. P. Pavlov 1849—1936）所说："无数不同性质与不同强度的刺激从外部和通过机体内部到达大脑两半球，有些刺激只是受到审视，另一些刺激则会引起高度多样化的有条件与无条件反射的效果。所有这些反射都会相逢、相互连结、相互作用，最终必然系统化、平衡化，形成一种'动态定模'（dynamic stereotype）"（Stones 1966：143）。对于这种基本相同的现象，有些心理学家不用"动态定模"，而用"图式"（schema）来描述。认知心理学家皮亚杰（Piaget）就是用"同化"（assimilation）和"顺应"（accommodation）图式理论来说明认知发展模式的成因的。他认为，在动作方面，由于常规动作的经常重复，各种体位的、触觉的、听觉的、视觉的刺激相互联结，最后形成图式。同样的原理，认知发展模式的成因也是如此。图式是指人类头脑中存在的对事物或物体的整体的认知结构。在图式里，事物的组成部分是以它们在时间或空间上的关系为纽带联结在一起的。例如，教室在人们头脑中一定有黑板、书桌、椅子、教师、学生。

2. 2　认知发展模式的基础

正如洛克（J. Locke 1632—1704）认为复杂的观念来自大脑对简单概念的组合一样，我们可以说复杂的认知发展模式来自简单的联想。联想是认知发展模式的基础，其作用是通过某种刺激而触发的，其方式通常不是孤立的简单反应，而是具有集成和连锁的性质。根据冯特（Wihelm Wundt）对联想的分析，我们可知联想的种类繁多，有直接联想、间接联想、上属联想（如小草—植物）、下属联想（如植物—小草）、并列联想（如小草—花）、对照联想（如长—短）、控制联想、自由联想、外部联想、复合联想、意义联想、表象联想、语言形式联想等。每种联想都需要大量的有意或无意的重复，本族语的人在自然环境中重复，学外语的学生通常在人为的环境中练习。在练习的过程中，大脑能够根据经验自动形成表象图式结构，并将原始的图式表象结构变成更复杂的心理认知结构（Lakoff 1987：280 - 1）。

3. 认知发展模式对词汇教学的启示

从以上对认知发展模式及其成因和基础的分析中，我们可以得出一些对英语词汇教学的重要启示。既然词汇习得过程同认知发展模式的四个阶段一样，是一个从低级到高级、从简单到复杂、从具体到抽象的不断发展的过程（这一过程我们可以从儿童习得词汇的过程——从 holophrases stage 到 two-word stage 再到更完善的词汇习得阶段中得到验证），那么，在英语词汇教学中，教师就应该遵循这个发展模式，不要急于求成，以免导致适得其反的效果。教师还可以尽可能地建立相应的词汇图式，或利用新的词汇知识激活已有图式，或建立新图式，以提高英语词汇认知能力。在认知发展模式中，由于最基本的联想原理，音、词、词组等单位都会具有自动反应性质，因而词汇和情景之间会在语用过程中产生较强的自动性联想。词汇的联想、类比、对照、推理均属于利用图式理论范畴。利用图式理论，可以使学生把词汇置于一个大的意义环境下，而联想组合愈紧密，词汇愈易于记住。联想还可以围绕一个主题或中心展开，如我们可以把这样一组词汇（meeting, conference, session, council, seminar 等）放在一起教。这种方法可以使学生在记忆词汇时，建构起相关的词汇图式，从而达到长时记忆的效果。词汇图式还可利用语义场来建构。学习者在掌握了相关语义图式的前提下，他们就可以利用推理、分析和对比等方法来理解、记忆词汇。另外，利用构词法知识、同/反义关系、词语的上下文关系等都属于建构词汇图式的范畴。在英语词汇教学中，教师要把认知发展模式成因中的图式理论恰当地运用到词汇教学中，使学生的长时记忆词汇能力大大提高，从而达到提高英语词汇教学效果的目的。总之，认知发展模式对英语词汇教学起着重要的理论指导和预示作用。

结语

我国教育学家胡春洞曾在《英语教学法》一书中提出：学英语＝学词汇。可见，在整个英语教学中，词汇教学是多么重要。针对我国目前英语词汇教学缺乏系统的理论指导和教学的输出、输入形式单一的现状，教师可以结合认知发展模式及其中的理论，如图式理论，找到提高英语词汇教学的最佳途径。在英语词汇教学中，教师可以利用图式理论中的联想、类比、对照、推理等进行教学。与此同时，教师还应尽量为学生提供运用语言的交际机会，因为交际才是语言学习的最终目的，而且，语言输出也能强化学习者对语言能力输入的理解和巩固（Swain1985）。只有这样，才有助于扩大学生的产出性词汇，丰富他们的表达，使他们真正掌握好所学词汇，从而提高英语学习效率，达到用英语进行交际的目的。但是，英语词汇教学过程中各种有效途径的结合还有待进一步探讨。

基金项目：湖南省哲学社会科学成果评审委员会项目，项目名称：教育语言学研究，代码：0606037B

参考文献

［1］Brown. J. Mind, *Brain and Consciousness*［M］. New York：Academic Press，1977.

［2］Lakoff, G. Woman, *Fire and Dangerous Things*［M］. Chicago：The University of Chicago Press，1987.

［3］Murphy, G. & Kovach, J. *History Introduction to Modern Psychology*（3rd ed）［M］. New York：Harcourt Brace Jovanovich，1972.

［4］Stones, E. *Educational Psychology*［M］. London：Methuen and Co. Ltd. 11 New Fetter Lane，1966.

［5］Swain, M. Communicative Competence：Some roles of comprehensible input and comprehensible output in its development. Gass, S & Madden, C(eds.). *Input in Second Language Acquisition*［M］. Rowley, MA：Newbury House，1985.

［6］Vygotsky, L. *Language and Thought*［M］. Mass.：MIT Press，1970.

［7］桂诗春. 实验心理语言学纲要［M］. 长沙：湖南教育出版社，2001.

［8］胡春洞. 英语教学法［M］. 北京：高等教育出版社，1990.

［9］吕道利. 英语词汇教学研究［J］. 外语研究，2004，(2).

［10］赵艳芳. 认知语言学概论［M］. 上海：上海外语教育出版社，2001.

［11］邹琼. 大学英语教学论［M］. 长沙：湖南师范大学出版社，2006.

（李永芳，长沙理工大学；曹志希，中南林业科技大学）

英语写作教学认知研究述评

引言

在中国，英语写作教学研究已取得了一些成果。20 世纪 80 年代，国内英语和二语写作理论研究开始起步，90 年代有了缓慢发展。21 世纪初，这方面的理论研究呈现出较大的发展趋势。近年来，中国外语写作教学研究引起了越来越多外语教育工作者的关注。从 2003 年起，通过研究国内多种外语类核心期刊上有关英语写作研究的文章，一些教师和研究者对我国英语写作教学和研究的历史和内容进行了综合、概括和总结（李志雪，李绍山 2003；姚兰，程骊妮 2005）。还有教师对国外第二语言写作研究的现状与取向进行了分析（王立非，孙晓坤 2005），通过对比呼吁我国外语教学研究加强外语环境下的二语写作研究。

但英语写作教学仍然面临不少问题。长期以来，怎样让学生在尽可能短的时间内，掌握地道的英语写作技巧，增强其语言能力和语用能力，是每一位教育工作者苦苦追求的。特别是自上世纪 90 年代以来，国内不少外语教师在课堂上强调意义交流而忽视了提高学生的语言知识水平，很多学生仍然难以用英语在真实场合进行复杂的思想交流，写作水平更是"不堪入目"，英语写作水平的总体水平没有"质"的提高。

因此当务之急是寻找一条更实用的英语写作教学途径。而近年来为大家所注目的认知语言学，为探索、研究英语写作教学所面临的困境提供了一个新的视角，认知法理论对解决这些问题具有较好的指导作用。

1. 认知法与英语写作

1.1 认知法理论

北京外国语大学王福祥教授和刘润清教授在给国家教委的一份报告（后发表在《外语教学与研究》1995 第 3 期）中曾指出"二十年之后，认知语言学将是最热门的课题。""认知"这个术语来自学习心理学。心理学的"认知"概念是"知道"的意思。而"知道"则有感觉、知觉、记忆、想象、构成概念、判断、推理等意义。认知心理学家重视感知、理解、逻辑思维等智力活动在获取知识中的积极作用。把认知心理学理论应用于外语教学的方法叫认知法。认知法（cognitive approach）又名认知符号法（cognitive code approach），是由美国著名心理学家 Carrol 于 1964 年提出。它是以心理学家 Piaget 创立的"发生认识论"、心理学家 Bruner 倡导的结构主义教育理论和著名语言学家 Chomsky 的转换生成语法理论为依据的。这种教学法重视对语言规则的理解，重视在外语教学中充分发挥学生智力的作用，是一套完整的外语教学法理论和一套极具科学理念的教育方法。认知法具有坚实的心理学、教育学和语言学理论基础。它有三个要素：① 外语教学要以学生为中心；② 学习外语的方式应是 S（stimulation）R（reaction）而不是 S→R；③ 规则性和创造性。

1．2　英语写作教学与认知法的关系

英语写作教学与心理学、教育学、语言学等密切相关，大学生只有遵循科学的认知原理，采取正确的认知策略，充分发挥人脑的智力潜能，才能做到事半功倍。认知法建立在认知学习理论基础上，它吸取了大脑生理、信息论、语言学的最新科学成果，它的对象是成年人，适应于没有语言环境下的外语语言学习，尤其符合我国当前的外语学习环境，它与英语写作教改有着千丝万缕的联系，两者之间存在许多契合。认知法历经四十几年曲折的发展过程，受到越来越多的专家、学者和一线教师的关注和研究。我们有理由相信，从认知法这一崭新的角度系统地、综合性地探讨英语写作教学的理论机制，尽可能还原人们使用和理解语言的认知过程以及大脑的认知环境，必能摸索出更实用快捷的科学方法，使大学生创作出符合英语本族人思维习惯的文章。认知法不仅能为写作知识结构化提供一个科学依据，而且能为培养学生良好的认知结构，实现有效性写作开辟一条新途径。

2．英语写作认知研究内容述评

以研究主题为标准，国内外英语写作教学认知研究可分为 5 个类别。

2．1　国外研究

近年来，国外从认知语言学和心理语言学的角度探讨二语习得（包括听、说、读、写、译）逐渐成为了一个热点。一方面，研究者发现二语习得有其认知和心理的基础，代表性的理论包括 Schumit（1990，1994）提出的 noticing hypothesis；另一方面，随着以任务为单位的教学方法的兴起，外语工作者也在尝试使用认知心理学的框架解析这些教学任务，并且取得了一定的成果，代表作包括 Peter Skehan 的《语言学习认知法》。例如，在口语研究中，比较有影响的是 Levelt（1989）提出的理论框架，它甚至被用到了写作研究中。通过这些研究，一些关于语言任务认知难度的理论框架被逐步完善，为后人的研究提供了基础。

2.2 国内研究

2.2.1 认知心理学研究

杨永林（2005）通过跨学科对比的方式，考察了西方写作理论的流变，得出"翻新多于立异，借鉴多于原创，传承多于革命"的结论。近些年来，中国语境中的英语教学实效性问题引他从理论语言学的最新发展入手，引入心理学和社会学的研究，并从较早的过程写作理论到新近的社会认知写作理论的发展变化出发，分析了西方英语写作的范式转变与理论传承。在心理学研究领域，杨永林对20世纪80年代以来认知心理学研究的发展及其对外语写作教学理念的影响进行了研究。在认知心理学理论的影响下，新的语言学习理论认为，有效的语言学习方法应当在课堂教学中充分体现协作学习的原则。他还分析了从传统的修辞选择理论到现代社会认知写作理论的历史发展变化。他指出"过去三十年间，西方写作理论研究获得长足发展，从最初的过程写作理论到新近的社会认知写作理论，呈现出一种'理论竞现、推陈出新'的局面。"

2.2.2 跨文化研究

丰国欣（2001）的"英语跨文化写作中的认知心理机制"有一定的代表性。丰国欣在文中对英语跨文化写作中认知心理机制的各方面，如语言习得与发展、思维心理和语用心理等进行了论述。丰国欣（1999）认为，认知心理处理是跨文化写作的核心和动力机制。由此他建议，对以汉语为母语的人在汉语环境背景下进行的二语写作的研究不能只停留在文本写作（即措词、造句、成段、谋篇以及对文章的错误分析和对比分析）这一层面上。他认为，从跨文化交际的角度来认识第二语言写作的本质更科学、更全面、更符合客观实际，不考察交际双方认知心理机制的第二语言写作研究是难以取得突破性进展的。

2.2.3 社会认知研究

邓志勇（2002）在"英语写作教学的社会认知模式"一文中提出了一个英语写作教学的社会认知模式。这一模式的主要特点是确定了写作过程中作者、主题以及读者之间的动态三角关系。根据这个模式，写作过程被看成是一个循环性而不是线性的过程，写作既是互动的过程也是劝说活动。

2.2.4 图式论研究

周遂的"图式理论与二语写作"（2005）探讨了图式论在二语写作中的应用。他从内容图式（即语言图式）和形式图式（即文章图式或文体图式）两个角度分析了中国英语学习者与英语本族人的图式差异给中国英语学习者英语写作带来的问题。为此，他从段落结构、衔接手段两大部分来进行英汉文体图式的对比，归纳出几点总体区别特征。最后他阐述了扩充和丰富学生写作图式的方法，以及教学中优化图式激活、增强目标语文化背景知识的必要性。

2.2.5 元认知理论研究

唐芳和徐锦芬（2005）介绍了近年来国内外元认知理论的构成和发展及基于该理论的英语写作研究成果，并在此基础上总结其主要贡献。他们重点介绍了Flavell元认知理论的重要观点：元认知是对认知活动的认知，即认知主体对有关自身任何认知活动的认识或调节，使认知主体关注并调控认知活动的知识与能力，包括元认知知识和元认知体验；这两方面相互联系和制约构成元认知整体。元认知至少是指认知主体所存储的既和自身有关又和各种任务、目标、活动有关的知识片断。根据唐芳和徐锦芬的综述，近年来国外基于"元认知理论"的研究成果主要有以下三项：第一，母语和二语写作认知模式的启示；第二，ESL写作者元认知发展评估；第三，ESL写作知识分析：写作成功者与不成功者的个案研究。

吴红云和刘润清（2004）的"二语写作元认知理论构成的因子分析"是国内第一项已发表成文的写作元认知实证研究。他们以 二语写作元认知理论构成 Flavell元认知理论框架中 理论上的改善，并在此基础上发展了中国环境中的二语写作元认知理论框架。

吴红云（2006）的"教学活动条件下大学生英语写作元认知的特点"根据Flavell的元认知理论框架，通过采用开放式问卷和周计调查，探究了在教学活动条件下大学生写作元认知的特点。周计调查表明：教学活动条件下，大学生的英语写作元认知特点反映出教学原则的构想，即英语写作元认知体现为元认知知识和元认知体验两大要素。元认知知识由任务知识、主体知识和策略知识构成，元认知体验分为积极与消极体验。开放式问卷结果表明：英语写作元认知有一定的发展性。这些结果验证并丰富了Flavell的元认知理论，对我国大学英语写作教学实践有着重要的启示。

吴红云（2006）还在"大学英语写作中元认知体验现象实证研究"通过纵向调查、横向调查、大规模问卷调查以及作文测试等多种定量与定性调查手段，探究了写作元认知体验的种类及其与作文成绩之间的关系，以及写作教学对元认知体验的影响。研究发现：① 元认知体验可分为积极体验和消极体验；② 写作元认知体验与作文成绩之间具有对应关系；③ 写作元认知教学对元认知体验有一定的积极影响。

3. 思考

目前国内有关英语写作方面的研究主要包括两大类（唐芳、徐锦芬，2005）：关于英语写作能力的影响因素的研究和英语写作过程的研究。总体上，大家对英语写作教学的理论研究关注还比较少。